Praise for

GOODNIGHT FROM

"Enriched with authentic ....don is
a fascinating, compelling ....nalist
in World War II London ....t experiences
firsthand the harrowing effects of the Blitz—and discovers love
when she least expects it."

—Jennifer Chiaverini, *New York Times* bestselling author
of *Fates and Traitors* and *Mrs. Lincoln's Dressmaker*

"Jennifer Robson's *Goodnight from London* is a beautifully written 'you are there!' novel. I was pulled right into the characters' struggles, victories, and catastrophes in World War II England and France. Every time we say 'good book!' I'll be thinking of this inspiring story."

—Karen Harper, *New York Times* bestselling
author of *The Royal Nanny*

"*Goodnight from London* is another masterpiece by Jennifer Robson—a novel draped in such rich detail that we are immersed in the joy and grief, hope and despair of World War II London through the lens of Ruby Sutton, an inspiring, strong reporter whose unrelenting passion for her work and those she loves is a triumphant tribute to the real heroines of history."

—Joy Callaway, author of *The Fifth Avenue Artists Society*

"*Goodnight from London* captures both the despair and the triumphant spirit of war-torn London through the eyes of Ruby Sutton, an American journalist, with precision and wit. Robson's novel is an ode to the heroes of World War II, a touching love story, and a marvel."

—Fiona Davis, author of *The Dollhouse*

GOODNIGHT FROM LONDON

Also by Jennifer Robson

Moonlight Over Paris
Fall of Poppies: Stories of Love and the Great War
After the War is Over
Somewhere in France

GOODNIGHT FROM LONDON

A Novel

JENNIFER ROBSON

um

WILLIAM MORROW

An Imprint of HarperCollinsPublishers

Grateful acknowledgment is made to Dr. Alexander Matthews and the Estate of Martha Gellhorn for permission to reprint an excerpt from "The Wounded Come Home" by Martha Gellhorn, which first appeared in *Collier's Weekly* (August 4, 1944).

FIRST EDITION

Designed by Diahann Sturge

Library of Congress Cataloging-in-Publication Data has been applied for.

ISBN 978-0-06-238985-5
ISBN 978-0-06-267557-6 (library edition)
ISBN 978-0-06-267355-8 (international edition)

17 18 19 20 21   LSC   10 9 8 7 6 5 4 3 2 1

In memory of Nikki Moir
1919–2014
A first-class journalist, a wonderful grandmother,
and the woman who led me to Ruby

PART I

You lay in the tall grass with the wind blowing gently across you and watched the hundreds of silver planes swarming through the heavens like clouds of gnats. All around you, anti-aircraft guns were shuddering and coughing, stabbing the sky with small white bursts. You could see the flash of wings and the long white plumes from the exhausts; you could hear the whine of engines and the rattle of machine-gun bullets. You knew the fate of civilization was being decided fifteen thousand feet above your head in a world of sun, wind and sky. You knew it, but even so it was hard to take it in.

–Virginia Cowles, correspondent for the
Sunday Times, Looking for Trouble (1941)

CHAPTER ONE

June 1940
New York City

Ruby had been marooned outside Mike Mitchell's office for going on forty-five minutes, perched on a hard wooden chair under a wanly flickering electric light. Not for *The American* a floor of grand offices in the modern splendor of the Rockefeller Center. Instead, America's fourth-most-popular weekly newsmagazine made do with a third-floor walk-up on a dismal stretch of East Forty-Seventh Street, and if anyone complained about the scarcity of telephones, or the need to wear an overcoat between November and April, Mr. Mitchell just gave them The Look, which everyone knew was shorthand for *If you don't want this job, there are ten people who'll take your place in a heartbeat.*

She hadn't so much as shed her coat that morning when his secretary had summoned her, and she was glad, now, with her stomach flipping and flopping, that she'd skipped breakfast yet again. Mr. Mitchell had said hello to her on her first day, and had nodded at her twice in the hallway, but for all that, she hadn't been sure he even knew who she was. And now he wanted to see her.

She'd thought she was doing well at the magazine. Already she'd earned two bylines of her own, and her name had appeared as a contributor to five other pieces. She'd even moved beyond the usual sob-sister fare on her most recent story, a profile of a family of Belgian refugees who were still in shock at their country's calamitous defeat.

Maybe she'd stepped on someone's toes. It wasn't hard to do, since your average newsman was as touchy as a cat in a room full of rocking chairs. Had she spoken out of turn at the last editorial meeting? Made the mistake of interrupting one of the old guard?

Mr. Mitchell had been awfully quiet this morning, which in itself was disconcerting. After her first few days at the magazine, Ruby had grown used to his hoarse bellow, which was a constant bass note amid the cacophony of the newsroom. Even when his office door was closed, which wasn't often, it was easy to hear him above the clattering of typewriters and jangling of telephones, shouting out his approval or disdain in equal measure. But a quiet Mike Mitchell . . . she'd no idea if that was good or bad.

"Miss Sutton! Still there?"

"Yes, sir," she answered, and gritting her teeth a little, she inched into his office.

She'd assumed it would be messy like the managing editor's office, which was overflowing with heaps of paper and books and marked-up page proofs. But Mr. Mitchell's desk was nearly bare. Two telephones, a lone piece of paper centered just so, an old coffee can stuffed with pens and compositor's pencils, and nothing else.

He'd been looking out his window, though the view beyond was hardly more than a plain brick wall, and as his chair swiveled around she forced herself to stand perfectly still. A strand of hair was tickling her cheek, but she resisted the urge to tuck it behind her ear. Fidgeting with it would make her look nervous, and to look nervous would be to imply she'd done something wrong. It was one of the first lessons she'd learned growing up at St. Mary's, and one of the hardest.

She cleared her throat and waited, and then, when he still said nothing, she spoke up. "You asked me to come and see you . . . ?"

"Yes." He indicated the chair in front of his desk. "Sit down, and remind me—how long have you been with us?"

"About six months, sir."

"You're happy here? Settling in well?"

"Yes, sir."

"Bill Peterson likes you. Says you work hard and keep your eyes and ears open."

That came as a relief. The managing editor was pleasant enough, but was a miser with compliments. "It'll do" was the highest praise she'd ever heard from the man.

"I—"

"Been reading your work. Not much of a stylist, are you? But then we don't leave a lot of room for that."

The American employed a distinctive house style that read like an expanded version of the cablese the wire services still employed to save money on overseas telegrams. Succinct, crisp, and to the point, it treated adverbs like caviar—rare and best regarded with suspicion—and ruthlessly excised any attempts by staff writers to spread their poet's wings.

Mr. Mitchell leaned back in his chair, his hands clasped behind his head, and regarded her steadily. "I've an idea to put to you. It would mean a big change."

It took a moment for her to process his words. "I don't understand. Didn't you call me in because I've done something wrong?"

"Hell, no. Why'd you think that? If you foul up, I'll let you know right away."

Sitting forward, he pushed the piece of paper across his desk and motioned that she should pick it up. "I just got this from Walter Kaczmarek, the editor of *Picture Weekly* in London. Go on—read it."

28 May 1940

Dear Mike,

I'll spare you the preliminaries and get to the point: with the Phoney War behind us, London is filling up with Yank journalists, and after running into at least a dozen of them over the past week I'm starting to think I could use one, too—the fellows I've met are keen and bright and unfettered by notions of politesse, at least where getting a good story is concerned. I don't have the budget to take one on full-time, but I could split the costs if you feel like sending one of your staffers over. If you have a girl to spare, so much the better—home-front news is our

bread and butter right now. Someone smart and indepen-
dent and not overly fussy about niceties like sugar in her
coffee, since both are in short supply in dear old England
right now, and likely to remain so.

If I'm barking up the wrong tree, let me know sharp-
ish. Same goes if you do have someone to send me.

Regards,
Kaz

"So? What d'you think? Are you game?"

Ruby stifled the urge to look behind her, half convinced he was speaking to someone else, and instead attempted to focus her wavering gaze on the letter.

"So you're saying you want *me* to go."

"Yes."

"Not one of the other staff writers? Tom Alfredson or Dan Mazur?"

"I may end up sending Mazur, but that would be to cover the war itself. If Britain and her allies ever get a toehold in Europe. Besides, Kaz says he wants the woman's perspective, and you're good at that human interest crap. I liked the piece you did on those Belgian refugees the other week."

"What about Frida Lindeman?" she persisted. It couldn't be her—he had to be confusing her with someone else.

"She has her parents to look after. No. Stop right there. I've already talked to Peterson. He says you don't have any family close by."

"Mr. Peterson knows about this? And he's fine with it?"

"'Course he is. So—do you have family here that need you?"

"No. Not close by." Not anywhere.

"Then what's the problem?" There was an edge of impatience to Mr. Mitchell's voice now. "Is there someone keeping you here? A boyfriend? Is that the problem?"

Ruby shook her head, her face growing hot. "No, sir."

"Do you want the job or don't you?"

"I do, Mr. Mitchell. I do. It's only that I . . . well, I don't have a passport."

"That's what's worrying you? For chrissakes—we'll help with that. Just bring in your birth certificate and one of the staff photogs will take your picture. I've a friend in the State Department who'll make sure there isn't any holdup."

Normally she was good at thinking on her feet, but this was a lot to take in. She looked around Mr. Mitchell's strangely tidy office, so different than she'd imagined, and then stole a glance at the oddly unthreatening figure of her editor. Perhaps this was just a dream. An amazingly detailed one, but a dream all the same. Nightmares, or even good dreams like this, did have a way of being that little bit off in the details. Mr. Mitchell being so nice, for example.

If she was dreaming, it was time to wake up and face the day. To hurry things along, she spiked her thumbnail into the tender skin of her opposite palm, and waited for the pain to wake her. Nothing changed.

"When would I leave?" she asked after a moment, her heart racing. She wasn't sure if it was from excitement or straight-up fear.

"In a week or two. Soon as your passport's ready. Are you in the middle of anything now?"

"A piece on the WPA program that's training domestic servants. It's—"

"Well, finish it off, then read up on the European war. Whatever's been printed in *Time* and *Newsweek*, and I guess the *Times* as well. Any other questions?"

"How would it work? Would you both run the pieces I write?"

"Depends on the piece. I like the idea of you writing something for us every other week or so. We could call it 'Letters from London' or something like that."

"I think the *New Yorker* is using that already for Mollie Panter-Downes's columns."

"Fine. Something else, then. And only if it's got some heft to it. No profiles of brave Spitfire pilots or plucky girls riding their bikes to the munitions factory. Any other questions?"

"Who will be paying me, sir? I'm sorry if that seems crass."

"Not at all. It'll be like Kaz says in his letter—we'll split your salary down the middle, and cover your expenses, same as here. No champagne lunches at the Savoy, obviously. Anything else?"

She had about a million questions, but it wouldn't be smart to annoy him now. And there were plenty of other people she could ask. "No, sir."

"The thing is . . ." he started, and a frown marked his brow. "It could be dangerous. We both know there's a better-than-average chance of the Germans invading England by the end of the summer. As an American, and a journalist, you'd be safer than most. But I need to warn you, all the same."

"I understand, sir." She doubted he'd have bothered warning any of the men at the magazine, but she was younger than most of her colleagues, and perhaps that was the reason he worried. "I'm not afraid. I'll take my chances."

"Good girl. On your way, Miss Sutton. I'll call along to Peterson now."

"Thank you, Mr. Mitchell."

He nodded, grinned, and then picked up the telephone receiver and swiveled away. Hoisting his feet onto the bookcase under his window, he leaned back so far she braced herself for the moment he toppled backward, but if there was a trick of balancing the chair just so, he had clearly discovered it.

Moments later she was back at her desk, which was wedged into the darkest corner of the newsroom with those of the other junior staff writers. She sat down heavily, out of breath though she'd only walked a matter of yards, and immediately drew the attention of her nearest neighbor. Betty Chilton had only been on staff a few months more than Ruby, and they shared a telephone and a typewriter.

Ruby had been apprehensive, that first day at work, when Betty had introduced herself with the clipped yet airy accent of someone who'd been born several rungs higher up the ladder than most and educated accordingly. It was, in fact, the same accent that Ruby herself had been trying to master for years, honed by repeated viewings of Myrna Loy and Norma Shearer movies at the cinema around the corner from her boardinghouse.

Betty was the kind of girl who bought her skirts and blouses from Bonwit Teller and had them fitted by the seamstresses in-store. Betty lived at her parents' pied-à-terre on Riverside Drive and spent her summer weekends in Narragansett. Betty hadn't needed to buy a used copy of Emily Post's guide to etiquette and read it over and over again until its precepts were glued fast in her head.

But Betty was friendly and sweet, and if she noticed that Ruby's clothes came from the sale racks at J. C. Penney and she only had one hat for summer and one for winter, or if she realized that Ruby turned down her invitations to go dancing at the Roseland because she didn't have a nice enough dress, she was too kind to say so.

"What's wrong, Ruby? Was Mr. Mitchell mean to you?"

"Not at all. He's sending me to England, if you can believe it."

"England?"

"I'm seconded to *Picture Weekly*. They're sending me to London. I might even get a column of my own." Saying it aloud didn't make it seem any more real. She was going to England. To cover a war. With only six months of experience under her belt, somehow *she* had been chosen.

"Lucky duck, you."

"I know. I can't quite believe it. Why did they pick me, of all people?"

"Why not you? Mr. Peterson's been happy with your work."

"I guess it helps that I'm at the bottom of the pay scale. And now they each only have to cough up half my salary."

"Perhaps, but they wouldn't have chosen you if Mr. Mitchell didn't think you were up to the job. So stop worrying and take a second to feel proud of yourself."

An unwelcome memory, fierce and galling, pushed itself forward. Sister Benedicta, her nostrils flaring with disdain, her hot breath puffing sourly against Ruby's face. Forcing her to hold out her small hands for the ruler, its metal edge so sharp against her palms. Making her repeat, in front of everyone, "I will never amount to anything. I will never amount to anything. I will never amount to anything."

She had dutifully parroted the words for Sister Benedicta, but with each biting jolt of pain to her tender hands she had made a different vow. *I will make something of myself,* she had chanted silently. *I will make something of myself.*

Ruby had known many disheartening and miserable days since then, days when she had been hungry and cold and so tired she could barely stay on her feet. And she had been grateful, each time, for Sister Benedicta and her cruelty. Giving up would have meant proving that the nun had been right, and the memory of the vow she had made to herself never failed to keep her standing and moving forward.

Betty reached over and patted Ruby's arm, her kind gesture instantly banishing the specter of Sister Benedicta. "You aren't worried, are you? The war's being fought in Europe, not England. London should be safe enough for the moment. And if the Germans do invade, I'm sure you'll be sent home. It's not as if *we're* at war with them."

Ruby nodded in acknowledgment, biting back any further protestations. Were Betty to be handed the same opportunity by Mr. Mitchell, she would certainly accept with grace and courage. "You're right," she said. "I know you're right."

"When do you go?" Betty asked.

"I'm not sure. I have to get a passport first." And that just made her stomach start to flip-flop all over again.

Mr. Mitchell had said they would need a birth certificate, which meant she would have to go over to Danny's place in Hell's

Kitchen that evening, and hope he wasn't too busy. Once she explained, though, he would definitely help. Once a St Mary's kid, always a St. Mary's kid.

It would be expensive—there was no getting around it. She'd have to go home and see how much was left in her rainy-day envelope wedged behind the top drawer in her bureau. And that meant she had to leave by five o'clock and not a minute later, since there was no point going to see Danny if he'd had more than a couple of drinks. Shaky handwriting on a birth certificate wouldn't get her across the Hudson, let alone the Atlantic.

CHAPTER TWO

30 June 1940
The Sinbad
The North Atlantic, somewhere north of Ireland

The knock sounded at her cabin door at seven o'clock on the dot. For the first time in two weeks Ruby felt close to human, and she had managed not only to dress herself, but also to brush the tangles out of her hair and sit up in her berth.

When she'd stepped on board the *Sinbad* in Halifax harbor, Ruby had been brimming with excitement at the adventures that awaited her: an ocean crossing, life in a new country, and demanding work at an exciting job. Within hours of leaving port, however, she had succumbed to seasickness, and it hadn't been the sort of vaguely unwell, delicately nauseous feeling that she'd always imagined when thinking of such a malady. It was a stomach-emptying, life-draining thing, her entire body trying to turn itself inside out, her world reduced to the bunk on which she was marooned and the bucket sitting next to it.

Today, however, she felt like she might just survive. Her head wouldn't stop pounding, likely because she hadn't been able to sit up for days and days, but it was worth it, if only because from this new perspective she could see out of her window. The view was nothing more than clear gray skies, and here and there a wisp of cloud far above, but it was a pleasant sight all the same.

The knock sounded again. "Come in, Davey," she called out.

Davey Eccles was the *Sinbad*'s youngest and hardest-working steward's boy. Only sixteen, he'd joined the merchant marine after leaving school two years before, and had served on three different ships already. His previous ship had been better, he'd explained, but it was laid up for repairs and he'd been restless after a week in a seaman's hostel in Liverpool. When a position had come up on the *Sinbad*, Davey had signed on for the dangerous North Atlantic route without thinking twice.

"I thought about joining the navy, but my dad wants me to stay in the merchant marine, just like him and Granddad, so I'll do my bit here."

"Aren't you afraid?" she'd asked.

"Aren't we all? Not as if Liverpool is safe, nor anywhere else in England, I expect. Besides, it's hard to be scared when you're busy with work."

And it was dangerous work. German U-boats were making a feast of ships in the Atlantic that summer, for the convoys stretched many miles from end to end, and it was impossible for the naval warships guarding them to be everywhere at once.

Yet there was no question of halting the convoys, for they were the lifeline keeping Britain afloat and undefeated. Passengers like Ruby were incidental to the convoys' true cargo: food, fuel, and war matériel from the Empire, and the enemy regarded every ship as fair game. If there were a more dangerous place to work in the summer of 1940, Ruby couldn't imagine where it would be.

Davey alone had seen to her well-being when she'd become sick, and if it hadn't been for his visits with weak tea, dry toast, and ample supplies of fresh sheets and towels, she was sure her lifeless body would have been slung overboard long ago.

"Look at you, sitting up already! You must be feeling better today."

"I am, thanks. I slept well, too."

"That'll put roses in your cheeks. Here's some breakfast for you. I had a feeling you'd be better this morning, so I brought some porridge with your tea and toast."

Ruby tried not to look at the porridge, since even thinking about it made her stomach churn, and not because of the sea-sickness. She'd eaten porridge once a day at St. Mary's, some-times twice when there wasn't anything else for supper, and when she'd left the orphanage for good, she'd vowed she would never eat it again. She would starve before touching the stuff, but there was no reason to hurt Davey's feelings by saying so.

"Thank you. This looks great. Any news this morning?"

After learning that Ruby was a journalist, Davey had made it his mission to share with her every scrap of information that came in over the wires and the ship's radio. When France had surrendered to Germany a little more than a week ago, he had woken her in the middle of the night, certain she would want to know.

"Nothing more from France," he said now. "Hitler's been to visit Paris—but I told you that already, didn't I?"

"Mmph," Ruby answered, her mouth full of toast.

"Let's see . . . they've started bombing England farther

north. The Germans, that is. I think they're trying to knock out the factories in the Midlands. At least, that's what the admiral was saying when I brought him his morning tea."

"Where are the Midlands?" she asked.

"I'm not sure how you'd describe them. North of London but not as far north as Manchester? With Birmingham in the middle? I grew up on the south coast, in Portsmouth, so I've never been there myself."

"Was anyone killed?"

"Admiral Fountaine didn't say. D'you need any fresh towels or linens?"

"No, thanks. I'm fine for now. Thank you again, Davey."

"It's no trouble at all, miss. I'll come again in an hour to collect your tray."

Ruby finished off her tea and toast at leisure, and when she still felt well a half hour later, she inched off her bunk and crossed to the window for a proper look outside. It was a very small window, and fogged with salt after nearly two weeks at sea, but she could see out of it well enough.

It wasn't quite as dull outside as she'd thought earlier, for the sea was darkly blue, glittering brightly as it swirled and broke into eddied waves, and the sky itself was growing ever more dazzling as the sun arched higher into the morning. Davey had warned her there would be no sign of land until they were practically on top of Liverpool, so she didn't fret at the endless horizon now, nor did she allow herself to scan the restless ocean for evidence of U-boats.

When she'd been seasick, the days had swirled together in a shapeless morass of misery, and it had come as a surprise, when she'd finally found the strength to sit up and keep down a few sips of broth, to discover they'd already been at sea for ten days. Usually, Davey informed her, the Atlantic crossing was far shorter, but their ship was part of a convoy, and could only travel as fast as the slowest ship in their group.

Back in New York, she'd been surprised when Mr. Peterson's secretary, who handled travel arrangements for the staff, had explained the indirect route she'd be taking for the journey to England. First Ruby would board an express train to Boston, then change to an overnight train to Halifax. From there, she'd make the crossing on a vessel that was part of the next convoy of troop ships and freighters leaving for England.

Ruby had known better than to ask if the magazine would be flying her over, for a one-way airplane ticket to England cost hundreds and hundreds of dollars. All the same, she had hoped there'd be room for her on a passenger liner sailing directly from New York.

"Too expensive," Miss Gavin had said flatly. "And none of them are going to England, anyway. Far too dangerous. Here are your tickets—do you have somewhere safe to put them?—and here's your passport."

The day before her departure, her colleagues at *The American* had treated her to an impromptu farewell party, and even Mr. Mitchell had stopped by for a slice of cake and a paper cup of rye-laden punch. As a farewell gift, they'd given her a brand-new Kodak Baby Brownie camera, which one of the staff photographers had insisted on showing her how to use, and a dozen spools of film. The fuss had been embarrassing, but at least no one had tried to make a speech.

Ruby knew only a few of her neighbors at the boarding-house, since she was never home for meals and Mrs. Hirsch two doors down, the one person who had ever bothered to talk to her, had died of cancer a year ago. Ruby had never met the woman who'd moved into the vacant room.

Although Ruby had lived there for nearly three years, it had only taken her an hour to pack. Everything she had fit into one good-sized suitcase, since she'd never been one for knickknacks and didn't have any keepsakes beyond a few photographs. The one thing she owned that she really and truly cared about—the sole possession she'd risk her life to save in a fire—was her Underwood Universal typewriter, and only because it had taken her almost a year to pay off in weekly installments.

On the advice of Betty and some of the other girls at work, she'd filled a second suitcase with stockings, soap, cold cream, bobby pins, chocolate bars, and three jars of peanut butter, all things they assured her were impossible to find in England.

She'd left New York with as little fanfare as when she'd moved there almost six years earlier, taking the train up the coast and across the border into Canada, finally ending up in Halifax. She'd waited three days as the convoy's ships were loaded and assembled, and she'd had a little taste of the war there, too, for the city had a blackout in place at night and some things, like fresh eggs and sugar, were getting scarce.

At last she'd been summoned from the hotel, a grand place just crawling with Canadian naval officers, and taken out to the *Sinbad* on a tender boat, and she was glad, now, that she hadn't known then how sick she would be in a few hours. Otherwise she never would have left dry land.

THEY DOCKED IN Liverpool less than forty-eight hours later. There was time for one last, hurried breakfast, brought to her cabin before the sun was up, and Davey lingered awhile, reluctant to say goodbye.

"You're sure you know where to go?" he asked her for at least the third time that morning.

"I think so. Down to the landing stage, then to customs, then to the railway station. Right?"

"Right. Don't forget to buy a through ticket for Euston, otherwise you'll have to queue up all over again. Do you have enough for the fare?"

"The woman who made my travel arrangements back home gave me five pounds. Will that be enough?"

"Enough to get you there and back again twice over. You'll go to Edge Hill first, then change for Lime Street, then to Euston. Can you remember all that or do you want to write it down?"

She smiled to reassure him. "I'll remember. Oh—I'm supposed to call the magazine where I'll be working."

"Do you have any coins for the telephone?"

"No, but they said I could reverse the charges."

"Then it's easy," he reassured her. "Tell the operator before you give her the number and she'll sort it out. There's a row of telephone kiosks in the main hall at Lime Street. And there'll be porters to help with your things, so don't try to carry everything yourself."

"I won't." She held out her hand for him to shake and then, since they were alone and she had become very fond of him, pressed a quick kiss to his cheek. "Thank you again, Davey, for everything."

"You're very welcome. You should know, well, you're a . . . a grand girl, Miss Sutton," he said, his voice catching. "I wish you well."

Her heart had turned over at his words, for he was such a nice boy and she couldn't stand the thought of him going back to sea again in a few days and playing cat-and-mouse with the Germans all the way back to Canada. He was so young, and he'd had to grow up far too quickly. So she said goodbye to him and turned away before she embarrassed them both by getting all weepy and sentimental.

She was off the ship and through to the train station before she even had a chance to feel nervous. With thousands disembarking from the convoy that morning, the customs officers seemed intent on keeping the line moving, and apart from a cursory glance at her passport and a stamp recording her entrance to the United Kingdom, no one so much as asked for her name. Only then did she stop holding her breath.

Davey had explained everything so clearly that she had no trouble navigating the route from one train station to the next. The telephone booths were just where he'd said they would be, and all she had to do was give the operator her name and the number at *Picture Weekly* and wait for someone to answer.

A woman with a brisk, no-nonsense sort of voice came on the line after only a few seconds, and when Ruby introduced herself and told her which train she'd be arriving on, the woman promised someone would be there to meet her.

Ruby was lucky enough to snag a window seat on the crowded train, and it provided a glorious view of England in high summer. It was the greenest countryside she had ever seen, and as soon as they'd left Liverpool behind, that's what it really seemed to be—nothing but mile after mile of fields and low fieldstone walls and impossibly picturesque villages. Every so often, a town would appear out of nowhere, a stark island of brick and masonry amid verdant seas of green.

The towering canyons of New York City's grand avenues had been strange and unfamiliar, too, when she had left New Jersey for Manhattan six long years ago. She'd been nervous and unsure of herself then, just as she was now, but she had conquered her fears. Against all odds, she had made something of herself, and she would do so again. No matter what awaited her in London, she would prove Sister Benedicta wrong.

"EUSTON! LONDON EUSTON! End of the line, ladies and gents— London Euston!"

Ruby woke with a start. The other people in her compartment were on their feet, reaching to retrieve their bags and cases from the overhead racks, and the platform outside was bustling with departing passengers. With a suitcase in each hand, her typewriter case slung over one shoulder, and her handbag in the crook of her free arm, Ruby lurched onto the platform and, shuffling, made her way along to the barrier. A guard was waiting to take her ticket, and when she didn't manage to retrieve it in time, she had to stand aside and dig through her pockets to find the silly thing.

"Miss Sutton?"

She looked up, astonished that the guard would know her name, and realized that another man, just on the other side of the barrier, had spoken to her. He wore the uniform of a British army officer and held a neatly printed sign that read MISS R. SUTTON.

"I'm Ruby Sutton," she volunteered.

"I'm Captain Bennett. Walter Kaczmarek asked me to meet you."

"Thanks," she said. "I appreciate it."

Captain Bennett was at least a head taller than her and looked to be in his early thirties, although Ruby was terrible at guessing people's ages. He had a disconcertingly direct gaze and a handshake to rival that of a circus strongman.

"Kaz and I are friends, and Tuesdays are his busiest day," he explained. "I happened to be in town and at loose ends, so he asked me to fetch you from the station. Is that all your things? You don't have a trunk to follow?"

"No. This is it."

"Very well." He turned to the guard, his brow creasing into a frown. "Let her through, will you?" Although it was posed as a question, his tone indicated otherwise.

"Oh, yes, sir," the guard replied, and obligingly waved Ruby past the barrier.

"Give me your cases, then," Captain Bennett said. "I've a car waiting for us outside."

He led them past the line for taxis at the station exit, instead approaching a car that was parked at the curb a few yards away. The driver got out, grumbling a little, and came around to take Ruby's suitcases. "Took your time there. Said you'd only be five minutes."

"Sorry. Miss Sutton's train was running late."

She got in the cab, still clutching her typewriter in its case, and the driver steered them away from the station.

"How was the crossing?" Captain Bennett asked.

"A blur. I was sick for most of it. But the convoy wasn't attacked, so I can't complain."

"I suppose not," he agreed.

"Where are we going?"

"The Manchester Hotel. That's where you'll be lodging. They've plenty of other boarders, and it's clean and safe. Not very grand, though."

"I don't care how nice it is, just as long as my bed stays put when I lie down on it."

The corner of his mouth began to curl into a smile, but then, as if thinking better of it, he smoothed his features into an expression of sober neutrality. "I promise it will."

Turning her head to look out the window, Ruby couldn't help but marvel at the passing streetscape. Unlike the ordered grid of upper Manhattan, there seemed to be no rhyme or reason to the arrangement of the roads they passed, and hardly any of the buildings she saw were more than three or four stories tall. It was quieter, too, with scarcely any traffic compared to New York. Most of the vehicles she saw were taxis or delivery trucks, though there was no shortage of horse-drawn wagons, and darting to and fro were any number of people on bicycles.

She glanced back at Captain Bennett. He had closed his eyes, perhaps glad of a moment of peace in his day. She had to admit, now she could stare without fear of his noticing, that he was as handsome as a movie star, with short-cropped hair that would probably curl if he let it grow a bit, and a high-bridged nose that wouldn't have been out of place on a Roman senator. The sweep of his long eyelashes couldn't camouflage the shadows under his eyes, though, or the echo of fatigue that was written across his features. This was a man who was tired down to his bones, and if she'd known him any better—or had he been an interview subject— she'd have insisted on discovering why.

He opened his eyes just then, as if he could feel the weight of her regard, and when he turned to meet her gaze, she realized they were a dark and quite mesmerizing shade of blue. "Is it very different here?" he asked softly.

"From New York? I guess so. You don't go in much for sky-scrapers, do you?"

"Not so much," he agreed.

"Have you ever been to New York?"

"No. I've never been to America. Although I always wanted to go. After the war, perhaps."

Their car turned a corner and drew to a halt in front of a large, dark building. "Manchester Hotel," announced the driver.

"Right, then. Here we are," said Captain Bennett. "Your new home awaits."

CHAPTER THREE

While Captain Bennett paid the driver and gathered up her bags, Ruby assessed the exterior of her new home. The name of her lodgings had conjured up visions of a grand manor house, but the Manchester was a gloomy pile of soot-stained bricks that looked more like a prison than a hotel. Her spirits sinking, Ruby followed him inside.

"Good evening," he said to the woman at the front desk. "This is Miss Sutton. There should be a reservation for her—it may be under *Picture Weekly*. She's just arrived from America."

The desk clerk's answering smile was warm and genuine, and immediately elevated Ruby's estimation of the hotel. "Welcome to England, Miss Sutton. I'm sure you're tired, so I'll go over things quick as I may. You're on half board here—breakfast and supper, and do let us know if you'll be missing a meal. Breakfast is from half six to half eight; supper's from half five to eight o'clock. Bed linens and towels changed every Saturday. Front door is locked after ten each night but you can ring the bell if you're late in. Here's your key—you're in 312. We've a shelter in the cellar, with cots set up but no blankets or pillows. Bring those down with you if you've got time after the siren sounds. And don't forget to keep your draperies well shut. If we're fined by the warden, we pass it on to you. There's a limit on hot water, so don't run the bath past the mark in the tub. And I'll need your passport, identity card, and ration book, please and thank you."

At this, Captain Bennett reached into his coat and pulled out a folded card, which he handed to the clerk. "Sorry. I ought to have given this to you straightaway. This is Miss Sutton's temporary ration book. She'll pass on her permanent one as soon as it arrives, together with her identity card. Until then I hope her passport will do. Miss Sutton?"

Ruby quickly handed over the document, anxious to be finished and off to her room, and was gratified when the woman did no more than page through it and note down its registration number.

With no bellboy in sight, if that was what they even called them in England, Ruby was resigned to lugging her cases to her room; but once again Captain Bennett gathered them up, together with her precious typewriter, and led the way up the nearest staircase.

"Avoid lifts whenever you can," he advised without looking back. "The mechanics who used to maintain them won't be back for the duration."

Her room was a narrow, dim chamber, made darker by the blackout curtains swathing the single window. A metal-framed bed stood along one wall, while a chest of drawers and small desk occupied the other. In one corner, to the left of the window, was a wall-hung sink. It wasn't fancy, but it was clean and private and about a thousand times nicer than the dormitory she'd shared with a score of other girls until she was fourteen.

Ruby went to the window and was relieved to see it faced over a warren of side streets; she'd take a quiet room over a pretty view any day. She turned, intending to shake Captain Bennett's hand and send him on his way, but he spoke first.

"No doubt you're tired, but will you let me take you to dinner? The place I have in mind is far nicer than the dining room here. If you need a few minutes, I can wait downstairs."

"Are you sure?" she asked. "I don't want to take up any more of your time than—"

"Very sure," he said, and there was something in his expression, something she couldn't quite pin down, that put her at ease. Perhaps a glimmer of humor behind his reserved and somewhat starchy veneer?

"That's nice of you. Is five minutes all right?"

"Take as long as you like. I'll be downstairs."

She shut the door behind him and went to the sink to wash her face, only there was no soap. Unlatching the smaller of her suitcases, she fished out a bar and ignored the siren call of the jars of peanut butter buried beneath her supply of Lifebuoy.

There was no time to change, and her clothes would all be creased anyway, so she washed her face, brushed her hair and teeth, applied powder and lipstick, and was downstairs exactly five minutes later.

"All set," she declared.

"Do you mind walking?" he asked, holding open the front door. "It's not far—about a third of a mile."

"Not at all."

She wasn't an especially short woman, but Captain Bennett was at least six inches taller, with correspondingly long legs, and he walked at a pace that left her nearly breathless. They continued on for five minutes or so, with the captain occasionally drawing her attention to points of interest, and then turned onto a side street that got progressively narrower and darker, the early evening sun ignoring it altogether.

"We're heading toward Clerkenwell," he explained, as if that ought to mean something to her. "You'll never see it mentioned in the guides for tourists, but it's one of my favorite parts of London. And this is one of my favorite places in it."

They had come to a halt in front of a narrow storefront. "The Victory Café," Ruby said, reading the lettering that adorned the window. Inside, past blackout curtains that had yet to be drawn, she could just glimpse a handful of tables, each draped in a red-and-white-checked tablecloth. Bennett opened the door, ushering her in, and they were instantly enveloped in the mouthwatering aromas of Italian cooking.

Until that moment, she realized, she'd been expecting him to take her somewhere that served traditional British food, like fish and chips or roast beef with, well, whatever British people ate with roast beef. He couldn't have known that her favorite place to eat in New York had been a little hole-in-the-wall Italian restaurant around the corner from work, and yet he'd brought her here, to a place that, judging by the smell alone, served exactly the sort of food she liked best.

"Bennett!" came a voice from the back. An apron-clad man came rushing forward, his careworn face wreathed in smiles, and shook Captain Bennett's outstretched hand with unaffected enthusiasm. "It is so good to see you, my friend. We were worried—"

"No need, no need. Jimmy, this is my friend Ruby Sutton. Miss Sutton has just arrived from America, and she had a hard voyage over. I thought she deserved a good meal."

"The best meal in London—that's what you get here at my café," Jimmy promised, shaking Ruby's hand only a fraction less vigorously. "Welcome, welcome. Come and sit, and I'll bring you some of Maria's bread."

"I've been coming here for years," Bennett explained. "Jimmy and his wife, Maria, run the place. It was her father's until he retired. He—"

Jimmy was back, with a basket of bread that smelled like heaven and a pair of handwritten menus. "You've heard the news?" he asked Captain Bennett, his expression solemn.

"I have. It's an awful thing. Did you know anyone on the ship?"

"One of Maria's cousins. We're so worried. Vittorio, you know, he's almost eighty."

"They're in Scotland still?"

"Last we heard."

"I'll ask around," Captain Bennett said. "If I find out anything, I promise to let you know."

Jimmy's face crumpled, and for an awful moment Ruby thought he was going to cry. "Thank you, Bennett. You are so good to us—so good to my family."

"It's no trouble at all. Your family has fed me well over the years. Oh, before I forget—do you have any wine?"

"Not much. A few bottles of Sangiovese, and one Brunello di Montalcino. What would you like?"

"May we have some of the Sangiovese? Say a glass each?"

"For you, Bennett, anything."

Captain Bennett waited until Jimmy was out of earshot before he spoke again. "He and I were talking about a ship, the *Arandora Star*. It was sunk by a U-boat off the west coast of Ireland this morning, probably around the same time your ship was docking safely in Liverpool. It was heading for Canada and was packed full of interned Italians, never mind that most of them were born right here in England."

"That's awful," she said, her appetite withering. "All those innocent people . . ."

"It's been a rough time for Jimmy and his family since Mussolini threw in his lot with Hitler. Maria's father and brothers were sent to a camp in Scotland—Jimmy was spared because he married into the family and isn't Italian himself. And the restaurant's name? It's the Victory Café now, but it was Vittorio's until a fortnight ago."

"They changed it to sound more patriotic?"

"They changed it because some pack of cretins tossed bricks through their front window on June tenth. The next week, a bucket of black paint was thrown over the boarded-up front."

"It's brave of them to start over."

"What choice did they have? Still, enough people in the neighborhood know and like them . . . they should survive. At any rate, you must be famished. Do you see anything you like?"

Ruby scanned the menu, which was short and not very descriptive. "'Baked pasta with Italian sauce'—do you suppose that's lasagna?"

"It is. Most Italian restaurants anglicize their menus, I assume for the benefit of xenophobic patrons. Shall I order it for you?" At her nod, he waved Jimmy over. "Miss Sutton and I will both have the lasagna."

Jimmy returned minutes later with two large plates, each one bearing a slab of lasagna at least four inches square and two inches deep. It tasted as good as it smelled, despite there being more carrots than meat in the sauce, and although she burned her tongue with her first mouthful, Ruby didn't pause, methodically eating bite after bite until nearly half her plate was empty. Only then did she force herself to slow down. After all, no one was waiting to take it from her if she didn't eat fast enough.

"Good?" Captain Bennett asked.

"Very good." She took a sip of wine, the first she'd ever tasted apart from Holy Communion, and tried not to wince. Like tea, red wine was something she'd have to learn how to enjoy.

"So," she began, "are you from London?" It wasn't curiosity that made her ask, only her natural interest in a close friend of her editor. The fact that he was handsome and interesting and had excellent taste in restaurants had nothing to do with it. Nothing at all.

"I am. I grew up not far from here."

She waited for him to elaborate, but he only sipped at his wine and watched her, his expression unreadable. "Were you in the army before the war? I mean . . . that *is* an army uniform, isn't it?"

"It is. I'm with the fourth battalion of the Oxfordshire and Buckinghamshire Light Infantry. Bit of a mouthful, isn't it? Easier to just say the Ox and Bucks. I joined up last fall."

"And before that?"

"Before that I was a barrister. What an American would call a lawyer."

"Why did you decide to become a barrister?"

"I didn't, not really. It was a family thing, I suppose you could say. And what about you? Where are you from?"

"New Jersey. Although I've lived in New York—the city, I mean—for years."

"Really? You don't have much of an accent. At least not one that I can detect."

That was a relief. "Do you mean like Jimmy Cagney? 'Youse guys' and all that?"

"I suppose so. I do beg your pardon if that seems rude of me."

"Not at all. Besides, a lot of New Yorkers do sound like that."

"But not you," he said with a quick smile, and turned his attention back to his dinner.

She looked to her own plate, and was surprised to see that she'd finished her lasagna. "I guess I must have been hungry."

"Did you enjoy it? The lasagna?"

"I did. It was much nicer than my lunch—all I had with me on the train were some stale crackers. I thought about opening one of my jars of peanut butter, but they were at the bottom of my—"

"*Butter* mixed with *peanuts*?" he interrupted. "Who on earth thought up such a thing? It sounds revolting."

Ruby couldn't help but laugh at the look of horror on his face. "It's not revolting at all. Just peanuts, made into a kind of paste. We use it as a spread. I put it on toast and crackers, and sometimes I even eat it with sliced apples—"

"Good God—stop right there," he pleaded, and drank down the last of his wine. "Peanut butter," he muttered, his voice warm with suppressed laughter. "You Americans and your strange notions of what constitutes food . . ."

"Says the man from a city where they eat jellied eels."

"A great delicacy, I assure you. Now, let's talk about tomorrow. Kaz asked me to tell you that he wants you there for half-past eight. Take your passport with you, and ask one of the staff photographers to take your picture. After work you can go to the police station on Bridewell Place, just to the south, and sort out your identity card. They should also be able to give you a gas mask."

"You don't have one," she observed.

"No, but you probably ought to carry one with you, if only because it's still considered an offense to leave home without one. Never mind that the Germans will never bother to gas us if a common or garden-variety bomb will do."

"What about my press card?"

"For that, you'll go to the MOI—the Ministry of Information. Kaz can help. And as I said at the hotel, your ration book is already being sorted. Got it?"

"Yes," she said, hoping she managed to remember everything he was telling her. It would be a shame to be deported because she'd forgotten to fill in a few forms.

He then produced a small book from his inside coat pocket and set it in front of her. On its cover was an abstract design of crisscrossing lines and the title *A to Z Atlas and Guide to London*.

"This is a map of every street in London. We call it the A to Zed—not 'Zee,' if you please. Guard this with your life, since it's next to impossible to get new ones." He thumbed through it rapidly, revealing page after page of detailed maps, before spreading it open on the table between them. "Here's the hotel," he said, circling it carefully with a pencil he'd pulled from his breast pocket. "You may have noticed that most of the street signs have been taken down, so try not to stray from the main roads just yet. To get to work tomorrow, you'll walk south," he explained, tracing a line with the pencil, "turning here at the cathedral, and then you'll walk west, along here, to Fleet Street. Bride Lane will be on your left. Turn onto the lane and you'll see some steps on your right. They lead up to the churchyard for St. Bride's. Just before the steps is number eighty-seven, and that's where you're going."

"Right. Number 87 Bride Lane."

"No, sorry—it's 87 Fleet Street. I should have said. There's a sign on the door, or rather just to the side of the door, around shoulder level. Just go upstairs; I'm sure they'll be waiting for you."

"Is all of London this confusing?"

"Nearly all of it," he admitted with a quick grin.

Just then Jimmy came by to clear their plates. "I'd offer you coffee, but I haven't been able to get my hands on any for weeks now," he said apologetically.

"That's quite all right. I really ought to be getting Miss Sutton back to her lodgings."

The bill for dinner, which Jimmy had written out on a piece of scrap paper, came to three shillings and sixpence. "Has anyone explained English currency to you?" Captain Bennett asked.

"No," she admitted. "I had to ask the ticket agent at the station in Liverpool to show me which coins to use."

"It doesn't make much sense to foreigners. I'll tell you on the way back to the Manchester."

They said good night to Jimmy and began the journey home. As they walked, Captain Bennett patiently explained pounds, shillings, and pence to her, and after a while it did begin to almost make sense.

It was rare for her to feel so at ease with someone on such short acquaintance, but there was something very reassuring about Captain Bennett. Perhaps it was the air of solid, dependable competence he projected, which she had to admit was really comforting on her first day in a new country. Certainly it didn't hurt that he was one of the handsomest men she'd ever met. If she wasn't careful, she'd end up batting her eyelashes at him and tripping over her words like some doe-eyed ingénue.

"I meant to ask earlier," he said as they waited to cross Long Lane, "if you know about the blackout."

"I do. I mean, they had one in Halifax on my way over. I know to be careful with the curtains."

"Yes, there's that. You should also be wary when you're out after dark. On cloudy or rainy nights, or ones without any moon, it is really and truly dark. You wouldn't believe how many people have been injured or killed by tripping over a curb, or getting knocked down by a car. And you're more at risk than most. Never forget to look to your right. That's where the cars are coming from—your right, not your left."

"I'll be careful. I promise."

They had arrived at the front door of the Manchester. "Good night, Miss Sutton," he said, and shook her outstretched hand. "Good luck tomorrow."

"Good night," she replied, and then, before she could stop herself, "Why are you being so nice? I don't mean to be rude. I'm just wondering why you went out of your way to help a complete stranger. That's all."

"Simply my impeccable English manners," he answered, and even though he didn't smile, she had a feeling he was teasing her, just a little. "Of course, if you'd borne the slightest resemblance to a grizzled old hack like Kaz, I'd have left you standing at the station."

"I'm relieved you didn't. Thanks for tonight."

"You're most welcome. If you do have any trouble getting on, please let me know. Kaz knows how to find me."

CHAPTER FOUR

Ruby awoke at dawn, and after rubbing the sleep from her eyes and muttering a prayer of thanks for a night spent in a real bed on dry land, she put on her robe and slippers and tiptoed down the hall for a quick, tepid bath. Twisting her hair back from her face, she secured it firmly with bobby pins and willed it not to frizz up, then turned her attention to her clothes for the day. They'd needed a pressing when she'd unpacked them the night before, but it had been too late to go in search of the hotel laundry, or to ask if such a thing as an electric clothes iron was available in England.

Instead she'd sponged her jacket, skirt, and blouse with a dampened facecloth and arranged them on the desktop to dry overnight. That had served to take care of the worst of the creases; and it wasn't as if anyone at the magazine would be expecting her to have stepped out of a bandbox.

She forced herself to sit down for breakfast in the dining room, which featured nothing more than strong tea, cold toast, and a very small amount of jam. The waitress, who introduced herself as Maggie, offered to make up a fish-paste sandwich for her to take to work, and it was all Ruby could do to maintain a neutral expression. Presumably it tasted nicer than it sounded.

"Thanks, but I should be fine for today."

"Another cuppa before you go?"

It took a moment before Ruby realized she was being offered a second cup of tea. "Oh, no. No, thanks."

"Suit yourself. If you want any of your tea ration back from your book, just let me know."

By eight o'clock she was en route, her bag and gas mask slung over her shoulder and her *A to Z* at the ready. With its help, and by following the landmarks Captain Bennett had pointed out, she found her way without too much trouble, though she was careful to pause every few hundred yards to check her bearings and take in her surroundings.

London was a beautiful city—the war hadn't changed that fact, at least not yet. Some of the buildings were ordinary enough, their bland facades quickly forgotten, but others reminded her of something from a fairy tale, with mullioned windows and crooked, cross-timbered upper floors that overhung the street below.

The larger shops she passed had their windows banded with tape, she assumed to guard against flying glass in the event of bomb blasts, and a few had even replaced their picture windows with wooden covers into which a smaller pane of glass had been inserted. Compared to store windows at home, where abundance was the rule, the displays of goods were modestly arranged. One shoe shop had a lonely pair of black lace-up ladies' boots, while a druggist's window nearby held a first-aid case, its contents lined up in neat rows around it.

And then she was standing at the corner of St. Paul's churchyard. Before her was the great cathedral, somehow plainer than she had imagined, and yet also the most beautiful building she had ever seen. With its restrained ornamentation and measured symmetry, it felt . . . reassuring. It looked, she decided, as if reason had been embodied in architectural form. What was a brash new skyscraper compared to *that*?

At last she was across Ludgate Circus, scurrying in the wake of other pedestrians to avoid being squashed flat in the street, and turning down Bride Lane. Just before the steps up to the churchyard, exactly as Captain Bennett had said, was number 87. A small, metal plaque was affixed to its bricks at shoulder height: PICTURE WEEKLY—RECEPTION FIRST FLOOR.

She opened the door, which gave directly onto a staircase—where was the first floor?—and marched upstairs to the landing. She went through another door, this one unmarked, and found herself in a small waiting room. At the far end, a woman was seated behind a desk. Seeing Ruby, she stood and came forward, her hand outstretched.

"Miss Sutton? Delighted to make your acquaintance. I'm Evelyn Berridge. We spoke on the telephone yesterday. Let me take your coat, and your hat, if you like. How was the crossing? Are you settled in nicely at the Manchester? Did Bennett meet you?"

"He did. It was really nice of you to send him along."

"Oh, that was Kaz's idea. Now, the editorial meeting starts in five minutes, so you've some time to meet the others. Would you like a cup of tea?"

"No, thanks. I only just had breakfast."

"I hope they're treating you well there. At the Manchester, I mean. It isn't easy to find lodgings these days, but Kaz knows someone who knows someone—you know how it is."

As they talked, Miss Berridge led them along a short hallway that opened to a larger room with individual desks arranged around its perimeter and a big, round table, surrounded by stools, at its center. They went straight to a desk in the far corner.

"This is where you'll be sitting. You've a telephone of your own—we've ten lines going out, so you shouldn't have any trouble placing calls—and a typewriter. I put pencils and a pen with a fresh nib in the drawer to the left, and there's a bottle of ink, too, along with some other bits and bobs. Paper clips and so forth."

Ruby hadn't expected much more than a dim corner and a shared telephone and typewriter, so her new working accommodations were a welcome surprise. "This is great," she enthused, wondering if everyone at *Picture Weekly* would be as nice as Miss Berridge.

"I'm so glad you like it. The meeting will start as soon as Kaz arrives—we sit at the big table." Miss Berridge checked her wristwatch and frowned. "Do you mind if I run back to my desk? I just have a few things to sort out before . . ."

"Go right ahead."

Everyone else looked to be busy, so rather than bother them right away, she sat down, pulled out her notebook, and stowed her handbag in the right-hand drawer. When she looked up again two people, a man and a woman, were standing in front of the desk. He was in his late twenties, she judged, with a slim build and pleasant face made almost memorable by a pencil-thin mustache. The woman next to him seemed a little younger, likely around Ruby's age, and was a dead ringer for Betty Grable.

"Are you the new girl?" the man asked.

"I am," she said, and held out her hand for them to shake. "Ruby Sutton."

"I'm Nell Fisher," the woman said.

"And I'm Peter Drury. We're staff writers here."

"Pleased to meet both of you. I guess we'll be starting the editorial meeting pretty soon."

"Soon-*ish*," Miss Fisher qualified. "We're waiting for Kaz and Nigel to arrive."

"Would you like us to introduce you to the others?" Mr. Drury offered. "We've been down to a skeleton staff for a while, so we're pleased as punch to have you here."

"Oh, yes," said Miss Fisher. "We've been counting the days since Kaz told us you were coming over. A year ago we had eight staff writers. With you, we're back up to three."

"*Three* staff writers for a weekly magazine? How do you manage?" she asked wonderingly.

"Some weeks it's a hard slog," Mr. Drury said, "but Kaz writes at least one big piece each week. So that helps."

"Our page count is down," Miss Fisher added. "We were running at seventy-two pages an issue before the war, and most weeks now we're only at twenty-four. Paper shortages, mainly. And we've fewer adverts, too."

"Do you have any photographers on staff?"

"Yes," Mr. Drury answered, "but only two. They usually hide out in their aerie upstairs—they've a studio and darkroom on the top floor. They'll come down for the meeting."

"Do you—" she began, but was interrupted by a shout from the hall.

"Morning!"

"That's Kaz," Mr. Drury explained.

"You really call him Kaz? Not Mr. Kaczmarek?"

"Nobody does," Miss Fisher insisted. "He's just Kaz. And he doesn't stand on ceremony."

"Nor do we," Mr. Drury added. "We're all on a first-name basis here. Come on—we'd better sit down."

She took the chair to Mr. Drury's—Peter's—right, and was surprised when the chair to her right was taken by a tall, rather shambling figure, his arms overflowing with folders and papers. He let everything drop on the table in an untidy heap before turning to Ruby. His eyes, much magnified by his eyeglasses, were a pale, almost icy blue, and gave her the impression he was the sort of man who missed *nothing*.

"Miss Sutton? Ruby?" he asked, his voice as deep and warm as a radio newsreader's.

"Yes, sir," she answered, and shook his hand, which was nearly as big as a catcher's mitt.

"Delighted to meet you at last. Was my friend Bennett kind to you?"

"He was, sir. Thank you for sending him."

"You and I shall have a chat later, but first—our weekly editorial meeting." He sat back in his chair and surveyed the assembled company. "All present? Who are we missing? Ah. Just Nigel. Very well. While we wait I might as well introduce our new colleague, Ruby Sutton. Ruby—I do hope you don't mind my using your Christian name—Ruby has been kind enough to abandon New York for the uncertainty of life with us here in wartime London, and for that we are most grateful. I believe you've made the acquaintance of your fellow staff writers?"

"Yes, sir."

"Then let's move on to our photographers, Frank Gossage and Mary Buchanan."

The table was too big for her to reach across and shake hands, so she simply smiled and nodded at them both. Frank looked a pleasant sort, unassuming and almost forgettable, but Mary was another matter entirely. She appeared to be in her late thirties, with sharp features, dark hair that was cut almost as short as a man's, and a perfectly tailored trouser suit.

"Welcome to *Picture Weekly*," she said, her Scottish accent evident in every rolled *r*. "I look forward to working with you."

"Thanks," Ruby answered, too intimidated by Miss Buchanan's direct gaze and confident bearing to say more.

"Now I should like to introduce you to Mr. Dunleavy, our librarian." Ruby exchanged a smile with the man, who had to be at least seventy years old, and was so slight that a sudden gust of wind might easily knock him down. "Mr. Dunleavy has been with us since the magazine's inception in 1935, and I daresay knows more about it than anyone else, myself included."

Another man came into the room just then, seating himself in the chair to Kaz's right. He was in his early thirties, of an age with their editor, and was rather handsome, with light brown hair that fell forward into his eyes. He reached across to shake her hand, blowing smoke from the cigarette that dangled from the corner of his mouth, and offered up a mumbled hello.

"Delighted you could join us," Kaz observed dryly.

"Sorry. Was on a telephone call. Is this Ruby from America?"

"Yes, this is Miss Sutton. Ruby, this is Nigel Vernon, our assistant editor, who presumably was busy with something pressing."

"Sorry—had to finish off a call. Will tell you about it in a moment."

"I can't wait. So, Ruby—our schedule. We start fresh every Wednesday while the previous week's issue is at press. Everyone takes a half day on Saturdays, and we're also off on Sundays, barring the need to chase down a story. Final proofs go out Tuesday evening, and then we start again the next day. Is that at all familiar?"

"It is. At *The American* we go to press on Thursdays, but otherwise it's the same."

"Then you're used to working quickly. Good. With that out of the way, let's begin. Nigel?"

"I just spoke to a man who was on Guernsey last week, within days of the Germans taking control of the Channel Islands. He wants to show us some photographs he took. I gather they show some damage from the air raids that happened just before the invasion. The MOI will need to clear them, and they may turn out to be rubbish . . ."

"Let's see what they're like," said Kaz. "If they're any good I'll write up a piece on the decision to demilitarize the islands, the fate of the islanders who stayed, and so on and so forth."

"Right," said Nigel, scribbling down notes between puffs of smoke. It was a wonder he could even see the paper in front of him.

"The *Arandora Star*," Kaz continued. "Thoughts?"

Ruby took a deep breath and spoke before she could think better of it. "What about a piece on naturalized Italians—is that a term you use here? I mean people who were born abroad but have lived here long enough to consider themselves British. With so many being interned, there have to be stories of families torn apart. People with no ties to Italy, or anything beyond distant memories, being interned."

"We can't get near the camps," Peter said, "but we could go over to Clerkenwell. St. Peter's will probably be holding some kind of service, and they've a parade of some kind—"

"The Procession of the Virgin," Kaz interjected.

"Yes, that's it. I'm fairly sure it's this weekend."

"Good. That's you started, Peter."

Ruby felt a twinge of disappointment, but Peter did know the area, from what she could tell, and the piece would be in better hands with him.

"How did you know about the *Arandora Star*?" Nigel asked her abruptly. "It wasn't in the morning papers."

"Captain Bennett took me to dinner at an Italian café last night. He spoke with the owners about the sinking."

"Of course. He loves that little wop café."

"Nigel," Kaz hissed sharply.

"Sorry," Nigel said, though he didn't sound especially apologetic. "I only meant to say that I wasn't surprised he took you there. It's a favorite haunt of our old friend. At any rate, we've only got enough to fill about eight pages so far. What else do we have?"

"What about Brighton?" Mary asked. "They've closed the beach for the duration."

"Aren't they blocking off all the beaches along the south coast?" Nigel asked. "Why a piece on Brighton in particular?"

"Just think of the pictures. The piers blocked off, barbed wire on the beach, the Royal Pavilion ringed round with sandbags . . ."

Kaz was nodding. "I like it. Let's send you and Ruby. But

not today—they're calling for rain. And you'd best check in ahead with local government. Otherwise some busybody's sure to peg you as fifth columnists. Ask Evelyn to help," he advised, turning to Ruby. "Until then, have a look through some of our back issues—Mr. Dunleavy will share them with you—and get a sense of what we've been covering. See if there are any holes that need filling."

"Anything else?" Nigel prompted the table.

"How about something on the extension of rationing to margarine and tea?" Nell asked. "Could take a man-on-the-street approach. Ask people which bothers them most. Might get some interesting answers."

"Agreed. You take that, Nell," Kaz said. "Peter—any decent letters this week?"

"Oh, yes. Plenty of outrage over our using photos that showed the sinking of the *Lancastria*. Height of insensitivity, doing Goebbels's job for him, et cetera, et cetera."

"I think that's enough to get started," Nigel said. "I'll ring up the chap with the Guernsey photos."

"And I'll ring Uncle Harry for the all clear."

As her colleagues moved back to their desks, Ruby approached Peter, curious about Kaz's last comment.

"Peter? May I ask—who is Uncle Harry?" It had been such an odd statement for Kaz to make. Was he actually asking his uncle for permission to write about certain subjects? Who was his uncle, anyway?

"Uncle Harry is our esteemed publisher. Harold Stearns Bennett."

"Oh. Any relation to Captain Bennett?"

"His uncle. Hence the Uncle Harry. I've never met him—he

lives out in the wilds of Kent, I think. Retired now, with pots and pots of money, and for some reason he wants to spend it on us."

"I see. Well, I guess I'd better get started. Which way to Mr. Dunleavy's office?"

"Straight through that door there."

Equipped with every issue of *Picture Weekly* since September 1939, Ruby read and made notes for the rest of the morning. At half-past twelve, just as her stomach was beginning to growl, her telephone rang. The noise so startled her that she almost knocked over a cup of room-temperature tea that Peter had brought to her several hours before.

It was Kaz, calling from his office at the end of the hall. "Time for lunch," he ordered. "We'll go next door."

She fetched her hat and coat and followed him downstairs, out onto the lane and immediately up the flight of steps to the right of the door.

"No lack of public houses on Fleet Street," he observed, "but this is my favorite. The Old Bell. The stonemasons who built Wren's churches used to drink here. Now it's full of old hacks like me."

The Old Bell looked exactly as she'd imagined an English pub ought to be: dark wood everywhere, polished brass trim at the bar, low ceiling beams to injure the unwary, and an unsmiling barman who regarded her with extreme suspicion.

"Hello, Pete. Brought in one of my writers for a quick lunch. Ruby Sutton. Came over from America to work for me."

"Well then," Pete said, his frown retreating by the smallest margin. "What'll you be having?"

"Cheese and chutney sandwiches, and—"

"Run out of chutney."

"Plain cheese, then, and a pint of bitter for me. What'll you have, Ruby? If you don't like beer you could have a half of cider. Or they might have some sherry."

"Just the sandwich, thanks. I'll have some tea when we get back to the office."

"So," Kaz said after they'd found a table and he'd wolfed down the first half of his sandwich. "I don't know much about you at all. Only that Mike Mitchell says you're good."

"There's not much to know. I grew up in New Jersey. Went to school there, too. When I was done I moved to New York. I was lucky to get my job at *The American*."

It was an answer she'd had plenty of time to think about and practice on her long journey from New York, and the words now unspooled with gratifying ease. Nothing she told him was wrong; it was all true, every word of it. She'd just left a few things out.

"Mike Mitchell sent along some of your clippings. They're good. Quite mature for someone of your age. I won't be so rude as to ask, but presumably you're still in your early twenties."

"I'm twenty-four."

"And how long were you at *The American*?"

"About six months."

"Not very long. Mike Mitchell must have a lot of faith in you. Did you know he's thinking of giving you a column?"

"He did mention it. But only if he likes what I send back. He said he's sick of the usual stories."

"Me, too. So don't write the usual stuff."

"I'll do my best."

He nodded, a faint smile playing about his mouth. "What did you do before you started at *The American*?"

"I was a secretary at an insurance firm. I started there after finishing night school. I went to a secretarial college. Not university," she added, wanting to be forthright about this one matter at least. The words were out before it occurred to her that he might have been told, by Mike Mitchell or someone else at *The American*, that she had a college degree. That he might be disappointed at her lack of education, or believe it meant she wasn't good enough for a job at his magazine.

To her relief, his expression didn't change. "Where did you learn to write, then?"

"I didn't. I mean, I read everything I could, and sometimes I'd write stories about things that interested me. Just for myself. To . . . well, to see if I could do it."

"And that was enough to land you the position at *The American*," he said, his pale blue gaze entirely focused on her.

She hesitated, not sure if he was stating a truth or asking a question. And she really, really wanted to start fresh at *Picture Weekly*, with nothing but truth between her and Kaz. So she waited and watched as he ate some more of his sandwich and drank down a few inches of beer.

"You said you grew up in New Jersey?" he asked after a moment.

"I did. In Newark."

"Did you always want to be a journalist? Don't look so surprised. Hasn't anyone ever asked you before?"

"No, not in so many words."

"So? When did you decide on it?"

"Not when I was little. I remember wanting to be a movie star for a while. And then I read a book about Anna Pavlova and wanted to be a ballerina. Silly dreams, I guess. I did like composition. It was one of the few things I really loved in school."

"What sort of stories did you write?" he asked, his sandwich finished, his beer almost gone.

"They were always about girls going on adventures, usually by stowing away on a convenient ocean liner. Not very original stuff. I'm sure if I read one of them now I'd be appalled. But they were fun to write at the time." She took a first bite of her sandwich; it was dry and somewhat tasteless, but would fill her stomach nicely.

"When I was taking night school classes," Ruby went on, "I met a woman who worked at a magazine in Manhattan. She was there to learn how to type and take shorthand, and she got me thinking. Maybe I could try for something more interesting than work as a secretary or file clerk. Maybe I could do something, like being a journalist, that I'd really love."

"Do you?"

"Oh, yes. It's the best job I've ever had. By a long stretch."

"What do you like about it?" he persisted.

She took another few bites of her sandwich, needing the time to consider her answer. "I like the work of finding a story, and then figuring out how to tell it. Everything is a puzzle, or at least to me it is. I just have to find the pieces that are missing. I hope . . . I mean, it does sound silly—"

He shook his head and leaned forward, propping his elbows on the table between them. "The thing is, Ruby, I already have two staff writers who are doing that. What makes you different? What can you bring to these stories? Beyond your curiosity and diligence and so forth."

"I'm not sure," Ruby said cautiously. "I guess it helps that

I'm an outsider. I'm not part of this war, not really . . . so perhaps I can provide a different perspective?"

He nodded, though from his owlish expression he was unconvinced by her fainthearted reply.

"I'm sorry," she admitted. "It's a fair question, and you deserve a better answer. In all the rush to pack up and get here, I guess I forgot to think about much beyond the practical things. Where I would live and how I would find my way around. That sort of thing."

"Understood. Well, think on it when you have a chance. We all bring something to the stories we tell. It may well be that your outsider's point of view, as you term it, is what sets your work apart—or it may end up being something else entirely. But it's worth thinking about."

CHAPTER FIVE

ot until Friday morning did the weather improve enough for Ruby and Mary's trip to Brighton. Gray skies bloomed sapphire blue, leaving only wisp-thin tufts of cloud, and with Kaz's blessing she packed up her things and took the Underground over to Victoria Station. Mr. Dunleavy had lent her a history of Brighton to read on the journey down, and as there were no express trains that late in the day, she would have nearly two hours to acquaint herself with the town and its lore.

Her ticket purchased, and with still ten minutes before the train was meant to depart, Ruby began to worry about Mary's absence. The photographer hadn't been at the office that morning, but Evelyn had said she or Kaz would telephone her at home. Ruby walked to the middle of the ticket concourse, a vast area that felt almost as big as a baseball stadium, and scanned the passing crowd for her colleague. It took no time at all to pick her out of the crowd.

Mary wasn't very tall, nor was she especially beautiful, not if compared to a Hollywood actress or some society beauty. But there was something about the way she held herself that would make anyone look twice, something arresting about the confident set to her shoulders, or perhaps it was the calm, almost unnervingly steady way she regarded the passing crowds. As if everyone was a potential subject, and she, the artist, stood apart.

The photographers Ruby knew in New York always had a satchel crammed full of gear, but Mary had brought only her camera in its case, slung casually over her shoulder, and nothing else. Perhaps the camera was some sort of new model that didn't require extra lenses or flashes or what-have-you.

"Hello, Mary," she called out, reminding herself there was no need to be nervous. "Do you have your ticket?"

"I do, aye. Ready?"

"Ready," Ruby agreed.

She'd been bracing herself for a crush on the train, and the possibility of having to stand until they were past the first few commuter stops, since Nigel had flatly refused to reimburse them for anything more than a third-class fare. To her surprise, the carriage they boarded was all but empty. She stood by as Mary chose a forward-facing seat by the window, and then sat opposite.

"When do we get in again?" Mary asked.

"At a quarter to two."

"I'll just close my eyes, then. Feeling a wee bit tired today."

It seemed to take forever before they were clear of the southern suburbs of the city. The countryside, at least what she could see of it from her backward-facing view, was markedly different from the region she'd passed through on the train from Liverpool to London. It was softer, she decided, with beckoning hills and quiet valleys threaded through with silvery brooks. The villages were especially picturesque, their cottages and squat ancient churches linked by hedgerow-lined roads that, with their gently meandering turns, made no concessions to modern notions of expedient travel.

Mary opened her eyes the instant the train arrived in Brighton, leaving Ruby with the unwelcome suspicion that the photographer had been pretending to sleep to avoid speaking with her, and together they made their way toward the main concourse of the station.

It wasn't hard to guess which of the half-dozen or so people waiting inside was their escort for the day. Middle-aged and precisely mustached, he wore the same sort of one-piece boiler suit in which the prime minister was often seen, along with an armband marked LDV in large appliquéd letters. All that was missing, Ruby mused, was a tin hat and bullhorn.

"You the ladies from *Picture Weekly*? I'm Bert Renfrew, from the Local Defence Volunteers here in town. Just a formality, but may I see your press passes and identity cards?"

He looked over their documents with care, though Ruby knew from experience that few people could tell a good forgery from the real thing, and handed them back with an almost sheepish grin.

"Can't be too careful these days. Speaking of that, Miss Buchanan, you really ought to have your gas mask with you."

Ruby had noticed, in her few days in London, that hardly anyone carried their masks with them; but as she was new to England, and didn't care to attract the wrong sort of attention, she had forced herself to sling her mask over her shoulder every time she left her lodgings. Mary, it was evident, had no such concerns. Rather than respond to Mr. Renfrew, she simply looked at him steadily, unblinkingly, until he flushed and stepped back.

"I, ah, I'm sorry I don't have a car for you. The request came in rather last minute, and we've . . . well, we've been rather busy here."

It was time for Ruby to play peacemaker. "I'm sure you have, and we don't mind at all."

"It's not far to the seafront," he added. "Only a half mile or so."

She remained in step with Mr. Renfrew on the walk, patiently answering his questions about her reasons for leaving America and her opinion of English people, English food, and the English countryside. Before long they reached the last block of buildings and emerged onto the seafront. Ahead lay the great sweep of the English Channel, vast and limitless, stretching unbroken to the horizon.

"I was told you want to see how the town is defending itself against invasion," Mr. Renfrew said. "It wasn't an easy decision to close the beaches, but it was a necessary one. From here, you see, the French coast is only seventy-five miles away, due south. The *enemy* is only seventy-five miles away."

Ruby took out her notebook and pencil, and began to make notes in shorthand. "How long does it take to cross to France? In peacetime, that is?"

"Oh, not long. Six hours, sometimes less if conditions are good."

They walked across the road, stopping at a set of railings that marked the drop to the beach below, and Mr. Renfrew pointed out the defensive measures that were being put in place. "Madeira Drive—the lower road, just down there—has been closed, and blocked off with barbed wire. The entire beach has been mined, of course, and the decking has been removed from stretches of the piers—you can just see the gaps from here. Even this railing will have barbed wire attached to it by next week."

"And those concrete structures? The things that look like children's blocks, but much bigger?"

"Ah. Those. We'd rather you didn't describe them in any kind of detail. Some are machine-gun emplacements, and some are simply barrier structures. In due course they'll all be camouflaged in some fashion."

"I understand," Ruby said, scribbling away. "The story and photographs will have to be cleared with the Ministry of Information, in any event, so you don't have to worry."

"It's strange, you know," Mr. Renfrew said. "Normally, on a summer day like this, the beach is packed with people. On Whitsun you couldn't see the shingle for all the crush. And now . . . now it's more than your life's worth to go down there."

"Is it affecting the town? You're a popular destination for tourists, aren't you?"

"Not anymore. Not for the duration. Most of the hotels have closed. No one wants to stay here, not so close to the coast, and not with a beach that looks like a battlefield. Still, we've got to grit our teeth and get through it. We're no different than any other town on the Channel."

"Are people worried about an invasion?"

He shrugged, his gaze fixed on the sea beyond. "No more worried than anyone else, I suppose. I know I'm sleeping better now we've got our defenses in place."

"What did you do before you joined the LDV?" she asked.

"I'm a clerk for the town. Still am, since there's no pay for local defense. Doing my bit, same as everyone."

As they talked, Mary kept busy with her camera, silently

walking back and forth, one moment focusing on the piers, the next on the beach, the next on the graceful facades of the seafront hotels. Although her work did provoke some curious glances from the few people they passed, Mr. Renfrew's presence was official looking enough to forestall any accusations of traitorous activities.

They continued along for a few minutes, eventually drawing near to a young woman and three children, one still in a pram.

"Hello there, Mrs. Goodsell," Mr. Renfrew said. "Nice to see you out and getting some fresh air."

"Hello, Mr. Renfrew. Keeping busy, are you?"

"That I am. These ladies are from *Picture Weekly* in London. Doing a story on the town and our defenses. Miss Sutton, Miss Buchanan, this is my neighbor from down the street, Mrs. Goodsell, and her little ones. Johnny, Stanley, and baby Carol."

"Very nice to meet you, Mrs. Goodsell. Would you mind if we photographed the children for the story?" Ruby asked.

"I guess not. Long as you don't say where we live or anything."

"No, we'd never do that."

They watched tolerantly as the boys tried unsuccessfully to climb the railings that separated them from the tempting obstacle course below, and all the while Mary's camera kept clicking away, so unobtrusively that the children likely had no idea they were being photographed.

"You must be tired," Ruby ventured, taking note of the dark circles under Mrs. Goodsell's eyes. "Taking care of three little ones must be a lot of work."

"Ooh, that it is. The boys were good babies, but Carol here is ever so fussy at night. Goes down without a peep, but then she's up like clockwork a few hours later. Still hasn't slept through the night. I've almost given up hope she ever will."

"She's a very pretty baby."

Mrs. Goodsell's expression brightened. "She is, isn't she? And she's good as gold during the day. It's just at night that she runs me ragged."

After that, the rest of the interview was easy. Ruby learned that Mrs. Goodsell and her husband had grown up on the same street in Brighton and had married when he was eighteen and she was seventeen, just as soon as they'd been able to persuade their respective parents. He was in the navy, and hardly ever home on leave, and Mrs. Goodsell fretted the children were forgetting him.

"What about the threat of invasion? Does that worry you, too?"

"Not so it keeps me up at night," Mrs. Goodsell answered, her attention focused on Johnny and Stanley. "The air-raid sirens are a bother, though. Forever going off just as I've got little Carol all settled."

The elder of the boys, Johnny, had tired of his attempts to scale the railings, and had come over to listen in on the adults' conversation. "But, Mummy," he pointed out, "you said it's better to be safe than sorry."

"Yes, I did," his mother admitted. "And it *is* best to be safe and listen to the siren." She ruffled his hair affectionately. "I'd best get you three home for your tea."

"Thank you for speaking with me," Ruby said. "The article will probably be in next week's magazine if you want to look out for it."

"I will, thank you. Hope you have a safe trip back to London."

They took a different route back to the train station, for Mr. Renfrew was keen to show Ruby the Royal Pavilion. The book Mr. Dunleavy had lent her had devoted an entire chapter to the unorthodox architecture and checkered past of the Prince Regent's seaside folly, but its arid prose had done nothing to prepare her for the reality of the actual pavilion.

It was . . . it was . . . how was she meant to react to such an edifice? Its onion-shaped domes, Moorish arches, and slender minarets gave it the appearance of a palace from the *Arabian Nights*, out of a fairy tale, really, and was absolutely the last building she'd have ever expected to encounter in *England*.

"I had no idea," she said, struggling to think of an appropriate response.

"That's how most people react when they see it. Of course, we're very fond of the pavilion here, but it *is* out of the ordinary."

Though there was no concealing the exuberance and grandeur of its architecture, the palace did look the worse for wear, its paint peeling in a few spots, and most of its windows boarded up or taped over.

"Does the royal family still use it?"

This provoked a honking laugh from Mary, who had been silent since they left the seafront. "They wouldn't go within a mile of it. Just look at the place."

This provoked a sigh from Mr. Renfrew. "Miss Buchanan is right. Queen Victoria sold it to the town many decades ago. We began a restoration of the interior a few years back, but that will have to wait until the war is over."

They said their goodbyes, and Ruby was relieved when

Mary managed a perfectly civil thank-you to Mr. Renfrew for his help. She didn't mind her colleague's lengthy silences, but it would help if she could refrain from offending the people who were meant to be answering questions. Hadn't anyone ever told her the rule about catching flies?

As soon as their train was under way, Ruby pulled out her notebook, intent on making more notes while the visit was still fresh in her mind. It would help the journey go faster, besides.

"You were good back there," Mary said into the silence. "With the LDV man, and Mrs. Goodsell, too. You've a real way with people, you know. Most people just rabbit on about themselves."

"What's the point in that? You'll never learn a thing if you're talking about yourself."

"Agreed. But you actually seemed interested in her answers."

"Of course I was. Besides, people can tell if you're asking questions just to soften them up. You have to care about what they have to say. You have to listen."

Mary nodded in approval. "It takes some people years to figure that out. Even Kaz in his younger days . . ."

"You've known him a long time?"

"Aye, for donkey's years. There's no better editor in London. Nor a finer man, for that matter." A ghost of a smile played around Mary's mouth, and she turned her head to look out the window.

Curious as she was, Ruby felt certain that the other woman would not welcome any further questions about her relationship with Kaz. "Were you able to get the photographs you wanted?" she asked instead.

"I think so." Pulling a packet of cigarettes from the breast pocket of her jacket, Mary tapped one into her hand and lit it, exhaling a thin plume of smoke in the direction of the half-open window. "I'd offer you one, but I haven't seen you smoking."

"I don't, but thanks all the same." The nuns had been quick to cane any girl who came home smelling of smoke, and then once she was working, it had seemed silly to take up a habit that was expensive and would leave her with a cough and bad breath.

"I was wondering . . . I mean, how long have you been a photographer?" She held her breath, hoping that Mary wouldn't decide to close her eyes and feign sleep, or, even worse, just stare at her as she'd done to poor Mr. Renfrew.

"Fifteen years? Yes, that's about right. I started as a writer like you, but I wasn't much good at it." Mary paused to remove a strand of tobacco from her upper lip. "Was much better behind a camera. I worked at a woman's magazine for a while. Hated it. Then a daily paper—hated that, too. Men there were vile. Not that the men at *PW* can't be idiots, but Kaz keeps them in line. Don't have to worry about getting my bottom pinched or anyone cornering me in the darkroom."

Ruby nodded, privately thinking that any man who tried to corner Mary would have to be crazy. "It was a bit like that in New York. Not the bottom-pinching, thank goodness, but some of the men were disgusting. The jokes they'd tell . . . and they honestly expected me to laugh along."

"Did you?"

"No. I always found an excuse to get away." They sat in silence until Ruby worked up the nerve to ask another question. At least it was good practice for reluctant interview subjects.

"I guess you're from Scotland," she stated, praying that she'd correctly guessed the origin of Mary's accent.

"Aye, tha' I am. From Dumbarton, no' far from Glasgow," Mary answered, exaggerating her brogue before abandoning the act with a wink. "It was beautiful there, but I couldn't wait to leave. Soon as I finished school I was off to Glasgow. Did a course in typing—hated it, of course—then came down to London to find my fortune."

"Do you miss Scotland?"

"Not really. I was never much for the outdoors. A city lass at heart, I suppose. London's my home now."

Mary had been looking out the window, but now she turned her head and looked Ruby in the eye. "I've been meaning to warn you. Peter and Frank are decent fellows, but try not to step on their toes. Like all men, they fight dirty, and I promise they'll get in your way if you get in theirs. D'you understand?"

"Yes."

"Most of all, watch out for Nigel Vernon. He's a good enough editor, but he didn't want you here in the first place. He may be over it, but be wary of him all the same. I don't trust him one bit, and I've known him for years."

"Why didn't he want me here? Is it because I'm an American?"

"Could be. Could be he didn't fancy having another woman on staff. Or he might've had a bee in his bonnet for some reason that has nothing to do with you. I wouldn't waste your time worrying about it. And Kaz will always have your back, no matter what. He's as different from Nigel as chalk and cheese."

It was disappointing, and more than a little disheartening, to learn the assistant editor had been set against her before she'd even set foot in England. It would be an uphill battle to prove herself, but at least she'd be prepared if things did get worse.

And it was good to know that Kaz could be relied upon to defend her.

"Thank you, Mary. I'm very grateful for your advice."

"You're welcome. Now I'm going to have another wee nap. Wake me when we get to London."

Dispatches from London
by Miss Ruby Sutton
July 9, 1940

. . . While visiting Brighton on England's south coast last week, a group of adults overheard some words of wisdom from Johnny, age 6. "It's better to be safe than sorry," he told his mother, and it's hard to disagree with him right now. The beaches there have been outfitted with enough defenses to make anyone think twice about setting a toe on their sands. It makes for a dismal sight for those in the mood for a sunny holiday, but they're a grand thing for anyone looking to sleep well at night . . .

CHAPTER SIX

September 7, 1940

I t had been such a nice day.

At work that morning, she'd helped Peter with a story he was writing on Vic Oliver. The comedian had been the top act in a series of sold-out shows at the Hippodrome, and despite the disruption of near nightly air-raid sirens, he hadn't yet canceled or cut short any of the shows. He was also the prime minister's son-in-law, although he had refused to talk about his ties with the Churchill family during the brief interview he'd given Peter.

Ruby had done the background research for the story, and with Mr. Dunleavy's help had managed to put together a fairly comprehensive biography of Mr. Oliver. He was Austrian by birth, although he had no accent to speak of, and he was also Jewish. According to more than one recent story she had dug up, he was on a list of prominent British Jews who were marked for arrest when Germany invaded. All the braver, then, for him to remain in the spotlight.

At one o'clock, the start of their weekend, everyone had trooped downstairs to the Old Bell for lunch. Encouraged by

Peter and Nell, Ruby had ordered a half-pint of cider with her cheese sandwich. She'd liked the taste of it well enough, but it had made her sleepy, and there was no way she was going to waste a half day off by napping.

As they were putting on their coats, Peter had asked her to the pictures. She'd almost said yes, for it had been ages since she'd seen a movie, but the way his face had reddened when he stammered out his invitation had led her, ever so gently, to decline. Best not to encourage any romantic feelings on his part, for she had neither the inclination nor the energy for anything beyond work. And it was true, as she'd told him, that she was tired and was planning on an early night.

She'd also been wondering if Captain Bennett might reappear at some point. She hadn't heard a word from him since their dinner together, though she hadn't expected to; he had, after all, just been doing his friend a favor. All the same, the memory of the man, so certain and sure and quietly strong, when set against the insignificant reality of Peter's timid presence, did the latter no favors.

"Perhaps, um, another time? When you're not so tired? We could go to dinner after work, and then the pictures?" her colleague persisted, his gaze fixed on a point past her shoulder.

"Perhaps," she said, praying that he didn't interpret her response as a guarantee of any kind. To her relief, he simply nodded, shook her hand suddenly, and bolted for the door.

Rather than walk straight home, she had lingered in the churchyard outside St. Paul's, letting the afternoon sun warm her face while she admired the stern simplicity of the cathedral's exterior. She hadn't yet worked up the nerve to venture inside. It had been years since she'd willingly gone to church, any sort of church, and even her curiosity wasn't enough, today at least, to propel her any further.

Eventually she wandered back to the hotel and, rather than take up the book she'd begun the night before, decided to type up the notes she'd made that morning. Would she ever tire of the sound and rhythm of her Underwood? The keys made such a pleasing noise as they struck the paper, and it was immensely satisfying to see the loops and dashes of her shorthand transformed into crisp, clean words. Secretarial college had been a long-drawn-out ordeal, but the skills she'd acquired had proved their worth many times over since then. Apart from Evelyn, she was the only person at *PW* who knew how to type properly—everyone else just picked away with their index fingers.

After an hour, perhaps more, she got up to open her window, for the room was becoming uncomfortably warm. She returned to her desk, her fingers poised above the typewriter keys, and that's when she noticed the noise. A rumble in the air, insistent and growing, unlike anything she'd ever heard. She went back to the window, leaned out as far as she dared, and craned her neck to see the sky above, though the neighboring buildings obscured all but a narrow strip of blue.

Where, a moment before, there had been nothing but empty sky, there was now movement. The strip of blue became a pattern, speckled with black dots that swam in and out of focus, and the pattern was moving, the shapes above advancing in perfect formation.

Airplanes, flying high above London.

She checked her wristwatch: a few minutes past five o'clock. It wouldn't hurt to go outside and get a better look at what was happening. Perhaps she would be able to tell which sort of planes they were—or, more likely, rely on someone else to tell her. If only she had read and committed to memory the articles on identifying enemy warplanes that all the papers had been running, or had thought to cut one out for future reference.

She had just started to lace up her shoes when the air-raid siren began to howl. The sound didn't startle her, for the siren had become a backdrop to everyday life in recent weeks. A few times over the course of the past month, an enemy bomber had made it past the RAF and dropped a payload of bombs on outlying suburbs, but casualties and damage had been slight so far.

There was no time to spare. She put on her coat, stuffed her notebook and pencil into her bag, and ran down the stairs to the hotel's basement. Her camp bed in the corner was waiting for her, and the same familiar faces of the other boarding guests were there, and nothing felt very different. Except she could tell that it was different. They all could.

She ought to be making notes—the sounds she could hear from outside, the demeanor of the other people in the basement, her thoughts as she waited for the all clear—but she couldn't bring herself to take out her notebook. Not yet. Not until she had a better idea of what was going on.

The sounds from outside were indistinct and impossible to interpret, muffled as they were by the basement's thick stone foundations. Of course that was a good thing, for whatever was happening must be far away, but it did make the waiting a much more fearful experience.

The rising drone of the all clear sounded after an hour, and rather than return to her room, Ruby went straight outside, as did most of the people who had been in the basement shelter with her. Nothing seemed all that different, not at first glance, but then she turned to the horizon, toward the roseate glow of the setting sun. And it dawned on her that she was facing east, not west.

She dug in her bag for the *A to Z* that Captain Bennett had given her, but even with its help she couldn't pinpoint the source of the fire, or fires, that were staining the sky red. Was it White-chapel or Stepney? Rotherhithe or the Isle of Dogs? Had the docks and warehouses been hit? There was no way to tell, not without a bird's-eye view of the city.

It seemed a bit pointless to just stand on the sidewalk, so she went back inside and ate her share of the meager supper—bread and margarine, jam and tea—the hotel's kitchen staff had been able to produce.

"No water coming in from the mains," Maggie explained, "and the gas has been switched off, too."

"I don't mind. I wasn't all that hungry, anyway."

"Best eat up, all the same. Never know when they'll be back."

At eight o'clock the sirens sounded again, so down they all trooped to the basement, guests and hotel staff sitting cheek by jowl in the dim and faintly damp shelter. A few stalwart souls tried to start up conversations with their neighbors, but earned only disapproving glares for their efforts. Instead, everyone seemed intent on charting the noises filtering through from outside. The rumbling hum of the bombers, the dull crump of falling bombs, the ineffectual bark of too few antiaircraft guns. Whatever was happening in the East End was still an abstraction, a calamity that felt palpably distant.

And yet, Ruby reflected, the simple fact that she could hear the bombs meant that she wasn't anywhere near distant enough.

In that moment, the opposite side of the ocean felt very much like the right place to be.

The all clear sounded just shy of dawn. Desperate for some fresh air, she stumbled up the stairs and straight outside, but there was no relief to be found. Smoke hung heavy in the air, overlaid by a terrible stench that clawed at her nose and throat. She fumbled in her bag for a handkerchief, desperate to dull the smell, and held it over her face.

"From the docks." One of the hotel cooks, still wearing his cap and apron, came forward to stand next to her. "Whatever was in the warehouses down on the docks is on fire now. Lumber, paraffin, sugar, tar, spirits. It's all on fire. That's what you smell."

Ruby nodded, her throat too dry to speak.

"I've got family down Stepney way," he said. "I hope . . ." he began, his words trailing off. He turned away, shaking his head, and went back inside.

Her eyes gritty from lack of sleep, or perhaps just from the smoky air, Ruby started walking. She didn't have a destination in mind, but anything would be better than returning to her room. She didn't have a radio, and the morning papers wouldn't have any news of what happened. She had to see for herself.

Fifteen minutes later she was at the Thames, a few yards from the northern end of Southwark Bridge. Others had gathered at its railings, likely feeling just as restless and bewildered, and she went to join them. Tower Bridge was due east, nearly a mile distant, its distinctive silhouette still intact, but every landmark beyond had been blotted out by spiraling towers of oily black smoke and a dawn sky painted crimson by fire.

She turned her attention to the people around her, and her

heart seized with sympathy. Haggard, disheveled, they were carelessly dressed in whatever garments had been at hand when the raid began. One man had belted a raincoat over his pajamas. All bore the same expression: exhausted, frightened, wary of what was to come, and yet grimly determined to endure.

THE BOMBERS RETURNED the next night, and the next, and the next, until it was hard to recall what life had been like before sirens and shelters and scattered moments of agitated, restive sleep. Only the unfailing routine of work kept her sane, or so she convinced herself; and she was needed at work, day in and day out, for the hours they spent in the shelters almost every day meant they were hard-pressed to get the magazine out on time.

Kaz never left the office, or when he did he only went home to bathe and change. He was there when she arrived at the crack of dawn, and there when she left in the late afternoon, for he insisted they all finish early in order to be home before the sirens began their nightly clamor.

Life settled into a wearying routine that was marked by four or five siren warnings over the course of the morning and afternoon, only one of which ever seemed to turn into an actual raid, and then the exercise in endurance of the nightly raids, which might easily last seven or eight hours. Day after day, week after week, until Ruby felt as flat and fragile as a scrap of tissue paper.

Little had changed outwardly at the office, although after a building across the lane had been hit, Kaz had enlisted everyone's help to move Mr. Dunleavy's library into the basement. There his precious store of back issues and reference books would be safer from the bombs, though not from flooding if a nearby water main were hit. This last thought Ruby kept to herself.

Stories of the Blitz, as people had begun to call it, became her and Mary's bread and butter, and much of what she contributed was sent on to New York for use in *The American* as well. The world was watching London, it seemed, and was avid for any insight into the wellspring of courage that had arisen to sustain the city's people.

Less than a week into the bombings, Ruby and Mary traveled east to Silvertown, a working-class enclave sandwiched between the Royal Albert Docks and the Thames, and ringed round with petroleum depots, a chemical works, a sugar refinery, a gas plant, and scores of warehouses packed full of flammable goods. A single spark would have been enough to set off a powerful blaze in Silvertown; a sustained assault by the Luftwaffe had been enough to level nearly all of it.

"It seems opportunistic," Ruby had protested when Nigel had assigned the story earlier that week. "We could end up doing more harm than good."

"Every other paper and magazine in the country is going there," he'd insisted. "But you want us to miss the story because you're worried about hurting some dockworker's delicate feelings?"

"I only meant—"

"I know what you meant," Kaz interrupted. "The thing is, we do need the story. That's a given. But you can get it without upsetting anyone. Ask as few questions as possible. Let people talk—that's what you need to remember. Just let them talk."

So they had gone to Silvertown and walked along its ruined streets and spoken with anyone who was in the mood to answer questions. Some turned away when they saw Ruby with her notebook and Mary with her camera. A few had broken down, unable to speak. But most had willingly, if not cheerfully, submitted to her questions.

The best interview, the one Ruby would remember for the rest of her life, was with the first man they met there. He was sitting on a block of rubble, his face and clothing coated in a layer of fine gray dust, a figurine of a Staffordshire dog clutched to his chest. Behind him were the smoldering ruins of a row of modest houses.

"Good morning," she said, her mouth dry with nerves. "My name is Ruby Sutton and I'm from *Picture Weekly*. This is my colleague, Mary Buchanan. I apologize for bothering you, but would you mind speaking with us?" She held her breath, certain that he would refuse.

"Pretty girls like you? 'Course I don't mind. Come round to see the pasting we got from Jerry?"

"I, ah . . ."

"Our boys chucked it back at them last night, though. Air raid warden was telling me so just this morning. Sent them limping back home to lick their wounds."

"They certainly did. Was . . . was this your house?"

"It was. The one on the end. Not much of it left now."

"But you rescued your dog."

He looked down, surprised by what she'd said, and realized she was talking about the figurine he held. "Oh, right. Only half the pair. Was my mum's. She'd be mad as a wet hen if she saw I'd let one of 'em get broken."

"Do you feel up to telling me what happened?"

"I was at the pub when the siren started. Near soon as we heard it go, the bombs started falling thick and fast. So we hid out in their cellar, tight as sardines, till the all clear sounded.

There was so much smoke that morning. Could hardly see my hand in front of my face. My house . . . it was gone when I got home, and most of the street with it."

"I'm so sorry."

"The couple that lived next door, they were nice, they were. Kept to themselves but still friendly. She needed a cane to walk, and he always said he'd never leave her behind. Warden said . . . he said they tried to hide under the stairs. But the house fell on them, and then the fire . . ."

He turned his head away, swiping at his eyes with his sleeve, and Ruby found herself blinking back tears as well.

"I felt bad, you know," he went on, "going down to the pub so early on a Saturday. My missus would've given me holy hell for it. But if I'd been home I'd have gone to the shelter on Oriental Road, since it's the nearest. And it got a direct hit that night. Everyone was killed."

"Your wife . . . ?" she asked gently, fearing the worst.

"She died a few years back. Would've done her in to see the house like this."

Ruby knelt in the dirt next to him, not caring if she ruined her stockings. "Do you have anywhere to go?"

He didn't answer, his eyes focused on a point just over her shoulder, and for a moment she feared she had gone too far. And then he straightened up, leveled his shoulders, and looked her in the eye.

"I'll be fine, don't you worry. My daughter lives down past Lewisham. She's on her way to fetch me now. Just came back today to see if there was anything I could fish out of the rubble."

"I'm so sorry this happened to you, Mr . . . ."

"Jemmett. But you can call me Bill."

"And you must call me Ruby. Is there anything I can get you? There's a mobile canteen down the road. I could bring you some tea."

"Nah, I'll be all right. Thanks anyway."

As Ruby and Bill talked, Mary had been taking pictures steadily, almost stealthily, and if it hadn't been for the click and zip of her camera, it would have been easy to forget she was there. She came forward now and tapped Ruby on the shoulder. "It's time to move on."

"Mary is right, I'm afraid. Would you mind if we used your name and photograph in the magazine? The article will probably run in next week's issue."

"Would I mind? I'll be the talk of the street. I, well . . ." Of course there was no street, not anymore.

"You're very brave," Ruby told him impulsively. "I'm sure your wife would be really proud of you."

"Nice of you to say so. You've got me wondering, though— what brought you all the way from America? If you don't mind me asking. Time like this, I'd have thought you'd stay put. Safer over there."

"But not half as interesting. I wouldn't have got to meet you if I'd stayed at home, would I? Good luck, Bill."

"And good luck to you, Ruby."

AT THE END of September, unable to sleep after the third cycle of siren, shelter, and all clear since dusk, she wrote an hour-by-hour description of living through a night of bombing: the call of the siren, the rush for shelter, the hours of waiting. The dreadful anticipation of what morning would bring.

She rewrote it at least a dozen times before working up the

courage to show Kaz, and still she was uncertain. The man read faster than anyone she'd ever met, but it was a long while before he looked up from her typewritten pages.

"I like it. I do, but . . ."

"It's not quite right, is it? I knew it. There's something missing, but I can't—"

"It's missing *you*," he said. "It's missing your point of view. Rewrite this in the first person. Tell the readers who you are, and how you came to be here."

"But it's not my place to editorialize," she protested. "I'm meant to stand aside so the reader—"

"Did you learn that at the knee of Mike Mitchell? As far as I know, Mike's never had to endure an aerial bombardment for— what day is it today?"

"Monday the thirtieth."

"For twenty-three straight nights and counting. Your first day here, you told me you were an outsider. You said you wanted to stand back and observe."

"I did. But—"

"So? Now you're in the thick of things. You're in the middle of this Blitz, same as we all are. You might as well be honest about it."

Dispatches from London
by Miss Ruby Sutton
September 30, 1940

. . . I don't think I could describe it if I hadn't lived through it. It's as simple as that. The fear of the bombs is real enough, and if there's a man or woman in London

who isn't scared during the raids I'd like to borrow some
of their courage. It's their good humor that surprises me.
How this city can paste a smile on its collective face and
still get to work more or less on time, still get the jobs done
that need doing, and apart from a wobbly moment here or
there, still find things to joke and sing and laugh about,
I haven't yet figured out. When I do I'll let you know . . .

CHAPTER SEVEN

October 1940

They were winding up their weekly editorial meeting when Kaz announced, to no one in particular, that he was going to a concert at the National Gallery that afternoon.

"Anyone care to join me? Mary?"

"All right."

"Nigel? Nell? Peter? Ruby? Come on. A little culture won't kill you."

The others mumbled their excuses, but Ruby was intrigued by the invitation. "What sort of concert?"

"Classical music."

"I . . ."

"Don't tell me you're one of those people who only like modern music. Swing bands with their drums and saxophones and screeching clarinets. Stuff of nightmares," he grumbled.

"You wouldn't say that if you'd been to a Benny Goodman concert."

Across the room, Nell let out a squeal of delight. "You've heard him play?"

"Only the once, about a year ago. It was *wonderful*." The concert ticket had been so expensive she'd nearly fainted, more than two whole dollars, but as soon as Mr. Goodman had stepped forward with his clarinet, she'd been in heaven.

"I insist you come to the concert," Kaz said, interrupting her reverie. "I'm certain you'll enjoy it far more than Mr. Goodman's startling syncopations."

"Very well," Ruby agreed. "If you insist." It would certainly be something new, and that couldn't be bad.

"When do you want to set off?" Mary asked Kaz.

"Oh, let's say a quarter to twelve? Just in case there's a queue. We can get something to eat from the canteen at the gallery."

They all wandered back to their desks, their respective assignments crowding out other concerns, and Ruby settled down to the business of figuring out how to structure the story she'd been assigned: a day in the life of a Women's Voluntary Service canteen worker. Nigel had suggested she ring up "someone" at the service and ask to be put in touch with a suitable subject, but Ruby would only adopt that approach as a last resort. A direct approach to the WVS would waste time, for there would inevitably be a tedious amount of official dithering as to who should be selected for the profile. There was also the likelihood of her being saddled with an interview subject whose personality was as lively as a piece of waterlogged cardboard.

"All set?"

She looked up to find Mary and Kaz in front of her desk. "Sorry. I lost track of time." She stuffed her notebook in her bag and hurried after them, only stopping to grab her coat and hat from the rack in the front room. "Where are we going again?"

"Trafalgar Square," Kaz answered over his shoulder. "The concerts are in the basement of the National Gallery."

They turned south, walking down to the Thames and, she assumed, toward Blackfriars Underground station.

"Why have the concerts in the first place? I'd have thought people were too busy for things like that."

"What are we fighting for, if not things of beauty like music and art?" Kaz all but barked, but then, as if realizing how harsh he sounded, he smiled at Ruby apologetically. "Sorry. It's a bug-bear of mine, this notion that we all have to put our noses to the grindstone and ignore everything else if we want to defeat Hitler. I disagree, and that is why I'm on my way to enjoy a concert of beautiful music. What can he do to stop me?"

"He can bomb the gallery," Ruby observed.

"He already has. They had to evacuate during a concert last week—I think an incendiary dropped through a skylight into an adjoining room. Didn't stop the show, though. They simply moved downstairs. Beautiful music won the day."

"Let's reserve judgment on the music," Mary said. "That last concert we went to was something awful."

"The Stravinsky? I loved it."

"Not my cup of tea at all," Mary insisted. "Give me Bach or Beethoven any day."

"Don't people complain?" Ruby asked. "They're both German composers."

"Yes, and to my sure and certain knowledge neither of them was a member of the Nazi Party," Kaz grumbled, "so I think we can listen to their music with a clear conscience."

"I didn't mean that—"

"I know you didn't, Ruby. Just me tilting at windmills. Right—here we are at the station."

A train was pulling in just as they descended to the platform. Though it was already crowded, Kaz insisted they squeeze on regardless. It was no more uncomfortable than the New York subway at rush hour, though, and it was only for a few stops.

"What music is being performed today?" she asked once they were under way.

"No idea," Kaz said. "Likely something traditional. From time to time they experiment with more modern selections—as with the Stravinsky that Mary was whingeing about—but they're not very popular. Most people want the old chestnuts."

"I've never heard an actual orchestra before," Ruby admitted. "Only Mr. Goodman's jazz band that one time." She didn't bother to mention the wheezing, out-of-key accordion that Sister Mary-Frances had played during Mass in the orphanage chapel each morning. That had been a torture device, not a musical instrument.

"It won't be an orchestra today," Kaz cautioned. "Likely just a chamber ensemble. A dozen musicians at most. Or maybe a solo pianist."

"First you tell the girl the music will be wonderful, and then you burst her bubble by saying it'll be one piano tinkling away," Mary said, directing a playful frown at him. "Make up your mind, won't you?"

"Pay her no mind, Ruby. She only comes for the sandwiches at the canteen."

"Yes, and why not? They're better than the cardboard and sawdust they serve up at the Old Bell."

Ruby wasn't sure how to insert herself into the conversation, or even if she should, so she simply listened to them bantering like the old friends they were. Was their closeness born of ease, the sort of comfort you might feel with another who had known you for years and years, had seen you at your worst, and still liked you? Or did it spring from true intimacy—the kind that arose from romantic love? She couldn't tell, and she certainly wasn't about to ask. But she did envy them, just a little, all the same.

As soon as the train pulled into Charing Cross, Kaz led the way upstairs. "It's a bit of a walk," he explained, "but it hardly seems worth the effort to change to another line just to go one more stop."

They walked for a few hundred yards along Villiers Street, turning left when they reached the Strand, and then the great open space of the square was before them. Only it wasn't empty at all, but rather was filled with statues and fountains and people, hundreds of people, most of whom seemed to be simply enjoying the glorious afternoon sun.

"This is . . . something," she said at last, trying and failing to find an appropriate adjective. "We don't have anything like this in New York."

"Not Times Square?" asked Mary.

"It's not really a square. More like a long sort of triangle. And it's the farthest thing from beautiful. Just a lot of neon signs hanging off buildings."

"More like Piccadilly Circus, then."

"I guess so." She had been past Piccadilly in a bus, late in the summer before the Blitz had begun, and it had reminded her a bit of Times Square.

"Over there," Kaz said, pointing to the south, "you can see

the elegant little shelter they built for the statue of Charles the First—the one who got his head chopped off." Ruby looked and had to laugh, for the statue had been hidden under a corrugated metal shell that looked like a windmill shorn of its sails.

She looked back toward the center of the square, to the largest pillar she'd ever seen, its base covered by protective hoardings and a layer of sandbags. She knew it to be Nelson's Column, and the hero of Trafalgar was still atop his perch, defiantly ignoring the bombers. The great bronze lions at the tower's base, each as big as an elephant, were also uncovered.

Around the square she could see a few small craters in the pavement, topped up with gravel while repairs awaited, and some boarded-up windows on nearby buildings. But the fountains were still full of water, the pigeons were still abundant, and the spirit of the square's occupants was, as far as she could see, still undaunted.

As they continued on toward the gallery, a building so large that it took up the entire northern side of the square, Ruby noticed a long and growing line of people snaking down the central steps and around to the right. "We'll never get in."

"Only a hundred or so," Mary said. "We'll get in, all right. Then you'll be sorry."

"Come on, you two," Kaz urged them, and they hurried forward to join the end of the line. Seen at closer quarters, the gallery really was gigantic, and seemed to Ruby at least as large as the Metropolitan Museum back home. She'd visited it several times, always emerging with the feeling that, no matter how often she went, she would only ever see a fraction of its treasures.

"You said the gallery is empty?" she asked Kaz.

"Yes. Right after war was declared, the—"

"Hello there!"

A man had come up on Kaz's other side and was shaking his hand. Peering around the large form of her editor, Ruby was surprised to see Captain Bennett. He moved on to kiss Mary's cheek and then, coming face-to-face with Ruby, bent his head to kiss her cheek even as she extended her hand for him to shake.

"Hello, Ruby. Lovely to see you again."

He was in uniform, though there was something subtly different about the insignia on his collar and shoulder tabs; if only she were better at remembering such details. He looked far less tired than he had in July, the shadows beneath his eyes much less pronounced. And his eyes—she hadn't forgotten how blue they were. As dark and deep a blue as a brand-new pair of denim jeans, and if there was a more American way to describe them, she couldn't imagine what it was.

Suddenly she realized she was staring. "You look well," she said, the imprint of his lips still warm on her cheek. "It's been a while since I saw you last."

"Yes. Sorry about that. I've been away since the summer."

She'd enjoyed their dinner, and it had been a bit disappointing when she hadn't heard from him afterward. Funny how she hadn't allowed herself to dwell on that last thought until this exact moment, standing in the sunshine, seeing him again.

And it was silly to let such a small thing bother her. She was not, and had never been, the sort of girl who would allow herself to sit around moping when there was interesting work to be done. Life was about far more important things than dinners with handsome British army captains.

"Glad you could get away," said Kaz. "They keeping you busy?"

"Not very," he said agreeably. "I'm working at the Inter-Services Research Bureau now," he explained for Ruby's benefit. "No one seemed to mind when I said I'd be taking a long lunch today. Shows my importance in the grand scheme of things."

They reached the doors, and there was a moment of détente when she tried to pay for her concert ticket and program, only to be ignored by Kaz, who paid for all four of them.

"It's the least I can do," he said, "since I all but blackmailed you into coming along."

"May I at least buy your lunch?" Ruby asked.

"You may not," he said gruffly, but softened his words with a smile.

The canteen, which was staffed entirely by volunteers, had been set up in an empty upstairs gallery. There were long tables filled with trays of ready-made sandwiches and slices of cake, and at one end a row of urns dispensing tea and coffee.

"Cream cheese and dates, ham and chutney, cheese and chutney, sausage roll," recited the volunteer who came forward to serve them.

"Ham and chutney, please," Ruby ordered, and was furnished with a sandwich that looked, as Mary had promised, far more tempting than their usual lunch fare at work.

"Station cake farther along, and tea and coffee, too. Cashier is at the end. Next, please."

The station cake, on closer inspection, was a sort of pound cake studded with bits of dried fruit. "Dried plums, my dear," explained the volunteer doling out slices. "Can't find glacé cherries for love or money these days. Would you like a cup of coffee or tea?"

"Oh, no thanks. I'll be fine with this." Ruby had learned to be leery of what passed for coffee in London, since it invariably turned out to be hot water tinted with a few drops of tinny-tasting coffee extract.

"Eat up, everyone," Kaz commanded. "We've only a quarter hour until the concert begins, and I don't much feel like standing."

Their sandwiches and cake devoured, they joined the stream of people making their way down to the basement and a large but low-ceilinged room. At its far end, a magnificent grand piano stood on a raised stage.

"I wonder how they got the piano down the stairs," she whispered to Mary as they took their seats about halfway back.

"Good question. Carefully, I expect."

She ended up seated between Mary and Captain Bennett, with Kaz on Mary's other side. "Can you see all right?" the captain asked. "We can switch seats if you like."

"No, I'm fine."

"When the concerts started last year, they were upstairs—I can't remember the name of the room. At any rate, the musicians were directly under a huge glass dome. Beautiful venue, but not a wise place to be during an air raid. No one wants to see Myra Hess skewered by broken glass."

"Myra Hess?" she asked. "Is she one of the musicians?"

"Yes, and the woman who had the idea of holding these concerts. Quite a remarkable person. If we're lucky she'll be performing." He pulled his program, now rather creased, out of his breast pocket and scanned it quickly. "Not today, alas. Haven't heard of either of the musicians, although they're usually pretty good. I do like the pieces they've chosen."

"Ah," she said, not willing to admit she knew as little about classical music as he likely did about baseball.

"They're starting with Mozart's Sonata for Violin and Piano-forte in A Major, then a short intermission, then Elgar's Violin Sonata in E Minor. The greatest of our modern composers. Beautiful piece, although I prefer his cello concerto."

"It sounds like you know a lot about classical music."

"My mother was a musician. A pianist, although she never performed professionally. Really more of an avid amateur."

"Did she make you learn, too?"

"Yes, although I was awful about it. Would much rather have been climbing trees or breaking the conservatory windows with a cricket ball. Of course I'm glad now that she made me keep on."

A round of applause signaled the arrival of the musicians, two men dressed in uniform who bowed before turning to their instruments. The violinist stood alone at center stage, while the pianist was joined by a young woman who sat on a stool to his side.

"To turn the pages," Captain Bennett whispered in her ear.

Silence . . . and then music, sublime music that filled her thoughts, her senses, obscuring all but the sweeping, plaintive notes of the violin and the precise delicacy of the piano. It was mesmerizing stuff, and Ruby leaned forward, eagerly drinking it in. What little classical music she'd ever heard on the radio had seemed stuffy and ponderous, but this was magic. This was sunshine made audible.

With one final flourish they were done, and so caught up was she in the performance that she jumped a little when everyone began to applaud. Glancing at her watch, she realized that nearly half an hour had passed. It had felt like only a few minutes.

"Did you like it?" Captain Bennett asked quietly.

"I did. I had no idea . . ."

"It's lovely, and not performed nearly often enough."

"There's more, though, isn't there?"

"Yes. They'll be back in a minute for the Elgar. It's very different to the Mozart, but I think you'll like it just as much. Possibly even more."

The Elgar sonata was indeed different, so heartfelt and romantic that it left her breathless and shaky and nearly dizzy with delight. She turned to Captain Bennett in astonishment as the musicians took their bows.

"I knew you'd like it," he said.

"Did you say the composer is English?"

"Was. Died five or six years ago. Why do you ask?"

"I don't know. Only that it's the most un-English thing I've ever heard."

"Why? Because it's so passionate?" he asked, and though he tried to put on a serious face, he couldn't quite keep his smile in check.

"I guess," she said, stifling a giggle.

"Hmm. I'd say you need to get to know us better. Come on—time to go."

They made their way outside, a slow process given the hundreds of people who had crowded into the basement, and waited for Mary and Kaz to join them.

"Mary and I are heading back to the office," Kaz said, "but you should go on home, Ruby. No point in coming back when I'm just going to send you packing an hour later."

"I'll come with you," Captain Bennett offered. "My flat isn't far from the Manchester."

"Don't you have to get back to work? It's only half-past two."

"We keep odd hours at the bureau. They won't mind."

Even bankers kept longer hours than that, but who was she to argue? They said goodbye to Kaz and Mary and walked north along Charing Cross Road, presumably in the direction of the nearest Tube station.

"I thought we'd take the Piccadilly line to King's Cross," he explained after a few minutes. "We can change there for Aldersgate. Unless you were wanting to go somewhere else?"

"No, home is fine. I have a lot of reading to do."

They just managed to squeeze onto the next train, and although it felt a bit uncomfortable, standing only inches from a man she hardly knew, she wasn't crazy about the idea of getting any nearer to the complete strangers who were pressing close on every other side.

"I'm sorry for having vanished," he said after a few minutes in which she studiously avoided making eye contact with him. She looked up, and was surprised to see that he really did look apologetic. "I've been away for months. I only returned last week."

"I understand," she said, wondering where he'd been and what he'd been doing, although if he'd wanted her to know, he surely would have explained.

"I did keep in touch with Kaz while I was away. He said your editor at *The American* has given you a column."

"He has. They call it 'Dispatches from London.'"

"Do you enjoy writing it? I presume you haven't had any difficulty in finding subjects to write about."

"None at all. Some weeks I don't know where to begin . . . there's so much I want to say. I usually fall back on describing something I've seen or experienced personally. Nights in the shelter, the morning after a raid. Conversations I've had with people who've been affected. That sort of thing."

"Kaz certainly likes what you're doing. Both your columns and the pieces you write for *PW*."

"He does?" And then, although it was pathetic of her to ask, "What did he say?"

"Among other things, he said you're able to make a story moving without manipulating the reader. And that you never cut corners, no matter how pressed you are to get a story finished."

"That's . . . that's very nice of him," she stammered. "I'm glad that Kaz is pleased with me."

"So you'll call him Kaz, but I'm Captain Bennett to you?"

The man was determined to confound her. Why should he care what she called him? "Your first name is Charles, isn't it?"

He groaned softly, his face twisting in mock disgust. "Yes, but I'm not fond of it. For some fool reason, my mother decided to name me Charles Stuart, always the both names together, after Bonnie Prince Charlie. Never mind that the man was an asinine dullard."

"So what am I supposed to call you? Charlie? Chuck? Chaz?"

"Ha. No, Bennett is fine. Just Bennett."

"All right. Bennett, then." Somehow this seemed even more daring than referring to her editor as Kaz.

"See? How hard was that?"

Once the train arrived at King's Cross, it took them a while to make their way from one platform to the next, since people had already begun to stake out spots in anticipation of the evening's raids. Ruby thanked her lucky stars, and not for the first time, that she had such a safe and congenial place to shelter each night.

The platform for the Piccadilly line was already crowded, and two trains came and went before one arrived that wasn't already bursting at the seams.

"So you were saying you'd just started at the—" she began, but stopped short when he frowned and shook his head.

"Not here—sorry. Too many people."

Only when they had left the train, and were walking up the steps at Aldersgate station, did he bend his head to explain, his words tickling at her ear.

"I am sorry. It's just that I'm not meant to talk about my work at all. Probably overcautious of me, I know."

"Not at all. None of us are meant to talk about anything important. At least that's what the posters on the Underground say. Is it interesting, though? The work you're doing?"

"In fits and starts. A lot of the time it's actually pretty boring. I wouldn't have thought it possible, but at times it's even more boring than being a barrister."

"I'd have thought being a lawyer—a barrister, I mean—would be really interesting. Being in court, you know, and standing in front of a judge. Arguing about life-and-death things every day."

"Not in my case. I specialized in international law. Trade relations and treaties."

"So you don't miss it?"

"I do, at times. I certainly miss my colleagues. What I don't miss is that damn wig."

"I . . . what? A *wig*?"

"In Britain judges and barristers wear wigs in court. A peri-wig, actually. Imagine the sort of thing your George Washington would have worn. They're made of horsehair, so they itch like mad."

"Where is your wig now?" she asked teasingly. "At the bottom of the Thames?"

"Now there's an idea. No, it's bundled away for the duration, along with my robes. God knows when they'll see the light of day again."

They'd been standing in front of the Manchester for several minutes, she realized. Perhaps he was going to ask her out for dinner.

His next words put paid to that notion. "I had better be going—I've another engagement this evening. Otherwise I would ask you to come to dinner again."

"I don't mind. I should try and get some work done before the first siren goes off. I can't believe we haven't had any yet today. Perhaps—"

"No, they're coming. Don't doubt that. Promise me you'll go to the shelter, will you? People are getting killed because they're tired and they stay in bed when the sirens sound. Even if the hotel isn't hit, there's the shrapnel to consider. It can fly through the window and cut you to pieces."

"Don't worry," she assured him. "I always go."

"Good. Well, good night, then."

"Good night, Bennett. Thank you for walking me home."

He turned away, crossing the street and disappearing back down the steps to the Underground station, and only after he'd vanished from sight did she go inside, to the solitary comfort of her room, to read and work until the siren began its nightly wail.

CHAPTER EIGHT

November 1940

They'd have taken the train north, but the station in Coventry was still being repaired after the air raids of the week before. Instead, Mary had called a friend of a friend, who in turn knew someone with a car they might borrow for the drive.

They'd agreed to meet outside the Tube station on Tottenham Court Road, which wasn't far from Mary's flat. Ruby was there promptly at nine o'clock, but it was closer to half past before her colleague came roaring around the corner in a jaunty little Baby Austin.

By the time they emerged from the tangle of London's streets onto the main road north, Ruby was feeling distinctly green around the gills. Not only did Mary drive at breakneck speeds, freely using her horn to communicate with other drivers, but she also smoked one cigarette after the other, explaining briefly that driving made her nervous.

"You really ought to learn how to drive," Mary observed. "It's important for a woman. Gives you freedom."

"I don't disagree with you. It's just that no one drives in New York, apart from the cabbies. There never seemed any point in learning." Nor had she ever imagined any circumstance in which she might aspire to own anything as expensive as a car, but that was a discussion for another day.

"Didn't you ever want to drive into the countryside? Breathe in some fresh air?" her friend asked, exhaling yet another lungful of stifling smoke.

Ruby wound down her window a few inches before answering. "That's what Central Park is for. Acres of green, and more than enough fresh air to go around. Anyway, I thought you said you hated the countryside. That's why you left Scotland."

"I didn't much care for it as a place to live, but I don't mind a wee visit now and again."

Ruby checked her wristwatch for the first time since she'd left; at the speed they were traveling, she judged, they'd probably reach Coventry by noon. That would give them time to visit the cathedral, or what little remained of it, and then attend the first of the mass funerals the government had arranged. Something like five hundred people had been killed on the night of the fourteenth, and they were still uncovering corpses a week later.

They would then attend the service, or rather stand by at a respectful distance, and capture the mood of the hour as discreetly as possible. On this, Kaz had been adamant, and had all but shouted Nigel down when the assistant editor had instructed Ruby to try to get quotes from people at the funeral.

"No, no, *no*. For the love of all that's holy—you want her to accost the mourners at a mass funeral? Are you out of your mind, Nigel? *No*." Waving off Nigel's sputtering objections, he turned to Ruby. "If anyone seems inclined to talk, by all means listen—but do not approach anyone before or after the funeral. Not even if every other journalist there is getting quotes."

"I understand."

"The images of the cathedral and the ruined city—that's what this piece will hang on. That's why you're going. A few months from now, it might be worth sending you back, but not now."

Armed with a road map from Mr. Dunleavy, Ruby had acted as navigator for the trip north without too much difficulty, a near miracle given the lack of road signs and her unfamiliarity with the region. And there was no mistaking Coventry as they approached its outskirts: the closer they got, the more bomb sites they passed, and the dread of what they were shortly to witness began to weigh upon her.

At Ruby's direction, Mary turned the car off the London Road and onto one of the ancient medieval streets just south of the cathedral precincts. On either side, the burned-out shells of shops and houses stood in mute testament to the firestorm they had endured. After only a few yards, however, Mary pulled the car to the side of the road and switched off the ignition.

"If I go any further I'll puncture a tire, and God only knows where I'd find a spare. We'll have to walk from here."

The street, narrow to begin with, was choked with rubble and debris, although someone had cleared a rough path down its center. Most of the buildings they passed were in ruins, and the few that had survived, some with only broken windows by way of damage, looked as out of place as a tree on a battlefield. They picked their way forward, moving slower than a snail's pace, and only when they were nearly at the end of the street did they notice the policeman standing at the far corner.

Since there wasn't much they could do if he decided to be

difficult, Ruby would have to win him over first. She pasted a friendly but serious smile on her face—she had mastered that smile over the past few months—and crossed the last few yards that separated them.

"Good morning, Constable," she said, praying she had interpreted his uniform insignia correctly. "We're with *Picture Weekly* magazine." She already had her press card in her hand, and held it out to him now. "If it's not too much trouble, we were hoping to get a little closer to the cathedral. But only with your permission, of course."

He inspected her card, and then Mary's, too, frowning all the while. "Come along with me, then," he said at last. "Watch your step."

They followed him along the street, progressing even more slowly as the piles of wreckage on either side grew higher and higher. Ruby winced as her stockings caught and tore yet again; looking down, she saw a thin line of blood trickling down her leg. She must have cut it on some broken glass.

"From London, are you?"

"I'm American, actually—I guess that was obvious as soon as I opened my mouth. And Mary here is a Scot," Ruby answered, resigned to the loss of yet another pair of stockings. "But we both live in London now."

"Hmm," he said, and then, after they'd gone another few yards, "I expect you've been having a hard time of it, too."

"Not as hard as you. This is awful. Were you on duty last week?"

"No. Probably the only reason I'm still alive. Station where I work took a direct hit." He didn't elaborate, and she knew better than to press him on it.

"When did it all start?"

"Around seven in the evening. Incendiaries were raining down like hailstones. The cathedral caught on fire around an hour later. They did their damnedest to fight it off, but what chance did they have? The roof leads just melted away."

The corpse of the cathedral, for how else was she to think of it, now loomed before them. They approached cautiously, silently, for it already had the feeling of a place of pilgrimage. Its masonry was streaked black with soot, and its delicate window embrasures were twisted and broken, their centuries-old stained glass lost forever. It was a desecration.

They walked around its perimeter, Mary taking photo after photo, and eventually they came to a space, in the shadow of the still-standing tower, where the great church's outer wall had collapsed entirely.

"I can't let you go in. We're busy enough as it is without having to rescue the pair of you," the constable stated gruffly.

"Of course," Ruby said. "We'll stay here."

So she stood and stared and tried to make sense of what her eyes were showing her. The cathedral was entirely open to the sky, for what remained of its roof had collapsed into a mountain of rubble, and every bit of its interior decoration, every treasure it had once contained, lay buried beneath the ruins. She was looking at a building that had stood for something like seven centuries, weathering all that history had thrown in its path, and in one night it had been obliterated.

"The king was here a few days ago," the constable said quietly. "He stood just where you are now. Had the same expression on his face as you have now."

"Did you speak to him?"

"No, he was ringed round by the mayor and people like that. But he walked by me, close as you are now. Never thought to see the king with my own eyes."

She nodded, fixing his words in her memory.

"The thing is . . ." he began.

"Yes?"

"What happened to the cathedral is awful. Standing here, looking at it, anyone would agree. But *five hundred* people died that night, maybe more, and hundreds more lost their homes. Seems like all anyone wants to talk about is the cathedral. And I'd have thought that all those people dying is worse. I mean, you can rebuild a church. But you can't bring the dead back to life, can you?"

"I'll talk about them. The people, that is. I'll write about them in my article."

He nodded, swallowing awkwardly, and then, turning away, scrubbed a hand across his face.

"We're meant to go to the funeral," Mary said, her voice soft and strangely tentative. "Is it at the cemetery we passed on the way in?"

"On the London Road, yes. Straight back the way you came."

"May I have your name?" Ruby asked the constable.

"John Stevens."

"And may I quote you, Constable Stevens? What you said about the people who died and so on? And use your photograph? Everything we print has to pass inspection with the Ministry of Information," she added, sensing his hesitation.

"All right, then," he said after a long pause. "I said it. Might as well stand by it."

They thanked him and shook his hand, and as they made

their way back to the car Ruby repeated his words in her head over and over, not wanting to forget or change them in any way. As soon as they were seated and Mary had reversed around for the journey to the cemetery, Ruby pulled out her notebook and scribbled down their conversation in shorthand. Mary's photographs would be the backbone of the story, but the constable's words would be its beating heart.

The funeral was easy to find, for they simply followed the trail of people dressed in black walking along the side of the road. Mary parked the car just inside the cemetery gates, pulling onto the verge next to a handful of other vehicles, and they walked the remaining distance to the burial site.

Seeing Mary's camera, a policeman directed them to an area where a clutch of other journalists was gathered. Ruby knew some by sight, having encountered them at the occasional MOI press conference, but apart from perfunctory greetings no one spoke.

They stood some yards distant from the graves, four endlessly long trenches that ran parallel to one another, and which were as deep as they were wide. The government had mandated this mass funeral—mass burial, to be brutally honest—as a measure against disease, and also to spare families the expense of burying their loved ones. The unacknowledged fact that so many of the dead had been burned beyond recognition had surely also been a factor.

The assembled dignitaries took their places as a convoy of trucks drew up nearby, the bed of each vehicle laden with plain, tarpaulin-covered coffins. One by one, the coffins were lowered into the trenches. Ruby stopped counting after a hundred and fifty.

The Bishop of Coventry, dressed in magnificent vestments and a steel helmet, said some words that were carried away by the wind, then another churchman recited the Twenty-Third Psalm, and that was all. No music, no hymn for the mourners to share. Only the distant drone, far above, of a pair of fighters that wheeled and turned like watchful eagles. "To stop Jerry from bombing the funeral," someone whispered.

The service at an end, mourners began to approach the trenches, silently setting down wreaths at the edge, or casting single flowers, many of them fashioned from paper, onto the rough, unadorned wood of the coffins below. Soon the graves were all but obscured by the tributes.

Ruby was glad of Kaz's injunction against approaching any of the mourners, many of whom looked to be still in shock; many were bandaged or hobbling on crutches. She hung back, as did the rest of the assembled journalists, and only once the mourners had dispersed did she go in search of her friend.

"Best be on our way," Mary said. "I don't much fancy trying to find my way around London in the blackout."

They stopped at a roadside café outside Daventry for a late lunch of greasy sausage rolls and astringent tea.

"I've been wondering—"

"Oh, no," Mary muttered.

"Wait until you hear my question. How come you don't carry around a load of gear? I've only ever seen you with your camera. Where are your lenses and whatnot?"

"Don't use them. I'm not much of a photographer, to be brutally honest."

Ruby rolled her eyes in dissent. "I beg to differ. I've seen your pictures, remember?"

"Thank you. What I mean is that I don't know much about photography, not technically, I suppose you could say. I know how *my* camera works, and I can get it to do just about anything I want it to do, but I'm rubbish with flashes and lenses and the like. What's the point of a long lens, anyway? I need to be close to someone to take their picture."

"Close enough to see the whites of their eyes?" Ruby said with a laugh.

"Pretty much, yes." And Mary picked the camera off the table and took three pictures of her, one—two—three, just like that. "There. Something for you to send home."

"Thanks. That's nice of you. Except, well, there isn't really anyone at home," Ruby said, her gaze fixed on the chipped spout of the teapot at her elbow. "I've no family anymore."

"What about friends? You seem like the sort of girl who'd have no end of friends." Mary's voice was gentle. Careful.

She shook her head. "Not really. The people I knew in New York were friendly acquaintances, but not much more. Not . . . not really," she ended, realizing too late that she'd repeated herself.

"Well, you've friends here already," Mary said. "Will you look at me a moment? Come on—you know I won't bite. There. Now listen to me: you have friends here in England. You do. And you mustn't ever forget it. D'you hear?"

"Yes, Mary," Ruby said, and then she had to look away again. That, or risk crying for the first time in living memory.

"Now finish up that wretched excuse for a sausage roll so we can be on our way."

They'd just passed Watford when Mary abruptly pulled onto the graveled shoulder.

"Do we have a flat tire?" Ruby asked.

"A what? Oh, you mean a puncture. No—the petrol's nearly gone. Need to top it up." Mary got out, tilted her seat forward, and pulled out a rectangular metal jerry can. "Hope this is enough to get us home."

"Isn't it dangerous to drive around with containers of gasoline? What if we got in a crash?"

"Didn't have a choice," Mary explained as she tipped the fuel into the Austin. "It's not my car, so I don't have my own petrol ration. Had to buy it off my friend. Oh, hell—I've gone and got it all over my hands. If Nigel gives me any guff about paying me back, I'll make him regret it, so help me I will."

They got back in the car, Mary still complaining about the smell of the gasoline on her hands, and set off again. They were both feeling very grumpy and hungry when they arrived back in central London, the light fading fast as Mary drove down Shoot-Up Hill.

"Why don't you drop me at the nearest Tube station," Ruby suggested. "You need to get the car back before the sun goes down."

"You don't mind?"

"I don't mind," Ruby insisted. "Look—we're coming up to Edgware Road. Just set me down here. See you tomorrow?"

"That I will. Not at the crack of dawn, mind you. I'll need a lie-in after today."

THE NEXT MORNING Ruby had been hard at work for a few hours before she happened to catch sight of the calendar hanging on the newsroom wall. Why hadn't it occurred to her before?

"I can't believe I forgot about it," she muttered to herself.

"Forgot about what?" asked Nell.

"Thanksgiving. It's today."

"Your American holiday? The one where you say thanks to the Almighty for your freedom from Mother England?"

"Ha, ha. No, Peter—it's more to do with the Pilgrims and their first harvest meal. At least that's what I learned in school."

"So what do you do? Go to church?"

"Most people just share a meal together. A big one, with roast turkey and potatoes and pumpkin pie. There's a parade in New York, too, with huge balloons and floats and sometimes even movie stars walking down the street, and the last float is always Santa Claus on his sleigh."

"Pumpkin pie? That sounds like something dreamed up by the Ministry of Food," Nell observed, her nose wrinkling.

"It does, doesn't it? But there's more cream and sugar in it than actual pumpkin. At least I think there is. I've never made one myself."

"You going to celebrate?" Peter asked.

"I don't know. I'm not feeling like there's much to be thankful for. Not this year," she said, adrift on a sudden swell of homesickness.

"You're alive, aren't you?" said Nell, not unkindly. "There's plenty of others who wouldn't mind being in your shoes."

"I know. You're right, I know."

"Sure I am. So let's celebrate your odd American holiday with a spot of lunch downstairs."

That night, huddled on her camp bed in the hotel's basement, waiting for the all clear to sound, Ruby let her mind drift across the ocean to New York. Last year she had watched the Macy's parade on her own before going home and eating Thanksgiving dinner with the other boarders. It had been a good day, if a bit lonely at times.

She'd lived in England for five months, and in all that time she hadn't written to anyone back in New York, nor had anyone there tried to keep in touch with her. Without quite meaning to, she had found a home in London. It wasn't forever, though, for the war would end one day, someday, and she would go back.

Back, but not home. For here, in this battered and stubbornly beautiful city, where death and destruction fell from the skies night after night, she had finally found a home. Here was the one place in the world where she truly belonged. And that alone, she decided, was reason enough for thanksgiving.

Dispatches from London

by Miss Ruby Sutton

November 26, 1940

. . . The foundations for Coventry Cathedral were laid in the 1300s, roughly two centuries before Christopher Columbus set foot in the New World, four and a half centuries before America won its freedom, and almost six centuries before the Empire State Building became the tallest structure in the world. Yet the end of 1940 sees it in ruins . . .

CHAPTER NINE

December 1940

Ten days later, Ruby and Mary were again traveling north, but this time by train. Their destination was Liverpool, and their assignment was to report on the Durning Road disaster of two nights earlier.

In Liverpool they would have the help of John Ellis, the longtime editor of the *Liverpool Herald*. "Gave me my first job," Kaz had explained. "Hired me straight out of university, even though I was an idiot in every measurable way. I'd walk on broken glass for the man, so be on your best behavior."

Mr. Ellis was waiting for them at Liverpool's Lime Street station when their train pulled in at midday. He was in his early fifties, with thick spectacles that failed to obscure his inquisitive eyes, and graying hair badly in need of a trim. He was also utterly exhausted, and Ruby felt a twinge of guilt that he would be spending his day showing them around when he so clearly needed to rest.

"Good morning, Miss Buchanan. Good to see you again."

"And you as well, Mr. Ellis. This is my colleague Ruby Sutton."

"Ah, yes. The American writer. Kaz sang your praises in his last letter. Shall we be off? My driver is just outside."

The car was an older saloon-style vehicle, about twice as big as the Baby Austin that Mary had borrowed for the trip to Coventry, and wide enough for Mr. Ellis to sit alongside them for their tour around the city. "I thought we might start here in the city center," he said as they got under way. "It will give you an idea of the damage Liverpool has seen so far. We can certainly go out to the docks, but I doubt the MOI will let you publish any descriptions or photographs, and you've only got a few hours here before you have to head back to London."

There seemed little to distinguish the streets of central Liverpool from those of London, at least to Ruby's untutored eye. The buildings they passed were a hodgepodge of styles, and the people doing their shopping wore the same sort of clothes as Londoners. There were even the same shops as she knew from the capital: Boots, Woolworth's, W. H. Smith, and more than one Lyons teahouse.

It was a warm day for early winter, and through the car's half-open windows she could hear snatches of conversation from time to time. Even to her ears the local accent was startlingly distinctive, and thinking back to her arrival in July, she recalled the first time she'd heard its expressive, almost musical cadences. The ticket agent at the train station had spoken just so, as had the train conductor, and she'd had to ask them to repeat their words several times before she had understood. It felt like a lifetime ago.

They circled through the central part of town, with Mr. Ellis pointing out significant buildings as they passed, many of them huge neoclassical edifices that, in their grandeur, reminded Ruby of the Capitol building back home. Not that she'd ever seen it in person; the farthest south she'd ever been was New Jersey.

"Have you lost any landmarks?" she asked.

"Not yet, no. Parts of the docks have been badly damaged, but places like St. George's Hall and the Customs House are still standing, as are all of the churches."

"So compared to London?"

"Compared to London we've barely been touched. Through September there were scattered raids with no rhyme or reason to them, or not as far as I could see. October was much the same. Damage, yes, but nothing like the East End has seen."

"And casualties?"

"Low if you set them against the numbers killed in London, but awful still. Three generations of one family were killed by one bomb last month, on Chapman Street, I think. Then, a few days later, ten children were killed in the same block of flats. *Ten*. I . . ."

"Yes?" she prompted.

"It's silly to try and quantify such things. Foolish, even. But the disaster at Durning Road is a turning point, for lack of a better expression. We've had a taste of the worst the war can throw at us, and it's bitter. By God, it's bitter."

They rode on in silence, broken only by Mr. Ellis's occasional directions to the driver.

"Where is Durning Road?" she asked.

"It's in Edge Hill, due east of here. A fairly typical working-class neighborhood. Close-knit. Sort of place where everyone knows everyone."

"What happened?" She knew the basics: a bomb had hit a shelter and killed a number of people in what the MOI had termed an "incident" in official briefings. As if such a bloodless term could properly express the limitless tragedy of what had befallen the people of Durning Road.

"It was a school. A training college. People had crowded into the basement shelter. Something like three hundred were packed into the boiler room. I imagine they thought it would be safer there, since the ceiling was reinforced with iron beams. But there was a direct hit, and the entire building, the entire weight of it, fell into the basement. Fell onto the people in the shelter. Those who weren't crushed by the beams and the bricks and everything else were scalded to death by water from the boiler. And then the gas from the mains caught fire."

"Do they have an idea yet of how many died?"

"The last I heard it was at least a hundred and fifty dead. Many of those who did survive are badly burned, so that number will certainly climb."

They turned off the main road and onto a wide street lined with brick-and-stucco shop fronts and older terraced homes. It was a tidy road, utterly unremarkable but for the smoldering ruin of bricks, stone, and blackened lumber in the middle distance.

"Mr. Ellis?" came the driver's voice from the front. "We're coming up to the, ah, college. Where'd you like me to stop?"

"Just ahead is fine. We'll walk the last block."

They approached quietly, tentatively, standing at the fringe of the crowd of onlookers, and all the while Ruby worked to fix the image of the collapsed building in her memory. It had fallen in on itself, its exterior walls folded upon its roof beams, which in turn rested heavily, crookedly, on layer upon layer of floorboards, plaster, stonework, and broken glass.

At ground level, near what once may have been a set of stairs, a group of men in steel helmets and boiler suits were pulling at the debris, shovels at the ready, their muttered instructions to one another barely audible above an undercurrent of noise that Ruby didn't at first recognize. It was a sort of low, keening cry, reminiscent of an animal in distress, and it made the hair on her nape stand on end and her breath catch in her throat. She turned her head this way and that, trying to discern what she heard, and then she realized it was coming from the people around her, men and women alike, some of them covering their mouths with their hands to contain their horror.

The sound rose and rose, and then the crowd parted before her, and she stood and watched mutely as two men shuffled past with a stretcher. On it was a blanket-draped body, far too small to be that of an adult, and as the men stepped free of the debris the blanket shifted, only a little, but enough to reveal a tiny shoe, its leather wizened and twisted by fire and water and . . .

The horror of that one shoe fell on her, a body blow that stole the breath from her lungs. She took a step back, closed her eyes, but the image would not flee, it was still there even in the darkness. She could see it, see the child's little foot, so still and cold. How was she ever to wipe such a sight from her mind?

"Deep breath," came Mary's voice in her ear. "That's it. And another. You'll be yourself in a minute. Come away with me. Come on and follow me."

"I'm sorry," Ruby gasped as Mary led her away. "I don't know why I reacted like that."

"You let yourself be human, that's all. I took a turn, too, when I saw that wee shoe."

"I'm fine. I will pull myself together——I promise I will."

"I know you will. Now, why don't we see where Mr. Ellis has vanished?"

They ran him to ground just around the corner, deep in conversation with a police officer.

"Sorry for wandering off, ladies. This is Sergeant Harris. Known him since he was a green recruit."

"Mr. Ellis here was telling me how you've come up from London to write a story about Liverpool. 'Bout time someone admitted the Blitz isn't just in London."

"That's why we're here," Ruby affirmed. "Mr. Ellis was telling us that the college took a direct hit."

"Was a parachute mine. One gust of wind in any direction and we wouldn't be standing here. Makes you sick just to think of it."

"Is there any hope of survivors? I saw, just now . . ."

Sergeant Harris shook his head decisively. "After what I saw last night? I doubt it."

"Do you think anyone might be willing to speak with my friends?" Mr. Ellis asked.

"Won't know unless we ask. But not here—people here are waiting for news. Best to go down the road a bit. By the mobile canteen, maybe?"

With their typical brisk efficiency, the ladies of the WVS had gotten to work feeding the neighborhood. Huge billy cans of soup and tea were steaming away, and slabs of cake were being handed out to any child who asked nicely.

Was that all it took to restore a child's spirits? A piece of cake and a cup of milky tea? When disaster had overtaken her life, she'd been about the same age as these children drawing hopscotch squares on the pavement with bits of broken plaster. It had been easy to placate her, too, with promises of fun and good things to eat. Only later, much later, had she grasped the import of her changed circumstances, and the grief of that moment had never left her.

A few women stood nearby, their hands wrapped around steaming mugs of tea, their faces drawn and pale, their eyes moving constantly, fretfully, between their children and the calamity of the ruin down the road. One, who looked even more tired than her friends, held a feebly fussing baby, well wrapped in blankets and a knitted cap, over her shoulder.

"Good morning, ladies. I've got Mr. Ellis here from the *Herald,* and two ladies from *Picture Weekly* in London." The women nodded, one by one, and did their best to smile.

There was nothing for it but to plunge ahead. "Thank you so much for speaking with us. Were any of you in the shelter at the college last night?" As Ruby talked, she pulled out her notebook and opened it to the first blank page.

They all shook their heads, and then the woman with the baby in her arms spoke, her voice wobbly with fatigue or shock. "Only by the grace of God we didn't go. Tommy is just getting over the whooping cough. He's that noisy at night, and I didn't want to bother anyone. So we sat under the stairs. Never thought I'd be happy to see him sick . . ."

"Do any of you know anyone who was, ah, in the shelter?" Ruby asked, and steeled herself for their answers.

"My neighbor down the road. Four of her kids died. *Four,*" said one.

The woman next to her nodded sadly. "We always thought it was the safest place round here. Big, solid building like that.

Seemed a sight better than those Morrison sandwiches they put up in no time at all."

"I beg your pardon?" Ruby asked. "'Morrison sandwiches'?"

"She means the surface shelters. Those places are death-traps," said another. "One good sneeze, and you're the meat in the middle of a shelter sandwich."

And then, from the woman holding the baby, "Are you an American?"

"I am," Ruby answered, still scribbling down the quotes that had come flying at her. "I came over in the summer. My ship docked in Liverpool, so my first sight of England was your city. I never thought . . . well, I'm sorry to be returning under these circumstances."

"If I was you, I'd hop on the first ship leaving for Canada," said an older woman at the fringe of the group.

"You know, there've been mornings it's crossed my mind. Especially after one of those nights when I've been back and forth to the shelter so many times my head is spinning."

Everyone nodded in agreement. "Those nights are the worst," someone said.

"But I usually think better of it once the sun is up. For better or for worse, I'm here for the duration. Now, would any of you be comfortable sharing your names with me? The story will likely run in next week's issue."

She was pleasantly surprised when all the women crowded around, perfectly willing and perhaps even a touch excited at the thought of seeing their names in print. As she copied down their names next to their respective quotes, she looked to Mary and waited for her colleague's signal. A nod meant they should move on; a shake of her head, and Ruby had to keep talking. Mary nodded.

"Thank you, ladies. I do appreciate your taking the time to speak with me." She shook everyone's hand, patted the baby's back and wished him good health, and then turned to follow Mary, Mr. Ellis, and the policeman back up the road.

They said goodbye to Sergeant Harris, and back in the car, Mr. Ellis asked his driver to return them to the city center. "Do you feel like you were able to get enough photographs, Miss Buchanan? And you, Miss Sutton? Do you have enough for your story?"

"I think so." She checked her wristwatch; they had ninety minutes before the train to London was due to leave. "We've got a bit of time left still."

"Then why don't I take the two of you to lunch? There's a decent place not far from the station."

"We wouldn't want to keep you from your work," Ruby protested, all too conscious of the poor man's fatigue. "Won't they be expecting you back at the paper?"

"I'm all but living there at present. They won't miss me for another hour."

"How is your wife?" Mary asked.

"She's well, thank you, and the children. Refuses to leave the city, no matter how often I ask. Won't agree to go without me."

"Do you live nearby?" Ruby asked.

"Fortunately, no. Our house is in Garston, a bit south of here. So far we've escaped the bombs, but I'm not fool enough to expect it to last forever. I only hope I can persuade Isobel to go to my sister in Wales if—when—it gets worse."

They passed a pleasant hour with him, and Ruby was content

to sit back and listen to his stories about a young Kaz, straight out of school and green as grass and given to blushing bright red whenever Mr. Ellis had so much as coughed in his direction. She couldn't remember, even an hour later, what she'd eaten for lunch at the public house near the station, but it had filled her stomach and calmed her nerves, and by the time they rose to leave she was feeling quite miraculously restored.

Mr. Ellis was kind enough to come inside the station with them and make sure their train hadn't been delayed, and only when he was satisfied that their journey home was assured did he shake their hands and accept their thanks for his assistance.

"It was my distinct pleasure, I assure you." He paused, his brow knitting into a frown. "The thing is . . . what happened in Edge Hill is only the beginning. Call me a Cassandra if you like, but I'm convinced the Germans have been toying with us. Here in Liverpool, I mean. When they decide to destroy the docks, life in this city will get much, much harder."

"So it's only a matter of time?" Ruby pressed.

"Oh, yes. The MOI won't let you print a word of this—I'm just telling you as one journalist to another. Britain lives and dies by what comes through these docks. War matériel, food, troops. Everything our empire can give us. The docks are a lifeline, in the most literal sense, and if they go . . ."

He surveyed the bustling station interior, his eyes heavy with exhaustion, his face pinched and drawn in an expression of utter desolation. "I'm sorry for sounding so bleak. If I were any kind of patriot, I would offer up something more encouraging. Something about the resolute spirit of Liverpool's people, perhaps? At least that part would be true."

The station clock chimed the quarter hour; their train was leaving in five minutes.

"Off you go," he instructed. "And make sure to embarrass Kaz with my stories as soon as you can. The next editorial meeting, if you can manage it."

"That's a promise," Mary said.

He turned to Ruby and shook her outstretched hand. "Good luck to you, Miss Sutton. Goodbye, and good luck."

CHAPTER TEN

Christmas 1940

Ruby hadn't expected to spend Christmas Eve in an air-raid shelter surrounded by strangers. Nor had she expected she would enjoy it so much.

With Christmas falling on a Wednesday, everyone at *PW* had worked well into the afternoon of the twenty-fourth. That way, they might then have Christmas Day off without falling too far behind. Before they left, Kaz treated everyone to dinner at a nearby chophouse that hadn't been aired out or given a good scrubbing for the better part of a century. Despite its scruffy interior, the food on offer was good and plentiful, and even included roast turkey as a main course.

Kaz produced a bottle of red wine, which they used to toast the king, the prime minister, and finally absent friends, among them Nell, who had gone home to see her fiancé, back on leave for a few precious days, and Nigel, who had declared to everyone that he detested Christmas and was going to stay with like-minded friends in Reigate.

As they ate, Ruby's friends regaled her with descriptions of the traditions and customs they observed in their families, and nearly all of them were unfamiliar to her.

"A Yule log, no. Pomanders, no. Bread sauce, ecch. Definitely no," she commented. "I did know people who left out stockings for Santa—Father Christmas, that is—but I never did."

"What did you do at Christmas?" Mary asked.

For a moment, she considered admitting the truth. Describing for them the grim reality of Christmas in an orphanage.

The charity baskets filled with cast-off toys and clothes that nobody else wanted. The bishop's annual gift of improving books that depressed rather than consoled. The knowledge that Santa Claus left presents only for children in real homes with real parents. It had been a relief to discover he wasn't real.

But what would that serve, apart from depressing everyone? Better to skim over the details and let her friends enjoy their lunch. "When I was young? Nothing very special, apart from going to church. And we would usually have turkey." But only if someone had been generous enough to donate a few birds to the nuns. Otherwise it was whatever would stretch to feed all the children. One year they'd only had porridge and molasses.

Nearly halfway through the meal, Mary finally asked the question that had been weighing on Ruby's mind all day. "Where is Bennett? I thought we might see him tonight."

"I've no idea," Kaz admitted. "I'd hoped to hear from him, but I expect he's busy with work. Not to worry, though. He'll make an appearance before long. Certainly before we ring in 1941."

At this, Mary's expression brightened. "There's another tradition for you. Hogmanay. Scots for the last day of the year."

"I've sung 'Auld Lang Syne.' Is that part of it?" Ruby asked.

"It is. Just after midnight is the important part. That's when you invite the first footer to pass through your door."

"'First footer'? Is that some kind of dance?"

"No, no. It's the first person to come into your house, to set foot in it first, after midnight. They set the luck for the year, so you need to choose just the right person. The best luck comes from a tall, handsome man. Bennett would be perfect."

"What about me?" Kaz asked plaintively. "Won't I do?"

"With that sandy head of yours? Not at all. You're bad luck. No, dark hair is best."

"Is that all?"

"Well, there's the gift to bring. My gran always preferred salt, but coal will do in a pinch. Or whiskey—I've never known anyone to turn up their nose at a bottle of good Scotch."

The sun had set long before they finished their supper, but Ruby wouldn't let Kaz ring up a cab for her. "There's enough moonlight still for me to see well enough, and I know all the shelters on the way home. I'll be fine."

He looked doubtful, but she stood firm and he had to accede. "Very well. Happy Christmas, Ruby. We'll see you on Thursday."

She wished the rest of her friends a happy Christmas and set off for home. She knew the best route to take, along roads that were wide enough to catch some moonlight, and even though it was a solid half-hour walk, she made it back before the first sirens of the night had sounded.

That didn't happen until nearly eleven, and although the all clear sounded less than an hour later, she decided to stay put in the basement. It was warmer there than in her room, to start with, and she knew some of the other long-term boarders well enough to wish them a happy Christmas and smile as they settled onto their respective camp beds.

It was usual, in the shelter, for everyone to observe a sort of informal curfew after nine o'clock or so, with no conversation above a whisper, and certainly no music or singing of any kind. But tonight was different, of course, and when a man on the far side of the basement began to sing "God Rest Ye Merry, Gentlemen," nearly everyone else joined in.

Ruby hadn't sung carols for years, not since she had been a very little girl, but the lyrics came back to her, and without quite meaning to she found herself singing "Angels We Have Heard on High" and "I Heard the Bells on Christmas Day" and "Silent Night," part of a choir of near strangers in a damp and rather smelly basement. And it was, with the possible exception of the concert at the National Gallery, the most beautiful music she had ever heard.

THAT SUNDAY AFTERNOON, Ruby and her colleagues worked hard to make up for time lost earlier in the week. She was struggling with her story, a piece on cosmetics shortages that felt irrelevant no matter what approach she took, and when Kaz called a halt to work at six o'clock she was more than willing to set it aside.

She had just switched off her desk lamp and slid the canvas cover over her typewriter when something made her look up. There, leaning against the doorway to the newsroom, was Bennett, and he was watching her. Smiling at her.

He had a black eye, she noticed suddenly, and a deep cut on the bridge of his nose, too. "What happened?" she asked.

"That bloody motorcycle again," Kaz answered, brushing past his friend. "He never learns."

Bennett simply grinned at her. "I lost a fight with a tree branch," he explained.

"See?" Kaz said.

"I'd have ducked if I'd known it was there."

"Are you back in London for a while?" she asked.

"A few days. We're long past due for a meal at the Victory Café. If you're free, that is."

"That would be really nice," she said, acutely aware that every one of her colleagues, Kaz included, was looking on and imagining far more than a simple meal shared by friends. "I'll just get my things."

They walked east along Ludgate Hill, moving slowly in the near-total darkness of the blackout. There was no moon at all, not even the thinnest crescent of waning silvery light, and it seemed to Ruby that her toes were magnetically drawn to every uneven patch of pavement and upended cobblestone. If it hadn't been for the support of Bennett's arm, she'd already have tripped a dozen times over.

"Did you have a nice Christmas?" she asked, hopeful for the solace of some easy conversation.

"Not really. It was rather lonely, I'm afraid. And you?"

"On Christmas Eve I had supper with Kaz and Mary and some of the others from work, and then I spent the night in the hotel shelter. We sang carols."

"Did you go anywhere on Christmas Day?"

"No, I just stayed at the hotel. I didn't mind, though."

"Do you have any plans for New—" he started to ask, but

the rest of his question was cut off by the rising wail of the air-raid siren. A heartbeat later, it was joined by the rumble of fast-approaching planes.

"Bloody hell," he swore. "A little notice would be helpful. We're not even at Temple Bar."

"What should we do? There's a shelter at the office."

"We're closer to the Tube station at St. Paul's. Can you run in those shoes? Yes? Then take my hand."

Together they ran through the night, his touch leading her forward through the swallowing darkness. They turned left, away from the churchyard, zigzagging through narrow, deserted streets that were completely unfamiliar to her.

"The dome of St. Paul's shines white," he explained. "On a dark night like this it's a beacon. We need to get as far away from it as we can."

Incendiary bombs were rattling down on the rooftops around them, here and there dropping onto the pavement to hiss and buzz impotently. "They won't explode," he cautioned. "Keep running."

They veered left again, onto an even narrower lane, but as they turned the corner her heel caught in a grate and she fell hard on her knees. Without a word, he dragged her to her feet, hoisted her into his arms, and set off running again.

"I'm fine, Bennett. You can put me down."

"We're almost there. Not until then," he said, his voice betraying no sign of exertion.

"I'm too heavy—"

"Nonsense. When I was in the infantry, my pack weighed twice as much as you."

He ran on, not halting until they were well inside the station's deserted entrance hall, and set her down at the top of the escalators.

"Switched off, naturally. Bloody things. Are you fine to go on?"

"I am. Lead the way."

They hurried down the escalator's stationary steps, first one long run and then another, drawn to the promise of light and refuge that beckoned, just out of sight, just around the corner. The platform was crowded, but Bennett, taller than most, spied a place where they might stand. It was at the very end, hard by the tiled wall that marked the beginning of the tunnel, and there was just enough room for the two of them.

The crowd was pushing her closer and closer to Bennett, and though she tried to maintain some kind of a decent distance between the two of them, before long she would have to choose between him or any one of a half-dozen strangers flanking her sides and back.

"Don't be shy," he whispered in her ear before gently pulling her forward. "I'll be on my best behavior."

It felt so wonderful to lean against him and let her head loll against his chest. Never, in all her life, had anyone comforted her so, and even the kisses she'd enjoyed from would-be boyfriends had been offered without the solace of a supporting embrace.

She nearly jumped out of her skin when the ack-ack guns started up. "We're near a ventilation shaft," Bennett explained, his voice calm and measured against her ear. "It amplifies the noise from outside."

"It was just . . . I was startled, that's all."

"Of course. Now . . . what were we talking about before? I was going to ask what you had planned for New Year's Eve."

"Nothing, to be honest. And you?"

"The same. And I'm leaving London again for a bit, otherwise I'd offer to take you to dinner. To make up for tonight."

"I see . . ."

"You know what we need? A diversion. Something lighthearted to talk about. Any suggestions?"

"I've plenty of ideas, but none of them are lighthearted." How was she meant to think of something joyful when fleets of bombers were doing their best to exterminate them?

"You're not making this easy. Let's see . . . how about your favorite poem?"

"My favorite *poem*?" It was such an incongruous thing for him to ask that she nearly burst out laughing.

"You tell me your favorite poem, and recite it if you're able. Then I tell you mine."

"I don't have one," she admitted. "We didn't really study poetry in school."

"You didn't? My ten-year-old self is exceedingly envious of you."

"I doubt that," she said, and this time she couldn't suppress a giggle.

"It's true. The horror of my childhood was being 'set' a poem. I was expected to memorize yards and yards of verse, and not only at school. My father was a great believer in making children memorize things."

"You poor dear. Do you remember any of it?"

"God, yes. They might as well be burned into my brain. What would you like to hear first?"

"Oh, you don't have to—"

"Of course I do. That's part of the game. And how else are

we to pass the time? Since our respective social calendars are all but empty."

"Fine," she agreed. "Go ahead and pick something."

"Hmm . . . let's start with some Milton.

"The mind is its own place, and in itself
Can make a Heav'n of Hell, a Hell of Heav'n.
What matter where, if I be still the same,
And what I should be, all but less than he
Whom Thunder hath made greater?"

He peered down at her inquiringly. "What do you think? It's from the beginning of *Paradise Lost*."

"How long is it?" she asked cautiously, not enamored of the few lines he'd recited so far.

"The whole thing? Goes on forever. I can only remember bits and pieces from the first book, though. How about some Shakespeare? There's Sonnet Ninety-Seven:

"How like a winter hath my absence been
From thee, the pleasure of the fleeting year!
What freezings have I felt, what dark days seen!"

He really did have the most beautiful voice, deep and hypnotic and perfectly modulated, and very nearly transporting enough to make her forget where they were. In a courtroom, she imagined, his voice alone must have made him a formidable opponent.

He finished that sonnet and recited a second one that spoke of love being a fever and desire feeling like death, and then, almost without pause, Keats's "Ode to Autumn," which she decided immediately was her favorite, and then a long poem by Wordsworth about daffodils. It was so comforting, the sound of his beautiful voice, and after a while, when the noise of the bombs had begun to lessen, and the smell of smoke wasn't quite so choking, she began to hope that the worst might be over, or at least close to being over.

"Did you learn about the Spanish Armada in school?" he asked suddenly. "No? The story has been polished and prettied until there's hardly any truth to it, but I loved it when I was a boy."

He told her how Spain had tried to invade England when Elizabeth was queen, and how, when the enemy fleet had first been sighted, and Sir Francis Drake had been informed, he'd decided to finish the game of bowls he was playing before sailing out to engage the armada in battle.

"It sounds too good to be true," Ruby said. "As if someone decided it would make an inspiring story after the fact."

"You're right," he admitted, "but it also says something about the way people thought of the man. Just imagine what they'll be saying about Churchill five hundred years from now."

"Is Drake your favorite hero? If you had to choose one?"

"If I had to choose one person from history? I suppose it would be Lord Nelson."

"The man from the top of the column at Trafalgar Square?"

"Him indeed. When he led our fleet into battle in 1805, he'd already lost an eye and an arm in previous battles. Can you believe it? And even though it made him a target for French sharpshooters, he insisted on wearing his full admiral's regalia, along with all his decorations. Partly it was vanity, I think, but mainly it was his way of leading from the front."

"He won the battle, didn't he? I do remember a bit of it from school."

"He did. It was a near-total rout of the French fleet, but he was shot through the spine before it was done. He died three hours later. One of the last things he said was 'Thank God I have done my duty.' When I read that for the first time I wept for hours. I was only six or seven, and my uncle had given me a children's guide to history for my birthday."

"Do you think Lord Nelson was ever frightened?"

"Undoubtedly. A truly courageous man is the one who knows what he is facing, is scared to death, and still does what he must—does his duty, as Nelson said. The man had many faults, but cowardice wasn't one of them."

She meant to answer him, but she was so exhausted it was an effort even to stay upright. So she simply stood in his embrace, and after a while she wrapped her arms around his middle and rested her head against his chest, and he didn't protest or move away.

And she was so very tired. Even through the lull in bombing over Christmas, she hadn't been able to settle into sleep. It had become a habit, the awful wakefulness that came with being blitzed, and although she was really good at taking catnaps during the day, and could sleep in a chair in a pinch, she longed for peaceful slumber the way a starving man might hunger for a crust of bread.

The ground began to shake in earnest, really heave and tremble as she was sure it must do in earthquakes, and the stench of smoke and cordite and God only knew what else drifting down through the ventilation shafts spoke mutely of the fires that were raging above and around them. Even then the bombs kept tumbling from the sky, closer and closer until she held her breath in heartsick anticipation.

"I thought I'd be braver than this," she told him. A confession, while she still had the chance.

He was a serious man at the best of times, but for some reason her words drew out his rare smile. "Who's to say you aren't? Brave, that is."

"Just look at me. My hands are shaking. *I'm* shaking. I thought I would be brave, but I . . . I can't stand it. I can't."

"You can. You will. And you're not the only one who's afraid. We all are."

The crescendo of explosions climbed to a heart-stopping pitch, and along the length of the platform hundreds fell silent, waiting and bracing themselves and praying that this one, this next bomb, would fall somewhere else, anywhere else. Not here, not tonight. Not yet.

"I'm so afraid," she confessed through gritted teeth.

His arms tightened about her. "I know."

"You won't let go, will you?"

"No. No matter what happens, I won't let go."

He held her close and tucked her head under his chin, and with his quiet strength he soothed her through the long, endless hours that followed. Her brain knew she was no safer in his arms, but her heart, illogical organ that it was, told her otherwise.

She lost track of time after that, for her next recollection was of the siren's rising wail and Bennett's soft touch as he brushed her hair off her forehead. "The all clear just sounded, Ruby. We made it."

His face was streaked with dust, all but hiding the bruising around his eye, and the cut on his nose looked so awfully sore. "I can't believe it," she said haltingly, her mouth and throat gratingly dry.

"Shall we get you home?" he asked, and rather than answer

she just nodded. He led her upstairs and outside, and though she was so tired that every step was a monumental effort, she somehow managed to climb the stairs and greet the day.

It had snowed overnight, just enough to whiten the pavement and rooftops, and were it not for the fires still raging in every direction, she'd have been delighted by the sight.

"The cathedral!" she cried out, remembering.

"Look south—see? The dome still stands. It survived, as did we."

Gently turning her, he led them north, along sidewalks crowded with others making their way home in the first light of dawn. It was almost impossible to see anything beyond the backs of strangers' heads and, far above, a sky still burnished red by fire. They were almost home, though, for they'd crossed over Manchester Avenue and—

"Ruby," he said, stopping short and pulling her close. "Oh, Ruby."

Only then did she look up and see. The Manchester was gone, and in its place was a smoking, devastated, and all-but-unrecognizable ruin.

PART II

Early September morning in Oxford Street. The smell of charred dust hangs on what should be crystal pure air. Sun, just up, floods the once more innocent sky, strikes silver balloons and the intact building-tops. The whole length of Oxford Street, west to east, is empty, looks polished like a ballroom, glitters with smashed glass. Down the distances, natural mists of morning are brown with the last of smoke. Fumes still come from the shell of a shop. At this corner where the burst gas main flaming floors high made a scene like a hell in the night, you still feel heat.

—Elizabeth Bowen, "London, 1940," *Collected Impressions*

CHAPTER ELEVEN

one, gone. All gone.

Her knees crumpled, but Bennett was too fast for her. He held her up, held her close.

All her clothes. Her books. Her last jar of peanut butter. Her camera. Her typewriter. The only photograph she had of her mother.

All gone.

And then, in a surge of panic, she remembered the people from the hotel. Maggie from breakfasts in the dining room and late nights in the shelter. Doris from the front desk. Betsy the maid, who lived in the garret with the other girls and always looked so tired. The other boarders—what had become of them?

"Miss Sutton!"

She whirled about to see Maggie rushing toward her, and without hesitating she swept the girl into a fierce embrace. Now was not the time to concern herself with respect for British reserve and propriety.

"Oh, thank goodness. I'm so relieved. Was anyone killed?"

"Not as I know of, though some people've been taken off to hospital."

"What happened?"

Maggie's pretty face crumpled at the memory, but she recovered her composure with admirable swiftness. "It was the incendiaries. They lodged in the roof and took out most of the building. Part of it collapsed straight off, and the warden says the rest will have to be pulled down soon. Your room, Miss Sutton . . ."

"I know," Ruby said, her last hope fading. "But I'm fine, and it looks like everyone else will be fine. That's all that matters."

"If you go see the woman from the WVS, you can fill out a relief claim. She's there at the corner."

"Thank you."

Ruby started walking toward the WVS official, but as she approached she saw the woman was busy with someone else. It seemed important to keep moving, though, so she turned the corner and kept going. She would walk for a while, and perhaps then her head would clear and she would know what to do.

"Ruby—wait up!" Of course. She'd walked away from Bennett. "Where are you going?" he asked.

"To work. I've nowhere else to go."

"Half of London is on fire. No one will be at the office."

She faltered, hearing this, but continued walking. "You're probably right."

His arm wrapped around her shoulders, the weight of it oddly comforting. It would be so tempting to simply stop and let him carry her. He would do it if she asked.

"Listen—just listen for a minute. I have a place for you to go. Come with me and I'll sort everything out."

"I'll be fine. I don't need your help. I'm used to taking care of myself."

"I know you are, and I know I could probably walk away and you would be fine. But you shouldn't have to manage on your own. I'm your friend, and I'd like to help. There's no shame in letting me help, is there?"

They had stopped walking a few minutes before, but she only realized it now. "I guess there isn't. But only until I can find a place to stay."

She was being sensible, that was all. Only a foolish or stupidly proud person would turn down a ready offer of help. She would accept his help today, and tomorrow she would start over. Tomorrow, once she'd had something to eat, and had rested, and had washed away the awful smell of smoke and loss that clung to her hair and clothes.

"Of course," he said. "Let's see if we can find a taxi, shall we? I don't much feel like braving the Underground."

They walked west until he was able to flag down a cab. "Twenty-one Pelham Crescent in Kensington," he said as they got in the car. "Just off Fulham Road."

"Where are we going?" she asked, not really caring.

"To my aunt's. We both could use a dose of Vanessa right now."

"WAKE UP. WE'RE here, Ruby. Time to wake up."

Rather embarrassingly, she had slumped against his side. She sat up straight and rubbed at her eyes. "Are we at your aunt's?"

"We are. Give yourself a shake and let's get out of this car."

They'd stopped on a gently curving street with large white-fronted houses along one side and a park or private garden on its other, the latter separated from the pavement by a high wrought-iron fence. After Bennett had paid the driver, he guided her up a short flight of steps and, not even bothering to ring the bell, ushered them both inside.

"She never bothers to lock the door," he explained, and then, "Vanessa? Jessie? Anybody home?"

From the back of the house came an answering cry: "Helloooo! Coming!"

The hallway where they stood was bright and spacious, its black-and-white marble floor softened by a long and rather threadbare Oriental rug. To their left was a sitting room, its tall, rather dusty windows crisscrossed with tape and hung with bottle-green velvet draperies. Nothing in the room was new or even vaguely fashionable, and some of the upholstery bore the signs of a cat's undivided and enthusiastic attention.

Hanging above the mantel, flanked by a pair of intricately carved wooden masks, was a portrait that caught and held Ruby's attention. Its subject was a young woman who wore nothing but a strategically arranged Kashmir shawl, her golden hair falling to her hips, and the expression on her beautiful face was both mischievous and beguiling.

"That's my aunt Vanessa," Bennett explained. "Although she's not really my aunt. My godmother, actually. The picture was painted when she was still performing."

"She was an actress?"

"Yes. Vanessa Tremaine. Her husband was Sir Nicholas Tremaine."

Ruby turned to him in wonderment. "I've heard of him. He played King Richard in that film years ago."

"*Winter of Our Discontent*, yes. Here he was better known for his theater work. Vanessa retired from the stage after Viola was born."

"Did you ever see her perform?"

"Sadly, no. I've heard that she was an unforgettable Lady Macbeth. I did see Uncle Nick in——"

"Bennett! My long-lost Bennett!"

Advancing toward them, her arms outflung in an anticipatory embrace, was an older version of the woman in the portrait. Vanessa Tremaine's hair was streaked with white and had been tied back in a messy bun, and the skirt and blouse she wore had to be as old as Ruby, but her beauty hadn't faded one bit. It was only reinforced by the dazzling smile she now directed at them both.

"Bennett, my dear, and a new friend. Welcome, welcome!" Ruby was swept into a rose-scented embrace, kissed on both cheeks, and then gently released so Vanessa might do the same to Bennett.

"I'll explain all in a moment, but introductions first," he said. "Miss Ruby Sutton, this is my godmother, Lady Tremaine."

"Oh, pffft—none of that," the lady in question protested. "The title came along with dear Nick's knighthood. The only time I bother with it is when I'm trying to reserve a table at Quaglino's. Do call me Vanessa."

"We've been up all night—were caught out in the raid," Bennett explained. "We sheltered at St. Paul's Underground station."

"The cathedral? Did it survive?" Vanessa asked worriedly.

"The dome was intact this morning. There may be some damage, but it's still there."

"Well, thank God for that."

"The hotel where Ruby has been lodging, though, the Manchester—it was hit. More than half of it burned down, including the wing where she had her room. She's lost everything."

It was hard to hear it like that, so bluntly stated, and a traitorous tear escaped before Ruby could blink it back.

"My dear, dear girl. Come here, you poor thing," Vanessa crooned, and enveloped her once more in an embrace, loosening it just enough to allow them to walk side by side down the hall. "Let's get you settled and comfortable. Oh, you poor, dear girl."

Vanessa led Ruby down the hall, past a second sitting room, a dining room, and finally down a short run of steps into a conservatory. It looked and felt like a luxurious greenhouse, and the air was warm and moist and smelled wonderful. A large tropical plant arched high over their heads, and there were pots of geraniums, violets, and ferns everywhere.

"Let's get you settled," Vanessa said, propelling Ruby toward a white wicker armchair softened by plump chintz cushions. "Bennett, be a dear and run downstairs to Jessie. We'll need some tea and biscuits."

Something brushed against Ruby's leg, and she looked down to discover a rumpled orange tabby cat looking up at her. "Mrrow," he said, and jumped onto her lap.

"Percy, you scamp. I'll just take him—"

"No, I don't mind. Honestly. I love cats."

"He certainly likes you. Normally he's a bit more standoffish."

"I see you're making friends." Bennett sat on the chair next to Ruby and nodded toward the cat. "Percy doesn't take to just anyone, you know."

"Did you find Jessie?" Vanessa asked.

"Yes, and tea is on its way. So . . . . I was wondering if Ruby might stay with you for a few days. It may take a while for her to find new lodgings."

Vanessa shook her head so hard that strands of hair escaped

from her bun and rose in a silver nimbus around her lovely face. "A few days? No, that won't do. Why on earth can't she simply stay on with me?"

"Oh, but I couldn't—" Ruby began, but Vanessa would not be deterred.

"Of course you can. It's only Jessie and me right now, and this house is far too big for the two of us. Do say you'll stay."

Ruby was prevented from answering by the timely arrival of Jessie, a stout, white-haired woman in her early sixties. "Here's your tea and biscuits, Lady T."

"Thank you. Jessie, this is Ruby Sutton. She was bombed out last night and will be staying with us from now on."

"I'm awfully sorry to hear it, Miss Sutton. I promise we'll take good care of you."

"I thought we'd put her in Vi's old room. Is the bed made up?"

"It is, but I'd rather freshen up the sheets. Won't take but a minute."

Ruby waited until Jessie had departed before protesting any further. "I haven't said yes. I don't want to be rude, and you have been so nice, but you don't know me. How can you be sure that you want me here?"

This last question appeared to baffle Vanessa. "I don't understand. Why wouldn't we want you? You're friends with Bennett, aren't you?"

"Yes, but—"

"And Bennett is my favorite godson—"

"Your *only* godson," he interjected.

"My *favorite* godson," Vanessa continued, "and his friends are my friends, too. So it's really very simple."

With this, and clearly believing the discussion was at an

end, she poured a cup of tea, dosed it with milk and sugar, and handed it to Ruby. "Go on. Drink it down."

Not daring to refuse, Ruby swallowed nearly the entire cupful in several long gulps. It still tasted awful, but she could feel the warmth of it all the way down to her toes. She closed her eyes and tried to marshal her thoughts.

"Just think of the fun we'll have as we get to know one another," Vanessa persisted. "Oh, *do* say you'll stay. It would make me so happy to have you here."

"What about my board? At the hotel I was paying—"

"La, la, la—we'll sort all that out later. I'm sure you'll let me know what's fair."

Ruby looked to Bennett, who didn't bother to hide his amusement at her plight, and then back to Vanessa. They had her cornered, for there was no gracious way to refuse, and they knew it. For that matter, why should she refuse? She had fallen into a tub of butter, and she was smart enough to know it.

"I guess I'll stay, then," she conceded. "Thank you very much."

"I'd better be going," Bennett said. "I need to check on my flat, and I want to make sure Uncle Harry is all right."

"I thought he'd decided to stay in Edenbridge for Christmas," Vanessa said.

"Not this year. Said he felt lonely. I've no idea where he actually spent Christmas Day—I wasn't even in town."

"What about my work?" Ruby asked, suddenly remembering. All this time she'd been sitting in cozy comfort, drinking tea and having her life arranged, while her colleagues were probably standing in the street and surveying the ruins of their professional lives. "I should go and see what happened."

"You stay put," he ordered. "I'll go by, and if there's no one there I'll ring up Kaz." Gulping down the rest of his tea, he got to his feet, his movements slow and almost labored. He had to be so very tired.

"Will you come back for dinner?" Vanessa asked. "The girls will be here—they were both working last night, for some odd reason, so we're having Sunday dinner on Monday this week."

"All right," he said. "But start without me if I'm late." He bent to kiss his godmother's cheek, and then, with a reassuring smile for Ruby, he was gone.

Ruby finished the last of her tea as Percy purred away on her lap, leaning into her hand as she stroked the soft fur behind his ears. It felt so lovely to sit there, in the warmth and comfort of the conservatory, and do nothing. Think of nothing.

"Did Bennett say how he got that black eye?" Vanessa asked, busily deadheading a nearby geranium.

"He said he ran into a branch when he was on his motor-cycle."

"That horrid thing. Why he takes such risks I'll never know." She snapped off the last of the withered blooms and turned to Ruby. "Would you like to see your room?"

"Yes, please." Not wanting to disturb the cat, Ruby picked him up and deposited him back on the chair. He turned around, wriggling into the cushion, and went straight to sleep.

Vanessa led her to the third floor and along a short hallway to an open door. The room they entered was huge and bright and, to Ruby's delight, overlooked the back garden. As charmingly old-fashioned as the rest of the house, it was wallpapered with a pattern of pink rosebuds and trailing vines, and was furnished with a tall chest of drawers, a desk and wooden chair, and a low, overstuffed armchair drawn up by the hearth. The room's centerpiece, however, was a high brass bed layered with pillows and eiderdowns and blankets. It was so wide that Ruby could lie down sideways with room to spare, and for a moment she contemplated doing just that.

"You've a bathroom of your own just through here," Vanessa explained, opening its door so Ruby might marvel at its white-tiled magnificence. "Although we are trying to conserve fuel, I insist that you run a bath that's as deep and hot as you can stand. At certain times, my dear, morale trumps austerity. Today is one of those times."

"It's so lovely," Ruby marveled.

"It is nice. Now, there's a robe on the back of the door. I presume you lost your clothes along with the rest of your belongings, so I'll rummage through the girls' trunks upstairs and see what I can find."

"Won't they mind?"

"Mind? Of course not. They'd be the first to suggest it. What else, what else . . . ? You'll need something more to eat than biscuits, so I'll have Jessie bring you some soup and a bun. I want you to have your bath, eat your lunch, and then have a good, long nap. I'm sure you didn't sleep a wink last night. Oh—and if there's a raid, we've a shelter in the garden. Bennett put it in for us, and he did something with a drain, or perhaps the floor. At any rate, it's stayed dry so far, and as long as we bring out enough blankets, we're able to keep warm."

"Thank you so much. I—"

"La, la, la. Off you go and pour that bath, and don't show your face until you've had that nap."

CHAPTER TWELVE

When Ruby woke from her nap, snugly cocooned in whisper-soft, lavender-scented blankets, it took a moment to remember where she was. And then, as the memories of the night before came flooding back, she resolutely closed her mind against them. This place, this room . . . it felt safe. Here she was warm and comfortable and safe.

Checking her wristwatch, she saw it was past five o'clock. She'd been asleep for nearly seven hours, the longest she'd slept since the beginning of September. She stretched languorously and, turning her head, saw that something had been left on the bed. Sitting up, she rubbed the sleep from her eyes and tried to focus. There, draped across the folded quilt at her feet, was a blue woolen dress with long sleeves and a cardigan to match, a full slip for underneath, made of cotton so fine it was nearly transparent, and a pair of silk stockings still in their package. Real silk, not rayon. She touched the dress, her hand shaking a little when she felt how fine and soft it was.

Ruby tiptoed downstairs a little before six o'clock, drawn by the sound of voices in the front room. Vanessa was standing by the fire, her hair and dress immaculate, and on the sofa in front of the window were two young women so alike they had to be sisters. One was in uniform, and the other, her hair several shades fairer than her sister's, wore a perfectly tailored suit.

All too aware that her own fine clothes had been borrowed from one of the sisters, Ruby lingered in the hallway. Perhaps she might simply creep back upstairs without anyone noticing. She took a step back, then another, but was stopped by Vanessa's sunny greeting.

"Ruby, darling—there you are. Do come in and meet my girls." The glamorous pair on the sofa stood in unison and came forward, their smiles unaffected and genuine. If they resented her sudden appearance in their mother's home, they certainly showed no sign of it. Or perhaps they were simply as talented at acting as their parents.

"Ruby, these are my girls. Viola and Beatrice."

Ruby shook their hands, sat on the chair she was assigned, and did her best to answer the questions they flung at her like confetti. Where are you from? How long have you been in England? How do you know Bennett? What sort of work do you do? Is your hair naturally curly or have you had a permanent-wave treatment?

They listened attentively to her vague and unenlightening answers, they insisted she drink a glass of sherry as they were doing, and they appeared to be genuinely horrified when Vanessa explained what had become of Ruby's lodgings and possessions.

"Thank heavens Bennett was there," Beatrice said. "He never loses his head, no matter how awful things get. Remember when Papa died? He was the only one of us who didn't fall to pieces."

"Such a dear boy. I don't know what I would have done

without him," Vanessa said, her expression melancholy. "Oh—there's the telephone. I'll just run and answer it."

She returned with the news that Bennett had rung to say he would be late. "He told me not to wait for him, so let's get started. Are you on duty tonight, Vi?"

"I am, so I'd best hurry. God only knows what Jerry has in store for us."

The dining room table was set with china and silver and fine white linens, and though it looked to Ruby as if the king was expected for dinner, she also suspected such finery was nothing out of the ordinary for the Tremaine family. Arranging themselves around the table, the sisters immediately began to complain about the food.

"I thought we were having mutton," said Beatrice.

"I did look, but the butcher only had a piece of scrag end, and I wasn't about to pay good money for nothing more than sinew and gristle. Jessie made toad-in-the-hole instead."

Seeing the look of alarm on Ruby's face, Viola rushed to reassure her. "Don't worry—there's no toad in it."

"Oh, yes—I ought to have said so," Vanessa chimed in. "We English do have the oddest names for food. It's quite prosaic, I promise. Nothing more than sausages with Yorkshire pudding on top."

"Not sausages *again*," Beatrice moaned. "The last ones were awful."

"I know, but that was an oversight on the butcher's part. He promised me that these ones are definitely made of pork."

"What was wrong with the other ones?" Ruby asked.

"You do *not* want to know," Beatrice hissed. "Let's just leave it at that."

"Such a gamy aftertaste, too," Viola commented mischievously.

"Enough, both of you," Vanessa chided. "Ruby needs a good meal and you aren't helping things. Pay them no mind, my dear. Apart from the toad—the main course, that is—we've mashed potatoes and onion gravy, and Jessie roasted the last of the parsnips from the cold store."

As they ate, the conversation turned to the Tremaine sisters' work. Beatrice, whose uniform was a striking dark blue, was a section officer in the Women's Auxiliary Air Force; before the war, she'd been a geography teacher at a girls' school. It had shut down for the duration, which had prompted her to join the WAAF. "It had the nicest uniform," Beatrice admitted with a laugh. "What was I thinking?"

Ruby looked to Viola, who wasn't in uniform. "Are you allowed to talk about your work?" she asked hesitantly.

"I am—it's not the slightest bit important, though."

"Nonsense," Vanessa insisted. "Vi is working two jobs right now, and I'm so terribly proud—"

"Honestly, Mama. I'm not doing anything out of the ordinary. Not compared to some."

"Allow me to disagree." Vanessa turned to Ruby, waving away her daughter's protests. "Vi inherited her dear father's talent. Before the war she was in show after show in the West End, but she's given it up to volunteer for ENSA."

"'Every Night Something Awful,'" Beatrice intoned solemnly.

"Horrid girl," their mother commented. "It's the 'Entertainments National Service Association,' in point of fact."

"I know," said Ruby. "We did a story on ENSA a few months ago. The group we featured were all musicians, though."

"There are all sorts in ENSA," Viola explained. "My group does a variety show, mostly at factories during the day. Our 'lunchtime follies,' we call them. Sometimes the shows are in the evening, but between the blackout and the air raids it's easier if we put on a quick performance during the lunch hour."

"Vanessa said something about a second job?"

"Oh, yes. Well, at night I'm a fire-watcher at my old theater. There's a group of us who do it."

"When do you sleep?" Ruby asked incredulously.

"I don't, not much. But I don't mind." Her expression grew somber. "I'm really sorry about your lodgings. Last night . . . it was endless. We stood on the roof of the theater and watched the bombs rain down, and there was nothing we could do."

"I'm sure that you and everyone else in the fire services did your best. You saved St. Paul's. That in itself was a miracle."

The rumble of a motorcycle outside brought the conversation to a halt. The front door opened and closed, and the sound of footsteps in the hallway grew louder.

"We're in the dining room," Vanessa called out.

Bennett appeared in the doorway, still shrugging out of a worn leather jacket. It was dampened by snow, as was the knitted watch cap he pulled off his head. His face was drawn and weary, and there were dark streaks of soot across his forehead and cheekbones.

"Sorry I'm late. Let me hang this up and wash my face. Then I'll be fit for company."

When he returned, his face and hair damp but clean, he

dropped into the chair next to Ruby and grinned at her reassuringly. "All settled in?"

"Yes, thanks. How are you?"

"Tired."

"Have you eaten? Let me fetch you something," Vanessa offered, and rushed off in search of Jessie.

"So? What did you find?" Ruby asked.

"My flat is fine—no damage at all. Uncle Harry is unhurt, although he lost his car. Left it parked on the street and an incendiary fell right on top of it. He was fit to be tied."

"And the *PW* offices?"

"Not so much as a scratch."

Vanessa returned, bringing with her a heaping plate of dinner. Bennett started eating, not pausing until he'd consumed more than half of it.

"Sorry. Was starving. Where was I . . . oh, the magazine. Your building is fine—I think I said that already—but St. Bride's is gone."

"The church next door? That's awful."

"The walls and steeple are standing, but the interior is burned out. The fire even melted the bells." He set down his fork and knife and rubbed at his temples, his shoulders slumping. "It was a Wren church. Built after the Great Fire."

"I don't know why you're so upset," Viola said, her voice oddly strained. "It's a building, not a person."

"Yes, but it was a masterpiece of—"

"It's a structure made of stone and bricks and wood. It can be rebuilt. But we can't raise the dead, can we?"

Viola stood, her eyes bright with unshed tears, and walked

quietly out of the room. Bennett followed her right away, his face a portrait of torment.

Vanessa reached across the table and grasped Ruby's hand. "Viola was engaged to an RAF pilot," she said softly. "He was killed in August. She struggles with it still, as I'm sure you can understand."

"I do. I visited Coventry after the bombings, and I met a policeman there who said much the same thing to me. How buildings can be raised again, but our dead are lost forever."

Bennett reappeared a few minutes later. "Vi will be down in a moment."

"Is she all right?" Vanessa asked.

"She is. I made my peace with her. We're all fraying around the edges."

"Won't you sit down and finish your supper?"

"Do you mind very much if I go? I have to leave at first light tomorrow."

"Very well, but won't you take anything with you?"

"No, I'm fine." He kissed his godmother goodbye, and then turned to Ruby. "Do you know how to get to work? I'm sure Vanessa can—"

"Don't worry. I still have my *A to Z*."

"Good. I did tell you I couldn't get you another. No, Vanessa—don't get up. I'll let myself out."

Ruby excused herself not long after, and as she lay in bed, hovering at the edge of sleep, she was overcome with a wave of gratitude for her good fortune. It was true that she had lost every one of her personal treasures, but they were only things, after all. She could replace her books and clothes. She would buy another typewriter one day. She could remember, just barely, her mother's face.

And she still had her job. Kaz and Mary and everyone at work were all safe. Thanks to Bennett, she even had a place to stay, and it was the most beautiful home she'd ever seen.

Home. She'd only been with the Tremaines for a few hours, but they'd already gathered her into their little family. Treated her as if she belonged. And it would be so very tempting to believe.

Of course it was kind of them to be so generous and welcoming, but she needed to remember she no more belonged with them than any other stranger seeking refuge from the cold. She was a grown woman, not the little girl who had prayed on her knees, every night for years, that her mother might somehow come back for her; and then, after she'd lost all hope of that, had yearned for a home with one of the nicely dressed couples who came, every so often, to pick a child from among the youngest, prettiest, and best behaved of the orphans.

But Ruby had never, not once, been taken to the parlor to be presented to the nice families. The day she had stopped hoping she might find a home with one of those couples was the day she had stopped believing in fairy tales.

And this? This was a fairy tale, no more, and she would do herself no favors by forgetting it.

CHAPTER THIRTEEN

February 1941

It was well past eight o'clock when Ruby emerged from South Kensington station and started on the short walk home. She'd stayed late to help Kaz go over the final page proofs, since Peter, who normally helped with that chore, had been laid low by a terrible chest cold. Kaz had sent him home to bed, complaining that the entire office would fall ill otherwise, and Ruby had volunteered to fill in. It was interesting work, and good practice besides, but she had missed her supper and, she feared, might well end up in a public shelter if she didn't get home before the first siren of the night sounded.

She, Vanessa, Jessie, and Percy had spent the last two nights in the Anderson shelter, and though it was dry and warm—Bennett's improvements had seen to that—she hadn't slept well at all. Percy had been restless, Jessie had snored relentlessly, and her narrow camp bed had left her back sore and stiff.

Ruby turned off Pelham Place onto the Crescent, skidding a little on the icy pavement, and was still trying to regain her balance when she heard a faint cry. She looked around, wondering if one of the neighbor's babies had its cot by an open window.

Another cry, a fraction louder this time, and it seemed to be coming from the gardens on the south side of the Crescent. She stepped onto the road, her eyes scanning the shadows beyond the fence, and was able to discern something, a slight rustle of movement, under some low-growing evergreens. A small figure detached itself from the gloom and came forward, its gait awkward and stiff.

It was a young cat, and the poor thing was in a complete state. His long fur was matted and dirty, and he was limping badly, as if his paws were very sore. Crouching down, hoping that no one would choose that moment to come barreling around the corner in their car, she held out her hand and made the same noise that Vanessa used when trying to coax Percy indoors.

"Tuk, tuk, tuk," she whispered, her heart in her throat. *Please don't run away*, she silently begged. *Please don't be afraid*. "Tuk, tuk, tuk. I won't hurt you. I promise I won't."

He stood there, trembling from his nose to his tail, and then, as if accepting he had nowhere else to go, inched forward. She let him sniff her hand and, when he didn't shy away, gently stroked his head. This close, she could smell his singed fur, and see where his whiskers had been burned off.

He looked up at her hopefully, his green eyes shining in the wan moonlight, and she was lost. Before she could think twice, she picked him up and cuddled him close. "Will you let me help you?" she asked, and his answering purr was all the confirmation she needed.

They were only a few doors away from home, fortunately,

and once she'd dug her key out of her bag and let them inside, she went straight downstairs to the kitchen.

"Is that you, Ruby dear?" Vanessa called out. "I'm in the scullery. Been trying for ages to shift an ink stain, but I'm not having much luck. I'll have to—oh, my goodness. What have we here?"

"I found him out in the street. At least I think it's a he. I didn't know what else to do. I hope you don't mind."

"Mind? Of course not. I'd have done the same. Come, come. Bring him here."

"He's limping, and I think he may have some burns. His whiskers are all singed off. I'm so worried about him, Vanessa."

"Let's just see what ails him first. Cats are sturdy creatures—you'll see." Vanessa let the cat sniff her outstretched fingers, but made no move to take him out of Ruby's arms. "He won't like it, but we need to start with a bath. That dust has to come off before he tries to lick it away."

"Have you ever bathed a cat?" Ruby asked.

"Not a one. Plenty of dogs, but never a cat. Well, there's a first time for everything."

After lining the scullery sink with a towel, and filling it half-way with warm water, Vanessa took the cat from Ruby's arms and set him down in his bath. Ruby stood by, fretting that he would fuss or claw at Vanessa, but apart from a few mournful meows for form's sake the cat didn't resist at all.

He was wearing a collar, which Vanessa handed to Ruby, but it was singularly unhelpful. "The tag only says 'Simon.' They might have thought to include an address or telephone number."

"We can put up a notice," Vanessa suggested. "But if no one claims him I don't mind if he stays."

A rush of emotion swept over Ruby, and for a few seconds she found it difficult to breathe. She knew what it was to be unwanted and hungry and desperate for love and attention. She, too, had once been a stray, alone in the world, and utterly dependent on the kindness of others.

Lathering her hands with the soap, Vanessa smoothed them gently over Simon's dusty fur, and then rinsed him with additional cups of warm water. He was shivering by the time she was done, and looked quite ready to fall over. "He won't tolerate much more tonight," Vanessa observed. "You open up that big towel, and I'll pop him on top. Try to soak up as much water as you can, then he'll do the rest if he's able. I'll make up a bed for him. And I had better scrounge up something for him to eat. Poor fellow is probably famished."

One wooden fruit crate and a square of ragged blanket later, and Simon had his bed. Satisfied that he was reasonably dry, Ruby set him in the bed and watched as he calmly washed his face and paws. His fur was longer than she had first thought, and was already drying to a beautiful shade of silvery gray.

"I found him something to eat," Vanessa announced. "Just some scraps from dinner, but they'll do until I can get some cat's meat at the butchers."

She set the bowl of food on the floor next to Simon's basket, and next to it a matching bowl of water. After sniffing at it suspiciously, he decided it would do, and set about inhaling the food with gusto. As soon as he had finished, Vanessa picked him up and carried him to the table. She'd already spread out a fresh towel and readied her box of first-aid supplies.

"Such a good cat, yes you are," Vanessa crooned as she ran her fingers through Simon's fur. Coaxing him onto his side, she inspected each of his paws minutely. "I don't see any glass, thank goodness, and none of the cuts seem very deep. Best to just leave them alone, I think."

"Will he be all right?" Ruby asked, her heart in her throat.

Vanessa glanced in her direction, and her answering smile was warm and loving and deeply reassuring. "Well, he's eating and drinking, and there's nothing wrong with his purr. All good signs. And he was well cared for before, which is fortunate. His owners had him neutered, which isn't cheap, so someone loved him. And it will make him a much nicer cat to have around. Far less smelly, to begin with, and no getting into fights with every tom on the street."

"May I keep him in my room?" Ruby asked, anxious to have Simon near at hand.

"Of course you can. But leave your door open so he can come and go."

"What if he runs off?"

"I doubt he'll try. Just listen to how he's purring. He knows he's landed on his feet. Besides, he won't be going outside at night— I don't want him getting run over in the dark. I've a box of sand in the cellar that Percy uses. Simon will find it on his own."

"Poor Percy."

"Oh, he'll be fine. I'm off to bed in a minute. Do you want anything to eat before I go up? I'm not good for much in the kitchen, as you know, but I can heat you up some soup."

"No, you go to bed. I'll make myself a sandwich."

"And you—are you all right, my dear?"

"I am. Thank you for letting me keep him."

"What sort of person should I have been to say no? Now, don't linger too long—you'll want to get in a few hours of sleep before the sirens start."

Ruby ate her sandwich as fast as Simon had eaten his dinner, and then carried him upstairs to her room. Shutting the door behind her, for fear that he might bolt, she returned to the kitchen to fetch his bed. Back in her room, she set it down in front of the cold hearth, and was pleased when he ventured over and curled up inside.

After changing out of her work clothes, she put on a warm pair of trousers and her heaviest sweater in anticipation of a night spent in the dubious comfort of the Anderson shelter. Crawling beneath the covers, she was only a little startled when Simon jumped on the bed a few seconds later. He curled up behind her knees, a welcome source of warmth in the chill of her room, and she quickly fell asleep to the lullaby of his soft and steady purr.

THERE WERE NO sirens that night, nor the following, but their run of luck ended on Sunday. Both of the Tremaine girls had come for dinner, the first time since January they hadn't been working, and in honor of the occasion Vanessa had charmed two pounds of stewing beef out of the butcher. It was just enough for Jessie to concoct a sumptuous boeuf bourguignon, albeit without a drop of Burgundy wine.

They had just started their dinner when the siren sounded.

"Oh, bother," Vanessa said, but with her next breath she picked up the casserole dish full of stew and set off for the shelter in the back garden. "Vi, you bring the potatoes and carrots. Beatrice, you bring the plates and cutlery. Ruby, you fetch Jessie, and collect the cats, too."

After a brief standoff in which Percy had asserted his supremacy in the Tremaine household, he and Simon had become friends. They hadn't yet been fed their dinner, which in any event would have been scraps left over from supper, and came running at her whistle. "Come on, you two," she said, scooping them up, and bore them out to the shelter. "There's some beef stew waiting if you behave."

Between the five women and two cats it was a tight squeeze, but they were warm and dry, their dinner was delicious, the noises from above weren't especially alarming, and they had, in the Tremaine family collection of anecdotes, a nearly inexhaustible source of entertainment.

"Have you told Ruby about Papa's Tour of Infamy yet?" Beatrice asked her mother as soon as they'd finished eating.

"You must, you must," Viola exclaimed. "I can't believe she hasn't heard about Mortimer the Charlatan."

"Or Papa's Dueling Scar," said Beatrice.

"Or the snowstorm in Alberta," said Viola.

"Enough, enough," Vanessa protested. "You're giving it all away. So. It was 1920, not long after we were married, and Nick was invited to do a tour of the United States and Canada. He'd just been in a film, his first cinema role, and his appearances were meant to build on the success of—what was it called again?"

"*A Fair Rose for the Crown*," Beatrice answered.

"Yes. Dreadful stuff. Nick played the hero's father, or perhaps his brother?"

"He was the hero's long-lost brother who turned out to be his father," said Viola.

"See what I mean? Ridiculous. In any event, we sailed across to New York in some style, and only when we arrived did we learn that Nick's role had been cut from the finished film. I think the back of his head was left in one scene, but that was it."

"He must have been so disappointed," Ruby said.

"He was at first, but when we saw the finished film we felt quite relieved. It was *awful*. Things then went from bad to worse when the impresario who had made all our arrangements—"

"Mr. Mortimer Hewitt Tucker."

"Yes, thank you, Beatrice—Mr. Tucker turned out to be a complete charlatan. Had booked Nick into one dismal place after another. Some were so seedy they made burlesque theater look respectable in comparison, and all of them were filled with men who weren't the slightest bit interested in listening to Shakespeare's soliloquies. One night, about a week into the tour, someone threw a broken bottle at Nick and it cut his forehead open, right down to the bone. He had to have a whole row of stitches put in."

"Yes," Viola added, "and when people asked about the scar, he always told them it was from a duel fought over Mama's honor."

"We'd only been married for a matter of months, and I began to worry I might have made a mistake. My parents had been entirely against my marrying him, you see. He was nearly twenty years older, and we hadn't known each other for very long at all before getting engaged."

"One week!" Beatrice crowed. "Can you believe it? One week!"

"Yes, well, that's a story for another day. At any rate, Nick was magnificent. He refused to scurry home in defeat, and before long he was winning over everyone. And we had *such* fun. We visited so many interesting places. Niagara Falls and New Orleans and San Francisco, and Canada was beautiful, too, although I mostly remember the endless train journeys between engagements."

"Viola said something about a snowstorm?"

"Yes. We were in Alberta, in the foothills of the mountains there, and our train got stuck in the snow. I've never been so cold."

"Did you go to Hollywood with him when he made *Winter of Our Discontent?*" Ruby asked.

"Would you believe it was filmed in England? So much easier for Nick, although I wouldn't have minded a winter in California."

"I loved that movie," Ruby said, a little wistful at the memory. Even though she'd been living hand to mouth at the time, her wages as a trainee stenographer so paltry that she'd had almost nothing left after paying her rent, she had always managed to scrape together enough money for a weekly trip to the pictures. "I saw it at least three times. Your husband was so handsome and charming. It was impossible not to sympathize with King Richard."

"He was wonderful in it, wasn't he? Such a shock when he fell ill. It was only a few months after the film came out, and he had so been enjoying the attention. Darling man."

"I miss Papa," Beatrice said. "I wonder what he'd have thought of all this. The war, and the Blitz, and having to sit in a shelter night after night."

"He'd have complained constantly," Vanessa said promptly. "And he'd have broken all the rules and had the warden by every night because he forgot to close the blackout curtains."

"And when we were in here, he'd have insisted on reciting his favorite soliloquies night after night, and he'd have used his loud voice, his 'Serious Theater Voice,' he called it, and the neighbors would have come round to complain," Viola continued happily.

"I'd much rather listen to music than *Hamlet*," said Beatrice. "Vi, will you sing to us?"

"All right. How about 'A Nightingale Sang in Berkeley Square'?"

At this, Jessie sighed happily. "Please do, Miss Vi. You sing it better than Vera Lynn!"

"I don't know about that," Viola said, but obligingly cleared her throat and began the song.

Hearing Viola sing, Ruby understood why she had been such a success in the variety theater. Her voice was clear and sweet and wonderfully expressive, and even without being able to see her face, lost as it was in the shelter's gloom, Ruby could feel everything that Vi felt, simply by listening to her song.

"I won't have a voice left for my performance tomorrow," Vi cautioned, "if you make me do all the work. Come on, you lot," and she launched into "Somewhere Over the Rainbow."

One song followed another, one hour flowing into the next, and when the all clear finally sounded Ruby was relieved to return to her room, yet also vaguely disappointed that the sing-along was at an end. She hadn't been brave enough to take the lead on any of the songs, but it had been fun to join in on the choruses and listen to the others.

Vanessa had insisted the girls stay until the morning, since the Underground had shut for the night and it was nearly impossible to find cabs so far west at that hour. They all piled up the stairs, Vi electing to share a room with Beatrice.

"And don't say a word about giving up your room," Vi warned Ruby. "It hasn't been mine in ages, and I'll be just as comfortable with Bea. Sweet dreams, everyone, and don't let the bombers bite."

CHAPTER FOURTEEN

May 1941

As Ruby helped Jessie wash the dishes from breakfast, she realized that she was content. For the first time in . . . well, as long as she could remember, she had woken up feeling hopeful. Happy, even. It was so unexpected she wasn't sure what to do with it.

For nearly a week they hadn't been troubled by a single air-raid siren, and that had meant nearly a week of deep, uninterrupted, restful sleep. She had a home, albeit a temporary one, where she was liked and treated well. She had friends. She had work that interested and challenged her. She had a cat named Simon.

Setting the last of the dishes in the rack above the draining board, she dried her hands and gave Jessie a quick hug.

"What's got into you today, Ruby?" It had taken months of coaxing, but Jessie had finally given in and had stopped calling her Miss Sutton.

"I'm feeling happy. That's all. I'm off to work now, but leave the rugs for me—I'll be home after lunch. I can help with the windows, too."

"I won't say no, but don't rush home on account of me."

"I won't—oh, good morning!"

Vanessa had come into the kitchen, already dressed for her morning trip to the shops. "Good morning. Such a lovely day, isn't it? And I have some good news. Did you hear the telephone ringing last night?"

"I did, but I was half asleep already."

"It was Bennett. He's back for a few days and wants to see us all."

"That is good news. Were you thinking of Sunday dinner?"

"Clever girl. Yes, since my two are already coming—but can you invite Kaz and Mary as well? He's keen to see them, too. Tell him half six for seven."

"I will."

Vanessa sat at the kitchen table and started writing out a shopping list on the back of an old envelope. "What do you think we should serve, Jessie? We've been careful with our coupons, so I should have enough for the butcher, and we can round out people's plates with potatoes and whatever is ready from the garden."

"I could do up a shepherd's pie if there's any mutton that looks half decent. Or braised rabbit might be nice."

Vanessa made a face but kept writing. "You know how I feel about rabbit, Jessie."

"I do, Lady T, but beggars can't be choosers. Just tell Mr. Gower that you're having your godson the war hero over for dinner and you have to feed eight. I'll figure out the rest."

With her basket on her arm and lipstick freshly applied, Vanessa set off a few minutes later, determined to be the first in line at the butcher's when he opened at eight o'clock. Ruby left for work soon after, her mood soaring even higher, and even a long delay on the Underground did nothing to dislodge her smile.

Kaz was already in his office, and after hanging up her coat and hat, Ruby went to pop her head round his door. He was working on his editorial for the week, as he did every Saturday morning, and didn't look up when she tapped on the doorframe.

"Kaz? Sorry to bother you. Bennett is in town and Vanessa wants you to come for dinner tomorrow."

He looked up briefly, smiled, pushed his glasses back up his nose, and set to writing again. He didn't type, so it would be left to Evelyn to interpret his nearly illegible scrawl.

"I know," he said. "Bennett rang me up at the crack of dawn. What time do you want me there?"

"Dinner's at seven, since Vi will probably be on duty later on. Anytime after half-past six. Oh—Mary is included, too. Is she in yet?"

"I doubt it. You know how she feels about mornings. I'll let her know when I see her."

Ruby greeted the rest of her colleagues and settled in to work. She was writing a short feature on paper salvage drives, and it had turned into an unexpectedly entertaining assignment. The government was urging people to hand in anything that might be pulped and reused for military purposes, and to that end had set up scrap-paper depots as collection points.

She and Mary had visited a depot earlier in the week, and it had been fascinating to see the sorts of things people were turning in: soiled paper from food wrapping, labels from cans and jars, old telephone directories, last year's magazines, last week's newspapers. One family had donated a thirty-year-old encyclopedia in fifteen volumes, very much the worse for wear, as it had been living in their cellar for at least a decade. It wasn't much of a loss, but it had been painful to watch, later that morning, as people brought in perfectly good books that went straight into the pulping bin.

Best of all was a group of young women who, having brought in their old love letters, were happily ripping them up and tossing the fragments on the scrap heap. Their donation didn't amount to much paper, but the pictures Mary had taken, together with some entertaining quotes from the women, had transformed the piece from a rather earnest piece of quasi-propaganda into something worth reading.

She was home by half-past one and immediately set to work on her chores. She shook out the rugs and hall runner, using the carpet beater on the latter, and then stood on a short ladder to wash the outside of the sitting room windows while Jessie tackled them inside. After that it was time to tend to the vegetable garden with Vanessa.

Spreading marrow vines had already smothered the earth-covered top of the Anderson shelter, and apart from a good watering didn't require much help, but the rows of carrots, bush beans, onions, and turnips needed to be weeded and inspected for pests, as did the potato patch on the opposite side of the garden.

Vanessa, who had been rummaging at the foot of the potato plants, now let out a triumphant hoot. "Look! Early potatoes!" She held up a tiny, pale tuber that was no bigger than a gum-drop. "As long as I'm careful, I should be able to get enough for all of us, and still leave the plants in peace."

"The first of the carrots are ready, too," Ruby added. "Do you want me to pull them?"

"Let's wait until tomorrow. We've both of us earned a rest."

THE NEXT MORNING Ruby slept in until nearly nine o'clock, and might have stayed in bed longer if not for Simon's decision to sit at her window and yowl at every passing bird.

After lunch, she and Vanessa dusted the main floor and polished the silver. With Jessie as the only remaining servant, the work that had once been the province of several maids now fell to Vanessa and, whenever she was home from work, Ruby. Not that she minded. Compared to the cleaning work she'd done as a girl, the few chores she completed each day felt like nothing.

When everything was done and the house was gleaming from baseboard to ceiling, Vanessa sent Ruby out to the garden, instructing her to bring back enough roses and lady's-mantle to fill the antique bowl on the sideboard.

As Vanessa worked to arrange the flowers, Ruby stood at her side and watched, fascinated, as the arrangement took shape. One day, if she ever had a garden of her own, she would grow flowers and put them in vases in every room.

"Do you know, I just realized it was a year ago today that Bennett came back from Dunkirk."

"He was at Dunkirk? He's never mentioned it."

"That doesn't surprise me," Vanessa said dryly. "He was among the last to be evacuated. I remember listening to the wireless, to the prime minister describing what had happened, and I was just sick with fear. I hadn't heard from Bennett for weeks and weeks, and I felt certain, by then, that he'd been killed or captured."

"What happened?"

"He rang me up later that day. Heaven only knows where he was. And then, twenty-four hours later, he was at the door. Had come to London on some sort of official business, and he'd persuaded his driver to stop by the house so I might see for myself that he was alive and unharmed."

"That was very thoughtful of him."

"Yes, he is good that way. Of course I was terribly upset when I found out later that he'd been decorated by the king and never told any of us. I just happened to see his name in the paper."

"So that's why Jessie called him a war hero yesterday. What medal did he receive?"

Vanessa turned the bowl this way and that, looking for flaws, and added a few more sprigs of lady's-mantle. "The Military Cross. Not something they hand out to just anyone."

"I remember him telling me, when we first met, that he was with the Ox and Bucks Light Infantry. I never thought to ask any more. I had no idea."

"Nor would any of us if it were up to him," Vanessa said. She gathered up the trimmings and put them in the compost bucket. "He doesn't wear his medals. Says they attract too much attention."

"But he still wears his uniform."

"Yes. Officially he's still with his old unit—at least I think that's the case. I suppose you could say he's been seconded elsewhere, rather like you and your magazines."

"Not quite," Ruby demurred. "I haven't been in the firing line."

"Haven't you?" Vanessa asked, and kissed her on the cheek. "Now, off you go. Read the paper or take a walk or even have a nap. I don't want to see you again until dinnertime."

Nearly the entire afternoon stretched before her. She skimmed through the morning papers, but nothing drew her attention. She did some mending, but only a loose button and a dropped hem awaited her attention. She picked up her book, a mystery novel that Vanessa had lent her, but set it down almost right away.

Simon looked up from his perch at the end of the bed, his expression hopeful. "Mrrrow."

"Yes, yes. You think I should have a nap with you. But it's far too nice to be inside. I'm going to take a walk."

Pulling on a cardigan in case it was cooler by the river, she said goodbye to Simon and slipped out of the house. It didn't take long, wandering through the pleasant streets of Chelsea, for her to reach the Albert Bridge, and after a longish break to admire the view from its central span, she continued across and down into Battersea Park.

There, life seemed almost normal. Children were playing, families were picnicking, dogs were running excitedly after sticks. Just another Sunday afternoon. But there were ack-ack guns occupying the running track, the park's flower beds had been replaced by allotment gardens, and the drifting shadows on the lawns came not from clouds but from barrage balloons far above.

She was home by four o'clock, and after helping Vanessa to set the table, she returned to her room to change. Normally she didn't spare a second thought for what she wore, even for Sunday dinner, but today she decided to make a little more effort than usual. It wasn't every Sunday that they had guests, after all, and she and Jessie and Vanessa had put a lot of effort into cleaning the house. It would be silly not to take a few minutes to ensure she looked reasonably presentable. So she put on her nicest skirt and blouse, the ones she saved for days when she and Mary went in search of their stories, brushed her hair until it bounced smoothly on her shoulders, powdered her nose, and dabbed on the faintest stain of lipstick.

She hurried downstairs and, before anyone in the sitting room caught sight of her, tiptoed along the hall to the back stairs and joined Jessie in the kitchen. She would help for a few minutes, and once her heart had stopped racing, she would return to the others upstairs. It was silly to be so excited about a dinner party. There was no one upstairs she needed to impress. No one she wouldn't see again before too long.

She set to scraping the carrots, but Jessie took the knife out of her hand after she'd reduced the first one to the diameter of a French bean. "Off you go, Ruby, before you leave me with a sink of carrot peelings. If Lady T asks, dinner will be ready in half an hour."

When she returned to the sitting room, she found the girls seated in a row on the sofa, chatting away merrily. Bennett and Vanessa were standing in front of the fireplace, deep in earnest conversation.

He'd shown up at the *PW* offices a few weeks before, looking as if he hadn't slept for days, and had promptly taken Kaz out to lunch. She had watched them leave and told herself the two men were old friends. Reminded herself that it was natural for them to want to see one another and there was no reason for her to have been included. When Kaz had returned an hour later, on his own, her heart had sunk into her shoes.

Kaz and Mary arrived just then. She greeted them, took their coats and hats, offered to fetch them drinks, and then, having helped herself to a thimble-sized portion of sherry, squeezed onto the end of the sofa next to Vi.

The conversation ebbed and flowed around her, and apart from answering the rare direct question put to her, she simply sat and listened and watched her friends. Bennett and Kaz were talking, or rather laughing, and she smiled to see the two of them in such fine spirits. Bennett looked the same as he always did, and fortunately bore no signs of any recent accidents with his motorcycle.

She stared at them, at *him*, not able to tear her gaze away. And it hit her, struck her like a blow to the face, and suddenly she knew. She had a crush on him, a stupid, childish crush, and that was the reason for her nerves. Her mouth went dry, her palms grew damp, and still she couldn't look away.

His eyes met hers, though surely she hadn't said or done anything to capture his attention. Something must have shown on her face, because he instantly left Kaz's side and came to crouch next to her.

"Are you all right, Ruby? Is something wrong?"

"No," she said, trying to smile. "Nothing's wrong. I just, ah . . . I thought of something I forgot to finish off at work yesterday. That's all."

"Surely it can wait for the morning," he said, his eyes searching hers, his expression troubled. "Kaz would never—"

"I know," she assured him. "And I'm not worried, not really. How . . . how are you?"

"Well," he said. "Busy."

He was so close, his face only inches away from hers. He smelled of soap, the plain, strong sort that was all you could get in the shops anymore, and as he spoke she caught the smoky scent of Scotch whiskey on his breath. He must have shaved only a few hours ago, for his beard hadn't yet grown in. If she touched his face, would his skin feel smooth? Or would she feel the rasp of his nascent whiskers against her fingertips?

"You look well," he said, his gaze intent on her.

"Thank you. Everyone has been so kind."

"I'm sorry I wasn't able to talk to you, that day when I had lunch with Kaz. I was only in London for a few hours. But he said you seem to be happy. Here with the Tremaines, I mean."

"I am. I love it. Vanessa and the girls have been so nice to me. I even have a cat now. I can take you to meet him," she added, knowing she was rambling but powerless to stop. "He's friendly but too many people send him running for the hills. He's probably asleep on my bed right now."

"What did you name him?"

"Simon. It was already his name. I mean, it was on his collar when we found him, but that was all. No address or anything else. We put up notices but no one claimed him. I think they must have been bombed out."

Why couldn't she stop talking? She had to stop talking—but if she stopped he might ask more questions, and he might press her on why she had looked upset a moment ago, and then she would have no choice but to get on the next ship leaving for Canada.

Jessie saved her then. Wonderful, wonderful Jessie. "Dinner is ready, Lady T."

Bennett stood, his expression faintly bemused, and let Ruby and the other women precede him into the dining room. Vanessa sat at the head of the table, Bennett sat at its foot, and Ruby was sandwiched between Vi and Kaz on one of the long sides.

Once again, Jessie had performed miracles. They had vegetable soup to start, then braised rabbit with carrots and the new potatoes Vanessa had harvested the day before. Bennett had brought a bottle of wine, which he confessed to having liberated from his uncle's wine cellar some months earlier. "Harry told me to help myself, since he's not allowed to drink it. Doctor's orders."

"This is delightful," Kaz said. "Shame that Jessie can't be persuaded to sit with us."

"She does when it's just the three of us, but otherwise she retreats into the kitchen," Vanessa explained. "I've tried, believe me, but she won't be budged."

As they ate, Ruby dipped her toes in and out of the various conversations that swirled around her. At one point she noticed that Vanessa wasn't eating much of her dinner. "Do you think your mother is all right? She's hardly eaten a thing."

"Mama won't eat rabbit," Vi hissed in her ear. "She's secretly convinced it's cat."

"It's not cat," Ruby whispered back, but only after she'd glanced at the bones on her plate. "The shape of the animal is entirely different. At least I think . . ."

"She's not convinced. And, believe me, we've tried. But she says that once the head is off and the animal is skinned, it might as well—"

"Please stop, Vi, or I won't be able to eat another bite."

To Ruby's right, Kaz and Bennett were arguing good-naturedly about postwar reconstruction. Kaz, to the surprise of no one who'd ever spoken with him for more than two minutes, was all for radical change across the board. But this was the first time she'd heard Bennett's views on the subject.

"I'm simply not sure the public will be comfortable with sweeping change. Isn't it better to address the worst inequalities first, and then move forward in measured steps?"

"When has that ever worked?" Kaz countered.

"What alternative are you suggesting? Stalin's model of change?"

"If you were in the cabinet, Bennett, what would you advise?" Mary asked. "What would you tell the prime minister to do? Not just after the war, but now?"

"I'd tell him to stay the course. Lend-lease is turning the tide in our favor. With the United States as our ally—"

Kaz was shaking his head. "Since when? I don't recall their declaration of war."

"You know what I mean. The Americans are our ally in nearly every way that counts. They certainly aren't aligned with the Axis states."

"So you think they'll sweep in to save us as they did in the last war?" Vanessa asked.

Ruby broke in. "Do you mind my answering, since I'm the only American here?"

"Go on," Kaz urged.

"It won't be anything so clear-cut. The U.S. will only declare war on Germany if we're forced to do so. If Hitler attacks us directly."

"And what if he doesn't?" Mary asked. "What if nothing changes?"

"Then we'll keep on keeping on," Bennett said, "and pray the Russians are as good to Hitler as they were to Napoleon."

"And in the meantime we're meant to ignore the failings of our society? You think we should 'keep on,' as you term it, and turn a blind eye to everything else?" Kaz asked indignantly.

"No. Of course we shouldn't. But we need to realize that no amount of postwar planning will help us if we lose the war.

Winning the war is the only thing that matters." Although Bennett said this calmly enough, his dark eyes were animated. Either he was very happy, or he was very angry. Perhaps it was a bit of both.

Kaz's face was bright red, the way it got when he was spoiling for a really good argument, and Ruby could tell he was working himself up for another salvo in his argument with Bennett. She elbowed Vi, hoping she would take the hint and divert them with another topic, but her friend simply said "ow" and continued eating.

"Shall I ask Jessie if there's anything for dessert?" Ruby asked loudly.

"By dessert, do you mean pudding?"

"Yes, Mary. Sorry. Pudding."

"Of course there's pudding," Vanessa confirmed. "Jessie made her one-egg cake, and we've the last of the rhubarb compote to go with it."

That had the effect of diverting the men's attention to the topic of rhubarb. Kaz thought it delicious; Bennett pronounced it an abomination. The conversation went steadily downhill from there.

"Are they always this argumentative with one another?" Ruby asked Vi.

"Nearly always. Kaz takes a stance, Bennett challenges him, and off they go. They both love it, Bennett especially. It's the barrister in him, I think. Why do you ask?"

"I guess I've never seen them together before, or not for any length of time. I'd no idea they acted like, ah—"

"Like thirty-three-year-old schoolboys?"

"Yes. Like that."

After dinner, the Tremaine sisters went downstairs to help Jessie with the washing-up, leaving Ruby to join the others in the sitting room. Vanessa had flatly refused her offer of help when they rose from the table, insisting that she'd done more than enough already.

She perched on the sofa, in the exact spot where she'd been earlier, and tried not to think about how amusing and articulate Bennett had been at dinner. A man like him, with his intelligence and abilities, was surely wasted in some desk position in an obscure ministry. He ought to be working with cabinet ministers, or helping to plan top-secret military maneuvers, or advising the prime minister on delicate diplomatic negotiations.

Then again, for all she knew he already *was* doing such things.

"There you are." Bennett sat next to her, his expression bemused. "I could hardly see you at dinner. Should have made Kaz switch places. The man's a mountain."

"The two of you were very entertaining. Are your conversations always so heated?"

"Almost always. I like to keep him on his toes."

"I know I can't ask about your work," she said, her nerve almost deserting her, "but don't you sometimes wish you were still with your old unit? Where are they now?"

The laughter fled from his eyes. "They're stationed on the south coast."

When he didn't elaborate, she floundered on. "Do you ever wish you were with them? Instead of at the . . . well, the place you work now?"

He didn't answer right away, his gaze locked on a spot in the middle distance. "No. Not anymore. Why do you ask?"

"It was something Vanessa said today. She, ah . . . she said you were at Dunkirk. That you'd been awarded the Military Cross."

"I was."

"Do you mind my asking why?"

He shook his head. "I don't mind. Only . . . it's not very exciting. I simply stayed on the beaches rather longer than I ought to have done. I wanted to know my men were safely away. And then . . ."

"Yes?"

"There weren't many of us left, and the shells were dropping around us like ungodly hailstones. Several of my men were hit. I carried them to the boats. It took a long while, and a few of them were dead by the time we got away. But I did my best."

"I had no idea . . ." she marveled.

"It's a bit embarrassing, really. The fuss everyone made. Hundreds of men were doing the same as me, but for some reason my actions were noticed. You know how it is. The next thing I knew they were hauling me in front of the king."

"And then? Why did you leave, and go to work for that bureau, or whatever you call it? You must have cared about the men under your command. Why not stay on with them?"

"Because I was asked to take up different work. It's as simple as that." For a moment it seemed like he might say something else, but he only shook his head. "Excuse me. I ought to see if the girls need my help in the kitchen."

He left the room quietly, unobtrusively, and since Kaz and Mary and Vanessa were deep in conversation at the opposite end of the room, she was left alone to fret. Why had she kept pressing him? She had secrets of her own. She knew what it felt like when someone dug too deep.

She ought to have left him in peace.

And she knew nothing, not one thing, about the work that had taken him out of active service and into a mysterious position at the Inter-Services Research Bureau. Everyone knew there were top-secret departments working on top-secret projects all over England. He might be working at a desk job, or he might be unraveling the inner workings of the German high command. For all she knew, he might have been parachuting into occupied France once a month for the past year. It simply wasn't her business to know, and it wasn't in his power to tell her.

She couldn't even cling to the notion that some kind of misplaced journalistic bloody-mindedness had driven her, for she knew full well that her curiosity was fueled by sentiment, no more. She was sweet on him, and it was her silly crush that had pushed the words out of her mouth tonight. As if knowing his secrets would also unlock the mysteries of his heart.

She was still fussing and fretting and torturing herself when he returned, a laughing Vi at his side, a few minutes later. He talked to Kaz and Mary, he embraced Vanessa and kissed the girls, and then he came to her, kissed her cheek without looking in her eyes, and walked out the door and into the night.

Somehow she endured another half hour of lighthearted conversation, unable to muster the energy to join in properly. She waited until everyone's attention was elsewhere—Vi was mimicking Gertrude Lawrence—and slipped out of the sitting room. A minute or two alone in her room, just until she was feeling herself again, and she would return to the party.

Opening her bedroom door, she all but tripped over a large object that was sitting on the floor just inside. A typewriter.

How long she stood there, just staring at it, not daring to

crouch down and take a closer look, she couldn't have said. Only when someone came up the stairs behind her did she tear her gaze away from the machine.

"You found it, then?" came Mary's soft voice.

"Yes."

"It took Bennett an age to track one down."

Ruby didn't reply. She couldn't.

"Care to tell me what's wrong?" Mary pressed.

"You . . . you noticed?"

"What happened between you and Bennett? Oh, aye. Was hard to miss. One moment you were all smiles with each other, and the next . . ."

"It was my fault. I asked him why he'd left active service, and I think he felt I was disappointed in him. But I didn't mean it, not one bit. I don't even know *what* he does, so how can I be disappointed? But now he's gone and I've no way of telling him I'm sorry, or to thank him for the typewriter." She rubbed at her eyes, swiping away the stupid, stupid tears. When was the last time she had cried about anything?

"Ring him up. He told Kaz he wasn't leaving until the morning. He should be home by now. Ring him at his flat."

"I couldn't."

"You can," Mary insisted. "Life is too short to leave things unsaid. If you hurt him, and if you want to put things right, call him now. Here—take this." She handed Ruby a slip of paper with a telephone number scribbled in compositor's pencil.

"How did you get this?"

"Kaz gave it to me just now. We both had a feeling you might want it."

"Thank you. I . . . I guess I'll call him now."

The telephone sat in an alcove on the main floor, in what once had probably been a closet of some kind, and had its own little table and a stool for calls longer than a minute or two. Quickly, before she could lose her nerve, she dialed Bennett's number.

"Chancery 8015."

"Hello? Is that Bennett?"

"Ruby."

Her hands were trembling, but somehow she managed to keep her voice steady. "I'm sorry to bother you. I know it's late. I just . . . Mary gave me your number. I wanted to thank you for the typewriter."

"You're welcome." His voice was flat.

"And I'm sorry. What I said earlier was wrong. I don't know what you do, obviously I don't, but I'm absolutely sure your work is important. It must be, because otherwise you wouldn't be doing it. And I'm so, so—"

"Ruby," he said.

"Yes?"

"I'm sorry, too. I . . . speaking about my decision to leave my unit is a sore point for me. If I could say more, I would. For now, though . . . I shouldn't have left without saying goodbye." A pause, as if he, too, were nervous. "Do you like the typewriter? It's one of those folding models. And it should be lighter than your old one, too."

"It's perfect. But it must have been so expensive—"

"Stop. Just stop. It took me a long time to find that damn thing, so you're going to keep it. Understand? I've no use for it—I never learned how to type. So you keep it, and use it, and if you run out of ribbons just let me know. All right?"

"Yes," she said, and found she was able to smile again.

"I had better ring off. I have to leave first thing tomorrow."

"Will you call when you're back in London?"

"I will. Good night, Ruby."

She put the receiver back on its cradle and stole back to her room, for she wasn't quite ready to rejoin the party. The typewriter was there, just as she'd left it. Only then, as she bent to pick up the machine, did she see the note he had typed out for her.

to Ruby

with my regards

Bennett

CHAPTER FIFTEEN

July 1941

Nearly everyone was late into work that morning. After weeks and weeks of clear skies and peaceful nights, the bombers had returned; and while it hadn't been quite as bad as the terrible raids in May, enough damage had been done to wreak havoc on everyone's morning commute. It had been a shock, coming so long after what everyone assumed had been the end of the Blitz, never mind that the government kept telling everyone to remain alert.

The bombing had gone on for hours and hours, the all clear not sounding until almost dawn, and come morning, the streets had been littered with unexploded parachute bombs and sizzling incendiaries. Ruby had walked far out of her way to get to work, and when she did arrive at almost nine o'clock she found the office all but deserted. Even Evelyn, who got up at the crack of dawn every morning for her journey in from Ealing and was never, ever late, had called Kaz to say there was a bomb in next door's garden and she had to wait for the bomb disposal crew to arrive.

The morning wore on, and one by one everyone appeared—everyone except Mary. Lunchtime came and went, and still she didn't come in.

"I rang her at home, but there was no answer," Kaz said worriedly. "Even for her this is awfully late."

"Why don't you go by her flat, then?" Ruby suggested. "Maybe she's under the weather and doesn't feel like getting out of bed to answer the phone. She did say she'd been feeling a cold coming on."

"Yes, that's probably it. I'll walk over now."

An hour passed, then another. Mary's flat was on Eagle Street, just off High Holborn, less than a mile away. It should only have taken Kaz a half hour, at the very most, to get there. So why hadn't he rung back with news?

Ruby waited and fretted and tried to work, and still there was no news. And then, when it was almost six o'clock and everyone else was packing up to go home, the telephone on her desk rang.

"*Picture Weekly*, Ruby Sutton speaking."

"It's Kaz."

"Where are you? Did you find Mary? Is everything all right?"

"I'm at University College Hospital. Mary . . . her block of flats took a direct hit last night." His deep voice broke. "It took a long while for them to . . . for them to dig her out."

"*No*. No, it can't—"

"They whisked her away. I had to find a cab and follow. I . . . I just got here, and no one will tell me anything."

"Tell me where to go. I'll be right there."

"The casualty entrance. I'll be there, or somewhere nearby."

She left seconds later, not bothering to see if anyone was still in the office to lock up. On the cab ride to the hospital, which felt like forever but took little more than fifteen minutes, Ruby pushed away images of the countless buildings she'd seen leveled by bombs and focused on the survivors she had interviewed. No one she knew was stronger, tougher, or more invincible than Mary. No one. She would be, *had* to be, all right.

Rushing through the doors to the casualty entrance, Ruby skidded to a halt in front of the duty nurse's desk. "I'm here to see Mary Buchanan. Mr. Kaczmarek asked me to come. He's already here."

"Yes, of course," the woman said, her expression carefully blank. "Come with me."

Kaz was slumped in a chair at the very far corner of the waiting area, his head in his hands.

"I'm here," she said, touching his shoulder.

He looked up, nodded, and motioned for her to sit next to him.

"Why are we waiting?" she asked.

"The doctors are still examining her. I don't know what's wrong with her yet. How bad it is. The nurse would only say that her condition is 'grave.'"

So they sat and waited, and no one came out to tell them what was happening, and minute by minute the pool of choking dread rose higher and higher in Ruby's chest, until it threatened to eclipse every thought in her head. Why was no one coming to tell them what was happening?

They sat in silence for another quarter hour, and then Kaz shifted, settling his elbows on his knees, and tilted his head to look at Ruby. "Did Mary ever tell you the story of how we met?" he asked.

"No. Only that she'd known you for years."

"She was the first photographer assigned to me when I came to London. I'd left the *Liverpool Herald* behind, convinced the grass would be greener in the big city. John Ellis had written a fulsome recommendation for me, far better than I deserved, and it had earned me a position at the very bottom of the editorial ladder at the *Evening Standard*. For my troubles I was sent out on the women's beat, and to my everlasting shame I considered it a blow to my pride. Mary was the photographer for my first assignment."

"I fear for you already," Ruby said. "What was the story?"

"We were sent off to some market town in the depths of the Cotswolds. I've forgotten the name. It was the end of September and they were having their Michaelmas fair. As far as I can recall, it was some sort of landmark year—their seven hundred and fiftieth anniversary or something like that.

"We were lent a little car, though again I've no memory of where it came from. Likely it belonged to someone at the magazine. Fool that I was, I insisted on driving, even though I barely knew the clutch from the brake."

"I've driven with Mary," Ruby said, recalling their breakneck journey up to Coventry. "She's not much better behind the wheel."

"Oh, she's a skillful enough driver. Just not a cautious one. So—we drove out there, and I was so, so nervous around her. She was about a hundred times smarter than me, and so glamorous and confident and regal that every bit of male pride I had just shriveled away."

"What happened at the fair?"

"Nothing very dramatic. I was convinced I could find an

edge to the story, some approach to it that would make my editor sit up and take notice of me."

"And did you?"

"Of course not. It was a country fair, more or less the same country fair that had been held in that same market town for three-quarters of a millennium. Insofar as there was a story, it was in the people we met. But I was so busy trying to impress Mary and find some different angle that I hardly talked to anyone there at all, and when I did I talked over them. I didn't ask questions and I didn't listen."

"What did she do?"

"She didn't give me a hard time, not at first. Mainly just let me blunder around like a great idiotic bear and scare off every single person who might have brought some life to the story. After a while, she suggested we have lunch at the local pub. It was probably early afternoon by then, and when we sat down to eat she told me to listen and not say a word until she was done. She told me I was new and evidently needed some help, and so she would give me some advice. She said that I was ruining the story and unless I learned how to shut up and listen I would never amount to anything as a journalist."

"Did she have that look on her face? The one where her eyebrows go up and she fixes you with the stare? The one you feel down to your toes?"

"She did," he said, and smiled at the memory. "I felt as if she'd reached over, pulled a stopper out of my chest, and let out all the hot air. I knew she was right, but I didn't know how to fix it."

"And?" Ruby prompted.

"And so I asked her what I should do. She told me to eat my

lunch, and then we would start again. This time, though, she wanted me to keep two rules in mind. One, I must never underestimate the intelligence of my readers. And two, I must never get in the way of my photographer. It worked."

"She does have an instinct for finding interesting people," Ruby said.

"She does. I let her take the lead, and she led me to people, and I just started talking with them. Not in an 'I am from an extremely important London newspaper and I should like to talk to you' way. More, I suppose, in a 'what a beautiful display of marrows' sort of way. 'Did you grow these? You did? How long have you been growing marrows? What got you started?'"

He clutched his head in his hands, his back bowed. "I fell in love with her that day," he whispered.

"Oh, Kaz. I did wonder, a few times. But the two of you were so discreet. I could never be sure if you were close friends, or if there was more."

"There was. Never quite enough, though."

"What do you mean?"

"When I finally worked up the nerve to tell her how I felt, a year or so after we met, she was kind. She didn't laugh at me. She didn't reject me, in point of fact. But she was clear. She might agree to be my lover, but she would never be anything more. She'd seen what happened to women who married and abandoned all their ambitions, and she swore it would never happen to her."

He looked up, his expression somewhat abashed. "I hope you don't mind my telling you this."

"Not at all," she assured him. "You are my friend, just as Mary is. But I am sorry. I wish . . ."

"I stopped wishing a while ago, and it was enough, I think . . ."

"Mr. Kaczmarek?" A doctor, not much older than Ruby, had approached as they were talking, and now stood a few feet away.

"I'm Walter Kaczmarek."

"I'm Dr. Bannion," he said. "Are you Miss Buchanan's next of kin? Your name is given on her identity card."

Kaz looked briefly surprised, but nodded readily. "I am."

"May I sit?" the doctor asked, and without waiting for a reply he pulled over a nearby chair and all but fell into it, exhaustion a stark veil upon his young, handsome face.

"How is she?" Kaz asked.

"I'm afraid it's not good. Miss Buchanan is suffering from extensive internal injuries, as well as a fractured skull and a subdural hematoma—a sort of injury to her brain. She was unconscious when they pulled her from the wreckage of her block of flats. I gather she and the other people in the building had been trapped in the cellar for some hours."

The horror of it was almost too much to bear. To know that her friend had been trapped and alone—that she had suffered alone for so long. Ruby looked to Kaz, whose face was twisted in a rictus of agony, and without hesitating, she reached for his nearest hand and grasped it tightly.

"The only way to remedy such injuries is through surgery," Dr. Bannion continued, "but we haven't yet been able to stabilize her condition. If we were to operate now, she would almost certainly die on the table."

"So are you saying . . . ?" Kaz faltered.

"I'm saying that Miss Buchanan's condition is too grave to allow for surgery. It's also the case that she has suffered such an acute head injury that, if she were to survive, I fear her faculties would be permanently impaired."

"I don't understand. Are you saying that you can't save her?"

"I'm very sorry, but I think it best if we do not intervene any further. Her injuries are too extensive, and there is no reasonable prospect for recovery."

"Is she still alive?" Kaz asked, his voice no more than a whisper.

"Yes. She is unconscious, and I doubt she will wake again. But she is not in any pain."

"May we see her?" Ruby asked.

"Of course. She's been moved to a bed on the ward, and there is room for you to sit with her. I don't think it will be very long."

The casualty ward was dim and quiet, with curtains drawn around several of its beds. Dr. Bannion led them to one of the nurses and, after a final, whispered apology, vanished down the hall.

"I'm Sister Milne. I'll be here for the rest of the night. I'll take you to Miss Buchanan now. We've drawn the curtains so you'll have some privacy."

Mary had been changed into a hospital gown, and apart from the bandages swathing her head she looked much as she always did, with no marks on her face or arms. A blanket had been tucked around her, and if Ruby hadn't known otherwise, she'd have thought her friend was sleeping.

Two chairs had been left in the curtained alcove, and now Ruby took one and drew it close to the bed. "You sit," she told Kaz. "Take her hand. I know the doctor said she's unconscious, but that doesn't mean she can't hear you. Now is the time for you to tell her everything. I'll wait outside."

"You won't go far?"

"No. I won't be far."

She closed tight the curtains, not wishing anyone to be a witness to Kaz's farewell, and walked far enough away that she couldn't hear him whispering to the woman he loved. She stood and shivered, wondering why they kept it so cold inside the hospital. Surely the patients needed to be kept warm.

Kind hands took her by the shoulders and directed her to a chair. "You're in shock," said Sister Milne. "It's quite natural. Wait here while I get you a cup of tea."

She accepted the mug, which was hot enough to scald her icy hands, and tried to take a sip. Her hands were shaking, though, and it was hard to drink without spilling.

"Go on," the sister encouraged her. "You'll feel better as soon as you've had something to drink."

Ruby gulped it down, hating the taste but grateful for its cloying warmth. Presumably hospitals were allocated extra sugar rations for moments such as this.

"If I had anything stronger I'd give it to you," the nurse said.

"This will do. Thanks."

She could just hear Kaz's voice, a murmur she didn't try to decipher. Eavesdropping now would be the worst sort of betrayal. So she sat and waited and drank all her tea, even the sugary sludge at the bottom of the mug, and hoped she would find the strength for what was to come next.

"Ruby?"

She was across the ward in a flash. "Yes, Kaz?"

"I'm done. I . . . do you want to sit with us?"

"Of course." Picking up the second chair, she brought it around to Mary's other side and, sitting, took hold of her friend's hand. It was beautiful, the fingers long and elegant. A strong, capable hand.

"She's barely breathing," Kaz said.

Ruby felt for the pulse in Mary's wrist. It was scarcely there, a whisper of movement, no more. Together she and Kaz sat and watched and listened, the space between Mary's breaths growing longer and longer, until nothing remained but a final, fading wisp of escaping air.

"Kaz," Ruby whispered.

"I know." Tears streamed down his cheeks, and he dropped his head to the bed, his back heaving with soundless sobs. Reaching out blindly, he took hold of Mary's cold hand and, turning it gently, kissed her palm.

This was agony. This was loss. This was love, and it was too late, now, for Ruby to do anything about it.

Too late to thank Mary for her friendship. Too late to tell her just how much she admired and esteemed her. In Kaz's pain she saw her own heartache reflected, for she loved Mary, too. Had loved her as the true friend she had been. Her first friend.

He stood, swaying for a moment, and Ruby rushed around the bed to steady him. "I'm all right," he said. "Do you have a handkerchief?"

"Yes, although it's a bit damp."

"I don't mind." He wiped his eyes, stuffed it in his jacket pocket, and straightened his shoulders. "There," he said. "I'm ready now."

RUBY AND KAZ planned the funeral while also working flat out on the magazine. There hadn't been any question of skipping publication for a week, not least because Mary would have been outraged at the idea. Kaz spent most of the week in his office, emerging periodically for editorial meetings that invariably ended with Nell in tears or Nigel shouting at someone.

Since Mary had never expressed any particular wishes on the subject of her funeral, it was left to Kaz and Ruby to try to arrange a memorial that would offend her as little as possible. "Probably a good thing she never said anything about it," Kaz observed at one point. "God knows what she'd have made us do. A Viking funeral pyre wouldn't have been out of the question."

"I think she'd have understood we're doing our best," Ruby had said, too tired and heartsick to find humor in Kaz's observation. "I did hear back from the vicar at the Scottish church in Covent Garden. We can have the service at eleven o'clock on Thursday. Vanessa has offered to host the reception afterward, too."

"That's kind of her," Kaz said absently.

"I can't help asking . . . have you heard . . . ?"

"From Bennett? No. I left a message with his work, but haven't heard back. If he can be there, he will."

"Of course. I had better get back to my desk."

"Ruby?"

"Yes?"

"Thank you for sitting with me. Having someone else there made it bearable. I'm not sure how I'd have managed otherwise."

"It just seems so unfair. To have lived through so many nights of bombing, and to be killed now. We've all been assuming the Blitz was over. Weeks and weeks without a raid, and then *this*."

"It *is* unfair, but that's true of nearly everything about this war. For that matter, life itself is unfair. Your only chance is to grab hold of happiness when you have it, and enjoy it for however long it lasts."

Their eyes met, and after a beat or two of almost unbearable silence, they both burst out laughing.

"She'd have had your head for that, Kaz."

"She would," he admitted. "Now, back to work you go. I'll let you know if I hear from Bennett."

BENNETT'S CALL DIDN'T come until the morning of the funeral. It awoke Ruby just past dawn, the phone ringing so persistently that she'd staggered downstairs, still half asleep, determined to slam the receiver down on the person who was so inconsiderate as to call at such an ungodly hour.

"Yes? Who is this?" she barked into the phone, forgetting Vanessa's insistence that she always answer by citing their telephone number.

"Ruby? It's Bennett."

"Where are you?"

"I'm in England, but I'm a few hours away. Ruby—I'm so sorry. I only got word this morning."

"Have you spoken with Kaz?"

"Yes," he said wretchedly. "He seemed to understand."

"Of course he does. I do, too. And it doesn't matter, because you're back now. Can you make it in time? The service starts at eleven."

"Yes. I'll be a bit rough around the edges, but I'll be there."

He walked up just as they were about to enter the church, and after embracing Kaz, he took her arm and they sat together in the front pew, flanked by Kaz and Vanessa. When it was time for the first lesson, it was Bennett who rose and made his way to the lectern.

"A reading from the book of Solomon:

"My beloved speaks and says to me:

Arise, my love, my fair one, and come away;

for now the winter is past, the rain is over and gone.

The flowers appear on the earth; the time of singing has come,

and the voice of the turtle dove is heard in our land.

The fig tree puts forth its figs, and the vines are in blossom;

they give forth fragrance.

Arise, my love, my fair one, and come away."

CHAPTER SIXTEEN

September 1941

A nother Monday morning, and as Ruby dragged herself up the steps to the *PW* offices she was assailed with the depressing knowledge that five and a half days of misery were waiting for her.

It had been a little more than two months since Mary's death, and Kaz showed no signs of emerging from the fog of grief that clung to him like so much poison gas. She had tried to help, asking tentatively if he wanted to talk with her, then inviting him to come to dinner with her and Vanessa, or even go to the Old Bell for lunch, but nothing could tempt him from his desk and the solace of work.

And there was no end of news to keep them busy. Crete had been lost to Axis forces at the end of May, the German invasion of the USSR had begun a month later, and by the end of the summer the Soviets seemed perilously close to defeat. And when that happened, Kaz never tired of telling anyone within earshot, Hitler would once again turn his attention to Western

Europe and the long-delayed invasion of Britain. It was only a matter of time.

Ruby was convinced that Kaz was drinking at the office, unremarkable behavior among most newsmen she knew but entirely out of character for her editor and friend. She'd smelled something sharp on his breath the week before, and later that afternoon he had tripped over his words more than once during their editorial meeting. It didn't help that he wasn't eating properly, his clothes all but hanging off his broad shoulders, and from the look of his hair and stubbled face he was long overdue for a good bath.

She tried calling Bennett at home, again and again, but he was never there, and Vanessa didn't have a telephone number for him at work. The only person who knew how to reach him was Kaz, and if Bennett had been in contact with his old friend, Kaz wasn't saying.

What made it all the harder was that she, too, missed Mary desperately. There were moments, over those bleak days of late summer, when Ruby would have given anything for a dose of her friend's canny advice, or a glimpse of her rueful smile. Even Mary in one of her foul moods would have been enough to leaven Ruby's spirits.

The instant she walked through the door, she knew something was wrong. Evelyn was crying—levelheaded, sane, endlessly sensible Evelyn, who never seemed to get upset, and had soldiered through the days and weeks after Mary's death with nothing more than reddened eyes.

"What is wrong?" Ruby asked, her heart seizing with fear. "Has someone . . . ?"

"No, no. It's only . . . Captain Bennett and Mr. Bennett are here. Kaz isn't coming back."

"What?" Ruby gasped. "*Ever?*"

"Sorry, no—just for a while. They'll explain it all, they said. You might as well go on in."

Ruby rushed down the hall, desperate to learn what had become of Kaz, but the door to his office was shut. Behind it, she could just make out Nigel's voice, rising and falling, and then Bennett's, more than an octave lower, measured and calm. Everyone else was in the main office, and by their expressions they shared her apprehension. If Kaz was leaving, what would become of them? What would become of *Picture Weekly*?

Evelyn came down the hall, and one by one they joined her at the big table. There were so few of them, really, for Kaz hadn't tried to replace Mary, instead relying on freelancers and agency photographs. Without Kaz, how would they put out the magazine? He was its beating heart—without him, what was left?

The door to his office opened, and footsteps sounded in the hall. First through the door was Nigel, who looked oddly pleased with himself. He was followed by an elderly man who had to be Mr. Bennett, their publisher. It didn't seem right, in that moment, to think of him as Uncle Harry. Ruby had pictured him as a rather doddery old fellow, but this man was tall and slim, with piercingly blue eyes under shaggy eyebrows. He had once been a judge, she recalled, and seeing him now, she was certain he had been a formidable presence in the courtroom.

Last of all was Bennett himself. His eyes met hers briefly, but there was time for nothing more, and she could discern nothing from his studiously neutral expression.

"Good morning," Mr. Bennett began. "As you all know, our dear Kaz has not been himself since Miss Buchanan's death. I confess I was unaware of how poorly he was feeling until I visited him over the weekend. I was so concerned that I rang up Captain Bennett, who is not only my nephew but also Kaz's oldest and closest friend. He immediately traveled to London, and together we were able to persuade your editor to take a short leave of absence." Mr. Bennett paused, allowing the weight of his words to settle over them all. "Kaz is coming to stay with me in Edenbridge until he is well enough to resume work."

"What will happen to *PW*?" Peter asked, giving voice to their concerns. "To us?"

It was Nigel's turn to speak. "Mr. Bennett has asked me to assume the editorship until Kaz returns. It is his hope that nothing will change, and I have promised him that we shall go on as we did before."

"I'm afraid we must ask most of you to shoulder some extra work," Mr. Bennett added. "Kaz has been trying to take on some extra staff for some time now, but the Ministry of Labor has been singularly unhelpful in that regard."

He turned to look at Ruby, his bright blue eyes capturing and holding her gaze effortlessly. "We hope, Miss Sutton, that you will agree to take on the role of acting assistant editor. Kaz was most insistent."

If the proverbial pin had dropped in that instant, she certainly would have been able to hear it. "Me? He wants *me* to do it?"

"He does."

The notion of her having been selected for the role, rather than Peter or Nell, was so startling and unexpected that she simply stared at the men sitting across the table, her brain struggling to attach words to the sentiments running through her head. Bennett nodded, his calm confidence lending her strength, and Mr. Bennett—Uncle Harry—appeared to approve as well.

But Peter's face was pale and drawn, and when she tried to meet his gaze, to offer up an apologetic smile, he frowned and looked away. The sneer that animated Nigel's blandly handsome features was similarly discouraging, and in that moment she was reminded of her conversation with Mary on the train back from Brighton, just days after she'd arrived in England. How men like Nigel and Peter wouldn't hesitate to fight dirty if she got in their way. How she had to watch out for Nigel most of all.

And then an even more worrisome thought occurred to her. Perhaps Kaz hadn't insisted. Perhaps it was all Bennett's doing—a way for him to be kind to her.

And if it were? What else could she do but accept?

"Thank you," she said, focusing on Uncle Harry alone. "I'm honored. I promise to do my very best."

"And that is all we can ask of you, my dear," he said. "I for one am perfectly confident you are up to the task."

Nigel cleared his throat and made a show of rustling the papers before him. "If you don't mind, Mr. Bennett, we still have this week's issue to put to bed. Let's all of us focus on that for now, and leave the glad-handing for another day. I'll be in my office if any of you wish to speak with me."

Bennett spoke up now, addressing Ruby directly for the first time. "We've agreed you can use Kaz's office while he's away. Would you like to come along with me now?"

She nodded, gathering up her bag and notebook, and followed him out of the main room and down the hall to Kaz's office, which looked as if a brief but intense hurricane had set down only minutes before. It might be more trouble than it was worth to clear a space for her to work.

Bennett closed the door behind them and turned to face her. "Say it. I could see the wheels turning in your head out there."

"Did you see Peter's face? He couldn't believe it. For that matter, neither can I."

"You will do a better job, Ruby. That's all there is to it—that's why you were asked. Even Nigel, when we pressed him on it, had to admit that your skills as an editor far surpass Peter's."

"So this isn't you looking out for a friend?"

"Absolutely not," he assured her. "This magazine is too important to Kaz to entrust the work of running it to someone who doesn't know what he—or she—is doing. The better question isn't whether you deserve the job, since we both know you do, but whether you actually want to do it."

"I do want it." And she did, she truly did. It would be a challenge, though, not least because of the man for whom she'd be working, and she felt ill just thinking about the circumstances that had brought it to her door . . .

"So?" Bennett prompted. "What is there to worry about?"

"Nigel, to start with. You saw the look on his face."

"That was the look of a man who had just been told he couldn't have his toady of an underling as his assistant editor. He'll get over it," Bennett promised, "and if he doesn't, he'll have me to deal with—and Kaz, too, when he's recovered." The expression on his face was sufficiently grim for her to almost feel sorry for Nigel.

His next words nearly eroded her meager store of confidence. "I have to warn you, though, that one of Nigel's conditions for taking on the role was that Harry and I remain at arm's length. That we not interfere in the editorial content of the magazine."

"Oh," she said, wishing she had something more worthwhile to offer than a single, feeble syllable.

"Since his leaving would mean our having to close up shop, we felt we had to agree. I'm not happy about it, but I didn't see any alternative. He'll take the magazine to the right—that's all but a certainty."

"I know. He's always complaining in meetings that Kaz is too liberal in his approach to stories."

"Yes. I'm not thrilled at the prospect of *PW* becoming a mouthpiece of Nigel's brand of last-stand, old-guard conservatism, but it won't be for long. At least I hope not for long."

"Will Kaz . . . will he be all right?"

"I hope so. I have to believe he will. Harry will take care of him, and Kaz has always loved the house in Edenbridge. He simply needs some time to heal. He will be back. I'm sure of it."

"Good. That should . . . well, that'll make it easier. At least I hope it will."

"If you're convinced Nigel is about to publish something truly objectionable, something that would ruin what Kaz has created here, you must let me know straightaway. Here's my telephone number at work if you need me." Bennett pressed a card into her hand.

"I will."

"If I'm not there, leave a message with one of the secretaries, and I'll ring you back as soon as I'm able."

"Thank you. For taking care of Kaz, and for—"

"You're very welcome. Now, unfortunately, I need to go—I'm sorry, but it can't be helped. And you do have a magazine to edit."

He kissed her cheek, so gently she scarcely felt it, and was out of the office and down the hall before she had so much as blinked.

The business card in her hand brought her back to the present. She looked down, curious as to what it would say.

Capt. C. S. Bennett
Inter-Services Research Bureau
Welbeck 1966

Nothing very enlightening, then, but she hadn't expected to discover his secrets engraved on a rectangle of cardstock. Tucking it away in her handbag, she went back to her desk in the main office, sat herself down, and got back to work.

NIGEL'S ASCENSION TO the editorship went pretty much as she had guessed, and rather worse, she suspected, than Uncle Harry and Bennett would have liked. Stories in the works that Nigel deemed too "soft" were canned, including one on female pilots in the Air Transport Auxiliary that Ruby had been working on for several weeks. He brought in a monthly column on military affairs, written by a press relations officer from the War Office, and he revived the letters page, ignoring her protests that they could make far better use of the editorial space.

Worst of all, he declined to pursue any of Ruby's story ideas. Week after week, he rejected her proposals, limiting her writing to the women's page he had instituted at the back of the magazine. As for her editorial contributions? Any substantive edits she made to his or Peter's pieces, or those of the increasingly conservative contributors who filled their pages, were soundly rejected.

"Now that we're down to sixteen interior pages," he was fond of saying at their editorial meetings, "we simply don't have room for any of that lightweight stuff that Kaz loved."

"Where does the 'women's page' fall in your estimation?" Ruby had asked the first time they discussed the subject. "I'd have thought you considered it far too insubstantial for our newly serious magazine."

"We're holding on to it for the advertising, no more. I'd like nothing more than to can it—but then how would you and Nell fill your days?"

He was especially nasty to Nell, who vowed again and again that she was about to resign. "The only thing holding me back is the fear of where I'll end up. If I quit, the Ministry of Labor is sure to send me somewhere even worse. Sewing parachutes, most likely, or ladling explosives into shell casings."

They tried to laugh together, for Nigel's antics could be amusing at times, particularly when he was shouting down the phone at some poor soul. "I've started marking off each day on my wall calendar at home," Nell admitted toward the end of October. "We've already survived six weeks of this. If Kaz does come back at the beginning of December, that means we're almost halfway there."

"And if it's still just as bad once he does return?" Ruby asked.

"Then I'm off to work in a munitions factory. But I'm sure he'll be back before long, and when he does he'll set everything to rights. Chin up, Ruby."

"Chin up, Nell."

Ruby did her level best to get on with Nigel. She kept her edits light. She tried her damnedest not to impose her point of view on the pieces that landed on her desk, some of them so shrill and unbalanced that they read more like satire than serious editorial content.

By the end of October she'd resigned herself to her role as a glorified copy editor, trusted to pick out typographical errors but not much more. Nigel had flat-out refused to let her accompany him to the compositors or the printers, and when she had objected, pointing out that he had always gone along with Kaz, Nigel had informed her that women weren't welcome, and that was that. For all she knew, it may have been true, but it stung just the same.

The covers that Nigel chose were even more objectionable than the stories they ran. Kaz had insisted their cover image be attached to a story, and the photographs they used—always photographs and never illustrations—had been, under Kaz's leadership, selected for visual impact but never for shock value.

Their first issue with Nigel fully at the helm marked a sharp departure from their usual fare. The cover was a close-up of two dancers from the notorious Windmill Theatre, the women wearing exaggerated stage makeup; and the picture was cropped so as to show only their heads and upper torsos, with a generous amount of cleavage underpinning the bottom third of the cover. It gave the impression that both women were entirely nude—as they might indeed have been, since the Windmill was known for its risqué tableaux. The article that ran inside, by contrast, was scathingly critical of the theater and others like it, and proclaimed them an affront to "true British values."

Ruby had felt sick to her stomach when the first proofs had arrived. Rather than challenge Nigel in front of everyone else, she had followed him into his office and, tossing the proofs on his desk, had gathered together every scrap of her courage and faced him down.

"This is the most hypocritical pile of *crap* I have ever seen, and you know it. How could you? Kaz will be mortified."

"Watch your language, Ruby."

"Oh, come on! This cover image is one of the most salacious photographs I've ever seen! Yet I wouldn't mind it so much if you'd chosen to couple it with a decent article. Something that actually gets to the bottom of why the Windmill is popular. Or what it's like to be a dancer there. Or any number of other subjects. But it's a diatribe—it reads like Oswald Mosley wrote the first draft."

He didn't even bother to look her in the eye, and instead was concentrating on extracting a speck of dirt from under his thumbnail. "Go ahead and resign, then."

"Not if it leaves this magazine in your hands. Kaz will be back soon, and everything will go back to how it used to be. You should be ashamed of yourself, taking advantage—"

His face reddened, but still he didn't look up. "What's shameful about it? I've been given a chance to show what I'm made of, and I plan to make the most of it."

"You'll be lucky if Kaz doesn't show you the door when he sees what you've done to *PW*."

"I doubt it. He'll see how well it's been managed and be grateful. Now, if you don't mind, I have some work to do. Shut the door behind you when you leave."

It didn't help that she was right in her prediction that Nigel would run the magazine into the ground: advertising revenues plummeted, together with newsstand sales, and before long they were solidly in the red issue after issue. Nigel refused to discuss it with her, insisting that the war was pushing down profits everywhere, but Ruby was unconvinced.

She knew Kaz was recovering well, for Uncle Harry's letters to Vanessa arrived like clockwork every Monday morning and he invariably promised that their editor would be back to work by the end of December, if not earlier. But what if there was no magazine left by the time he returned?

Nearly at breaking point, she shut herself into Kaz's office one morning in late October and, fishing out the card Bennett had given her, dialed through to his work.

"Good morning, Inter-Services Research Bureau, how may I direct your call?"

"May I speak with Captain C. S. Bennett?" she asked.

"I'm afraid he isn't in the office today. May I take a message?"

"Could you tell him . . ."

"Yes, miss?"

What could she tell him? Nigel had insisted on control of the magazine, and Bennett had given it to him. They'd published some awful stuff since then, but nothing so terrible that it would put Kaz in his grave. Surely, she reasoned, both Uncle Harry and Bennett had seen some of *PW*'s recent issues. If they truly hated what Nigel was doing, they would have acted by now.

"Sorry. I'll call back another time."

She would give it another month. If things got any worse, she would write to Uncle Harry and let him know. Kaz would be back before long, and the damage Nigel wrought could be undone. Surely all would be well in the end.

CHAPTER SEVENTEEN

November 1941

I t was Sunday morning, the only day of the week that Ruby didn't wake up and instantly feel gloomy, for an entire day free of *PW* beckoned. She rose early, went for a walk to the river and back, and was finishing off the morning with some satisfyingly aimless work mending socks and turning cuffs. If only every day could be so pleasant.

"Ruby!"

She looked up from her darning and spied Vi in the front hall.

"Hello to you. You're early."

"I am. I was thinking of going through the trunks in the attic again. Nearly everything I have is threadbare."

"Do you want to take back any of your clothes? I hate to think you've gone without nice things because of me."

"No—I should have said I was looking for something to make over. A frock for evenings out. Even if I come across something that's hopelessly out-of-date, it shouldn't be too hard to have it altered. I'm sure I can find a tailor or seamstress to help."

"I can help," Ruby offered. "I was taught to sew by nuns. If there's one thing they're good at teaching, it's needlework. The rest of my education didn't amount to all that much, but I do know how to sew." In point of fact she hated to sew, but the look of delight on Vi's face more than made up for any tedious moments she was bound to suffer.

"That would be lovely—thank you. And I think we still have Mama's old sewing machine up in the attic."

They trooped upstairs and began sorting through a trunk of Vi's old things, most of them fancier dresses that had been packed away for the duration. They were gorgeous things, for the most part, but the change in fashions over the past couple of years hadn't been kind to them. Everything they pulled out was awash in excess fabric, the skirts too full and long, the bodices too unstructured and voluminous.

"These will be easy to fix," Ruby promised. "They just need a more, well, military cut. It's really a case of removing material. If it were the other way around, we'd be in trouble."

"What do you think of this frock?" Vi asked. "Do you think we can save it?"

She held up a dress—a gown, really—made of silk chiffon, each layer a steadily lighter shade of blue. It was swoony and romantic and almost comically dated.

"I think so. Just hold it up so I can see. Yes, yes . . . I think we can do something with it. I'll unpick the waistband, flatten out the layers in the skirt, and take out enough to straighten the lines. I can add in a few darts, too, so everything fits properly. And I'll do the same to the bodice. See how the sleeves are so full here? I just have to unpick them, take out the excess, and sew them back on. It's the work of an afternoon, no more."

Vi hugged her suddenly, crushing the dress between them. "You're a genius, Ruby. I'd never be able to do this."

"Oh, it's easy enough once you know how. Do you want to try it on? I'll find some pins—I think I see your mother's sewing things over there."

Vi took off her skirt and blouse and slipped on the gown, which, considerations of current fashion aside, really was beautiful. As she was changing, Ruby rummaged through Vanessa's old sewing box and found a pincushion, its pins still sharp and rust-free.

"This looks like something you'd wear to a ball," she said as she got to work.

"It was. I wore it to a ball in Oxford, at the college where Hugh was an undergraduate, the summer before the war. It was a magical night. I hardly knew him—I was only eighteen, and he wasn't much older—but I'd already decided I was in love with him."

"What was he like?"

"So very handsome. A bit like Ronald Colman, only without that silly little mustache. Ever so funny and kind. I know it happens that sometimes you lose someone, and before long you start to realize they weren't as wonderful as you'd believed. That they had feet of clay like everyone else. But Hugh was different. He really was just as perfect as I imagined him to be."

Ruby knelt by her friend, busily pinning back layer after layer of chiffon. "I'm sorry I never got to meet him."

"He'd have liked you very much. He'd been to America with his family when he was younger, and he loved it. He promised me we would go there after the war. He was so certain I'd become a movie star in Hollywood."

Ruby kept pinning, methodically, gently, taking care not to scratch Vi's skin. She was so close to her friend that she couldn't fail to notice how Vi was trembling.

"He signed up straightaway. I knew he would. He'd joined a flying club when he started at Oxford. It was a sort of lark to him and his friends, you know. They all signed up. They're all . . . they're all dead now."

"Oh, Vi."

"There were five of them, and they were killed last summer. Hugh was the oldest, and he was only twenty-one. It was before I knew you, of course. Were you living in England then?"

"I'd only just arrived. I was still learning my way around. Finding my feet, I guess you could say. I didn't realize, then, what they were doing. How they were saving all of us."

Vi nodded, just the once, and breathed in deeply. "It was such a beautiful day. The sky was so blue that it hurt my eyes to look at it. He was . . . Hugh was on his third sortie of the afternoon. He hadn't slept properly in weeks, so he must have been terribly tired. There were so few of them, you know, and each day there were fewer. He went out and he never returned. I didn't find out until the next day. His parents had been sent a telegram, and his sister drove through the night so she might tell me, face-to-face, and spare me the shock of a telephone call or telegram. I'll always be grateful to her for that."

Ruby was working on the sleeves now, the pins marching south along Vi's slim arms. "Had you been engaged for long?"

"Only since that Christmas. After he was killed, I wore the ring for a while, but it had been his grandmother's, and it didn't seem right to keep it. I gave it back to his mother."

"Do you have a photograph of him?"

"Oh, yes," Vi said, and the smile she gave Ruby was wide and tremulous. "It's in my handbag. Remind me to show you before dinner."

"I'm all done. Let me help you out of it. Slowly now, so you don't get stuck with any of the pins."

As Vi was changing back into her skirt and blouse, she paused for a second to wave her hand at the still-open trunk. "You should choose something. Please do."

"Oh, no. I already took too many of your things when I moved in with your mother. I don't need anything more."

"Of course you do. Christmas will be here before you know it, and you'll want a pretty frock. Oh—and I've a charity evening with my ENSA company coming up next week. You'll need something nice for that. Did anything catch your eye earlier? Be honest—I really and truly do want you to have something."

"If you're sure . . . perhaps that red dress? Only it looked almost new."

"If it's the one I'm thinking of, I bought it on a whim and never wore it."

Vi delved into the trunk and emerged with the exact dress Ruby had admired earlier. It had a long, swirling skirt, not too full, with little puffed sleeves and a sweetheart neckline. It was a dark tomato red with tiny white polka dots, and had a row of delicate mother-of-pearl buttons down the front.

"The color is awful on me," Vi said, "but it will be wonderful on you. I insist you take it."

RUBY WORE THE dress, which had only needed the tiniest bit of alterations, to Vi's ENSA show the following Friday evening. It was held at the Fortune Theatre in Covent Garden, just next door to the Scottish church where Mary's funeral had been held. Vanessa came to the show, too, but was unimpressed when the usher at the theater's entrance informed them they were sitting upstairs.

"You're in the upper circle, ma'am. Up the stairs and all the way to the top. Usher there'll show you where to go."

"I hadn't realized we'd be seated on Mount Olympus," Vanessa grumbled as they trudged up the stairs.

"Yes, but we'll be able to see everything so well," Ruby said brightly, too excited to care a bit where they were sitting. "Is this the same show Vi does on her factory visits?"

"I believe it's an expanded version," Vanessa answered, a little out of breath from their ascent. "They've done it a few times for fund-raisers."

At the top of the stairs, a waiting usher handed them a program and directed them to their seats. It had been worth the climb, for they were seated in the front row of the upper circle, with a terrific view of the entire stage.

"There she is," Vanessa said, pointing to Vi's name on the program.

ENSA Proudly Presents
A Variety Showcase
In Aid of the British Red Cross
Starring
Danny Styles and His Swingin' Syncopators
Morton and Milly
Arthur Latimer
Eva and the Starlettes

Jimmy Cole
Miss Viola Tremaine

***

There will be a brief intermission
Refreshments are available at the bar

Mr. Styles and his band began the show with a round of popular music, the highlight of which, for Ruby, was "Chattanooga Choo-Choo," one of her favorite tunes. It was all she could do not to get up and dance in the aisle. The band was followed by Morton and Milly, a pair of tap dancers who offered a credible imitation of Fred and Ginger, and then by Arthur Latimer, who performed several brief but showy piano solos on a gigantic Steinway that was rolled out from the wings.

After a brief intermission Eve and the Starlettes, a troop of acrobatic dancers, took to the stage, and then it was time for the comedian.

"He's awful," Vanessa warned Ruby as the man took to the stage. "It's the worst sort of jingoistic tripe. Why they keep him on I have *no* idea."

"Too bad Nigel isn't here. He'd probably love it."

Vanessa wasn't wrong. The man was a cretin, and after an especially distasteful limerick about "Japs, wops, and krauts," Ruby was ready to put her fingers in her ears.

"I can't believe people are laughing," she whispered in Vanessa's ear.

"I suppose he appeals to the lowest common denominator. But at least—oh, thank goodness. Off he goes."

As soon as the stage was empty again, the lights went down

and the audience fell silent. A circle of light appeared at center stage. Out of the darkness, a lone figure appeared. It was Vi, costumed in the chiffon dress Ruby had altered, her hair swept back from her face to fall in loose curls around her shoulders.

"Good evening, everyone. My name is Viola Tremaine, and I'm here to share some songs with you."

She paused, her hand coming out to steady the microphone on its stand. And then her voice rang out alone, sweet and true and achingly beautiful.

"I'll never smile again . . ."

"I love this song!" Ruby hissed in Vanessa's ear. From the cheers coming from the audience, she wasn't alone in that opinion.

Vi waited until the applause had died down, smiling and laughing as GIs in the audience called her name and shouted out song requests. Then she launched into "When the Lights Go on Again," and the bittersweet yearning of its lyrics left Ruby struggling to catch her breath.

Taking only the briefest pause, Vi moved on to "Why Don't You Do Right?" and "I'll Be Seeing You," another standard that left Ruby hovering on the edge of tears.

"Thank you, everyone, for your generosity in coming out tonight and supporting the work of the British Red Cross," Vi said. "We've just enough time for one last song, and it's a favorite of a dear friend who is here tonight. Ruby—this is for you."

"Somewhere over the rainbow . . ."

This time, without any encouragement from Vi, the audience joined in, singing of lemon drops and bluebirds and happiness forever out of reach. The final bars of music faded, everyone leaped to their feet, and the rapturous applause that ensued was positively deafening.

"Should we try and go backstage?" Ruby asked when the applause had died down and the audience was making for the exits.

"We'll never get through, I fear. There will be GIs ten deep outside the stage door. And we will be seeing her on Sunday."

Ruby had known Vi could sing—that had been apparent from their first sing-along in the shelter. But the woman she'd seen onstage tonight? She was a different sort of creature altogether, her talents so superior to everyone else who'd preceded her that it was almost laughable. Vi was Ruby's friend, but Miss Viola Tremaine? She was a star.

RUBY WAS STILL in a wonderful mood the next day, and not even the prospect of seeing Nigel could faze her. She left for work early, hoping to have some time to herself; Evelyn would certainly be there, but Nigel wasn't likely to roll through the door until closer to nine o'clock, and perhaps even later since it was a Saturday.

The office was silent when she arrived, and after hanging up her coat and hat, Ruby walked down the hall to Kaz's office. She opened the door, but the chair behind the desk was occupied.

Kaz had returned.

She stared at him, tears gathering in her eyes. "I thought you weren't coming back until the end of December."

He was marking up a piece that Nell had left for Ruby the night before, his head bent low, and when he did look up she was taken aback by the weight of sorrow in his pale, wise eyes.

"I felt better," he said, and smiled. "How are you?"

"Seeing you at your desk? So much better than when I woke up this morning."

"I see you'd set up shop in here. Do you mind if I reclaim my office?"

"Of course not. And I only came in here when I needed a bit of quiet."

"Or to get away from Nigel?"

"That, too. From time to time. Are you . . . are you better?" It felt wrong to ask, and yet it would be worse to pretend that nothing had happened.

"I am, or as better as I'll ever be. Losing Mary was a wound that won't ever heal. I had to learn how to live with the pain. To accept that my life isn't over and I have useful work to do. Not to mention friends who care for me and want me to be well."

"We do," she insisted. "I ought to have made that clearer to you. We all should have."

He grimaced theatrically at this. "Remember that the rest of us are English, and we'd rather chew on broken glass than talk about our feelings." His expression grew somber. "I read through the back issues this morning. I've a lot of damage to undo."

"I know you and Nigel are old friends," she began, not wishing to offend or further distress him, "but it was awful while you were gone. Nell and I were counting the days."

"I've spoken to him, and he has tendered his resignation. He's gone already."

"Oh," she said, taken aback by the speed of Nigel's departure. "Will you be able to find anyone else?"

"I think so, but I wanted to speak with you first. The position is yours if you want it. If you see yourself turning away from writing, at least for the time being."

"Are you sure? It's not as if Nigel gave me much to do."

"I am sure, Ruby, and once again I feel very badly that he

was so obstructive. But the question remains: Do you want the job of assistant editor? Or would you rather be a staff writer?"

It would be a step up, a big one. Certainly it would be sensible of her to accept. But she didn't want to be an editor—she was a writer down to her toes, and that was the work she wanted to do.

"If you need me to help with the editing, I'll do it, but I really have missed the writing. Nigel preferred to bring in freelancers. I don't think I've written an original piece since you left."

"I know, and *PW* has suffered for it. Consider yourself freed from editorial purgatory."

"Thank you. And I will stay on until you find someone else. You did say you have someone in mind?"

"I do. An old friend. Czech by birth, but he spent most of his childhood here. He worked in Germany for a number of years—the man speaks half a dozen languages—and was imprisoned by the Nazis for a time. Fortunately, he had the good sense to come here as soon as he was released in early 1939, otherwise God only knows where he'd be now."

"Where has he been working since coming to England?"

Kaz's expression darkened. "Nowhere. He was sent to an internment camp last year, and despite my best efforts, and those of Harry and Bennett and a host of other friends, he remained in detention until earlier this summer. None of it makes any sense— Emil is the most fervent opponent of fascism I've ever met."

"There's another story we should be covering—conditions in the internment camps. I've wondered about them before. How people are treated there."

"Emil says the camp where he was sent was pretty decent, but his point of comparison is a Nazi prison. I think for the average interned person, simply being deprived of his liberty is injury enough. We could put them all up at the Savoy and it would still be unjust."

"Have you asked him yet?"

"No. I was waiting to speak with you. In case you wanted the job."

"Then what are you waiting for? Can you ring him up? See if he's free for lunch one day soon? That way you can introduce him to all of us."

"And allow him to make an informed decision as to whether he wants to sign up to work in this madhouse?"

"Yes, Kaz. Exactly that."

EMIL BERGMANN MET Kaz and Ruby at the Old Bell later that week. Slight and slim, with thinning hair that was carefully combed back from his brow, and elegant hands that fluttered around his face when he talked, he looked many years older than Kaz, though Ruby suspected they were about the same age.

He was friendly but reserved, the sort of man who listened while others spoke, but when he did offer his opinions they were thoughtful and considered. He let Kaz tell him about the struggles the magazine faced, the need to reclaim readers who had been driven away by Nigel's disastrous stint in the editor's chair, and apart from nodding his head, and occasionally murmuring "of course, of course," he remained silent throughout.

"So? What do you think? Are you interested?" Kaz asked.

"I am. As far as turning the magazine around, it will take time. To begin with, you need a big story. Something that gets everyone's attention. Gets readers talking. But not in a reactionary way, as your previous editor attempted."

"Have any ideas?"

"Yes. It is not an easy subject. I think your readers may find it difficult to read about. It will certainly be difficult to persuade the Ministry of Information to let you run it. But I think it can be managed. I think they'll agree it will help the war effort."

"Go on."

Emil leaned forward, his gaze fixed on the dregs of his beer. "This past summer, the Catholic bishop of Münster gave a sermon that condemned the Nazis' so-called euthanasia program of invalids, which was nothing more than the targeted extermination of innocents. The program has since been wound down, which is to say it has simply gone underground, and the bishop has been placed under house arrest. I wouldn't be surprised if he ends up in one of their gas chambers."

"Gas chambers?" Ruby asked.

"That's how they kill them. Children and cripples and old people who've become senile. They kill them with poison gas. Tens of thousands under the official program. And heaven knows how many more are being killed in secret. We won't know the full extent until the war is over, but my gut tells me it will be the stuff of nightmares."

Kaz took off his spectacles and began to rub at his temples. "Do we have any firsthand accounts? Anyone who can speak to the full extent of the horrors?"

"Not as yet, but it's only a matter of time. For the moment, I propose that we print a translation of the bishop's sermon alongside your editorial. It will cause an uproar. It may even become a point of debate in the House of Commons. And it will remind readers that *Picture Weekly* is a force for good in this country."

CHAPTER EIGHTEEN

December 7, 1941

O ver the past few months, Ruby had gotten into the habit of sitting with Vanessa and Jessie in the library after dinner. It was smaller and cozier than the sitting room, and it also held the wireless, as Ruby had come to think of it, in its grand wooden case.

That Sunday evening, Vi had been absent from dinner; she'd been performing at a Christmas party for factory workers somewhere north of the city. Beatrice left by eight, for she had an early start in the morning, and Jessie had gone off to bed complaining of a sore back.

That had left Ruby and Vanessa alone in the library, quietly knitting and listening to the rather feeble programming the BBC supplied on Sunday evenings—church services, hymns, improving lectures, and the like. Ruby had turned down the wireless earlier, not caring for the nasal tones and banal remarks of the clergyman who'd been rambling away for the past quarter hour; but as the clock chimed nine she returned the volume to its normal level so they might listen to the evening news.

"Here is the news, and this is Alvar Lidell reading it."

"Don't you love that voice? 'Here is the news,'" Vanessa intoned, mimicking the newsreader perfectly. "Can you imagine a plummier voice? It sounds as if he gargles with vintage port every—"

"Shh, Vanessa. Something's happened . . ." Ruby turned up the volume even higher, straining to hear.

". . . attacks on United States naval bases in the Pacific . . ."

"My God," Vanessa gasped. "Can it be true?"

". . . from Tokyo say that Japan has issued a formal declaration of war against both the United States and Britain. The Japanese air raids were made on the Hawaiian Islands and the Philippines. Observers' reports say that an American battleship has been hit and that a number of the Japanese bombers have been shot down . . ."

"When did this happen?"

"It's happening *now*, Vanessa—hush!"

". . . Roosevelt has told the army and navy to act on their secret orders, has called a meeting of ministers, and is preparing a report for Congress. In London, Mr. Winant has seen Mr. Churchill and both houses of Parliament have been summoned for tomorrow afternoon to hear a statement on the situation. In further news . . ."

Her fingers suddenly nerveless, Ruby let her knitting slip to the floor, grabbing for it just in time to feel an entire row of stitches pop off the needles. Clutching the tangled bundle to her chest, she stared sightlessly at the wireless. Could she have imagined it?

"'Further news,'" Vanessa muttered, switching off the wireless. "Unless Axis troops are landing in Kent, I doubt anything else can be of interest tonight."

It was so hard to believe. Tensions had been running high

between the United States and Japan, but she'd never have imagined *this*. And for Japan to have declared war on Britain, too, was almost impossible to credit.

"What are you thinking?" Vanessa asked softly.

"That I can't quite believe it, I guess. We're at war with Japan, and probably with Germany, too. We'll be fighting a war on two fronts, on opposite sides of the world. And yet . . ."

"Go on."

"I feel relieved. Isn't that awful? To be glad that my country is at war? And I'm not, not really. But to know that we're your ally now, and that Britain isn't alone, is such a relief. After all this time, after all this country has endured . . ."

"Well, nothing much is going to happen overnight," Vanessa said. "Put aside your knitting and go on up to bed. Kaz will have you run off your feet tomorrow, so you'd best get some sleep now."

Vanessa was right. Kaz threw out half the magazine in the morning, sent them off in search of new stories, and completely rewrote his editorial. The final proofs went out the door on Tuesday a few minutes shy of midnight, but then, exhausted as they all were, Kaz insisted they be back at their desks by eight o'clock the following morning.

Emil proved his worth many times over in those busy days of early December. Not only was he an astute and sensitive editor, but he was also an elegant writer. He worked harder than everyone else, staying late nearly every night. When Ruby tried to encourage him to go home on time, he always demurred, explaining that there was nowhere else he'd rather be.

"I'm simply making up for lost time," he explained. "When I was trapped in that internment camp, prevented from doing any meaningful work and bored out of my mind, I promised myself that if I was ever released, I would never let an idle hour pass by again. I intend to keep that promise."

The news kept coming, and it seemed to get worse every day, so much so that Ruby longed for just one solid day, even a single waking hour, when she might be free of it. When she might empty her mind and simply daydream about Christmas dinner and gathered friends and a bright future for all of them. When the awful period of waiting and wondering might be over, and she and the rest of the world might be confident of what would happen next.

INSTEAD OF HAVING everyone come to Vanessa's for Christmas, Uncle Harry had suggested they travel out to the house in Edenbridge for luncheon. It would make a pleasant change of scenery, he had argued in his letter to Vanessa, and it would also save her and Jessie the burden of cooking for everyone.

With the trains running often enough to make a day-trip practicable, it was agreed that everyone would meet at Victoria Station on Christmas morning, Jessie having gone to her sister's in Wapping the day before. Bea appeared promptly at ten o'clock, as agreed, but Vi surprised no one by being late.

"What time did you tell Vi to meet us?" asked Bea for at least the third time. "You ought to have said a quarter to ten," she went on, not waiting for her mother to answer.

"She'll be here," Vanessa insisted. "And she's a grown girl. If she misses the train, she can catch up later. Stop fussing about it."

So they waited and checked their watches and scanned the crowds, and just as the station's clocks began to ring the quarter hour, Ruby caught sight of a familiar face. She stood on tiptoe, craning her head this way and that, wishing the crowds would thin just a little.

"I think I see her—yes, there she is," she confirmed.

Vi was dressed in the nicest of her suits, its dove-gray color the perfect foil for her brunette hair and bright blue eyes, and she had on a new hat that Ruby hadn't seen before, a jaunty little cap that looked a bit like something a sailor might wear. She strode through the station as if it belonged to her, and she was so beautiful, so impossibly glamorous, that passersby were stopping and staring and whispering behind their hands.

"There you are, Vi!" Bea called out. "We were starting to worry."

"Well, I made it, so no need to fuss. Happy Christmas, all of you. Where are Kaz and Bennett? It won't be the same if they aren't there, too."

"If you'd listened to me when we spoke on the telephone earlier in the week, you'd know the men are there already. Now let's hurry up—if we miss our train we'll have to wait another hour, and you know how Harry hates it when luncheon is late."

"Do Kaz and Bennett always spend Christmas with your family?" Ruby asked once they were under way.

"Nearly always. The first Christmas he was at university, Bennett asked if he might bring a friend," Vanessa explained. "Kaz's parents had gone to live abroad, I believe, and he'd nowhere else to go. He's come for Christmas every year since."

"And Bennett?"

"Him, too. His mother died when he was only thirteen. She was my dearest friend, you know. And then his father died only a few years later."

"How did you meet Mrs. Bennett?"

"We attended the same finishing school in Switzerland, and we bonded over our mutual dislike of all the other girls. Terrible snobs, all of them. When I returned to England at the end of the year, she came for a visit. That's when she and David—Bennett's father—met, and it was love at first sight. Never mind that they ought to have been all wrong for one another."

"Why should that be?" Ruby asked.

"Well, she was French, to begin with, and very high-spirited and romantic and given to grand gestures. And he was exactly as you'd imagine a very senior barrister to be. Terribly traditional and fond of hearing his own voice, and not one to suffer fools gladly. But they were happy together, and he was simply devastated when she died. We all were."

"And Bennett?"

"My husband and I took him under our collective wing. He needed attention, which his father wasn't able to give him for some time, and he needed a place to be a boy. He found that here, and also in Edenbridge with his uncle Harry. In due course his father recovered, and they were close again, but then the poor man keeled over from some sort of undiagnosed heart ailment."

"What was he like when he was young? Bennett, I mean."

"He was ever so funny," said Bea, giggling a little at the memory. "Remember how he would make us all laugh with the stories he told?"

"He did have me in stitches most of the time. And he was terribly naughty. Forever getting into trouble at school. His father would be so stern, and Bennett would promise he was sorry, but there was always that light in his eyes that promised more mischief to come."

"I guess he changed when his father died," Ruby said, unable to reconcile the Bennett she knew with the laughing, merry boy he had once been.

But Vanessa was shaking her head. "No, even that didn't alter him much."

"Then what—"

"It was Dunkirk. That's when he changed. That's when we lost the old Bennett." She sighed, and then she straightened her shoulders and aimed a dazzling smile at Ruby. "Oh—listen to me being so gloomy, and on Christmas morning, too. Let's talk of nicer things. Vi, why don't you tell us where you've been performing. Have you been anywhere interesting recently?"

"Do the Cambridgeshire Fens count as interesting? Because that's where I was all week."

Vi's description of her rainy trek from one sodden airfield to the next kept them entertained through their change of trains in East Croydon and their arrival, not long after, in Edenbridge Town. They were the only passengers to alight in the village, which was so quiet as to appear deserted.

"Not far now," Vanessa assured Ruby. "We used to make this trip nearly every bank holiday, didn't we?"

"It felt faster when Papa had the car," Beatrice observed.

"Yes, but then we didn't have the fun of the walk up to the house. We're taking the back way. The main entrance is all the way around to the north, but there's a path just ahead that takes us through the woods to the bottom of the gardens."

"We'll have to bring you back in the summer," Vi added, catching hold of Ruby's arm and urging her along. "It smells like heaven when the roses and clematis and lavender are in bloom. Absolute heaven."

"Have you met Uncle Harry before?" Bea asked Ruby.

"Just the once. He came to *PW* when Kaz began his leave of absence. I didn't have much of a chance to speak with him, though."

"You'll like him," Vanessa declared. "Dear old fellow. Although you'd never know he was once a high court judge. All he talks about now is his rhododendrons and azaleas."

They came up to the top of a little hill, and there was the house itself, an ancient, rather shambling structure that exactly conformed to every one of Ruby's preconceived notions of what an English cottage should look like. Its slate roof was thick with moss, and hung low over a half-timbered upper story. The main floor was made of brick, soft and rosy, with short runs of a dark gray stone at intervals, and its windows and doors were set into the exterior in a charmingly haphazard fashion. There wasn't, at least as far as Ruby could see, a completely straight line in the entire building.

Closer to the house, the garden had been planted out as a vegetable patch, its dormant beds flanked by rows of elegantly skeletal fruit trees. A stone bench sat in a patch of pale winter sunshine under one of the trees; and stretched upon it, fast asleep, was Bennett.

"I'll wake him," she said. "The rest of you go on inside."

It seemed a shame to rouse him. His face was so peaceful, the lines around his eyes and the deeper groove between his brows smoothed out by the calm of sleep. But he wouldn't want to miss the party and the chance of seeing them all together, not after being absent for so long.

"Bennett," she said, crouching by the bench. "It's Ruby. Time to wake up. Will you wake up for me?"

He opened his eyes, instantly alert, and then, hesitantly, as if she might shy away, he reached out to trace the curve of her cheek. "If I didn't know better, I'd think you were a dryad come to steal me away," he said huskily.

"A dryad?"

"A tree spirit. Although no self-respecting dryad would be caught wearing a cardigan."

"It's winter. My swansdown cape isn't nearly warm enough."

"I thought so," he said, a smile tugging at the corners of his mouth. "What time is it?"

"Almost noon."

He sat up, stretching his arms behind his back. "We'd better go on in. Harry will start tearing up the floorboards if we don't sit down to lunch soon."

Standing, he looped his arm through hers, and led her around to the front of the house.

"Has Harry always lived here?" she asked.

"Since he retired. This was actually my father's house."

She stopped short, surprised by his admission. "And it's Harry's now?"

"Well, no, not exactly. I inherited it, but I'm happy for him to live here. It leaves him free to spend his money on other things."

"Such as *Picture Weekly*?"

"Just so."

They went inside through a wide, heavy door of wood gone nearly black with age, and into a simply furnished hall awash in boots, Barbour jackets, and dogs of all shapes and sizes, all barking and yipping with joy at their arrival.

"I'm here, I'm here," Bennett crooned. "Time to settle. Calm down, calm . . . calm . . . there you are. Say hello to Ruby. Come on, now."

She held out her hand, a little nervous as she'd never spent much time around dogs, and one by one they came over to sniff and lick at her fingers. "What are their names?"

"Let me see. The old yellow Lab is Tilly, and the younger version is Joey. The terrier is Dougal, the lurcher—this odd-looking fellow with the shaggy coat and long legs—is Mickey. And this one"—here he bent to pick up a rotund little dachshund—"is Spitz. Not a German spy, I assure you, despite his name."

"Why so many?" she asked, stroking Spitz's long, silky ears.

"Harry is incapable of turning away a stray or the runt of a litter. At one point I think he had ten dogs living here, but in recent years I've been encouraging him to find other homes for dogs as they're brought to him."

"I like them," she said. "Spitz especially. Even if he does look like a ham with four legs."

"You go ahead while I put the dogs outside. Otherwise we won't have a moment's peace during lunch."

Following the sound of conversation, Ruby wandered down the hall and into the sitting room, a modest chamber with an enormous open hearth as its focal point. In its decoration, the room reminded her of Vanessa's house, with well-worn easy chairs, polished antiques, and a gallery's worth of oil paintings hung closely on every vertical surface.

Their host heaved himself to his feet as she entered. "Ruby, my dear. How good to see you again."

"Happy Christmas, sir. Your house is beautiful."

"Did you meet the dogs?"

"I did, and they were very sweet."

"I just spoke to Cook, and she said lunch will be ready in an hour," Bennett announced from the door. "Do any of you mind if I show Ruby around the house before we open our gifts?"

"Not at all," Harry insisted. "We'll just have a little aperitif while we're waiting. Kaz, would you mind doing the honors? It's the last bottle of Pol Roger from my cellar."

Bennett led Ruby back the way they'd come, through the sitting room and the dining room, past several smaller chambers, one of which looked to be Harry's library or study, and up a narrow, creaking staircase.

"How old is the house?" she asked.

"The oldest parts are from the early fifteenth century. It's a bit of a jumble, as I'm sure you noticed."

"So what? I think it's charming." They'd reached the landing and were at the end of a long and very crooked hallway.

"Up to a point. If you only knew the number of times I've cracked my forehead open on beams in this house. I probably have a dent in my skull," he grumbled.

Laughing, she touched her fingertips to his brow, sweeping them back and forth, as if to check for evidence of past injuries. His eyes met hers, and she noticed, once again, how very blue they were, like India ink straight from the bottle.

Her hand fell away.

He took a step back and cleared his throat. "Let me show you around."

The full tour took a long while, for Bennett was intent on showing her everything: from medieval graffiti scratched on a pane of stained glass, to the adze marks left by carpenters shaping the ceiling joists more than five centuries ago, to the loose floorboard in his childhood bedroom where he'd once stowed all manner of treasures.

"How long did you live here?"

"Only until I was thirteen. After Maman died, we returned to London and Harry took over the house. I visit on holidays, but I haven't lived here for a long time."

"Do you think you'll ever live here again?" she asked, though it wasn't any of her business.

He looked around his old room, its furniture hidden under dust sheets, and shook his head. "I don't know. It's hard to look ahead any farther than a few weeks. But it was a good place to be a boy. If I ever . . ."

"If?"

"Never mind. We'd better get back to the others."

After learning they would be traveling out to Edenbridge for Christmas lunch, Ruby had knitted scarves for the men with wool she'd scavenged from some old cashmere cardigans that Vanessa had unearthed. They pronounced themselves delighted with her creations, as did Vanessa and her daughters with the delicate lace shawls she'd knitted from the unraveled remains of a fine lamb's-wool dressing gown that had once belonged to Sir Nicholas. In return, and rather to her surprise, she received an automatic pencil from Kaz, a diamanté brooch from Vanessa, a bottle of Sauternes dessert wine from Harry, and a copy of *For Whom the Bell Tolls* from Vi and Beatrice.

The last gift she opened was from Bennett, and it all but took her breath away. It was a small oil painting, not much bigger than a sheet of typing paper, and it was a view of St. Paul's Cathedral from the banks of the Thames, the great dome almost lost in the mist of a rainy day.

"I think the artist must have been standing on Blackfriars Bridge," Bennett explained. "But he painted it before the railway bridge went up, so that puts the painting at 1850 or earlier. The dealer wasn't able to tell me much more, and we couldn't make much of the signature. All the same, I hope you like it."

"I do. Very much." There was so much more she could have said, but not without embarrassing them both. "Thank you."

With the gifts unwrapped, it was time for luncheon, so they trooped into the dining room and took their places around the expansive table. Its polished wood had been left bare, with lace mats in lieu of a cloth, and at its center a mass of chrysanthemums had been gathered into a sparkling crystal vase. Heavy silver flatware flanked blue-and-white china at each place setting, and appetizing smells floated from covered serving dishes.

Harry had laid in a sumptuous feast: roast pheasant, sent by a cousin with a shooting lodge in Scotland, roast potatoes, and brussels sprouts, which Cook had prepared with what looked like a year's ration of bacon. To finish, there was plum pudding made with grated apples and carrots and a handful of precious raisins, and set aflame with a dribble of brandy that Bennett had discovered at the very back of the drinks cabinet.

"Now eat up," Vanessa encouraged everyone, "or we'll miss the king's message."

At three o'clock they gathered around the wireless in the sitting room, everyone standing in accordance with Harry's wishes. "In my day you didn't sit to listen to the sovereign. You stood, and you toasted the man when he was done."

"We will, Harry. Now hush so we can hear."

So they stood and listened, and each time the king hesitated over a word they held their collective breath, but he got through his speech without too much difficulty. Ruby couldn't remember how she had learned about his stammer and his work to overcome it, but whatever measures he had taken seemed to have worked.

"You don't think he writes the speech himself, do you?" she asked.

Kaz shook his head. "Doubt it. Probably has some equerry do the job."

"I thought it was lovely," Vanessa said.

"You always say that, Mama. And you always say he was ever so brave, and didn't he manage well, and so on."

"Enough, Bea." This was from Bennett. "Your mother is right. It was a good speech, and the king did well by it. Did you notice the allusions to 'Dover Beach,' though?"

Kaz groaned. "You and your poetry."

"'Nor fortitude, nor sacrifice, nor sympathy'? It's as plain as day."

"What poem are you talking about, Bennett?" Ruby asked, not caring if it made her look like the most ignorant person alive.

"'Dover Beach.' Written almost a hundred years ago, though Matthew Arnold might have been talking about the present war. Listen—here's the last few lines:

> "... *let us be true*
> *To one another! for the world, which seems*
> *To lie before us like a land of dreams,*
> *So various, so beautiful, so new,*
> *Hath really neither joy, nor love, nor light,*
> *Nor certitude, nor peace, nor help for pain;*
> *And we are here as on a darkling plain*

Swept with confused alarms of struggle and flight,
   Where ignorant armies clash by night."

"How wonderfully festive of you," Vanessa observed, and Bennett, looking a little embarrassed now, did a mock bow. They were saved from further awkwardness by the timely delivery of mincemeat tarts and tea. Only after everyone had been served, and a single pie remained on the platter, did Ruby notice that Bennett had vanished.

"Did you see where Bennett went?" she asked Kaz.

"Likely the garden. If not there, then the library."

She found him in the same spot he'd been when they'd arrived, sitting on the bench, a nimbus of cigarette smoke hanging around his head. In all the time she'd known him, she'd never seen him smoke or smelled it on his clothes. For some reason it disappointed her, even though half the people she knew were smokers.

"Since when do you smoke?" she asked.

"Hardly ever," he said. "It's a nasty habit I thought I'd left behind years ago." He dropped the cigarette to the ground and crushed it beneath his heel. "Vanessa will have my head if she finds out. It's what killed Uncle Nick, you know. Poor man was dead in six months. That's when I stopped for the first time."

"I have to agree with Vanessa," she said as she sat next to him. "Any length of time sitting with smokers and I feel ill."

He turned to grin at her. "I'd no idea you were such a delicate flower, Miss Sutton."

"Why are you out here?"

His smile vanished. "I am forever misjudging the mood of the hour. I love that poem, but it was idiotic of me to recite it like that. As if anyone needs a reminder of how grim our lives have become."

"I wouldn't say it was idiotic. Although the king's message was perhaps a touch more hopeful than your poem."

"You would think that," he muttered. "You writers are all dreamers at heart."

He tilted his head back, as did she, and together they surveyed the infinite dome of stars blanketing the night sky.

"Makes you think, doesn't it? How insignificant we are. How little our cares and worries mean to the universe. We're specks of dust, and all our dreams . . ."

"What of them?" she whispered.

"They come to nothing, don't they? As all dreams must. I . . ."

She waited and waited, the silence between them stretching tighter than a bowstring, until she couldn't bear another second of it.

"When are you off again?" she asked. A stupid question, since the answer was sure to be some variation of "soon."

"Tomorrow."

"Will you be back for New Year's? Vanessa was so hoping you—"

"I doubt it."

"Is what you do dangerous?"

"Don't do this. Please, Ruby."

"I'm not asking what you do. Only if I ought to worry."

"I'm not worth your worry. Swear to God I'm not."

She reached out, through the dark night that separated them, and set her hand on his knee. "It's not your decision to make. You can't stop me from worrying."

"I suppose not."

"What do you think is going to happen now?" she asked, letting her hand fall back onto her lap.

At last he twisted around to face her. "Now, as in this evening? Or now, as in the foreseeable future?"

"The latter."

"I've no idea. Only that the war won't end next year, or even the year after. The rot I've heard over the past few weeks—as if it'll be a cakewalk from here on in. As if we'll be walking through Berlin by the summer."

"I never thought—"

"If ever we do get a real toehold in Europe, we will have to fight for every yard, every inch of ground. The years to come will be drenched in blood, and we haven't even begun to plumb the horrors of what is happening to civilians in Axis territory. That article you ran in *PW* about the Nazis' euthanasia scheme was only the tip of the iceberg. If I told you all I know, you would never sleep again."

"Bennett—it's Christmas," she pleaded, her heart aching for him. Could he not let the weight of the world slip from his shoulders, if only for a few short hours?

"I know, I know. But how can I find it in me to be cheery, knowing what I know? How am I meant to care that smoking will kill me twenty years from now?"

"I care," she whispered. "And there *are* things to be cheerful about."

"Name one."

"Christmas puddings that taste almost like the real thing. Hand-knit scarves. A sky bright with stars. Friends that love you."

"Don't. Just . . . don't."

It was hard to answer him, after that, without her voice wobbling. "I won't, then. But Merry Christmas. Happy Christmas, I mean."

He didn't answer her right away, and simply to sit there and wait and wonder what was going through his head was unbearable. She stood, ready to flee to the warmth and certainty of the sitting room and their waiting friends, but his hand upon her sleeve stopped her.

"Ruby—wait. I'm sorry."

He rose to his feet and kissed her fleetingly, fitting his lips to hers for the length of a heartbeat, no more. "Happy Christmas," he whispered.

Then he was gone, past the blackout curtain and into the house, and she was alone in the garden, sheltered only by stars, her world turned upside down.

PART III

At the Savoy on Monday night, the American correspondents had everybody worked up to slapping backs
and singing "O say, can you see . . ." On Thursday night,
there was little emotion and no singing. Instead, there
was a feeling that the war was going to be tougher from
now on, that it would certainly be longer than people
had expected, and that this country and America may
easily have to take some knocks which will make the
loss of a couple of capital ships seem like chicken feed.
—Mollie Panter-Downes, columnist for the *New Yorker*
(December 20, 1941)

PART III

CHAPTER NINETEEN

April 1942

It was six o'clock on a Friday, at the tail end of a long week that had featured very little by way of good news, when Ruby's phone began to ring.

"*Picture Weekly*, Ruby Sutton speaking."

"Ruby. Dan Mazur here. How are you?"

The last time she'd seen her colleague from *The American*, at her farewell party, he'd been three sheets to the wind and about to usher one of the secretaries into a coat closet. She hadn't spared more than a passing thought for him since.

"Very well, thank you. When did you arrive? I assume you're calling from London."

"Sure am. Got in a couple of days ago. Hell of a crossing. Don't know why they wouldn't cough up for a plane ticket. Anyway, I'm at some rinky-dink hotel on Cockspur Street, wherever the hell that is—"

"Near Piccadilly," she told him. "Not a bad place to be. You're around the corner from our embassy, and Whitehall is just down the road."

"If you say so. Haven't actually left the hotel yet. So, where was I? Oh—Mitchell said I should look you up. Said you might have some pointers for me on how they do business here. I know you've been stuck on the women's pages and all, but—"

"*Picture Weekly* doesn't have women's pages, Dan. I work on the same stories as anyone else. Not to mention my column in *The American*."

"I wouldn't count on that. No room for filler during a war. Mitchell's looking for hard news, not—"

"I'd hardly call reporting on the Blitz 'filler,' Dan."

"All right, all right. Calm down. You know I didn't mean anything by it. So what do you say? Do you want to meet up somewhere?"

"How about Monday evening?" she said after a pause. She'd had to unclench her teeth and remind herself that he was a colleague and it was only civil and courteous to help him. Not that he'd ever have done the same for her. She recalled, suddenly, how he'd once delighted in asking her to fetch him cups of coffee, even though the percolator had been within arm's reach of his desk. "I can spare some time after work. There's a Lyons Corner House not far from you, at the junction of Coventry and Rupert. I'll meet you there at half-past six."

"Sounds like a plan. See you then."

She left work early on Monday, having explained her obligation to Kaz, and arrived exactly on time.

The teahouse was packed to the rafters, and from what Ruby could tell, the war hadn't slowed down business one bit. It helped that restaurants were off ration, and since the set menu was a reasonable one-and-six, it was a popular destination for families and young couples alike. She'd been a few times, most recently with Vi, and was always impressed with the efficiency of the waitresses in their black-and-white uniforms and smart little caps. For some funny reason they were called Nippies, perhaps because they nipped from table to table so swiftly.

At twenty minutes to seven she made eye contact with a passing Nippy and ordered a cup of tea, a soft-boiled egg, and two slices of buttered toast. She had nearly finished her egg, the first one she'd eaten in weeks, by the time Dan made his appearance at a quarter past seven.

"Sorry I'm late," he said, after shaking her hand and taking his seat across the table from her. "I got turned around. Guess they never got the hang of the grid system here."

"I guess not. Although that's often the case with cities as old as London."

"Fair enough. So what do they have here? The food at the hotel is god-awful." He opened his menu, read it swiftly, and turned it over. "Is this it?"

She glanced at her own menu; it was the same as his. "I'd say you're spoiled for choice. It's a set menu, so for one-and-six— that's one and a half shillings, which is about thirty cents—you get a main, a dessert, and a cup of tea or coffee. You could try the vegetable hot pot, or there's the sausages and mash if you want something a little more filling."

He made a face and scanned the menu again. "I was hoping for a steak, or at least a couple of pork chops. I'm ready to chew off my own arm."

"Well, meat is in short supply here, and has been for a while. You do realize this is an island, don't you? An island that's been under siege for two and a half years?"

"Ha, ha. Explains why everything looks so run-down. Fine,

then." He flagged down a passing Nippy and placed his order, though not before questioning her closely on the composition of the sausages.

"I've heard stories about the sausages over here. Full of sawdust and horsemeat."

The Nippy's bland expression crystallized into a rictus of extreme horror. "I assure you, sir, that our sausages contain nothing but the finest—"

"Please excuse him," Ruby interjected. "He's new in town. I'll set him straight."

"Very good, madam."

"So," Ruby said, turning her attention back to Dan. "You said you wanted my advice on how to get around."

"It was Mitchell who suggested it," he said, his expression reminiscent of a disgruntled adolescent. "Said you'd show me the ropes since you've been here awhile."

"And I'm happy to do so. Let's start with the basics. Do you have a press card yet? No? Then you'll need to head over to the Ministry of Information and get that sorted."

"Sounds straightforward enough."

"You'll also need an identity card and ration books for food and clothing," she continued. "I'm not sure where the nearest police station is, but the staff at your hotel will know. Food in restaurants is off the ration, but if you decide on half or full board at your hotel, you'll need to give them your ration book."

"What do you do?" he asked. "Are you in a hotel?"

"Not anymore. I live with friends and we pool our rations. It's cheaper than eating out all the time."

Their Nippy delivered his supper, which looked and smelled

wonderfully appetizing, and after poking at the sausages several times Dan overcame his initial doubts and began to eat heartily.

"In terms of clearance for your pieces," Ruby plowed on, "you'll have to talk it through with your information officer at the MOI. I have to admit I'm not sure what the process will be for approval."

"I'll need British government approval for pieces being published in an American magazine? You've got to be joking."

"Dan, listen to me. I am not joking. None of us like having our work censored, but it's a fact of life here—and I'll bet a year's pay that it'll soon be a fact of life back home, too. My work goes through the MOI as a matter of course, so the pieces that end up in *The American* have already passed the censor here. Do not, under any circumstances, try to send anything back to New York without approval. That's the fastest way to get your press card pulled—I guarantee it."

"So I'm supposed to work with some government pencil pusher breathing down my neck?"

"There's no point complaining. Just find out what your information officer expects and don't try to do a workaround."

"How do you stand it? All these controls over what you can write—over what you can eat, even."

"I don't have a choice," she said. "So why bother whining? Now, if you don't have any more questions I had better get home."

"You're going to leave me alone to eat my mystery-meat sausage? And drink this sludge they call coffee?"

"I am, but I'll let you in on a little secret before I go. People here have been through a lot. For that matter, I've been through a lot—and I'm not complaining. I'm just stating a fact. In 1940 I lived through fifty-seven straight nights of bombing, just like most of the people sitting in this restaurant. I lost everything I owned when my lodgings were blitzed that December.

"But I'm getting on with it. I'm managing without coffee or chocolate or any one of a hundred little luxuries I used to accept as my due. And I am not going to whine about it, because there's no point. It just wastes time and irritates people." She stood, ready to summon a Nippy and pay her share of the bill. It was getting late, she was exhausted, and she would much rather be at home with Vanessa than sit with Dan Mazur for one more minute.

"Ruby, hold on. I'm sorry. I really am. It's just . . . well, I'm a little nervous, that's all. It's my first time overseas, and I didn't think it would be so different here, you know?"

Ruby sat down, took a deep breath, and reminded herself that she, too, had been nervous and uncertain when she had first arrived in England. "It *is* different," she agreed, "but those are surface things like accents and unfamiliar words and warm beer. The important stuff is the same. The questions you'll ask are the same. 'How are you doing?' 'What do you think?' 'How does this work?' It's really pretty simple, when you boil it down."

"I guess you're right. You know, Ruby—and don't take this the wrong way—but I was surprised as hell when they sent you here. You'd hardly written a thing for the magazine, and you looked like you'd faint if anyone said boo to you. I couldn't figure out why Mitchell chose you."

"Thanks a lot."

"Let me finish," he said, holding up his hands defensively. "That's what I thought *then*. But I've been reading your pieces as they come in, and they're good. They're really good. And, well, I'm glad Mitchell sent you. Even if it's only because that means I know one person in London now."

"You do, and you'll make more friends in no time. Just try to keep a lid on the complaints, at least until you know people better."

By the time she got home, her irritation had faded. She sat in the kitchen with Vanessa and told her everything, and only then did it occur to her that she might have inadvertently stepped on just as many toes upon her arrival in England.

"I do hope I wasn't *that* annoying."

"I doubt it," Vanessa said calmly, "otherwise Bennett or Kaz would have set you straight."

"And Mary," Ruby said, smiling at the memory of her friend's inability to suffer fools gladly. "For that matter, can you imagine if she'd been there tonight?"

"Nothing less than a bloodbath, I expect."

"I don't doubt it. Oh, Vanessa——if you could have seen the look on that poor Nippy's face when Dan accused the restaurant of serving sausages made of horsemeat and sawdust. She didn't know what to do, poor girl."

"For my part I'd have thumped him, and been sacked for my troubles. Oh, well——you set him straight, and in far nicer a way than anyone else would have done. Good for you."

Dispatches from London

by Miss Ruby Sutton

April 14, 1942

. . . People here don't complain, and it's something worth remembering as America gets used to life during

a war. They may whinge, which is their term for letting
off steam, but they don't whine. They just get on with it,
which means darning their socks until they're more darn
than sock, and drinking their tea without sugar or milk
most days, and some days without much tea at all . . .

THE NEXT MORNING dawned bright and fair. The sun was shining, it was warm enough for her to go without a coat for the first
time that year, and best of all, she'd been successful in her quest
for new stockings. Vi had rung up to say that Selfridges had new
stock of both cotton lisle and rayon stockings, and even though
Tuesdays were the busiest day of the week at *PW* Ruby hadn't
hesitated: she'd been waiting when the department store's doors
had opened that morning at eight o'clock, and had managed to
buy three pairs—enough to get her through the summer and
even the autumn if she was careful with them.

With that one critical errand finished, she had left the store
and walked north along Baker Street. It would be faster to take
the Underground from Oxford Circus, but she didn't feel like
shutting herself away from the sun just yet.

It was the first time she'd been in this part of London. There
wasn't anything particularly notable about Baker Street itself,
which was a long and boring run of office buildings, blocks of
flats, and shop fronts. Some of the buildings were so new and
modern, in fact, that they reminded her a little of Manhattan.

She couldn't say, later, what had caught her attention about
the man crossing the street ahead of her. He was dressed in uniform, like so many other men she'd passed already, but there was
something familiar about the way he held himself. It couldn't

be—but it was, for when he turned his head fleetingly to check for traffic, she recognized his profile. Bennett.

She was so surprised that she stopped short, hardly even noticing when a man walking behind bumped into her and, cursing under his breath, brushed past her roughly. Still she stood frozen, her heart racing. He was much too far away for her to catch his attention or even hear her if she called out his name, so she hurried after him, hastening her pace until she was all but running.

Before she could catch up, though, he vanished inside a nondescript building. If she hadn't seen him go in, she'd have walked right past, for there was nothing remarkable about it at all. Nothing, apart from the small plaque by its door. INTER-SERVICES RESEARCH BUREAU, it read. Just as he had once told her.

She stood on the sidewalk for several minutes, trying and failing to think of a single decent excuse to follow him inside. It was an awfully vague name, even for a government department, and nothing she saw about the building, or the people who came and went as she stood there, looked the slightest bit suspicious or even interesting.

Rather than continue to hover outside, which was not only pointless but also a bit pathetic, she continued north to the Underground station at the top of the street and headed off to work. All that day she kept herself busy as they rushed to get the issue out the door and off to the compositors, not letting herself dwell on the questions that clamored for her attention.

Bennett didn't call that afternoon, nor that evening—he didn't even ring up Kaz, which she'd assumed he always did when he was in town. What was he doing in London, when she and all his friends had been led to believe he was somewhere else? And what sort of work was he doing at the Inter-Services Research Bureau? Was he a minor cog in an obscure, bureaucracy-driven ministry? Or was there something more to the bureau than the carefully dull facade of its offices might suggest?

The next morning she finally took a moment to chase down her suspicions. Her first call was to a contact at the Ministry of Labor. "I was wondering if you might put me in touch with someone at the Inter-Services Research Bureau," Ruby explained. "We're thinking of doing a story on the ways that different ministries and departments are reducing waste by working together."

"Ah. Yes. May I take your details and ring you back presently?"

A few hours later her telephone rang, but instead of the woman from the Ministry of Labor, it was the same information officer from the MOI who handled most of her stories. The man was as slippery as an eel, but he'd been reasonably helpful the few times she'd needed to deal with him directly.

"Miss Sutton? Robert Tuttle here. You were asking about the ISRB?"

"Yes. Can you connect me with anyone there?"

"Unfortunately I can't. The ISRB is actually part of a scientific ministry whose workings are classified. You know how it is."

"I guess so."

"What was the story you were working on? I may be able to help you."

"Oh. It was, ah . . . I was hoping to speak to someone about efforts to avoid duplication of efforts between government ministries. How you're freeing up manpower and resources for the war effort by coordinating your efforts. That sort of thing."

"I see—it sounds like a very interesting story. Well, here's what I can tell you off the top of my head . . ."

TWO WEEKS LATER, Ruby was waiting for a press conference to start at Macmillan Hall in Senate House, which was the headquarters for the Ministry of Information's press operations in London. She was early, for the press conference on Churchill's visit to Washington and his meetings there with the president wasn't due to begin for another twenty minutes. That left her with enough time to scribble down a few questions and read through the memos she'd picked up on her way in.

She was vaguely aware when the chairs behind her were taken up by a pair of men, one American, one English, but as she recognized neither of their voices, she didn't bother to turn around and greet them.

"D'you think it was the crew from Baker Street who got Heydrich?" the American whispered.

"No way of knowing," came an equally furtive reply. "I'm certainly not about to ask."

"Can you imagine?" said the first man, who had a vague sort of transatlantic lilt to his accent. Either he'd lived in England for a while, or was affecting it to better fit in. "'May I ask if anyone from the Inter-Services Research Bureau was involved in the planning and commission of Reinhard Heydrich's assassination?' Heads would roll for sure."

Ruby couldn't believe what she was hearing. Surely they were mistaken.

"I heard a new cover name the other day. Ministry of Agriculture and Fisheries," said the Englishman.

"That one's new to me, too. There's the Inter-Services

Research Bureau, the Inter-Services Signals Unit, the Joint Technical Board, the Ministry of Economic Warfare . . ."

"Have you ever been inside?"

"Their HQ on Baker Street? Not for all the tea in China," said the American. "Have you seen some of the types who come and go from there? Give me the chills."

"I'm with you there. You know, I did hear from one fellow— he works at arm's length from them, but knows just enough to get himself in real trouble, if you know what I mean. He told me they're sent out with nothing more than a cyanide tablet to do themselves in, and a garrote to take care of anyone who gets in their way."

She couldn't breathe. What they were saying . . . it all made sense now. Horrible, terrible sense.

"Thank God we have them on our side."

"I suppose. Still, it—oh, right. Better leave off for now. You never know who might be listening."

Ruby didn't take any notes during the press conference, nor did she ask any questions. For the rest of the day, and the night that followed, she could think of nothing else. Nothing but trying to assemble the puzzle pieces of what she'd heard. Assuming what the men behind her had said was true, and further assuming that Bennett was actually a part of it, what was she to do?

Nothing. As dawn came, as a new day began, she had her answer. And she'd known it all along. If she were to keep asking questions, keep burrowing away in an effort to exhume the truth, she would endanger Bennett. She might even cause a terrible breach in security.

It wasn't a question of doing her job or exposing the truth or even getting her hands on a great story. None of that mattered, not set against Bennett's safety and that of his colleagues. The truth would come out one day, but when it did, the story would be told by other writers. And that was a price she was more than willing to pay.

CHAPTER TWENTY

October 1942

I t had been a week since Mrs. Roosevelt's arrival in London, and Ruby, along with every other journalist following the first lady on her goodwill tour of Great Britain, was half dead with fatigue. The woman got up at the crack of dawn, no matter how busy she'd been the day before, and was a perpetual motion machine from the moment her eyes opened.

Yesterday had been a blur, and today promised to be no better. Kaz had told Ruby not to worry if she couldn't keep up; as long as she and Frank captured a representative sample of Mrs. Roosevelt's activities, that would be more than enough for a story. But that seemed like giving in, and she couldn't stand the idea of pulling back and missing something truly newsworthy. The day before, for instance, the president's wife had not only gone to visit U.S. Air Force personnel at Bovingdon airfield, but she'd also crawled into the cockpit of a B-17, no small endeavor for a tall and stoutly built lady in her fifties.

It had been an effort, but Ruby had managed to drag herself out of bed on time and to work by just past eight o'clock. It was

Saturday, which meant a half day of work and then home for a long, long nap. Unless, of course, Mrs. Roosevelt had other plans.

Evelyn, who was never late and never anything less than immaculately dressed, greeted Ruby with an understanding smile. "This just arrived for you," she said, and handed her a small envelope.

"Thanks." She looked it over, but there was no return address. "Wonder what it could be?"

"Go on and open it."

30 October 1942

Dear Miss Sutton,

The pleasure of your company is requested by Mrs. Eleanor Roosevelt at an informal luncheon for American journalists to be held tomorrow, October 31st, at 11:30 A.M. at the American embassy, 1 Grosvenor Square.

Yours sincerely,
Doreen Wolfort
per Malvina Thompson

"Goodness. It's an invitation to a luncheon with Mrs. Roosevelt. *Today.*"

Ruby looked down at the outfit she'd chosen, which was serviceable but by no means attractive. Her shoes needed a good polish, too, and she'd worn the oldest and plainest of her hats.

"Will I do? Or should I go home and change?"

Evelyn shook her head. "I wouldn't bother. I don't mean to insult Mrs. Roosevelt, but she isn't what you'd call a snappy dresser. Do you think she'll care? Or even notice, for that matter?"

"I doubt it. And it's sure to be a cast of thousands. If I'm lucky, I'll get close enough to shake her hand, but no more than that."

It wasn't quite a cast of thousands, in the end, but the reception room at the embassy was packed full of journalists, nearly all of them unfamiliar to Ruby. Of course she'd only been at *The American* for a matter of months before moving to London, and since then she hadn't socialized with other journalists beyond her modest circle of colleagues. With the exception of her dinner with Dan Mazur, she hadn't spent any time with other Americans—not unless you counted jostling shoulders in a press scrum.

Today they were all on their best behavior, all doing their best to look responsible and sober. It didn't change the fact that nearly every guest there would have happily pushed his or her own grandmother in front of an Underground train for the chance of a lively quote from Mrs. Roosevelt.

A door opened at the far end of the room, the ensuing commotion offering ample proof of the first lady's arrival. A flock of aides came forward, some in civilian dress, others in Red Cross uniforms, and marshaled the guests into a long receiving line that stretched nearly the length of the room. It was that, or risk having Mrs. Roosevelt trampled.

Ruby was near the end of the line, not having been audacious or desperate enough to insert herself closer to its beginning, and as the minutes ticked by she began to worry that Mrs. Roosevelt, or one of her aides, would decide that enough was enough and it was past time she moved on to her next event.

And then the great lady was before her, much taller than Ruby had expected, and she was wearing the same shabby coat she always had on, with an enormous fox-fur stole slung around her neck and a truly awful hat, a round of dark velour that sat on top of her head like a forlorn and very wrinkled pancake. And Mrs. Roosevelt was shaking her hand, the hand of a girl who had no right to be in her presence, let alone meeting the most famous woman in the United States, and she was introducing herself to the first lady.

"Ruby Sutton, ma'am. I'm a staff writer with *Picture Weekly* here in London."

"A pleasure to meet you, Miss Sutton," Mrs. Roosevelt said, her homely face transformed by her smile.

People were always going on about her looks, and it was true that she was far from beautiful—until she smiled. Her smile was so warm, so entirely genuine, that it left Ruby feeling as if the first lady had actually enjoyed meeting her. As if that instant of connection between the two of them had been the high point of Mrs. Roosevelt's day.

The next person in line received the same, equally heartfelt smile, and the next, until the receiving line was finished and the boldest of the guests surged forward around the first lady, and soon all Ruby could see of her was the top of that terrible hat.

With that kind of crowd, there was no chance of getting close enough to even hear what Mrs. Roosevelt had to say, let alone speak with her. And it did mean she and the remaining guests had first crack at the luncheon buffet. The food wasn't much to speak of, little more than corned beef sandwiches and pickled vegetables, but it would get her through the day.

She scanned the crowd, but didn't see Dan Mazur. As far as she knew, he was still in London. Perhaps he felt a luncheon with the first lady, as opposed to the president himself, wasn't worth his time. Perhaps he had gotten turned around on his way to Grosvenor Square. This last thought left her smiling, but only until she happened to glance down at her watch. It was a quarter past twelve, and at twelve thirty she was meant to be at a press conference for British magazine writers, again hosted by Mrs. Roosevelt.

She wasn't late, not yet, for the guest of honor was still standing on the far side of the reception room. She still had time, assuming of course the press conference wasn't miles and miles away. Unlike the first lady, she would have to travel by Underground or bus to get to her next appointment.

Ruby returned her plate to the buffet table, which had been all but denuded of its modest lunch, and ran into the hall. She dug through her bag, trying and failing to unearth the memo she'd received earlier that week with details for the press conference. It had been there yesterday, so what had happened to it since?

It wasn't there. She would have to ring up the office, and hope the memo was somewhere on her desk. Failing that, it might be in her room at home, except that Vanessa was probably out doing her volunteer work at the hospital, and Jessie was so hard of hearing that she would only hear the phone ringing if she was standing next to it.

"Drat, drat, drat," she muttered, only just resisting the temptation to hurl her handbag and its incomplete contents down the hall. "Of all the days . . ."

"May I help you?" came a pleasant voice. Ruby turned to see a group of women approaching, two in Red Cross uniforms and one in civilian clothes.

"Sorry about that," Ruby said, smiling a little sheepishly. "I'm meant to be at the press conference for Mrs. Roosevelt that starts soon, but I lost the memo with the address. I could just kick myself right now."

"Isn't that for British journalists?" one of the Red Cross women asked, not unpleasantly.

"It is, but I work for *Picture Weekly*. I've a foot on both sides of the pond, I guess you could say."

The woman in civilian dress, her face vaguely familiar, looked up from the day diary she'd been examining. "You can come with me," she offered, and extended her hand for Ruby to shake. "I'm Malvina Thompson."

"Oh, ah, thank you, Miss Thompson," Ruby stammered, recognition dawning. "That's really nice of you to offer."

Miss Thompson. Tommy Thompson. Mrs. Roosevelt's personal secretary, press secretary, and chief aide, all rolled into one terrifyingly capable person. Miss Thompson, who had just offered to give Ruby a ride across town.

"It's no trouble at all, since we're going there, too. The ladies here will show you out to the car—I'll be right behind you."

Ruby dutifully followed the women in uniform outside, to a parking area at the side of the embassy where an enormous black car was waiting. Guarding it were two extremely serious-looking soldiers in U.S. Army uniforms.

"Can't let you go any further, miss."

"It's all right, Private Dunn," said one of the Red Cross ladies. "Miss Thompson is giving her a lift."

"I see. We'll need to see your identification, miss."

Ruby dug in her bag again, and fortunately was able to unearth her pocketbook right away. "Here's my press card, and I've also got my identification card." She prayed he wouldn't ask to see anything else, for her passport and birth certificate had both been lost when the Manchester had been blitzed.

"These look fine. In you go, Miss Sutton. Won't be long."

She thanked Private Dunn and the Red Cross women, and got into the car. The interior was huge, far bigger than a black cab. It seemed a bit bold to take one of the forward-facing seats, so she pulled down one of the jump seats and perched on it, wondering how long Miss Thompson was going to be.

The car door opened. Ruby was very glad she had taken the jump seat, for Miss Thompson was preceded into the car by Mrs. Roosevelt herself.

"How are we for time, Tommy?"

"Only a few minutes off the mark, Mrs. R. We'll make it up at the press conference. Oh—this is Miss Sutton from *Picture Weekly*. We're giving her a ride."

"Good, good. I'm sorry we didn't have more time to talk, Miss Sutton."

"Oh, no. I mean, there's no need to apologize, ma'am. You're the busiest woman in England right now."

"Ha! Well, I don't know about that, but I'm glad you understand."

If Ruby had been dazzled during their introduction back at the embassy, she was utterly star-struck now. Of course she noticed the aspects of Mrs. Roosevelt's appearance that critics were always going on about: the protuberant teeth, the unfashionable clothing, even her high-pitched and somewhat singsong voice. She noticed, and then she instantly forgot, because those superficial details faded away to nothing when set against the things that did matter: the brightness of Mrs. Roosevelt's gaze, the warmth of her regard, the acuity of her interest in the person before her.

Only then did it dawn on Ruby that a heaven-sent opportunity had just fallen into her lap, and that she would be no kind of journalist if she didn't pull herself together and at least attempt to pose a few questions.

"Have you had a busy day so far?" she asked.

"Fairly busy, I'd say. Tommy?"

"Oh, busy enough, Mrs. R."

"We started with Mr. Winant, who took me to see a photo exhibit. Very interesting—showed the damage done by the RAF to targets in occupied Europe. Then I had a visit from the president and foreign minister of Czechoslovakia, and then a short visit with the Dutch queen. I thought it was very kind of her to come into London to see me. Don't you agree, Tommy?"

Mrs. Roosevelt plunged on, not waiting for an answer from her secretary, who was busily annotating a stack of documents. "Then we were off to the British Red Cross to see parcels being made up for prisoners of war. I am concerned that the parcels are only going to men whose families can help pay for them. Would you make a note of that, Tommy, so I can follow up? Last of all was our little luncheon just now. Did you get anything to eat?" she asked Ruby, motherly concern animating her face.

"Oh, yes, ma'am. Thank you."

"So now we've got this press conference, which should be

interesting, and then I'm off to see the Duchess of Kent, poor woman. I wish I could stay with her longer. And then what?" she asked, turning to Tommy.

"We said we'd visit some of the YWCA centers in London, and there's a Halloween dance for servicemen after that."

Eight engagements in one day alone, with barely a moment to sit or eat or even gulp down a cup of coffee.

"I honestly don't know how you do it, Mrs. Roosevelt," Ruby admitted. "We're all of us—the press who've been covering your visit, that is—we're just about to fall over trying to keep up with you."

This provoked an especially broad smile from the first lady. "There's no secret, you know. You simply get up and start your day and keep going. You don't get tired because you don't have time to be tired. If I could, I'd do more, but Tommy won't let me."

"It's for your own good," Miss Thompson said, not looking up from her papers.

Ignoring this, Mrs. Roosevelt turned back to Ruby. "How did you end up working for a British newsmagazine, Miss Sutton?"

"I was seconded, I guess you could say, from *The American*. They wanted someone in London, and *Picture Weekly* needed another staff writer."

"Do you still write for *The American*?"

"I do, although they don't use as many of my stories as they used to. Mainly because they've another staff writer over here now. But that's fine. *PW* keeps me busy enough."

"How long have you been in England?"

"Since the summer of 1940, ma'am."

"So you've been here through thick and thin," Mrs. Roosevelt observed.

"Through the Blitz? Yes. It was awful, just awful, but I'm glad I was here. It was . . . I'm not sure how to put it. A privilege? I mean, how many people get to witness something so extraordinary, in ways that are both bad and good?"

"What did you see that was good?"

"Nothing about the Blitz itself was good—I don't mean that at all. I guess I mean the way people reacted to it. The courage I saw every day. No matter how bad it had been the night before, people would get up and go to work. Even if they had to climb through wreckage to do it. Even if they had to walk for miles. I saw people working in offices and shops with the windows blown out, and they'd find a way to joke about it. I remember one sign in a shop that said, 'Even More Open for Business,' and this was a place with its windows just gone, even the front door gone, but they'd opened and were working as if it was a normal day."

"You say this as though you weren't doing the same thing yourself," Mrs. Roosevelt observed.

"Well, the *Picture Weekly* offices escaped any real damage. We had a few windows shattered, but that was it."

"You lived through the same nights of bombing, didn't you?"

"Yes, ma'am."

"Was your home damaged at all?"

"It was. I was living in the Manchester hotel, but it burned down at the end of 1940. It was the same night that St. Paul's came so close to being destroyed."

"Yes," Mrs. Roosevelt said, nodding gravely. "I remember that night."

"A friend found me a place to stay right away. I've been very happy with the family who took me in, so I can't complain."

"I think you are a very brave young woman," Mrs. Roosevelt said decisively.

"With the greatest of respect, ma'am, I'm no braver than anyone else," Ruby insisted. "I came to London to report on the war, and I knew it would be dangerous. So I can hardly object when danger came calling."

"Well said, Miss Sutton."

"Thank you, Mrs. Roosevelt. The thing is, though, if anything happens to me, the world won't stop spinning. Far from it. But you take a lot of risks by traveling overseas and working yourself to the bone, and there are some people who say it would be better for you to stay at home, or that you should confine yourself to the sort of good works first ladies have always done. What would you say to such people?" Ruby readied her notebook and pencil, hoping and praying to get the sort of quote that journalists across England would faint over.

"Well, of course it's hard work. Anything that is truly worth doing is going to be hard and difficult and even dangerous at times. But peace will only be won with sacrifice and hard work, and I believe I must set an example for others to follow."

"May I ask what you think of England and its people?"

"I hold them in the highest regard. I can't help but admire their sense of obligation in fulfilling their duties, for I see it everywhere I go. From the ordinary man on the street to the king himself, I have observed, in my time here, an unswerving devotion to duty, no matter the cost to self. And I firmly believe such devotion to duty will win the war."

"We're here, Mrs. R," Miss Thompson observed.

"Good, good. Did you get enough from me, Miss Sutton?"

"Oh, yes, ma'am. More than enough."

The car drew to a gentle stop; outside, a crowd of reporters and photographers already lay in wait. Mrs. Roosevelt sat up straight, adjusted her awful hat, and shook Ruby's hand with the vigor of a lumberjack. "It has been a pleasure speaking with you, Miss Sutton. I shall look out for your work."

"Thank you, Mrs. Roosevelt, and thank you as well for allowing me to come along."

"That was Miss Thompson's doing. Onward, Tommy?"

"And upward, Mrs. R," her faithful aide replied. The car door opened, the crowd surged forward, and Mrs. Roosevelt was off, striding forward, shaking hands and dazzling everyone with the glow of her attention.

"Are you coming, miss?" Private Dunn asked, coming round to peer inside the car.

"Oh, yes—sorry. Was feeling a little bowled over. Is she always like that?"

"Always. Never forgets anyone's name, always has a smile. Always doing nice little things for us. 'How are you today, Private Dunn?' she said to me this morning. 'Have you had a letter from your wife this week?'"

"I'd always thought the stories about her . . . well, they seemed too good to be true."

"And now?"

"Now? Now I feel like doing cartwheels down the street!"

"You do that, Miss Sutton—but wait until after the press conference. And you'd better hurry on in. Time, tide, and Mrs. Roosevelt wait for no one."

Dispatches from London
by Miss Ruby Sutton
November 3, 1942

It's a strange thing to sit in a car across from the most famous woman in the world and have the gift of her attention for a few minutes. She's the busiest woman in the world, too, and she does more in one average day than most of us manage in a week. If ever a woman were fitted for her place in history, our First Lady belongs to this time and this place . . .

CHAPTER TWENTY-ONE

June 1943

Ruby's exclusive interview with Mrs. Roosevelt, which was greeted with surprise and not a little jealousy by her colleagues at rival publications, quickly led to bigger and better things. On the strength of it, she was granted interviews with Clementine Churchill, who was lovely; Nancy Astor, who was awful; and Dame Myra Hess, the organizer of the classical music concerts at the National Gallery, who welcomed Ruby into her home near Hampstead Heath, performed an impromptu private concert of Beethoven and Schumann, and sent her home with a jar of homemade quince preserves.

Just that afternoon she'd interviewed the Marchioness of Reading, a friend of Mrs. Roosevelt's and the formidably capable founder of the WVS. While perfectly friendly, Lady Reading had clearly been a woman with a purpose, and that was to talk at length on the mission, current work, and long-term aims of the Women's Voluntary Service. Ruby had filled nearly an entire notebook with her shorthand scribblings.

She'd do her best to interpret them tomorrow; for now, all she wanted was a quick listen to the nine o'clock news before bed. She had just switched on the wireless when a knock sounded at the front door.

"Were you expecting anyone?" she asked Vanessa.

"No. Perhaps it's one of the neighbors. Would you mind seeing who it is?"

The knock sounded again, louder and more insistent. Whoever could it be?

She opened the door, feeling more than a little apprehensive, and discovered two men waiting on the stoop. One, overweight and balding, was dressed in civilian clothes. The other, his features blandly unremarkable, wore the uniform of a British army captain.

"Hello," she said. "May I help you?"

The man in civvies spoke first. "I'm Detective Inspector Vickers of the Metropolitan Police." He didn't introduce his companion. "We need to speak to Miss Roberta Anne Sutton."

"I'm Ruby Sutton," she said, her insides twisting with abject, piercing fear. They had come to tell her about Bennett. They had come to tell her that he had been killed.

"We need to ask you some questions about your reasons for being in this country."

Sweet relief—and then apprehension, chill and clammy, began to claw an icy path up her spine. "Wo-would you like to come in?"

The man in uniform took a step forward. "You are being detained under the provisions of the Defense of the Realm Act. You need to come with us."

"What on earth is going on?" Vanessa had come forward to

stand behind Ruby. "I am Lady Tremaine, and I demand to see your warrant card."

Detective Vickers offered it to her, and once she'd inspected it, accepted the card back without comment.

"What is this all about? Why does Ruby need to come with you?"

"We're not at liberty to say," the man in uniform said. "You have one minute to fetch your coat and bag, Miss Sutton."

"I'll get them," Vanessa said. She returned seconds later. "What should I do? How can I help?"

Bennett could be anywhere, and even if he were in London, he might be unable to intervene, constrained as he was by the secrecy of his war work. There was only one other person who might be able to help. "Call Kaz."

"Where are you taking Ruby? I insist that you tell me." Vanessa was using her most imperious voice, the voice that made ordinary people freeze in their tracks, but the men ignored her. Already they had taken hold of Ruby's shoulders and were leading her down the steps.

"If you cooperate, we won't need to restrain you," Detective Vickers said. Not wishing to be manacled, Ruby walked obediently between them, and made no protest when they forced her inside the waiting police car. Squashed between the two men, unable to see where they were going, she had no choice but to endure. If she were compliant, if she did as they told her, perhaps someone would decide to explain what was happening.

The faint glow of a police station's blue light, dimmed for the blackout, eventually heralded their destination. The car turned left into a courtyard, stopped suddenly, and then she was hustled up a dark flight of stairs, in through a pair of double doors, and along a deserted corridor.

A door opened. Her handbag was torn from her arm. She was pushed forward, into a small room made bright by a single, swaying lightbulb. The door clanged shut behind her, a lock clicked into place, and she was alone.

The cell was smaller than her cabin on the *Sinbad* had been, with no fixtures apart from a narrow bench along one wall. She sat, her knees suddenly unable to bear her weight. Would Vanessa know how to find Kaz so late at night? Did she even have his telephone number?

She'd taken off her wristwatch to help Jessie with the dishes and had forgotten to put it back on, and of course there was no clock in the cell. Time stretched thin, and after a while—it might have been half an hour or half the night—she began to feel very tired. Deciding that she might as well sleep while she could, she took off her coat and cardigan, folded the latter into a pillow, and, stretching out on the bench, covered herself with her coat.

It was cold in the cell, though, and the light was so very bright, and she couldn't stop her fears from burrowing a poisonous path into her heart. So she sat up again, shivering, and waited for whatever might come next.

The door opened suddenly, swinging wide on screeching hinges. "Get up," Detective Vickers said. "Come with me."

Gathering her things, she followed him down the hall and into a larger room. The army officer from earlier was seated at a large table.

"Sit down, Miss Schreiber," he said, indicating a chair on its opposite site.

Ruby froze. It had been years since she had heard that name.

"Didn't you hear me? Sit down."

Detective Vickers took his place next to the unnamed officer. "It has come to our attention that you are in this country under false pretenses. We believe that you knowingly entered Great Britain with the aid of counterfeit documents on the second of July, 1940, for purposes yet to be determined—"

"My passport was genuine," she broke in. "My employer handled the application process."

"Really? Do you have it in your possession for us to examine?"

"No. It was destroyed in the Blitz. My lodgings burned down at the end of 1940."

Detective Vickers frowned, and then scribbled something in a notebook he'd pulled from his coat pocket. "I see. Do you have any other supporting documents? A birth certificate, for instance?"

"No," she admitted. "My birth certificate was destroyed as well."

"So you have nothing to prove that you are Roberta Anne Schreiber, alias Ruby Sutton, formerly of New York City?"

"Not as such."

"And the name of Schreiber?" the army officer prompted. "Is it familiar to you?"

"Yes," she said, although she knew it would damn her. "It was my birth name."

"So Sutton is your married name?"

"No. I . . . I changed it."

"Because Schreiber is a German name," the officer stated.

"No—I mean, yes, it is a German name, but that isn't the reason I changed it. I changed it long before I came to England."

Again it was the officer who spoke. "With the intention of implanting yourself at an English newsmagazine? And thereby finding a way to place false information, or possibly encoded information, in the stories you wrote?"

"What? Oh, my God—*no*. Of course not. I changed it because I thought I'd have a better chance of getting a job if I had a more American-sounding name."

"Did you change it officially?" Detective Vickers asked. "Presumably there are mechanisms for making such changes in the United States, just as there are here."

"No. I mean . . . it never occurred to me. And so what if I changed my name? Plenty of people do. You aren't chasing down Cary Grant or John Wayne, are you?"

"If we discovered they had provided false documents for the purposes of obtaining a passport and entering this country, we would," said the officer. "Because that's what you did. Your passport, as registered upon your entry in 1940, was under the name of Roberta Anne Sutton, born in New York City on July 12, 1916. Is that how it was made out?"

She nodded.

"And since you have already admitted your change of name was not formalized in any fashion, you must have obtained your passport by providing the United States government with a false birth certificate."

He had her there. "Yes," she admitted.

"And you did so in order to obtain a passport and gain entry into this country."

"Yes, but only so I might take up the job I had been offered.

They'd have given it to someone else if I'd told Mr. Mitchell the truth."

Detective Vickers and the officer exchanged knowing glances. "By 'truth,' do you mean the truth about your name?" the officer asked. "Or were there more lies?"

Detective Vickers leaned across the table, his brow creased in a forbidding frown. "I must warn you, Miss Schreiber, that you are on extremely shaky ground here. Anything less than complete honesty—"

"I lied on my job application to *The American*. I said I attended Sarah Lawrence College, but I didn't. And I grew up in New Jersey, not New York."

"Where in New Jersey, Miss Schreiber?"

"St. Mary's Orphan Asylum. In Newark." This provoked a further round of note-taking.

"I only did it so I could get a job," she added, even though it was clear they weren't interested in hearing her excuses. "I tried again and again, but no one would hire me. If I'd had a more American name, or if I'd had a better upbringing, they might have considered me, even without a college degree. But all of it, together, put me at the bottom of the list of candidates every time."

"Is your employer here in England aware of these fabrications?" Detective Vickers asked.

"No—of course not!"

"We'll have to call him in. See what he knows."

If this was calculated to break her composure, it was working. "He knows nothing," she insisted, her voice rising. "He has nothing to do with this, nor do any of my other friends. Am I . . . may I please speak with a lawyer?"

"No," said the officer.

"So what are you going to do? Keep me here indefinitely?"

"Only until we decide what to do with you," he said, his tone indicating an utter lack of interest in her well-being. "If you are deemed to be an ongoing security risk, you'll be sent to an internment camp. If not, you'll be deported to the United States, presumably to face criminal proceedings there."

She was done for. Slumping in the chair, Ruby covered her face with her hands and tried to gather together what was left of her dignity. She would not cry. No matter what, she would recover her composure, and she would not cry.

There was a knock at the door, and Detective Vickers got up to answer it. He went outside, shutting the door behind him, and a heated conversation ensued with whoever had been at the door. A minute later, the army officer got up from his chair and joined the others in the hall. The conversation continued, still muffled enough that she couldn't make out the least part of it.

The door opened again. The officer stood at the threshold, his gaze fixed at a point on the far wall. "You're free to go," he said.

"What? I don't understand."

"It has been determined that you pose no threat to public safety or to national security. If you will come with me, I'll have your bag returned to you."

She got up, still not quite grasping what had taken place. He stood back as she passed him to leave the room, his lip curling in disgust.

". . . friends . . . high places . . . ." he muttered.

"Pardon me? I didn't hear what you said."

"Nothing. Come on."

Someone handed over her bag, which had been rifled through thoroughly, and Detective Vickers, his expression just as disapproving as the officer's, showed her to the station's side door.

Not wishing to linger, just in case they developed second thoughts about letting her go, Ruby ran down the steps and away from the station, not stopping until she was at least a hundred yards away. She was free of them—but she also had no idea of where she was.

CHAPTER TWENTY-TWO

Ruby walked on through the dark, hoping to chance upon a rare street sign that hadn't been removed for the duration, but the nearest intersection was barren of information. Perhaps she ought to keep moving. She might come across a public house that was still open, or some recognizable landmark.

"There you are," came a familiar voice. She turned, squinting in the gloom, and was just able to make out the figure of a man, standing next to a motorcycle, only a few yards from the next corner.

"Who is it?" she called out.

"You know very well who it is," the man said. She took a step forward, then another, and finally his face emerged from the shadows. Bennett, his expression set and grim.

"How did you know where to find me?" she asked.

"That may be the stupidest thing you have ever said. Come on. I'm here to take you home."

"On the back of *that*?"

"Yes. I don't have a car, and I didn't have time to flounder around looking for a cab. There's nothing to it—just hop on."

"What if I fall off?"

"I think that's the least of your problems right now. Get on. *Now*."

He'd already kicked back the motorcycle's side stand and had swung a leg over the machine. Its engine roared to life, all but deafening her.

She climbed up behind him, and it was just as unpleasant as she'd feared. Sitting astride the machine left her feeling horribly exposed, her skirt riding so high that the tops of her stockings were visible. Despite the warmth of his back, for she was pressed right against him, she was chilled through in seconds.

He was a precise and careful driver, navigating the darkened streets with ease, even though the shuttered headlamp of his motorcycle illuminated little more than a narrow yard of road in front of them. "Almost there," he called back after they had traveled for what felt like miles and miles, and still she hadn't been able to make out any recognizable landmarks.

He turned onto a narrow side street and braked almost immediately. If they were near Vanessa's, it was a part of the neighborhood she'd yet to visit.

"Get down," he told her, and switched off the ignition. He hauled the motorcycle onto its center stand and then, grasping her arm, steered her back to the main street and along for nearly half a block. He stopped at a modest entryway next to a cobbler's shop, unlocked the door, and motioned her forward. "Upstairs," he said flatly.

She walked up one flight of stairs, then another, and then he was brushing past her to unlock a second door.

"Where are we?" she asked.

"Gray's Inn Road. This is my flat." He motioned for her to

enter. "You and I need to talk, but I don't want to do it in front of Vanessa, and we can't talk in public."

He switched on the lights, revealing a small and sparsely furnished sitting room. There was no art on the walls, no shelves full of books, no knickknacks or photographs.

"How long have you lived here?" she asked.

"Ages. But I'm hardly ever here. Most of my things are stored at the house in Edenbridge. Do you want anything to drink?"

"No."

"Fine. I'd better ring up Vanessa. Assuming she hasn't died of fright already."

A bottle of Scotch and several glasses stood on the room's lone table, which also held a telephone. He dialed with one hand, the telephone receiver cradled in the crook of his neck, even as he poured a healthy measure of spirits into one of the glasses.

"Vanessa? It's Bennett. She's fine. I'll have her home to you soon—she'll explain everything to you then. You don't have to worry. Yes, I promise. Yes. Good night."

He hung up the telephone, took a healthy swig of whiskey, and finally turned to face her, his dark eyes glittering with emotion.

"Are you angry?" she asked, though she knew full well what his answer would be.

"Seething." He downed the remainder of his whiskey in one long swallow. Returning to the bottle of Scotch, he poured another inch of spirits into his glass, then crossed the room to sit on the lone armchair.

"Why?" he asked. "Just tell me why you never thought to tell me the truth. Make me understand."

"Of course you don't understand. You grew up surrounded

by people who loved you. I had no one. After my mother died, there wasn't one single person in this world who cared whether I lived or died. Not one."

He motioned to the sofa. "Sit. And tell me more."

She perched on the sofa and took a deep breath. Where to begin? "My mother was a maid in a hotel in Atlantic City," she said at last. "I don't know who my father was. She never told me his name. And I was so young when she died . . . I barely remember her, to be honest."

"What happened to her?" he asked, his voice softening.

"She died a few years after the war. In one of the later flu epidemics. I was five. I guess I was sick, too, but I don't remember it."

"Had you no other family?"

She shook her head. "No one. Or no one who would admit to it. I was sent to St. Mary's Orphan Asylum in Newark."

"A regular Jane Eyre," he observed.

"Not really. St. Mary's was no Lowood. Yes, I've read the book—don't look so surprised."

"What was it like there?"

"The nuns were decent, apart from one who hated me on sight. Sister Benedicta was awful, but most of the others were kind enough. I was never made to stand on a stool for hours." This brought a thin smile to his face, but it vanished with her next words. "We were hungry most of the time, and cold, too. Our uniforms were hardly more than rags."

"What about school? Did you receive any sort of an education?" he asked.

"We got the bare minimum. I guess there didn't seem much point to it, since we were all sent out to work when we were fourteen. Mainly as domestic servants, although some girls went to clothing factories. I was lucky."

"In what way?"

"I was sent to work as a live-in maid. The family took no notice of me. As long as I got my work done, they didn't care what I did in the evenings. So I saved up my wages and started attending classes at night. It took me four years to earn my diploma from secretarial school. As soon as I was done, I moved to New York and found work as a stenographer."

"You didn't remain one."

"No. When I was at secretarial college, I met a woman who worked at a magazine, and she just loved her work. When she talked about it, I could see myself at a magazine or newspaper. Writing stories for a living. Doing work that I really enjoyed."

"But? I sense there's a 'but' at work here."

"I couldn't get my foot in the door. I applied for so many positions, but I hardly ever got a response. The few times I did hear back, they said I needed experience first. I think that was just their way of turning me down.

"Only once did I get as far as an interview. It was for a position as an editorial assistant at a woman's magazine. There was another girl waiting at the same time as me. She didn't have any experience in journalism, but she had a college degree. And she had a plain American name. Emily Miller—I still remember it. Of course she got the job. And it made me wonder if that was all I needed. A different name.

"So I did it. I changed my name and said I had a degree I hadn't earned. It was wrong. I knew it then, as I know it now. But I did what I felt I had to do at the time. Can you say you would have done any differently?"

A long pause. "No. I can't."

"It was a lie I told once, after five years of dead ends, and haven't repeated since. I had hoped I could leave it behind—the lie, that is. I figured that if I ever needed to look for another job, I'd just put down my years at *The American* and that would be enough."

"Lies are dangerous things. They'll eat you up from the inside eventually."

"Really, Bennett? *Really?* Because you are the last person who should be lecturing me about the importance of truthfulness. Your whole *life* is a lie—"

"Hold on—"

"Do you honestly think any of us believe that you're a pencil pusher in some obscure ministry? I've heard the talk, you know. About all the false names and made-up departments, and how you're really all a pack of—"

"*Stop*. Just stop. You know I can't talk about it. To begin with, if I did, and if I were found out, I would end up in prison for a very long time. That is not an exaggeration designed to make me look mysterious and dashing—it's the truth. But it's also the case that I took an oath, a solemn and binding oath, to keep quiet about my work. And that's what I have done—I have kept quiet. I haven't lied to you, not once. Name one instance."

"You say you work at the Inter-Services Research Bureau."

"Which is one name, among many, for the branch of the government that employs me. More than that I cannot say. Anything else?"

"That time you had a black eye and scratches all over your face. You said you'd been knocked off your motorcycle by a tree branch. Is that what happened?"

"Yes. That's how I was injured. And since we're being honest with one another, I will admit that I have been hurt other times over the course of the war, but never seriously. Never badly enough that I was in hospital for more than a few days."

"Have you ever left England? As part of the work you are doing?"

"Yes."

"Is it dangerous? Could you be killed?"

"Yes. But that's true of any soldier or officer in this war."

"Were you the reason they let me go?"

Rather than meet her eyes, he focused on the dregs of whiskey in his glass. "Not directly," he said. "I've a few well-connected friends, that's all. I vouched for you, and that was enough."

"But why? You said earlier that you were angry—why didn't you just let them deport me, or send me to an internment camp?"

He looked up, his expression aghast. "Do you think so little of me, so little of our friendship, that I'd allow such a thing to happen? I was—I *am*—angry with you, but not because you lied about your name and education, and came to England with the help of doctored papers. I don't care a fig about that. I'm angry because you endangered your future, your entire career, over a few silly lies. If only you'd told me, Ruby, I would have helped. I would have believed you."

"I know," she said. "I want to believe. I want to have friends I trust. It's only that . . . I was alone for a long time. I learned to be careful. And it's a hard habit to break. Can you at least see that?"

"I can. But can you also see that I am your friend? That I care about what happens to you?"

It wasn't a protestation of love, not really, but it tore at her heart all the same. "I can," she said at last.

"Good. I'd better get you home."

"I guess Vanessa will be waiting."

"At the front door, if not on the stoop. And you need to know—I wasn't talking out of school just now. I *will* help. It shouldn't be too difficult to get a copy of your original birth certificate sent over, and once you have that, you can apply for a new passport from your embassy here. I'll make sure there are no roadblocks."

"So I'm back to being Ruby Schreiber? It doesn't even feel like my real name anymore."

"I don't see why you can't keep writing as Ruby Sutton—your nom de plume, if you will. Although Schreiber *is* a fitting last name for someone in your profession."

"Really? I don't speak a word of—"

"It means 'writer,'" he said with a fleeting smile. "And that is why it fits."

CHAPTER TWENTY-THREE

s Ruby had hoped, but hadn't dared to presume, Vanessa's reaction was comforting, loving, and entirely lacking in judgment. She was also angrier than Ruby had ever seen her over the incivility of the arresting officials.

"I feel ill thinking about what might have happened. What if we hadn't been friends with Bennett? You'd still be stuck with those awful men and we'd be completely in the dark."

"To be honest, I feel guilty about it," Ruby said. "No—don't say I shouldn't feel that way. I do. I ought to. I did break the law, even though it wasn't for the reasons they said."

"But the way they treated you—"

"That's why I'm feeling guilty—I had a friend who intervened. What about people who don't have a Bennett? People who are dragged off in the night and interrogated, and if they don't supply the right answers are sent to an internment camp or put on a ship to Canada or Australia. What happens to them?"

"I think you've worried enough for tonight, and for many nights to come," Vanessa stated. "Now you ought to have a bath. Make it as long and hot as you like, and I'll fix you something to eat. Then off to bed."

"You're right. And I do need to get to work early so I can speak with Kaz. I've no idea how much Bennett will have told him. I can't stand the idea of him worrying the whole night through."

"Well, don't. It's just gone two o'clock in the morning, my dear—you'll be speaking with him in no time at all."

RATHER TO HER surprise, Ruby slept well and awoke without much difficulty at seven the next morning. After dressing hurriedly, she wolfed down her breakfast and was running up the road to the Underground only a quarter hour later, arriving at the office a few minutes before eight.

Evelyn had just hung up her coat when Ruby walked in. "Good morning, Ruby."

"Good morning. Is Kaz in yet?"

"Do I even need to answer?"

He was there, his mane of sandy hair even more disheveled than usual, his back hunched low over the desk as he concentrated on the notes he was writing. When did the man sleep? Vanessa hadn't said how she'd run him to ground last night—had he been at home, or still at the office? She very much hoped it had not been the latter.

"Kaz?" she whispered, not wishing to startle him. "Kaz? May I come in?"

"Yes, and shut the door," he said, not looking up. "Just let me finish this thought."

He scribbled away for another minute, perhaps the longest

minute of Ruby's life, and then he capped his pen, set it on the desk, and stared at her owlishly.

"You're alive, then. That's good."

"Thank you for your help last night. Did Bennett . . . did he tell you what happened?"

"He rang me from his flat last night, after he'd seen you home. He said he'd fixed the problem, and that you would tell me the rest. So . . . ?"

"I was detained because I used a false birth certificate to obtain my passport," she said, praying that her nerve wouldn't fail before she was finished. "I then used the passport to gain entry to Britain, and the reason I did it was because of a lie, or a set of lies, that had helped me get a job at *The American*. My true last name is Schreiber, not Sutton, and I don't have a university degree. I finished school at fourteen and did a secretarial course at night school, but that's all."

He said nothing, so she plowed on, desperate to get to the last of her confession and so learn what her penance might be. "I am so sorry. To the bottom of my heart I am sorry. You, and everyone else here, have been so kind to me—but especially you, and to deceive you in such a fashion was inexcusable."

Still he said nothing, and with that, the last of her resolve drained away. "I guess I'll just go and collect my things . . ."

He shook his head, rather like a lion might do when awakening, and jabbed a forefinger in her direction. "Stay where you are. Have I said anything about your leaving?"

"Well, no, but when you were silent for so long—"

"I was simply trying to make sense of all this. You changed your name from Schreiber to Sutton, correct?"

"Yes."

"Presumably because you thought you might be more employable with a run-of-the-mill name?"

"Yes."

"Well, *that* I understand," he said. "I'm probably the only person in England who knows how to spell my surname properly. And what else? Oh, right—you fudged your credentials. Said you'd been to university."

"Yes. I planned to go one day, but I had to save up first. And to do that, I needed a better-paying job."

He nodded, his fingers steepled under his chin, his gaze fixed on the desktop between them. "And is that the sum of it?"

"Not quite. The worst part is that I used a forged birth certificate to obtain my passport. I went to a man who'd been at the orphanage with me. Danny was good at things like that. I . . . I may be prosecuted for it when I return home."

"I doubt it. Bennett will make sure you aren't bothered again."

"Do you have any idea how they found out? I've been think—"

"I do," he said wearily. "I'm fairly certain it was Peter Drury."

"*Peter?* But I thought . . . I mean, we were always friendly. This doesn't make any sense. Why would he do such a thing?"

"I'm not sure. When Bennett rang last night, he asked if there were anyone here who might bear you a grudge. Anyone who might be unhappy at your presence at *PW*. It made no sense to me, but then I recalled something Peter had said a few weeks ago. He came in one morning, shut the door, and asked why you'd been chosen to come here. Of all the staff writers at *The American,* why had it been you, since you were so young and inexperienced, at least compared to others there who might have been interested. It seemed an odd thing for him to ask, not least because he'd never shown any interest in the subject when you first came to England."

"What did you say to him?"

"I said I'd specifically asked for a woman, and that obviously they had chosen you because you were the best of the female staff writers they had."

"It was actually because I was the only one without a husband or family that needed—"

"*Ruby*. Another day I shall take you to lunch and set you straight on a few things. At any rate, I thought that was the end of it, but he kept on at me. Wanted to know why you'd been given the chance to interview Mrs. Roosevelt, for example."

"It was an accident—a miracle, really. I just ended up in her car."

"That's what I told him. So then he . . . what is going on out there?"

The office was always a noisy place, but the voices outside were louder than normal; angrier, too. The door burst open. Peter all but tumbled into the room, struggling free of Emil's restraining arms, his own limbs flailing wildly.

"I knew it! I knew you'd be here, telling Kaz your side of things, making him believe your lies."

"Why, Peter?" Ruby asked. "Why did you do this? I thought we were friends. You were so nice to me when I first arrived."

"And look what that earned me. Before you came, *I* was the one Kaz took to lunch. *I* was the one he confided in. *I* was his friend here at *PW*—not you."

"No," Kaz insisted, shaking his head. "Nothing changed

when Ruby came here. If I was kind to her, it was because she was on her own. She was new here, and she needed friends."

"Everything changed," Peter went on, his voice rising steadily, "and there was nothing I could do. I just had to stand there and take it as she got all the best stories, all the best chances. And when I tried to be friends with her, to get to know her better, she acted like she was too good for me. Like she'd rather do anything than spend a few minutes with me after work. But then I ran into Dan Mazur, and—"

"Who?" Kaz asked perplexedly.

"A staff writer at *The American*," Ruby broke in. "Remember? I met up with him just after he was posted here. I wouldn't say we're friends, but we're not exactly enemies."

"You should have heard what he had to say about her," Peter sneered. "He told me he couldn't understand how Ruby had landed a job at *The American* in the first place. He said he'd noticed that her accent would slip sometimes, just enough to make him curious. No college girl he knew would talk like that, he said. He said he figured she was hiding something.

"It was easy to unravel," Peter went on, not noticing, or perhaps not caring, that his colleagues had begun to regard him as they might do an earwig. "I wrote to *The American* and asked them to send me a copy of Ruby's bio. It said she'd gone to Sarah Lawrence College. So I checked, good reporter that I am, and they had no record of her attending.

"That made me wonder what else she was hiding, so I decided to find out where she was born. It turned out there were no records of a Roberta Anne Sutton, birth date July twelfth, 1916, in New York, New Jersey, Connecticut, Rhode Island, or any other neighboring state."

"This is demented," Kaz observed bitterly.

Peter ignored him. "So I wrote back to the state registrars, and asked if anyone with a similar name had been born on the same date. That's when I discovered a Roberta Anne Schreiber had been born in Newark, New Jersey, on that date, to a woman named Annie Schreiber. There wasn't a name for the father on her birth certificate, which didn't surprise me one—"

"Enough!" Kaz roared.

"She grew up in an orphanage. She lied about her name, her education, *everything*, and you welcomed her like a long-lost sister. You even gave her the best stories—"

"She thought up those stories," Emil interrupted. "If her ideas were better than yours, you have only yourself to blame."

"Every time I turned around she was there, worming her way in. She even sat next to you at Mary's funeral. And where was I? Standing at the back of the church like some *nobody*. How could you do that to me?"

"Get out," Kaz said. "Collect your things and get out."

"She's the one who has to go! I told the police everything. They said it was a grave offense—they said she'd be deported."

"Nothing is happening to Ruby. Emil? Can you help Peter clear out his desk?"

"With pleasure," Emil said, and went to grasp Peter's arm.

"You can't do this," Peter shouted, twisting free. "I'll go to the papers. I'll tell them *everything*."

Kaz rounded the desk with astonishing speed for such a big man. Looming over Peter, cold fury in his eyes, he was a daunting sight. "You will say *nothing*."

"You can't stop me," Peter squeaked, marshaling the last of his bravado.

"Perhaps not, but I've friends who can. And I'm not above pulling them into this to ensure you keep quiet. I'll not let you ruin Ruby's life because of your wounded pride."

Peter turned to Ruby, his face so twisted by loathing that she could see little of the affable colleague she'd once known. "It was Bennett, wasn't it? Of course it was. He's up to his neck in—"

"One. More. Word," Kaz enunciated, his words dropping like stones into a soundless lake. "One more word from you, and I will pick up this telephone and call him. Is that what you want? Is it? You have to know what the consequences will be."

"No," Peter mumbled, his face sweaty and pale. "I'll go." He shambled from the room. At a nod from Kaz, Emil followed.

Ruby lingered, not wanting to see Peter again. And she still had so many questions. "I thought you'd be angrier," she said once they were alone.

"Last night I was, a bit. Only at first. Apart from your name, though, you didn't lie to me. Your first day here, when we were at lunch, you told me you grew up in New Jersey and that you went to secretarial college. You didn't say anything about going to university."

"You remember that? Even three years on?"

"I remember everything," he said, his pale eyes meeting hers. "Now, off you go. We still have a magazine to get out, and we're down a staff writer. Time we got back to work."

CHAPTER TWENTY-FOUR

December 1943

At their Wednesday editorial meeting, the last of the calendar year, Emil had almost finished enumerating his list of story ideas for the week. "I'm not sure about this last one. We've had an invitation from the Hornchurch Cottage Homes in Essex. They'd like us to do a story on their annual Christmas party for the children. It's this Saturday, the eighteenth, so we can just fit it in. Kaz? What do you think?"

"Hmm. In theory I don't object, but I don't want something syrupy about rosy-cheeked orphans. I'm not—"

"I'll do it," Ruby said, surprising even herself.

"Are you sure?" Kaz looked uncharacteristically anxious.

"I don't mind. And I don't think there's any chance of my making it syrupy."

"True enough," he agreed. "Very well. Let me know how you get on. Frank—do you mind going with Ruby?"

"Not at all."

Saturday morning saw Ruby and Frank on a District line Underground train to the wilds of Essex. When they arrived, a scant hour after leaving the *PW* offices, they discovered the home's superintendent had sent his car and driver to fetch them.

"This bodes well," Frank whispered, and she had to hope he was right.

The "cottages" were substantial two-story brick houses, no more than fifty or sixty years old, and were set well apart from one another, with no lack of green space between. Altogether the institution looked pleasant enough, but Ruby wasn't inclined to pass judgment until she'd seen and spoken with the children who lived there.

Their car pulled up to what looked like a chapel or hall, and there they were greeted by the superintendent himself, Mr. Oldham, who was well into his sixties and had a disarmingly friendly smile.

"Welcome, Miss Sutton, Mr. Gossage. Welcome to Hornchurch, and happy Christmas to you both. Let me show you inside."

"Is this where the party is being held?" Ruby asked.

"Yes—the hall is the only place here that's big enough to hold all the children. We've nearly three hundred at the moment."

The first thing Ruby noticed, as they entered the hall, was the noise. She'd expected silence, for the nuns at St. Mary's had been quick to punish anyone who spoke above the merest whisper at Mass, at gatherings, or even in the dormitories. But here the children were talking and laughing with one another, their assembled voices a happy chorus, and no one seemed to be afraid of how the adults would react.

In true institutional style the girls had their hair cut short; no fussing with braids and ribbons here. But the children were dressed neatly, their shoes were polished, and their faces were clean. Ruby saw no bruises or evidence of mistreatment, though such things were easy enough to hide beneath clothing. Of course she would need to speak with—

"Don't you agree, Miss Sutton?" Mr. Oldham asked.

"I'm sorry—I didn't hear you just now. I was busy watching the children." Frank, she now saw, was on the far side of the hall, melting into the background as he took his photographs.

"I was saying only that the fresh air, here in the countryside, really seems to bring out the best in the children. Most are from Clerkenwell, you see, and often are in a rather sad state when they come to us."

"I know that part of London," she said, turning to the superintendent. "I used to live nearby. Are all the children here orphans?"

"Some, but not all. Quite a few have a surviving parent who simply can't manage."

"What sort of schooling do they receive?"

"The same state-funded education as any other child. They finish at fourteen, and at that point most are placed out as domestics or, as with many of the boys, in apprenticeships of one sort or another."

"May I speak to some of the children?"

"Of course, of course. I do ask that you be sensitive in the questions you ask. Nothing about their parents or how they came to live here, please. That sort of thing has a tendency to upset even the most levelheaded child."

"I'm sure it does. I promise to be gentle with them."

In the end, speaking to the children wasn't much different from any other interview. She asked them their names, how old they were, if they had been good, and if they were excited about the visit from Father Christmas. In turn she explained, more than once, that she had a funny voice because she was from America, that she didn't know any film stars personally, and that she sadly hadn't brought any chewing gum or chocolate with her.

"I think that's mostly the American soldiers who have things to share," she explained solemnly, "but I haven't been back to the United States in a long time. I'm very sorry."

As she spoke with them and scribbled down their answers, she remained alert for any signs of distress or fear, but detected none. No one from the home came to hover at her elbow to intimidate with their silent presence. The children didn't cringe or fall silent when Matron or one of the nursemaids wandered past. Best of all, when it was time for the Punch and Judy show, they reacted as healthy children ought to do, with shrieks of laughter at Punch's alarming antics and shouted warnings to the other puppets.

At last it was time for Father Christmas, who arrived with a bulging sack that contained a small gift for every child. His costume was a little moth-eaten and his cotton-wool beard was far from convincing, but the children didn't seem to notice or care.

By then, Ruby had returned to Mr. Oldham's side, and they watched as Father Christmas doled out the contents of his sack to the waiting children.

"How do you afford gifts for everyone?" she asked softly.

"It's a struggle, especially with the war on. But local businesses are very generous, as are our churches here in Hornchurch. And our staff work year round to knit mittens for everyone. Add in a pencil and a handful of sweets, and they're happy. Or as happy as we can make them. I'm afraid children like these are destined to have modest expectations, not only of Christmastime but life in general. We do our best, though."

"I can see that you do."

All too soon, the party was over and it was time for Ruby and Frank to return to London. As soon as they were safely on the train she sat back in her seat, let out her breath, and tried to put her thoughts and feelings into some kind of order.

"You all right?" Frank asked quietly.

"Yes. It wasn't . . . I mean, it was nicer than I was expecting," she said after a moment.

"It was."

"You know about . . . ?"

"You growing up in an orphanage? Yes. Couldn't help it, really, what with the way Peter was shouting about it that day."

"Oh," she said. "Of course."

"I grew up in one of Dr. Barnardo's homes. My dad died when I was little, and my mum couldn't take care of all of us. So she handed over me and my younger brother. Kept the four eldest with her."

"I'm so sorry, Frank."

"I was young, but I still remember that day. They had to tear me out of her arms. I was kicking and screaming like a banshee." He began to fuss with the buckle on his camera bag. "I don't talk about it much. I suppose it's the same back in America. People get that look on their face when they find out."

"They do. Did you ever see her again?"

"No. She died when I was ten or eleven. Long after I'd given up hoping she'd come back for me."

Ruby nodded. "I remember that feeling. Even though my

mother was dead, and the nuns never stopped reminding me of that fact, I still hoped. And then, one day, I just stopped."

"Stopped hoping?"

"Yes. An awful thing, when you think of it. That a child so young should feel such despair."

Frank nodded, and for a few minutes neither of them spoke.

"Every so often people would visit the orphanage," Ruby began, half-forgotten memories crowding in on her. "Couples who wanted a child. They'd sit in the parlor and the nuns would bring out a few children for them to inspect. When I got to be a bit older, I asked one of the nuns, one of the nicer ones, why I never got to go to the parlor. I'd already figured out I wasn't pretty enough, and I assumed that's what she'd tell me. But she said . . ."

Frank reached out and took Ruby's hand, and the solidity of his touch, the understanding that radiated from him, helped her to go on.

"She said my mother had been a woman of low repute. A whore, in her words, although I knew she'd been a maid in a hotel. I can just remember her, dressed in her uniform, going off to work. So I knew what Sister Joan said wasn't true."

"Who took care of you when your mum was at work?"

"I don't know. I don't remember anyone else being there. I think, maybe, she might have left me alone. In the room we shared. Somehow I must have known not to cry . . ."

She stopped there, not sure of her voice anymore. When she was feeling more composed, more like herself again, she squeezed Frank's hand and gave him her best smile. "The home today wasn't perfect," she said. "Places like that never are. But the children . . . they seemed happy enough."

"They did," he agreed.

"Did you see their faces when Father Christmas arrived? That's when I knew they were all right. That they were being cared for."

"How?"

"They still believed. All those smiling, trusting little faces, and somehow, in spite of everything, they still believed."

BENNETT REAPPEARED A few days into the New Year, coming through the front door of the *PW* offices just as Ruby was preparing to go home for the day.

"Hello, Ruby."

"Hello," she said, feeling awkward for no good reason at all. "You're back."

"I am. Are you free for dinner?"

"No. I mean yes. I mean—I'm not really dressed for an evening out."

"I was thinking we could go to the Victory Café. See what they have on the menu tonight."

"I'd love that."

"Right. Just let me pop my head into Kaz's office before we go. Won't be a minute."

Night had fallen by the time they left the office, but the moon that greeted them as they stepped outside was full and fair and cast enough light, at least to Ruby's blackout-attuned eyes, to cast every detail of the streetscape into sharp relief.

Rather than turn left and continue along to the street, Bennett paused and, looking over his shoulder at the ruins of St. Bride's, asked, "Do you mind?"

"If we visit? Not at all."

Although the steeple rose high above them, the church beneath was a barren shell. Its roof was gone, burned away by the same fires that had destroyed Ruby's lodgings, and within the nave nothing remained but cold, old, soot-stained stone.

"Everyone talks about St. Paul's having survived," Bennett said as they stood at the edge of the fenced-off ruin, his eyes fixed on the desolation before him. "Yet something like fifteen Wren churches were destroyed during the Blitz. Just look at this place."

"Did you ever visit it before it was destroyed?"

"Many times. I'm the furthest thing from a religious man, but I loved this church. And this is only one example of what has been, and still will be, destroyed. Europe will be a charnel house by the time this war is done."

"It's a building, Bennett. I don't know . . . I can't find myself moved to care. Not the same way I care about what happens to people. So many have died already. So many are starving or suffering."

"I don't disagree. The thing is . . . no one remembers the tide of human suffering from the last war. Never mind we were all brought to our knees by grief. No matter that we vowed it would be the war that put an end to war. Yet here we are, a quarter-century later, and we've forgotten. All that grief has been washed away, and with it our memories."

"It won't last forever. You know it won't. And when it's over, you can create new memories. Happy ones."

"I wish I could believe you. I wish—"

"We should go," she said, though she was reluctant to interrupt him.

"Yes, you're right. Enough of my pontificating. I brought my motorcycle with me—do you mind?"

"No," she said, although she was a little nervous of it. At the same time, she rather looked forward to sitting behind him, her arms locked around his middle, the heat of his body keeping her warm.

Jimmy and Maria greeted them joyfully, and their dinner—a carbon copy of the one they'd shared when she'd first come to London—was as delicious as she remembered from her first visit to the café.

Ruby told him of Christmas with the Tremaines, Kaz, and Uncle Harry, and how they'd made do with braised rabbit for lunch and, horror of horrors, elderberry wine for the toast to the king, since Harry's wine cellar had finally been depleted. Bennett admitted to having missed Christmas lunch entirely, and though her heart seized at the idea of him alone and hungry while she'd been happily surrounded by friends, she didn't press him for details. And then, lingering over the bottle of vinegary wine that Jimmy had unearthed, they talked of nothing much at all, until it was nearly ten o'clock and Bennett was hollow-eyed with fatigue.

The house was still and quiet when he brought her home, and as she couldn't bear to see him go, not just yet, she asked him to stay on and share a cup of tea in the kitchen. Sitting at the homey old table, the cats twining around their legs, gave Ruby the odd and entirely unreliable feeling that all was right with the world. But perhaps, just perhaps, it was a taste of a future, of a shared life, that might yet be.

"You're leaving again," she said at last.

"I am. I won't be back for a long while."

"Will you come back to us? To . . . to me?"

His hands enveloped hers. "I hope I will. I want it more than anything."

"I want it, too. I want you safe and whole and free of the obligations that take you away from me. But you need to know that I do understand why you must keep the promises you made. I do. Because if you broke them, you see, you wouldn't be the man I know. The man I . . ." She faltered, unable to go on.

He nodded, but rather than say anything, he simply looked in her eyes, and it was a long time before he spoke again.

"I must go."

They started up the stairs, Ruby a few steps ahead, but when they were only halfway up he caught at her hand and gently turned her around.

"Ruby," he said, his eyes darkened by grief. He framed her face with his hands, his big hands that were so warm and gentle, and he kissed her with such sweetness, such yearning, that she felt she must surely die from the pain of it.

At last he pulled away, his mouth coming to rest against her ear. "Don't come to the door with me. Don't look back."

And she obeyed him. She let him brush past her, heard him walk down the hall, heard the soft click of the front door as it latched behind him. And only then did she sit on the stairs, her knees giving out, as she, the girl who never cried, let the tears stream down her face until her eyes were dry and she could cry no more.

PART IV

Then we saw the coast of France. As we closed in, there was one LCT near us, with washing hung up on a line, and between the loud explosions of mines being detonated on the beach, one could hear dance music coming from its radio. There were barrage balloons, looking like comic toy elephants, bouncing in the high wind above the massed ships, and you could hear invisible planes flying behind the grey ceiling of cloud. Troops were unloading from big ships to heavy barges or to light craft, and on the shore, moving up brown roads that scarred the hillside, our tanks clanked slowly and steadily forward.

—Martha Gellhorn, correspondent for *Collier's Weekly*
(August 5, 1944)

CHAPTER TWENTY-FIVE

June 1944

Everyone at *PW* was gathered around the wireless set in the main office when Ruby arrived at work that morning.

"What is it?" she asked.

"Shhh," Nell chided. "It's happening. Our forces are landing in France."

Ruby let her coat fall to the floor and rushed to stand close to the wireless.

"A new phase of the Allied air offensive has begun." This sentence opened what was described as an extremely important warning broadcast in our European service this morning by a member of the staff of the supreme commander of the Allied expeditionary force. This new phase, the speaker said, will particularly affect people living roughly within twenty-five miles of any part of the coast. The supreme commander of the Allied expeditionary force has directed that wherever possible an advance warning shall be given to . . ."

"Emil, I want you down at the MOI this morning," Kaz said. "Ring me with updates as often as you can. We just might be able to pull through a half-decent cover story by this afternoon."

"Isn't it better to leave the issue as it is?" Emil observed mildly. "How much more are we likely to know by this afternoon?"

"I'm not saying we should scrub everything," Kaz said. "I'll rewrite my editorial. Explain that we were going to press as the landings began, but will have a special issue next week. If we can find an image that's strong enough for the cover, we can go with that, and link the cover image to my editorial. That way the issue won't be stale-dated by the time it goes on sale."

"What about a map for the cover?" Ruby suggested. "One with the landing sites, and graphics with as much information as—"

Kaz was shaking his head. "That's fine for the interior, but not the cover. I want faces on the cover."

"What can I do?" she asked.

"You and Nell can go through our photo library. See if we've any decent shots of Eisenhower. Even better if he's standing next to Churchill or the king. Frank, you get on the phone with the agencies and see if anyone has shots from yesterday. Soldiers waiting with their kit, for instance."

There was no time to talk or even think beyond the task at hand. Ruby and Nell spent the hours that followed paging through hundreds of contact sheets that dated as far back as the beginning of 1942, yet no matter how long they searched the pile of possibilities, what they unearthed remained disappointingly modest.

They gathered around the wireless again at one o'clock. The

news was encouraging, at least in terms of what was being reported. Kaz, unsurprisingly, remained skeptical.

"We won't know the truth of it for a while," he insisted. "They're not going to tell us about the casualties, not yet, but they've got to be significant. I've been to those beaches in Normandy. They're flat and rocky and there's nowhere to hide. What did Churchill say just now? 'The fire of the shore batteries has been largely quelled'? Perhaps, but not before the landings began. God only knows how many men were killed before they set foot in France."

They listened to the remainder of the reports, and then it was back to work for another hour. Kaz summoned them at two o'clock with the happy news that Emil had unearthed a series of photographs, taken the day before, of GIs waiting to board their ships for the first leg of their journey to France.

"They're still being vetted by the MOI," Kaz explained wearily, "but Emil is confident they'll pass."

It was just enough. They pulled a double-page spread from the front of the book and replaced it with Kaz's editorial, several of the photos, and a map of the landings that Mr. Dunleavy had drawn. On the cover: a picture of an American soldier, his pack on the ground beside him, his eyes fixed on the far horizon.

"Well done, everyone," Kaz pronounced. "I'm off to the printers. Go home and get some rest. Everyone except Ruby. I need you for a minute."

She followed him to his office and watched as he rummaged through one of the drawers. Coming around the desk, he motioned for her to sit down, and then he held out an envelope.

"What is this?"

"I had a call from Uncle Harry last night. He was concerned

about Bennett. You see, when Bennett is 'away,' as it were, Harry receives a card on the first of every month. It's a form, really, that says he continues to be in good health, or something along those lines."

"Harry hasn't received this month's card," she said, her voice so calm that it surprised her.

"Nor the previous month's card. And they've come like clockwork before. Each time Bennett has been away, doing whatever he does for months and months, the cards have come."

"Do *you* think something has happened?" she asked, very glad that she was sitting and not expecting her legs to hold her up.

"I don't. In the absence of any real proof, I refuse to accept that Bennett is injured or dead. But I did make him a promise, and I'm carrying it out now."

Kaz placed the envelope in her hand. "He told me about the postcards before he left this last time. He asked me to give you this if they stopped coming."

"What's in it?"

"I don't know, but you should probably read it in here. I have to go to the printers now, but I'll be home tonight. You can ring me there if you want to talk about anything."

He squeezed her shoulder, as if to warn her, and then he was gone.

My dearest Ruby,

I've thought of writing you such a letter any number of times, but something always stayed my hand—fear of saying too little, or perhaps of saying too much. And I was always certain I would come back to you, always, until today. In a few hours I will leave England again, and I cannot be sure that I will return.

I do not say this to upset or hurt you—quite the contrary. Only to prepare you, if you do receive news that I have not survived, for you have borne enough shocks already in the course of this long and terrible war.

You have been my friend, Ruby, and more than that, I think. You have been my North Star, my point of light in a darkened sky, the steadfast beacon guiding me home. (I beg your pardon for such poor poetry, but these are the words that come to mind as I leave you.)

If I were a braver man, I would have told you this to your face, your lovely face that haunts my dreams and blesses my waking hours. I so wanted to empty my heart and confess all, that last night when we sat in Vanessa's kitchen after dinner at the Victory Café. I very nearly did.

I hope to return to you—I long for it more than anything—and yet I know it is unlikely. So I will say farewell, and I will thank you for your friendship and regard and, if I have not misjudged you entirely, your love.

All I ask of you, now, is that you be happy—do not look back and mourn what might have been. Go on and be happy and never stop writing, no matter what. Write your stories and discover the world, and if you think of me, think only that I loved you for you, you alone, you and nothing more. Only you.

Bennett

WHEN RUBY ARRIVED home, well past seven o'clock, it was to find Vanessa and Jessie preparing a late supper in the kitchen. There was comfort to be found in peeling potatoes and scraping carrots, and by the time they sat down to eat she felt calmer, if not happier. She would never be truly happy until she was certain Bennett was safe.

Their talk at dinner was light, for they needed a respite from the drama of the day's events, but when the hour drew near to nine o'clock Ruby followed Vanessa into the library and stood by the wireless for the news. It began with the king's address to the nation and the empire; and if his voice was rather more halting than usual, his message was all the more steadfast and determined.

> *"Once more a supreme test has to be faced. This time the challenge is not to fight to survive, but to fight to win the final victory for the good cause. Once again what is demanded from us all is something more than courage, more than endurance. We need the revival of spirit, a new unconquerable resolve."*

"Nicely done, once again," Vanessa said, bending to switch off the wireless. "The dear man struggles so, but it does make you—Ruby? Whatever is wrong? Why are you crying?"

"This," she said, and pulled Bennett's letter from her cardigan pocket. "Kaz gave this to me. Bennett has disappeared. He's had no news—Uncle Harry, I mean. He usually gets a postcard from Bennett's work at the beginning of every month, but there's been nothing for more than two months now."

Vanessa read it through, and when she looked up again her

eyes, too, were swimming with tears. "My darling girl," she said.

"If only I'd told him how I felt. If only . . . I don't know how I can bear it."

"It was his choice," Vanessa said, and she took Ruby's hands in hers. "Obviously he has never said a word about what he does, not one word, but he did tell me, once, that it was his choice. He had no wife, no children, and his parents were dead. He said it was better for him to risk his life than a man with people who depended on him."

"What about you?" Ruby sobbed. "He's a son to you, and a brother to the girls. And what will Kaz do? First Mary, and now his best friend?"

"And you, my dear? Don't you need him, too?"

"Vanessa, don't. Please don't."

"There, there. I understand. I do. And I don't think you should give up, not just yet. A few missing updates are not the same as a death notice. For now, I choose to believe he is alive— and I think you should, too. Focus on your work, just as he is surely doing—"

"And find my unconquerable resolve?" Ruby whispered.

"Yes. Just as the king said. Find your resolve, and it will see you through."

CHAPTER TWENTY-SIX

With D-day came the V-1 flying bombs, as many as a hundred a day. Though the destruction they wrought was nothing like as lethal as the bombardment of the Blitz, the panic they induced was nearly as awful.

There was never any warning. Before long, Ruby lost count of the number of times she had been walking down the street, feeling reasonably cheerful, the sun full on her face, and the next moment found herself cowering behind the nearest post office box or parked car as a building at the end of the block exploded into flames. People nicknamed them doodlebugs, but she couldn't think of one thing that was funny about the flying bombs and the terror they sowed.

A month passed, then another, and there was no renewal of the reassuring postcards to Uncle Harry. Yet Ruby couldn't bring herself to give up on him, not without any definitive news that he was lost. It was that scrap of belief that she clung to, a buoy of hope in a sea of despair.

Work was another solace, although she soon began to chafe at the restraints that Kaz continued to place on her and everyone else at *PW*. No matter how many times she asked to go over to France, to report from a safe distance behind the front lines as so many others were doing, he flatly refused. Instead, Kaz relied on freelancers for stories from France, claiming that it was cheaper for the magazine to do so, at least until the Allies had gained a firmer hold on Europe.

Ruby tried to be patient, yet it was agony to be left behind—and all the more so once she read Martha Gellhorn's description of stretcher-bearers ferrying wounded to the hospital ships, or Lee Miller's dramatic accounts of field hospitals, devastated French villages, and pockets of German resistance amid the ruined streets of Saint-Malo. The nadir was a copy of *The American,* sent to Kaz by Mike Mitchell, which featured a cover story by Dan Mazur on the liberation of Cherbourg.

"It's an overcooked piece of tripe, Ruby. I don't know why it bothers you," Kaz observed calmly.

"You know why. You know I could have written that story ten times better."

"Yes, but I don't much care what happens to Dan Mazur. If you get yourself killed, however, I won't have a decent night's sleep again for the rest of my life."

"If I were a man, you would let me go," she persisted. "And you wouldn't make him feel guilty for asking."

"Perhaps. I don't know. Certainly my reasons for holding you back have nothing to do with your sex. You're as capable as any male journalist I've ever met, and every bit as tenacious and brave. Far more so than that cretin Dan Mazur."

She ignored his praise, though it would make a fine memory to focus on as she tried to fall asleep that night. "Well, then? If I'm so good—"

"You are, but we both know the War Office has been refusing to accredit women as war correspondents. And without a pass you can't go to France."

"Promise you'll let me go if they do start accrediting women."

"Fine. I'll send you—but only if you can get a pass, and not until I think it's safe for you to go."

AS JULY GAVE way to August, and as resistance from Axis forces was steadily if bloodily quelled across France, Kaz's opposition melted into resigned acceptance.

"So I ran into an editor at the *Evening Standard* yesterday," he mentioned one morning. "He said they've applied for a war correspondent's pass for Evelyn Irons."

"Did she get it?" Ruby asked eagerly.

"Not yet. Apparently the War Office is still thinking about it. But it might be worth starting your application now. God knows how long it'll take for them to make a decision."

"May I go to Macmillan Hall now?"

"Let me talk to Frank first. You can't go to France on your own—don't even think about fighting me on this—and there's no point in getting stories without photographs to accompany them. But you know Frank. He hates being away from home, so I know he's going to kick up a fuss."

It was hard to imagine mild-mannered Frank being difficult about anything, and in the end he couldn't have protested all that much, for Kaz gave them permission to head over to Macmillan Hall later that morning. By eleven o'clock she and Frank were sitting across the desk of Captain Tuttle, Ruby's favorite among the information officers at the MOI's London headquarters, and the same man who had given her the run-around when she'd asked for information on Bennett's mysterious employer.

"Getting you a pass for the European theater of operations, Mr. Gossage, is no trouble at all," he said after they'd made their case for accreditation. "But regretfully I can't do the same for you, Miss Sutton."

"Surely I'm not the only woman correspondent to ask," she protested. "You can't be turning *all* of us down."

"We aren't. A few, a *very* select few, are being considered, but only for work well behind the lines. And even then, I have to tell you, my superiors are not at all enamored of the idea."

"So what am I meant to do? Just sit out the rest of the war in England?"

Captain Tuttle leaned forward, his voice thinning to a conspiratorial whisper. "Are you asking me what would I do, hypothetically speaking, were I in your shoes?"

"Yes. Hypothetically speaking," she hissed back.

"In that case, as an American, I would speak to someone in press relations at SHAEF. I would ask for Captain Zielinski. That's what I would do, if I wanted to get to France before the end of the month."

"Aren't the SHAEF offices all the way out in Bushy Park?" Frank asked. "That's past Twickenham. More than an hour on the train one way."

Captain Tuttle shook his head. "Fortunately, they have a satellite office here at Macmillan Hall. I believe Captain Zielinski is here today." He sat back and, speaking at a normal volume again, gathered together the forms he had filled out for Frank. "I'll have your photographer's pass ready for the end of the week, Mr. Gossage. Is there anything else I can do for the two of you? No? In that case, have a pleasant day—and good luck, Miss Sutton."

Half an hour later they were speaking with Captain Zielinksi, who listened intently as Ruby described her credentials and experience.

"That all sounds fine to me. I can accredit you for thirty days, beginning on the date you sail for France. Do you know when you want to leave?"

"That's it? Don't you need anything else? Don't I have to fill out some forms?"

"Nope. You'll have to sign your war correspondent's pass, but that's all. And I do know who you are, Miss Sutton. I've been reading your column in *The American* for years. You might actually send back some stories worth reading—unlike some of the sausage makers we've got over in France already. At any rate, when do you want to leave?"

"I don't know. Kaz didn't say."

"Let's check with him. What's your number at *PW*?"

"Central 1971."

The captain began to dial even before she'd finished reciting the number. A few seconds later he was talking to Kaz.

"Mr. Kaczmarek? Tim Zielinski here, calling from SHAEF press relations. I've got your Miss Sutton here. Wondering when you'd like me to date her press pass. Yeah . . . yeah. Uh-huh. Thirty days. There is that, I agree. No, I doubt they'll open the press camps to women. Yeah, got it. Good. Thanks. I'll get on it now."

He hung up the receiver and grinned at Ruby. "You're all set. We agreed on August twentieth as your departure date. Come along with me and we'll get your picture taken for your pass. I'll grab your insignia, too. Pins for your collar and cap, a shoulder badge, and we'll get some dog tags made up. You'll have to supply your own uniform, though—one of the girls here can tell you where to find an outfitter. And I think that's about it. Oh, hold on—you'll need a field manual, too. Spells out all the rules and regs."

RUBY WAS IN a triumphant mood when she returned to *PW* late that afternoon.

"See?" she told Kaz, handing over her war correspondent's pass so he might inspect it. "Accredited for thirty days. And here are my insignia and dog tags. I just have to get a uniform jacket and skirt, but apparently there's a tailor—"

"We can talk about that later. Did Zielinski say where he's sending you?"

"Yes. I can't stay at any of the official press camps, since they're still closed to women, so they're sending me to an evacuation hospital. It's the hundred and twenty-eighth, about halfway between the landing sites and Paris. And then, when Paris is liberated—he said it's sure to be anytime now—we can go there. Can you believe it? Paris!"

"But only once I give the go-ahead, and only if it's safe to do so."

"Yes, yes. Of course, only once it's safe."

"No heroics. No venturing off the beaten path. Don't even think about going out after dark, and make sure Frank sticks to you like glue. Understood?"

"Understood. Thank you, Kaz."

"Make me proud, Ruby."

CHAPTER TWENTY-SEVEN

Vanessa had received the news of Ruby's forthcoming journey to France stoically enough, but when the time came to say farewell, she was unable to hide her misgivings.

"How shall I bear it if anything happens to you? Already I can't sleep at night because I'm so worried about Bennett, and now you're going there, with goodness knows how many Nazis still on the loose . . ."

"Vanessa. Listen to me. I am going to an evacuation hospital that is well out of the way of the fighting. Miles and miles away from it. And I will only go into Paris after it's been liberated and made safe. I'll have Frank with me all the time."

"He's a sweet fellow, but I can't think he'll do much to protect you."

"I can protect myself. Remember how I grew up. I'm as tough as nails, and you know it."

"I suppose you're right."

"Of course I am. Now—you haven't said what you think of my uniform." Ruby had been sitting with Vanessa on the sofa, but now she stood and took a few steps back. "Do I look the part?"

The tailor, recommended by one of the WACs who worked with Captain Zielinski, had supplied her with a woman's khaki jacket and matching skirt, a pair of trousers for cold and rainy days, and two men's-issue uniform shirts, size extra small, together with a men's khaki tie. Once her insignia had been pinned to her jacket, and her cap badge had been added to her smart little uniform hat, Ruby had felt every bit the accredited war correspondent.

She was traveling light, taking only a single musette bag packed with clothes and toiletries, and her typewriter in its hard-shell case. The folding model was so much lighter and easier to carry than her old one had been, although she did think of Bennett and worry about him every time she looked at it.

A knock sounded at the door; her taxi to the station had arrived.

"Promise to write as often as you can," Vanessa said, enveloping Ruby in one final hug.

"I will. Please say goodbye to Jessie. I hope she isn't too upset." Jessie had retreated to the kitchen, too distressed to stay and see Ruby leave. Nor had Simon ventured inside to say farewell, although he had carefully inspected her packed bag and even tried to crawl inside.

And then she was out the door and into the taxi, with hardly enough time to roll down the window and wave a final goodbye to the woman who had become the mother she'd never realized she needed.

Frank was waiting for her at Waterloo Station; together they took the train to Southampton, arriving in the late afternoon.

The ship that was ferrying them over to France, the *Duke of Argyll*, had just docked and was off-loading patients into ambulances that had been driven right onto the wide quay. Ruby soon lost count of the men on stretchers, but there were at least several hundred and possibly even more.

Their ship was an older steamer, probably a ferry before the war, now painted white and emblazoned with red crosses to indicate its status as a hospital vessel. Ruby and Frank were escorted inside, to the officers' mess, and were cautioned to stay there for the voyage, as the ship's crew would be busy cleaning and refitting it for their next complement of patients.

Ruby had eaten nothing at lunch, wary of being sick, and though she did feel rather uncomfortable once they set sail, she was able to push back the nausea by fixing her attention on the view from the room's large window. Six hours later, she woke from a fitful doze—it was past midnight—to discover they had docked at the Mulberry harbor at Gold Beach in Normandy.

"We're here, Ruby," Frank said, shaking her awake. "Best be getting off the ship before they turn her around and head back home."

They stayed by the harbor overnight, sleeping in tents alongside the ship's medical staff, and at first light were roused for their ride to the 128th evacuation hospital. A truck had been loaded with medical supplies for the hospital and the driver was willing to take them—but not if he had to wait. So into the truck they climbed, hungry and tired, and began the long journey to Senonches.

"Takes about four hours," their driver said. "That's assuming we don't have to make any detours because the road's been hit or the krauts have started lobbing shells in our direction again."

The roads they took were cratered and potholed, enough to rattle Ruby's teeth out of her head, and traced a depressing path through countryside laid waste by war. The first ruined town they drove through nearly brought her to tears; by the tenth, she hardly blinked.

In one muddy field they passed, British soldiers were digging holes to bury a herd of cattle that had been killed. The animals, about a dozen of them, lay on their backs with their legs pointed straight up, their bodies bloated but otherwise intact.

"Blast force from a shell," their driver said. "Waste of good meat, that."

On and on they drove, hour after hour, stopping only once so they might relieve themselves by the side of the road. Wary of land mines or other surprises left for the unwary by retreating German troops, Ruby positioned herself by the truck's rear wheels and prayed that no one would come along and catch her in the act.

They arrived at the hospital as the sun was setting, at which point Ruby's stomach was so empty it had given up on growling at her. But food had to wait: their first order of business was Colonel Wiley, who'd left orders that they be brought to see him as soon as they arrived.

"You're not the first journalists to pay us a visit," he said, his tone affable enough, "and you won't be the last. I don't mind you being here, since it helps with the war effort and all that, but if you get in my way, or in the way of anyone else here, I'll have you back in England by the next morning. Understood?"

"Yes, sir."

"We don't have the time or patience to coddle you, so here's a few rules. Don't bother my staff when they're working. If they aren't on duty, don't bother them if they say they don't want to talk. Don't talk to patients without permission from the doctor on duty. Don't leave the hospital. And, no, I can't spare a jeep to take you to Paris, so don't piss me off by asking again."

Ruby was given a spare cot in one of the nurses' tents, while Frank was quartered with the junior officers. It had been easy to make friends with the nurses, who were friendly and open and curious about Ruby's work, and they had been quick to invite her to join them for meals in the canteen that everyone shared, soldiers and officers alike.

Three days in, she was sitting with them, listening as they talked about home and the things they missed most.

"What about you, Ruby?"

"Me? I guess I'd say it's coffee. The stuff you have here isn't bad, though. And anything is better than tea. Plain hot water, even. There were times I—"

"Hey there! Ruby Sutton!"

She swiveled around, searching for the owner of the voice, and was taken aback to see it belonged to Dan Mazur. "Oh, boy," she muttered under her breath.

"Friend of yours?" one of the nurses asked.

"That's stretching it. He's not a bad guy, just—Dan! How are you?"

"Well enough. Surprised to see you here. I thought the Brits weren't keen on girl correspondents."

"They're not," she said, and pointed to the U.S. war correspondent shoulder patch on her jacket. "Did you just get here?"

"Here, meaning the one twenty-eighth? Yeah. I landed on D-day plus ten," he said, evidently a point of pride for him. "Been all over since then. Just back from Falaise. Was there with the

Canadians for a while, but when it got quiet I decided to spend a day or so getting some softer pieces while I wait for the go-ahead for Paris."

The most senior of the nurses, a captain in the Army Nursing Corps who had been overseas since the summer of 1942, arched an eyebrow at him. "'Softer'? Is that what you think it's like here?"

"I'm forgetting my manners," Ruby said, hoping to cut Dan off before he irritated the nurses any further. "Let me introduce everyone. Ladies, this is Dan Mazur from *The American* magazine. We used to work together before I moved to London. Dan, these are some of the nurses who've been showing me around and answering my questions. Captain Gladys Kaye, First Lieutenant Sally Greene, and First Lieutenant Edith Geller. They're veterans of the campaigns in North Africa and Sicily, just so you know. And they were the first nurses to arrive in Normandy. What day was it again?"

"D-day plus six," Gladys answered, her expression coldly daunting.

"Well, uh, good for you," Dan said. "I'm sure you all have a lot of stories to share."

"Colonel Wiley has given permission for Miss Sutton to observe one of the surgeons at work," Gladys told him. "If you want to join us, I doubt he'll object."

Dan swallowed uneasily, but nodded all the same. "Sure thing. What time?"

Gladys looked at her wristwatch. "Right about now. All set, Ruby?"

"All set."

CHAPTER TWENTY-EIGHT

They followed Gladys, Sally, and Edith to the foyer of the operating tent, where sinks had been set up for the nurses and surgeons to scrub up. Following the nurses' instructions, Ruby washed her hands and forearms with carbolic soap so strong that it made her eyes water, and held them in front of her, still wet, as she'd been told.

Gladys, who had already scrubbed up, dried Ruby's hands and forearms with a clean towel, then carefully opened a fresh gown from a neatly folded stack and directed her to slide her arms into the sleeves. After fastening the gown, she slid gloves onto Ruby's hands, covered her hair with a cap, and placed a surgical mask over her nose and mouth.

"Stand right there and don't touch anything," Gladys warned. "If you do, we have to start from the beginning. I need to wash my hands again and get Mr. Mazur gowned, then Mr. Gossage."

Gladys repeated the procedure for Dan and Frank and then, after washing her hands yet again, she swabbed down Frank's camera and tripod with cotton lint dipped in rubbing alcohol. He would be standing at a distance, so his camera might come into the operating room; but Ruby and Dan, who were going to be much closer to the patient, would have to work without their notebooks.

"Can't sterilize paper," Gladys explained, "and pencils and pens are just filthy. Mr. Gossage, remember that you need to stay well clear of the surgeons."

"I'll remember. No point in coming closer, anyways. The censors will never let us use anything that shows blood and guts."

"Good. Now wait here while I scrub up for surgery."

The three of them stood like statues as Gladys went through the routine of washing her hands and gowning herself with the help of another nurse. She was joined at the sinks by Major Ewing, one of the hospital's surgeons, and the man they'd be watching today.

"Major Ewing, sir, these are the journalists who are joining us. Ruby Sutton and Frank Gossage from *Picture Weekly*, and Dan Mazur from *The American*."

"Welcome. I believe Captain Kaye has read you the riot act?"

"Yes, sir," Ruby answered promptly.

"Then let's get started." They followed him into the operating tent, which was large enough to hold four tables at a decent distance from one another. Doctors and nurses were already busy at three of the tables.

"Here we are," Major Ewing said as he approached the nearest table. Another surgeon was waiting at the table, and an anesthesiologist was seated on a stool by the patient's head. Gladys, who was assisting, took up her position at the major's side. "Miss Sutton, Mr. Mazur, you can come and stand at my patient's feet. A little ways back—yes, that's good."

The patient, who was already asleep, was covered with sheets that left only his right leg exposed from the knee down. Thick pads of gauze covered an area from a few inches below his knee to just above his ankle. His foot was so close to Ruby that she could see the fine, fair hairs on his toes.

"What happened to him?" she asked softly, not sure if Major Ewing would mind her asking questions.

"I'm not sure. I'll have a better idea once I get a good look under these dressings."

"Did the medics give you any notes?"

"Not that I can read. He's German."

Dan made a strange sort of choking noise. "You're operating on a kraut? When American soldiers are waiting for their turn on the table?"

"I don't give a fuck what country he fights for—pardon my French, Miss Sutton, Captain Kaye. All I see is a man, a boy, really, who needs our care as much as anyone else."

"He looks young," Ruby said.

"They all do. I doubt he's more than eighteen years old. Now, let's see what we can do about this leg. Just give me a moment to dig in and I'll let you know what I find."

He removed the dressings, layer by layer, dropping them onto a metal tray that Gladys held out. A foul smell rose from the wound, like blue cheese but far stronger, and for a terrible moment Ruby was afraid she might be sick.

"Breathe in through your mouth and out through your nose," Gladys advised. "That should help."

The wound, once revealed, was every bit as awful as Ruby had feared. It was deep and wide, and amid the torn flesh and oozing blood she could see flashes of white. The bones of his leg, she realized, one of them sticking out of the wound at a disconcerting angle.

Major Ewing was talking softly with the other surgeon, and as they talked they prodded gently at the wound with metal instruments that looked like large pairs of tweezers.

"Can you see inside the wound well enough?" Major Ewing asked.

"Yes, thank you," Ruby replied. *All too well*, she thought.

"I'm guessing a shell fragment was the culprit here, given the size and irregular shape of the injury to this man's leg. See, here, how the fibula is shattered? And the tibia, too, although that break is cleaner. What a goddamn mess."

"What is that smell?" Ruby asked. "Is that normal?"

"It's a sign of infection. Have you ever smelled meat when it goes off? This is what human beings smell like when their flesh is rotting. And that is a problem, a very serious one. On top of that, his foot is ischemic—see how the skin has gone gray and cold? Not a good sign. And then . . . oh, boy. Here's another complication. Evidently the wound was left to fester rather longer than we thought. Just look at this. These fellows don't hatch overnight."

He held up the surgical instrument he'd been using to probe the wound. Caught between its tips, wriggling feebly, was a small, gray-white *something*.

"Jesus H. Christ," Dan muttered. "Is that a maggot?"

"Yes. Not uncommon in wounds that have been left untreated for a few days. I could spend hours on this leg, and even then I doubt I'd be able to save it. Better, I think, to take it off."

Ruby stole a look at Dan. He was pale under his tan, and

drops of sweat were sliding down his forehead. She looked back at Major Ewing. "So you're going to amputate his leg?"

"Yes. You don't have to stay, but if you feel up to watching the procedure, I think you'll find it interesting. I should be able to keep the knee, which will make all the difference for this man later on. Much easier to fit prosthetics."

"Ah," Ruby said. The lights shining on the table were so very hot, and the smell was inescapable, no matter how carefully she breathed in through her mouth and out through her nose. How did the nurses and doctors stand it?

She heard a low groan, followed by a heavy thud as a body hit the ground. Turning, she saw that Dan had passed out.

"Major Ewing . . . ?"

"I know. Marked him for a fainter the minute he walked in. He'll be fine there for a minute or two. Now—tell me about your time in England. I lived in London before the war, you know. Worked at a hospital in the East End. Some of the stuff I saw there would turn your hair white . . ."

By concentrating on her conversation with Major Ewing, and by studiously looking over his shoulder and not letting her gaze drop to the operating table, Ruby was able to stay on her feet—just. It was a near thing, especially when the mangled mess of the boy's leg was bundled away, leaving an empty space where a healthy limb had once been, but she summoned up every ounce of willpower she possessed and did not embarrass herself by collapsing as Dan had done.

"Right. I think we're nearly done," Major Ewing finally announced. "We'll leave the wound open for a few days, since it's easier to monitor for infection that way. I'm off to the canteen for some lunch. Would you care to join me? Miss Sutton? Mr. Gossage?"

Frank shook his head; he, too, was looking pretty green around the gills. "Thanks for the invitation, but I'm going to lie down for a bit."

"Miss Sutton?"

"I'd be delighted to join you. Although I don't think I'll be eating anything."

As soon as they were out of the operating tent, and away from the terrible odors and heat, Ruby began to feel better, though not well enough to dig into a full meal as Major Ewing was doing.

He reminded her a little of Bennett, though his hair was receding at the temples and streaked through with silver. Like Bennett he was far too thin, and looked as if he hadn't slept properly in years. The lines of weariness engraved around his mouth and eyes had nothing to do with how old he was, she suspected. Here was a man who had probably aged a decade since the beginning of June.

"Do you mind if I take notes while we talk? I'll check everything with you before including it in any of my pieces."

"Go right ahead," he said, trying and failing to stifle a yawn.

"Are you as tired as I think you are?"

"More," he said, and smiled a little. "Our first two weeks in France we had something like three thousand men come through this hospital. About nine out of ten needed surgery. It got to the point where I couldn't sleep. I'd just drink another cup of coffee and keep going."

"Where was the hospital when you first landed?"

"Boutteville. About six miles in from Utah beach. An awful

place. Rained all through the last part of June, and then, about five minutes after each storm, the dust clouds would roll in. Coated everything. And then there were those damned orchards. No one around to tend them, so there were rotting apples everywhere. And the flies—my God, the flies. Not a surprise, since this entire region is carpeted with the bodies of men and livestock." He looked down at his plate and pushed it away. "I'll never forget all those flies."

"How has it been since you moved here?"

"Better, on the whole. Although last week and the week before, when they were closing up the Falaise pocket, were rough. I'm just hoping this lull lasts for a while. We all are."

"How long have you been a doctor?"

"I finished medical school fifteen years ago. Worked in Boston for a while, doing general and thoracic surgery at one of the big hospitals there. Then I got it in my head that I wanted to see more of the world, so I came to London for a few years. It's a long story, but I ended up at the London Hospital in Whitechapel. Have you heard of it?"

"I have, and it's a fine hospital. Their staff should all have received medals for the work they did during the Blitz. I only wonder . . . why did you go there? I can think of half a dozen other hospitals in London with far more modern facilities and equipment."

"There are, but I wanted to work with their head of general surgery. I'd been reading his papers in medical journals and wanted to learn from him."

"And did you? Learn from him, I mean."

"Oh, yes. He's one of the finest men I've ever known. He was a combat surgeon on the Western Front during the last war, and although he didn't talk about it often, he did say that medicine had advanced a great deal since those days—in part because of what he and other surgeons had learned during the war."

"What was his name?"

"Robert Fraser. I've been thinking of him a lot since we got here. Thinking of what he must have seen and done and endured. And every day I count myself fortunate that doctors like him paved the way for doctors like me."

Dispatches from London

by Miss Ruby Sutton

August 24, 1944

. . . The wounded soldiers I've met at the 128th Evac Hospital are men, some by virtue of age, but most by virtue of what they have seen and done in the months and years since they left civilian life behind. Some are so young they have down on their cheeks and they blush when I speak with them. But they are all men now, their boyhood stripped away, and they will fight and die as men in this foreign land . . .

AT BREAKFAST THE next day, the hospital was abuzz with news from Paris: at dawn that morning, Free French and Allied troops had entered the city, and had encountered next to no resistance. Liberation day had come at last.

Ruby was thrilled for the people of Paris, and more than a little excited at the prospect of reporting from the freed capital, but she and Frank still had no way of getting to the city.

"I don't know what to do," she complained to Gladys. "I can't ask Colonel Wiley for a jeep, and short of walking out to the main road and trying to hitch a—"

"I'll give you a ride." Dan had come over to stand behind her as she was talking. She was so annoyed at him that at first she didn't realize what he was offering.

"You do want a ride, don't you?" he pressed.

"I do, of course I do. Thanks so much."

"Well, you helped me out when I first came to London, and then, the other day, you could have scored some points off me. But you didn't. So that's why I'm offering."

"By 'the other day,' do you mean when you fainted in the OR?" Gladys asked.

"Yes. That. Thanks for saying it straight up. Makes me feel so much better."

"When do you want to leave?" Ruby asked. "Frank and I can be ready in a few minutes."

"My jeep and driver are arriving sometime this evening. Sorry it isn't sooner."

"We'll be ready. And thanks again, Dan. I owe you one."

As soon as he was out of earshot, Gladys began to laugh. "Well, he certainly redeemed himself just now. Although I do think he's a bit of an ass all the same."

"He can be," Ruby agreed. "But he can be the biggest jackass in the world and I won't complain. Just as long as he gets me to Paris."

CHAPTER TWENTY-NINE

Although they didn't leave until well past ten o'clock, Ruby was hopeful they might arrive in Paris by midnight; even taking a southerly route through Chartres, which kept them well clear of recent fighting, it should only have taken two hours at most to cover the seventy-odd miles between Senonches and the outskirts of Paris.

But she'd forgotten about the condition of the roads, which were so perilously potholed that it was suicidal to drive more than thirty miles an hour, and she also hadn't reckoned on their driver getting lost within minutes of their leaving the hospital.

At one o'clock, still twenty miles south of the city—or so she estimated, for the map in the Michelin guide that Mr. Dunleavy had given her was difficult to read in poor light—the driver announced he was too tired to drive any farther, and pulled abruptly to the side of the road. Dan alternated between pleas and threats, but it was no good.

"I haven't slept in three days, sir, and if we go any farther we'll end up in the ditch, or worse. Give me until dawn, and then we'll be on our way again."

The driver—his name was Tony, Ruby had learned, and he came from Jersey City—stretched out on the ground beside the jeep and fell asleep instantly, as did Dan, for all his complaining. Frank had nodded off ages ago, and hadn't woken when they'd pulled over, so Ruby decided to leave him be. She felt exposed sitting in the open jeep, so she sat on the ground and leaned against one of the back tires. It was a warm night, luckily, and she'd slept in worse places. At least no one was aiming bombs at her tonight.

She would look at the stars for a few minutes, she told herself, and hope that Bennett, wherever he was, might be doing the same. One day, when she saw him next, she would ask him.

She closed her eyes, just for a moment, and opened them to the thin, pale light of early dawn. Tony was stomping around, trying to wake himself up, and Dan and Frank were yawning and stretching wearily.

"How long, do you think, until we get to Paris?" she asked Tony.

"We passed a sign not long before we stopped last night. Said thirty kilometers to Paris. What's that—about twenty miles?"

"Sounds about right," Dan agreed.

They passed through the Porte d'Orléans at seven o'clock on the morning of August 26. The streets were quiet and eerily peaceful, despite the irregular noise of shellfire in the distance, and still littered with wilting flowers and abandoned tricolor rosettes and flags. Every so often they had to edge past the remains of barricades, most no more than piles of rubble, broken timber, and scavenged gates and railings.

"If only I'd scared up a driver a day earlier," Dan fretted, another variation on the same theme that had been consuming him since their departure from the 128th. "Everyone else will have filed their stories already, and I'm left out in the cold. Mitchell will have my guts for garters."

"You were never going to break the story," she told him for perhaps the twentieth time. "Remember that you work for a weekly. No matter how fast you file it, whatever you write will be a week behind the dailies. So why don't you stop worrying and start taking notes? There's plenty of material for stories here."

"Like what?"

"Oh, come on. I shouldn't have to tell you this. Just start with what you see and go from there."

He fished around for suggestions for the rest of their journey, but she steadfastly refused to offer any ideas. And she had plenty of ideas for stories, beginning with her firsthand observations of Parisians and their city.

Outwardly, the city seemed to be in better shape than London. An air of shabby neglect clung to the buildings they passed, though the grandeur she'd hoped to see, especially once they reached the central neighborhoods, was still present. The city's boulevards continued wide and straight, its buildings remained pictures of refined elegance, and its cathedrals and churches endured in all their ancient glory.

The suffering of France was written, instead, on the drawn and haggard faces of her people, not one of whom failed to stop and wave and call out blessings to Ruby and her friends as they continued north through the city.

"I'm going to the Hôtel Scribe," Dan announced as they approached the Seine. "Most of the press pack is staying there."

"Then we'll try to get rooms, too."

"They've all been booked up by the big papers and wire services. But you can probably find something nearby."

The Scribe was a fitting name for a place crammed from cellar to attic with journalists tapping away on typewriters, fighting over its too-few telephones, and arguing with the censors who'd set up shop and were tasked with inspecting every outgoing story. Anyone who wasn't busy writing, chasing down leads, or harassing press officers had congregated in the bar that adjoined the lobby, and the loudest of them all was Ernest Hemingway.

He and his acolytes had taken over most of the tables, and though it was not quite nine in the morning, they were working their way through what looked like a bottle of brandy. The great man himself was impossible to miss, his large frame clothed in sweat-stained khaki, his voice drowning out everyone else's as he described, likely not for the first time, how he had personally liberated the Hôtel Ritz the day before.

After a long wait to see the concierge, she discovered that Dan had been correct: the hotel was fully booked.

"May I suggest that Madame try one of the establishments on the rue Daunou? They are rather modest, I'm afraid, but they may have rooms available. And you are of course most welcome to make use of our facilities for your work."

The first two hotels she and Frank tried were full, but they found a pair of rooms at the third, which unfortunately had no lift and only one bath per floor.

"You go first, Ruby," Frank kindly offered. "I know you've been wanting a proper bath for days now."

"That's really nice of you. I promise not to use up all the hot water."

As RUBY WAITED for her hair to dry, she worked her notes into a short piece on entering Paris at dawn. Frank had knocked on her door earlier to announce he was taking a nap, and not wanting to bother him, she decided to head back to the Hôtel Scribe and brave the lineup for the censors. Once she received approval for the piece, she could send it back to *PW* via air courier, so that even if Frank's photos were delayed they might marry her piece with something from one of the agencies.

The Scribe's lobby was, if possible, even more crowded than it had been earlier in the day, and as she stood in line for the censors she was pushed and jostled so many times she felt ready to scream at the next rough-mannered man who barged past her.

Just then, a careless elbow knocked her off balance and sent her reeling into a passerby. Her story, which she'd typed out so carefully, was immediately lost beneath a stampede of passing feet.

Rather than continue on his way, the man she'd bumped into crouched down and helped her gather up the scattered pages. He was older than most of the other journalists, in his midfifties at least, with auburn hair that had faded to white at his temples.

"Are you all right?"

"I'm fine. Thanks for your help," she said. "Ruby Sutton. With *Picture Weekly*."

He shook her outstretched hand. "Sam Howard. With the *Liverpool Herald*."

"John Ellis's paper. I met him—oh, it was back at the end of 1940, I think. November, perhaps? I went up to Liverpool to write about the Durning Road disaster, and he was kind enough to help."

"Hold on," Mr. Howard said, his face brightening with recognition. "You work for Kaz. Sorry—I ought to have made the connection right away. I knew him years ago, when he was just starting out, and I've bumped into him a few times since. How is he?"

"He's well," she said. "Have you been at the *Herald* for a while?"

"Going on twenty years. My wife is English, so I wanted a job that kept me on this side of the pond. We lived in France for most of that time, but came back to London in the fall of '39. Thought it would be safer. Then the Blitz began, and we felt like we'd gone from the frying pan into the fire."

"But you all . . . ?" she asked tentatively, bracing herself for the inevitable story of loss and woe.

"We all survived. Nothing more than broken windows. And you? How long have you been at *PW*?"

"Since the summer of 1940. I was bombed out that December, but I've lived with friends ever since. Compared to some, I've been very lucky. Do you think you'll come back to France to live?"

"One day. Ellie is desperate to return, but this war isn't won yet, and I won't risk her safety, or that of the children. Never mind that they consider themselves all but grown. The eldest joined the ATS as soon as she was able, and spends her weekends stripping back lorry engines."

"Are you staying here?" she asked.

"No. I'm across the road at the Grand. And you?"

"At a little place on rue Daunou. A better match for our budget at *PW*."

"Next!" called the censor, and looking ahead, Ruby realized she was at the front of the line.

"I guess that's me," she said.

"It was good to meet you, Miss Sutton. Give my best to Kaz when you get home. And keep your head down. Paris has been liberated, but not everyone is happy about it. Be careful whenever you're out and about—promise me?"

"I promise. Goodbye, Mr. Howard. And good luck."

Dispatches from London

by Miss Ruby Sutton

August 26, 1944

. . . Compared to London, Paris looks as if it needs little more than a good scrub and a few coats of fresh paint to bring it back to life. I speak of the city itself, its buildings and squares and wide-open boulevards. Its people are in far worse shape, and I cannot begin to imagine how long it will take for them to recover from four years of Nazi oppression and terror . . .

BY ONE O'CLOCK that same afternoon, Ruby and Frank were in place on the Champs-Élysées for the anticipated victory parade. It had proved impossible to reach the front of the crowd, which stretched to ten people deep where they were standing, but the spot they had chosen, half a mile from the Place de la Concorde, boasted a clear view of the avenue as it rose toward the Arc de Triomphe in the west, and by standing on the very tips of her toes and craning her neck, Ruby was able to watch the parade of dignitaries and Allied military might for nearly the entire distance.

Charles de Gaulle himself had just marched past, his height and regal bearing making him impossible to miss, and Ruby, not wishing to forget even the smallest detail, had ducked her head to scribble in her notebook.

Without any warning, strong hands grasped her arms and swung her around. "Ruby," a voice whispered in her ear, and the man pulled away just far enough that she might see his face. It was all but obscured by a scruffy mustache and beard, but wonderfully familiar all the same. Bennett.

He kissed her fiercely, one hand grasping the back of her head, only pulling away when the people around them began to stamp and clap and cheer. "Your room number at the hotel— which is it?" he whispered in her ear.

"Thirty-two."

"I'll be there at nine tonight."

He vanished into the crowd before she could say anything, and she was left to stand among strangers, mute from shock, and try and make sense of what had just happened.

Bennett was *alive*. He was alive and unharmed, and she would see him again in a few hours.

A frantic voice brought her back to earth. "Are you all right? Say something—did that fellow hurt you?"

"No, Frank. Just a bit of high spirits. That's all."

"Gave me a fright, he did, when I saw how he was manhandling you. I tried to get to you in time, but there were half a dozen people between him and me. I'm so sorry."

"I'm fine. Honestly I am. Besides, I doubt it's the last kiss I'll get from a stranger today."

She was right. Their uniforms made them the center of unfettered and crazily exuberant displays of affection from Parisians, whose expressions seemed to indicate that they, too, were perplexed by their compulsion to greet perfect strangers with such a disconcerting lack of decorum. Yet it didn't stop them from hugging and kissing and dancing down the streets with anyone and everyone they encountered in an Allied uniform.

Moving away from the crowds that flanked the Champs-Élysées, Ruby and Frank walked north, in what she hoped was the general direction of their hotel. Away from the parade route, the streets were far less crowded, less noisy, and altogether less overwhelming.

Ruby smiled until her face ached, accepted the many flowers that were pressed into her hands, and tried unsuccessfully to unearth someone who spoke English and might be able to tell her what the last few weeks had been like. But the people she approached couldn't understand her questions, or perhaps they simply didn't want to talk about serious things on such a day.

They walked and walked, and Ruby filled her notebook with observations of the people they encountered. The sun was beginning to set; she checked her wristwatch and realized it was almost seven o'clock.

"Do you want to find somewhere to eat?" she called to Frank, who was trying to extricate himself from the embrace of a large and extremely affectionate nun.

"Yes, please!" he shouted, and she grabbed his arm and pulled him away and down the nearest quiet street. It had no shortage of cafés and restaurants; the problem, though, was that most were closed.

They were standing before one such establishment, trying to summon up the strength to continue along, when its front door burst open and they were confronted by a young man in an apron, his face wreathed in smiles.

"Vous êtes américains? Anglais?"

"Oui," Ruby said, and then she produced the only useful French phrase that she knew: *"Est-ce que vous parlez anglais?"*

"Yes, yes—but of course we speak English for our American friends! Please come in and allow us to feed you. It is our pleasure. Please come in."

It quickly became apparent, since they were the only people in the dining room, that the staff had opened the restaurant especially for Ruby and Frank; and it was also evident that they were being treated to the best the chef and his staff could provide.

After the first bite of bread, fresh-baked and spread with real butter, Ruby knew she'd be dreaming of this meal for years to come. Roast chicken and new potatoes and green beans followed, and then they were served a cake studded with fresh apricots, and by the time they emerged from the restaurant, buoyed by the embraces and gratitude of the staff, she felt as if she were floating on air.

The walk back helped to clear her head and calm her nerves, and once they reached the hotel, a few minutes before nine, Ruby felt she might, just might, be able to get through the next hour or so without bursting into tears at the sight of Bennett, or otherwise embarrassing them both.

"I'm off to bed," Frank said as they collected their keys from the concierge. "How about you? Planning on a visit to the bar at the Scribe?"

"Not tonight, I think," she said, and followed him up the stairs. "Good night, Frank."

She waited until he'd gone into his room and she was alone in the hall. Waited until she could hear past the drumming heartbeat that filled her ears. And then, only then, did she open her door and slip inside.

CHAPTER THIRTY

Bennett was there, waiting for her, as she had hoped and believed he would be. He'd been sitting on the room's only chair, which belonged to a small table by the window, and now he stood and faced her. Between them loomed the bed, too wide for one person and not quite wide enough for two. She hoped it was not the sort of bed that squeaked if you so much as breathed on it.

He was dressed in workman's clothes, clean but ragged, his coat hung carefully on the back of the chair. His hair had grown out in the months since she'd seen him last, and now had some curl to it, as she'd always thought it would. His mustache and beard were threaded with silver, and his face and forearms were tanned.

For long seconds she stared at him, drinking in the sight of his features, his form, everything about him. He was too thin, too tired, but he seemed to be uninjured.

"How did you find me in that crowd?" she asked.

"I'd been keeping an eye on you since you landed in France." Of course he had.

"I got your letter," she said.

"I know. I wish I hadn't left it. Looking back, it seems so ridiculously self-centered. To leave you with *that* as a goodbye. It would have been better to simply vanish."

"No," she insisted. "Never say that. I treasure that letter. Would you believe I have it memorized? Just like you with your poems."

"There was nothing very poetic about it," he grumbled.

"I disagree. And what does it matter now? We're here. We survived. What do you say to that?"

He smiled, his teeth a flash of white against his tanned face and dark beard, and took a step toward her, then another, until his knees bumped against the bed.

She moved forward, too, her heart hammering in her breast, and before she could think twice she unbuttoned her uniform jacket. A shimmy of her shoulders, enough to make Bennett's eyes darken with hunger, and it fell to the floor.

"Ruby," he rumbled, his deep voice roughened by desire. "If you only knew how many times I've thought about this moment. Tried to conjure up every last detail. Wondered if I'd ever have the chance."

"I know," she said, emotion clogging her throat. "I wondered, too."

She unbuttoned the cuffs on her shirt, untucked it from her skirt, and not once did she look away from his face. Another step forward and she was kneeling on the bed. A heartbeat later and she was in his arms, enveloped in his fierce embrace, and he was kissing her, his mouth pressing against hers with growing and near-desperate urgency, his beard deliciously rough against her shivering skin.

She unbuttoned his shirt and dragged it down his arms, and as soon as it was gone she pulled his undershirt loose from his trousers and pulled it off, too. His skin was pale, apart from the tan of his forearms and throat, and contrasted sharply with the dark, softly curling hair that dusted his upper chest. All the easier, then, for her to see the marks that told her more about his work than she had ever wanted to know.

There were too many bruises to count, some fresh, some fading, and there was a long, puckered scar, newly healed, across his tautly muscled stomach. He stood there, let her run her fingers over the evidence of past wounds, and not once did he protest, not even when she found the mark by his collarbone. An older scar, raised and circular, no bigger than the diameter of her baby finger.

"Were you shot?" she asked, touching it lightly. Afraid it might still hurt.

"Yes. It happened a while ago."

She swept her fingers over his back, where a scar from the bullet's exit wound ought to be, and found nothing but smooth skin. "Is the bullet still inside you?" she asked, her mouth going dry.

"No. Someone dug it out. I'm embarrassed to say I passed out before she was done."

"She?"

"The village midwife. And a nun, as it happens. Risked her life to save me."

"Perhaps, one day, you might return to wherever it was, and thank her."

"Perhaps," he agreed. "Are you almost done with your inspection?"

"Almost. What about this one? On your stomach?"

"What about it? I survived, didn't I? And they look worse than they are. Even the tiniest scratch leaves a mark on me."

"These aren't scratches," she whispered, her lips brushing over each scar. "They're badges of honor."

His skin was surprisingly sensitive, jumping and twitching wherever her mouth landed, but she didn't halt, didn't even consider it, until he took hold of her chin and tilted her head back just enough that he might look her in the eye.

"I don't want to think about any of that tonight," he said, and then he kissed her again, his mouth tracing a glowing line from her lips to the fluttery place just below her earlobe, and from there down to her collarbone and the rising swell of her breasts.

She began to unbutton her uniform shirt, but this time he pushed aside her hands and did it himself. Then he was unfastening her skirt, which he whisked over her head before she could protest, and she was left in nothing more than her brassiere, panties, garter belt, and stockings.

"You are so beautiful," he whispered reverently. "Everything about you is lovely. Everything."

"I love you," she said. "I feel as if I've loved you forever."

"I know. I love you, too. Such a gift, to be able to say it to your face. There were so many times when I thought I would never get the chance."

"How long do we have? I mean until you leave."

"Only until the morning."

"Then what are we waiting for?" she asked, and this time it was her turn to kiss him.

RUBY WOKE BEFORE dawn, her head tucked against his shoulder, feeling so content that she couldn't imagine ever wanting to move. The curtains were thin and worn, and did little to mask the brightening sky outside, but she didn't care, for she planned on memorizing every detail of his face and form before he disappeared into his work again.

There was nothing about him that she didn't like, from the soft, dark hair on his chest to the wash of freckles across his pale shoulders. Even his hands were lovely, with long, straight fingers.

Only then did she notice the marks around his wrists, horrid purple welts that had broken and scabbed over in a few places.

"What is this?" she whispered, her throat closing in.

Nearly a minute passed before he answered, his eyes still shut tight. "I was caught. Beaten. There was a hook in the wall. They tied me to it and left me dangling for a few days. But that, and a round of kicks and punches, were the worst of it. They couldn't have been that suspicious or I wouldn't be here now."

"When did this happen?"

"A few weeks ago."

"And when you say 'they,' who do you mean?"

"The Milice. The collaborationists' militia. If it had been the Gestapo proper, I'd be dead."

"What did they accuse you of doing?" she asked, so nauseous she thought she might have to run for the bathroom down the hall.

"Nothing. They never asked me a thing. My walking down the street out of uniform was enough. Perhaps they were bored, and I was a way for them to pass the time."

"Were you afraid?"

"Of course I was. Only a fool forgets to be afraid. But I knew as long as I kept my head they would probably let me go. My papers were in order, and I speak French without an accent. I simply had to endure until they found someone else to torment."

"All those times you were away, when you disappeared for months, were you in France?"

"Sometimes. That's all I can tell you."

"I heard some people talking once. They said that people like you were given a cyanide tablet and a garrote, and not much else."

"A knife is better. Quieter and faster."

"So you . . . you've had to kill people?"

"Yes."

"Was that the hardest thing you've ever done?"

"I . . . no. No, it wasn't." He covered his eyes with his forearm, as if to block out the sight of his most painful memories. "It's not simply the case that I'm secretive, you know. I don't want you to know such things because I don't want you to be burdened by them."

"But that's part of loving someone. Sharing the weight of the burdens they carry. If you want to tell me, then go ahead. I won't break."

He swallowed, the muscles in his jaw convulsing, and her hand, resting against his chest, began to thrum from the drumbeat of his racing heart.

"I was working with another man. He was captured by the Gestapo. He killed himself before they could get anything out of him, and they decided to retaliate.

"I'd had just enough time to hide. Was high up on a rooftop that overlooked the village square. They dragged in the handful of young men who were left—most had been taken away to labor camps—and they hanged them from the plane trees around the perimeter of the square. One after the other, as their mothers screamed and begged and pleaded with the Germans. Seven of them, and the youngest was fifteen. He was only fifteen.

"I had to watch them die. There was nothing I could do. I'd have given myself up to save them, but I had to send out a message. My colleague hadn't enough time to get it out before he was captured. I can't tell you what it was about, but it was vital. I knew that thousands of lives, perhaps tens of thousands, would be spared if I could get that message sent. And so I stayed hidden and watched them die. It's been more than a year, but when I close my eyes I can still see their faces."

"If they had caught you," she asked carefully, "would we have known? Would someone have called Uncle Harry?"

"Yes. You'd have known that I was dead, but that was all."

"We were worried earlier in the summer. Harry stopped getting the postcards from your office."

His arms tightened about her. "I am sorry about that. They lost track of me, and it wasn't safe for me to let them know I was alive. Once I was able to send out a message, I did pass on the news, but that was less than a week ago. You were already on your way to France."

"What now? What happens next?"

"We make love. We say our farewells. And then you return to your work, I return to mine, and we both do our level best not to get killed."

"And after the war?"

"I will come home to you. It may be months or even years, but I will come home to you."

CHAPTER THIRTY-ONE

Ruby and Frank were back in England by the middle of September, arriving in Southampton the very morning her thirty-day war correspondent's pass expired. There was time enough, as they waited for their train to London, to ring home with news of her homecoming, and when Ruby's taxi pulled to a stop in front of the house, Vanessa was waiting at the door.

As soon as she'd set her free from a long and nearly smothering embrace, Vanessa pointed Ruby in the direction of the stairs. "I am *agog* to hear every last detail, but first you must have a bath and something to eat. Jessie is heating up some soup for you now."

"You're a mind reader, Vanessa. Thank you."

An hour later she was ensconced on the sitting room sofa, Simon was curled up on her lap, Vanessa was seated inches away, and it was time to tell the story of her month as an accredited war correspondent, albeit with a few prudent omissions.

Although she'd written Vanessa every few days when she was

away, Ruby had saved the telling of Dan Mazur's ignominious collapse in the operating room for this moment, and if she embellished his faults in the retelling, it was only to amuse her friend. She also took pains to describe, in as much detail as she could summon, the delicious meals she and Frank had eaten in Paris, the beautiful buildings they had visited, and the fierce dignity of the French people.

"You haven't said anything yet about Bennett," Vanessa observed. "How was he?"

"Well enough. Alive."

"That was when you'd just arrived in Paris?"

"Yes. He found me in the crowd. But he wasn't able to stay for long."

"Long enough, I hope!"

"*Vanessa.*"

"Oh, don't mind me. Although . . . how did you, ah, leave things?"

"He promised to come home to me. And I believe he will."

"As do I."

They sat in silence for a minute or so, the two of them listening to Simon's purr.

"Did you read any of my pieces? The ones from France?" Ruby asked, suddenly anxious for Vanessa's approval.

"Of course I did—every last one. I adored the story about the American hospital. Simply wonderful stuff. You've such a knack for capturing a sense of place. I really did feel I knew those nurses and that doctor by the time you were done. And the poor boys they were trying to save. Just thinking about it, now, brings tears to my eyes."

"Did you see my piece in last week's issue?"

"The one about the building where the Gestapo tortured people? Yes. I don't know how you were able to bear it."

"After Frank and I were finished there, after we'd seen everything the French wanted us to see, we walked back to our hotel. It was only about a half mile away but it seemed to take forever. I got back to my room and I had to be clean. I had to wash that evil place off my skin. So I went down the hall and ran a bath and I scrubbed and scrubbed until the water was cold and I'd run out of soap."

Standing outside the unremarkable building on the rue de Saussaies that morning, she'd had only the faintest notion of what she would find inside. The French authorities had said it was a place of detention, of torture, and of execution. She had heard the words clearly enough, but she hadn't understood.

Not until she had toured through cell after cell, their barred windows offering a monstrous view of the inner courtyard where, after days of unrelenting torture, countless men and women had been tied to a post and shot, did she understand. A reprieve from execution, their guide explained, had meant only a one-way journey to Nazi death camps in the east. No one had escaped number 11, rue de Saussaies. No one.

Many of the cells had writing on their plaster walls; what amounted to epitaphs, Ruby had realized. *J'ai peur,* one had said. *I am afraid.* Others offered farewells to loved ones or, defiant to the last, condemned Nazi barbarity. The hardest to read, the one that nearly brought her to her knees, simply said, *la vie est belle.*

Life is beautiful.

A gentle touch on her arm brought Ruby back to the here and now. "Did you leave Paris after that? Go farther north?"

"No. So much of France isn't yet secure. And I probably

wouldn't have been given permission to get any closer to the fighting. Frank might easily have gone alone, but he refused to leave me."

"Such a lovely man. It was a comfort to know you were with him."

"He was so keen to be back with his wife. I hope he doesn't come up for air for days."

"And you?" Vanessa asked. "Will you go back to work to-morrow?"

"I will. I sent Kaz a telegram a few days ago, just to let him know we were on our way home. He sent me one by return that said he'd had a letter from my old editor at *The American*. Apparently Mr. Mitchell is wondering when I'll be returning to the States."

Vanessa looked as if she were about to cry. "Please don't tell me you're even considering it. I can't bear it."

"I'm not. I love my country, I do, but everyone who matters to me is here. If I go back to New York, I'll be alone again."

"And we can't let that happen," Vanessa said, blinking back tears.

"No. I've come too far for that."

THE NEXT MORNING, still shy of eight o'clock, Ruby was back at *PW*. After a jubilant greeting from Evelyn, she made the rounds of the office with promises to share her stories later that day. And then, before she knew it, she was standing in front of Kaz's open door.

"I'm back."

"I know. Come in and sit down while I finish this thought." She sat, watching him fondly as he scribbled away. At last he set down his pen and looked up at her, his pale eyes aglow with affection. "It's very good to see you. Did you have a happy reunion with Vanessa?"

"The happiest."

"And Bennett?"

"He was well, or at least he was when I saw him last."

"Does he have any notion of when he'll be home?"

"No," she said, shaking her head. "Though I can't imagine it will be before the end of the war."

"Yes—the end of the war. Have you given any thought to what you want to do?" Kaz the editor was back, and there was something in his serious expression that made Ruby sit up a little straighter in her chair.

"I have," she said. "Is this about the letter you got from Mike Mitchell?"

"In part. You know he's keen for an answer as to when I'll be sending you back. The man seems to think you have a bright future at *The American*. As do I, for that matter. Assuming that's what you want."

"What if I don't?" she countered. "What if I want to stay here?"

"You certainly can. You know you've a job with me as long as you want one. You ought to know, too, that I don't enforce any sort of marriage bar here at *PW*."

It was a good thing Ruby wasn't given to blushing, otherwise her face would have been fire-engine red. "A marriage bar?"

"Yes. The antediluvian convention whereby women are given the sack upon marriage. I never—"

"I know what it *is*. I just don't understand why we're talking about it *now*."

It was Kaz's turn to blush. "I do beg your pardon. I had assumed that you and Bennett had, ah, come to an understanding."

"We haven't. I mean, not in so many words. Oh, please—can we talk about something else?"

"Of course. Let's focus on your having a job here as long as you want one. Will that do?"

"Yes."

"And that's what you want? When this war is over and done?"

"I think so. I mean . . . I've never thought beyond the end of the war. I know I want to stay here, and I know that I love Bennett. But that's all I can be certain of right now."

"That's everything, though. Everything that matters. You've a home here, friends who care for you, work that you love. Don't you see?"

"I do." And the realization of it, the certain knowledge that Kaz was right, made her heart grow tight in her chest. "Do you remember my first day? How nervous I was? I'd no idea of what sort of writer I wanted to be, let alone what kind of person I wanted to become."

"And now?"

"Now I know. I was so unsure of myself back then. As if I had everything to prove, and nothing to lose."

He nodded, his expression warm with understanding. "But that was five years ago. How do you feel today?"

"Excited. Still a little nervous. Ready for what's next."

"Good," he said decisively. "So—shall we have an editorial meeting? Just to bring you back up to speed? And then lunch at the Old Bell?"

"I wouldn't miss it for the world."

A TELEGRAM WAS waiting for her when they returned from lunch. She knew not to panic, for bad news about Bennett would never come by telegram. He'd told her as much when he'd kissed her goodbye that morning in Paris.

"I'll send you a telegram each week, plus or minus a day if I can't get to a dispatch office. If anything does happen to me, you'll find out from Harry, who's just as likely to saddle Kaz with the news. So don't be alarmed when the first telegram makes its way to you."

She opened the envelope with care, for she didn't want to tear the flimsy piece of paper inside. It was the same message he'd sent her three times already, and once again it comforted her beyond measure.

DEAREST R. ALL IS WELL. I WILL COME HOME TO YOU. B.

CHAPTER THIRTY-TWO

May 8, 1945

A dvance, Britannia! Long live the cause of freedom! God save the king!'"

As the final words of the prime minister's V-E Day address to the nation faded away, Kaz produced a bottle of Scotch and proceeded to splash an eye-watering ration into each of the mugs that Evelyn had set out earlier on the center table in the main office.

"To victory in Europe!"

"Hear, hear!"

"To His Majesty the king!"

"Hear, hear!"

"And to absent friends," he finished.

"Hear, hear!"

Ruby swallowed a great mouthful of whiskey, the first she'd ever tasted, and the unexpected rush of molten lava down her throat left her eyes streaming and her lungs bursting for want of air.

"Easy, now," Frank soothed. "Not all in one go. You'll be falling over."

"And now I want all of you to return home," Kaz commanded. "The issue is in the bag, thanks to everyone's hard work last night, and you can begin your celebrations with a clear conscience."

Ruby didn't need to be told twice. With one final round of hugs to her friends, and a last kiss to Kaz's stubbly cheek, she ran out the door, her departure coinciding with the first joyous peals of the city's church bells. It was the first time she had heard them since coming to England.

Vanessa was waiting in the front hall. "I couldn't help my-self—I rang your office, and Miss Berridge said you were on your way home. Oh, Ruby—at last, at last!" Together they danced down the hallway and around the house until they both collapsed on the sitting room sofa.

"The girls are coming," Vanessa gasped, thoroughly out of breath. "We'll have an early dinner, and then I thought we could see how close we can get to Buckingham Palace. Won't that be fun?"

Vi and Bea rolled through the door well before six o'clock, and after a hurried meal of beans on toast, and heartfelt promises to Jessie to be careful, they were on their way. Vi had persuaded her mother to take the Underground, explaining that it was only two stops and there was no other means to get close to the center of things, and though Vanessa had to hold her daughter's hand the entire journey, and was very pale by the time they stepped off the jam-packed train, she recovered her spirits as soon as they emerged from Hyde Park station and were swept up in the mass of jubilation swirling about them.

"Hold on tight," Vi insisted. "We don't want to be separated. And follow me!"

It took ages to make any headway in the crowd, but Vi was persistent, and after a solid forty-five minutes they were within sight of the palace. Another ten minutes took them to the edge of Green Park, but after that the crowds were too dense for them to go any farther.

By standing on her tiptoes, Ruby could just make out the balcony at Buckingham Palace. Before them, the great open space around the Victoria Memorial and along the Mall was a buoyant sea of joyful people, tens of thousands of them, their voices rising in a single, chanted demand: "We want the king! We want the king!"

"Heavens," Vanessa said suddenly. "I almost forgot." She pulled a spyglass from her handbag, the kind of object that Lord Nelson might have held up to his lone eye. "This was in the library, and I thought it might be useful. Bea—you're the tallest. Tell us what you see."

Bea extended the telescope and fitted it to her eye just as a roar surged through the crowd.

"What is it, what is it?" Vi implored.

"It's the king! And the queen!"

"What about the princesses?" Vanessa asked.

"No, only the king and queen—oh, and they're waving!" She looked a moment more, and then she handed it to Vi. "No telling how long they'll be out—have a look and pass it on."

There was just time for Ruby to catch one quick glimpse of the king, so tall and handsome in his uniform, and the smaller figure of the queen, who was dressed in a light-colored dress and hat that made her easy to spot against the stonework of the balcony.

"What now?" Bea asked, and together they decided to walk on to Trafalgar Square, since there was no rush to get home, and the lights were all on anyway.

"After all those years of blackout, it feels as bright as day now," Vanessa observed, and she was right—to see London lighted up at night, after half a decade of gloom and darkness, was just about the most inspiring sight that Ruby could imagine.

At Trafalgar Square they wandered around for an hour or more, watching people splash around in the fountains and sing at the top of their lungs, and it was no trouble to persuade Vi to climb up and stand between the forepaws of one of the great bronzed lions, and from there to lead a sing-along of "Jerusalem," "Rule Britannia," and "God Save the King."

"More! More!" people shouted, but Vi's voice was almost gone and they were all beginning to feel tired.

Next they walked down to the Thames at Westminster, hoping the crowds would be a little thinner there, and only as they approached the Houses of Parliament did Ruby think to look east along the river. Searchlights were forming a huge V in the sky above the dome of St. Paul's, and on the Thames itself the tugboats and fireboats were chugging back and forth, the latter sending arcs of water high into the air.

They walked all the way home, their feet aching but their spirits light, and were still chattering and laughing as they burst through the front door just shy of midnight.

"Is that the wireless?" Vanessa asked. "I don't remember leaving it on."

"Perhaps Jessie was having a listen before going to bed," Ruby suggested.

"I suppose. Let me just switch it off and—Ruby!"

"What is it?"

"Just come here. And, girls—upstairs with me now. Quietly, though."

Wondering at the fuss over a wireless left on, Ruby hurried down the hall, stopping short at the welcome sight awaiting her. Bennett was in the easy chair next to the wireless, Simon on his lap, and both were fast asleep.

She stood in the doorway and simply looked at him, letting her eyes take in every beloved feature, every detail of his appearance. He had shaved off his beard, and his hair was military short again. He wasn't as thin as he'd been when she'd last seen him, though his uniform made it hard to be sure.

"Bennett," she said, but he didn't rouse. She crossed the room and knelt at his side, reaching up to brush her fingertips across his brow and down his cheek. "Bennett, my darling. You've come home to me."

His eyes fluttered open. "Hello," he said, his voice raspy from sleep. "I only meant to sit down for a minute and listen to the news."

"When did you get back?" she asked.

"Just before nine. Did you have fun? Jessie said you went out right after supper."

"We did. It was so much fun—we even saw the king and queen."

"How'd you manage to get close enough?"

"We didn't. Vanessa had an old spyglass of Nick's. We all took turns."

This made him smile. He stood, taking Simon with him, and gently set the cat on the floor. Then he turned to Ruby. "It has been exactly two hundred and fifty-five days since I saw you last." There was a glint in his eye that reminded her, suddenly and wonderfully, of the night they'd spent together, and the nights he'd promised would follow once the war was done.

"I know," she said huskily. "I was counting, too. Will you stay this time?"

"Yes," he said, and then he kissed her until she was breathless and shaky and ready for far more than was possible in a house filled with other people. When he finally dragged his mouth from hers, it was only so he might hug her close, her head tucked just so under his chin, her ear pressed close to his heart.

"Ruby? Will you sit down for a moment?"

"Why? Is something wrong?"

"Shh," he said, and as soon as she was seated on the chair he knelt before her. "I've been rehearsing this in my head for months. You'll throw me off." He fished about in the breast pocket of his uniform jacket and pulled out a little box. "I'd have been home earlier today, but I had to stop in Edenbridge for this."

"Is this . . . ?" she asked wonderingly.

"It is." He opened the box and took out the ring inside. "It was my mother's, but if you don't like it, or it doesn't fit, we can find another."

The ring was a trio of stones in a filigree platinum setting, the central ruby flanked by diamonds, and it all but took her breath away.

"I thought, at first, that I would preface this with some poetry. But I've waited nearly a year to say these words to you, and I'm not going to wait any longer. Ruby, will you marry me?"

"Yes," she said, pleased by how firmly she'd answered him.

He slid the ring on her finger, and it was only a little bit too big. "We'll have it sized. Do you like it?"

"Very much. When are—"

"Is it safe to come in?" Vi called out from the hall. "We have champagne. Remember, Ruby? The bottle you brought home from France."

"What say you?" Bennett asked. "Are you ready to share our news?"

"Yes. Mainly because I want some of that champagne. It will help to erase the memory of my first taste of Scotch this afternoon. Awful stuff."

"I'll pretend you didn't say that," he whispered, and then, for the benefit of the Tremaine women, "where's that champagne?"

They turned to face everyone, though Bennett kept his arm around her waist, and Ruby's heart nearly cracked in two at the look of hopeful anticipation on Vanessa's face.

"Ruby and I have some news to share. A moment ago I asked her to do me the honor of becoming my wife. And to my very great relief, she has accepted."

Vanessa burst into tears, which set Ruby to crying, and then Vi and Bea, too. As they embraced and wept and the other women admired Ruby's ring, Bennett set to work opening the champagne and filling their glasses.

"To king and country and glad days ahead," he offered.

"To glad days ahead."

The instant their glasses were empty, Vi took her mother by the arm and propelled her toward the door. "It's about time we let Bennett and Ruby talk. You only gave them five minutes alone before you insisted on rushing in."

As soon as they were alone again, for even Simon had vanished, Bennett steered Ruby to the narrow settee by the window. "Happy?" he asked, his hands twined in hers.

"Very. What now?"

"We plan our future. Have you given any thought to where you want to live? Where you'll work?"

"You'd let me work?"

This earned her a suitably reproving glare, though it was rather undone by his smile. "Roberta Anne Sutton. What kind of question is that? Do you not know me at all? Of course I would."

"I want to work. And I'll be staying on at *PW*—Kaz asked me a while ago."

"You truly wish to live here in London?"

"I do. This is where I belong. This is where my friends are, where my family is. And this is where I want to tell my stories."

Dispatches from London

by Miss Ruby Sutton

May 8, 1945

. . . Tonight I stood with my family and friends as we said a toast to glad days ahead, and for the first time in years I can feel them around the corner. Of course the war in Japan is still to be won, and the world will yet see many hard days in the months to come. All the more reason, on this day of victory, to raise a glass to hearth and home, to freedom and liberty, to those we have lost, those who are still in peril, and to the promise of glad days ahead. May they arrive sooner than any of us dare hope. Until then, goodnight from London.

ACKNOWLEDGMENTS

Once again I would like to thank everyone who has embraced my books so enthusiastically. I am very fortunate to have such devoted readers, and I am deeply grateful to each and every one of you.

In the course of researching this book, I relied upon the collections of a number of libraries and archives. I would specifically like to acknowledge the Bodleian Library at the University of Oxford, the British Newspaper Archive, the Mass-Observation Archive at the University of Sussex, the Museum of London, the National Archives (UK), the National Library of Scotland, the New York Public Library, and the Toronto Public Library.

I would also like to offer my thanks to Aaron Orkin for once again patiently answering my questions related to medicine, to Susan Coates for casting her keen editorial eye over the final manuscript, and to Stuart Robson for once again reading through my final draft so diligently.

I would like to acknowledge the debt of thanks I owe to the women who participated in the oral history project I undertook as part of my doctoral research in 1993-1994, the results of which I drew upon while researching this book. Though the participants in my project remain anonymous here, in keeping with a promise I made a quarter century ago, I have never forgotten the hours I spent with them, and I am deeply grateful to each of them for taking the time to speak with me so frankly and honestly.

To my literary agent, Kevan Lyon, and her colleagues at the Marsal Lyon Literary Agency, in particular Patricia Nelson, I once again extend my heartfelt thanks.

I am deeply grateful to my former editor, Amanda Bergeron, for her understanding and support throughout the entire creation of this book, as well as to my current editor, Tessa Woodward, for her generous and able counsel. I am also very grateful to Elle Keck in editorial, as well as my publicists Camille Collins, Melissa Nowakowski, Emily Homonoff, and Miranda Snyder.

I would like to thank everyone who supports me and my books at William Morrow, in particular Martin Karlow, Serena Wang, Diahann Sturge, Robin Barletta, Amelia Wood, Jennifer Hart, Samantha Hagerbaumer, Molly Waxman, and Carla Parker. The producers at HarperAudio have once again created a beautiful audiobook and I am most grateful for their hard work. I also want to thank all of the sales staff in the U.S., Canada and the international division, as well as the wonderful team at HarperCollins Canada, among them Leo Macdonald, Sandra Leff, Cory Beatty, Shannon Parsons, and Kaitlyn Vincent.

Closer to home, I'd like to thank my friends for their love: Amutha, Ana, Clara, Denise, Erin, Jane D., Jane E., Jen M., Kelly F., Kelly W., Liz, Mary, Mary Ellen, Michela, and Rena. To Kate Hilton, Marissa Stapley, Karma Brown, Chantel Guertin, and Elizabeth Renzetti, my fellow members of the coven, my deepest gratitude for your friendship and support.

My heartfelt thanks go out as well to my family in Canada and in the U.K., especially my aunt, Terry Lindsay, and my uncle, John Moir, who patiently answered many questions about my late grandmother's life and work; my father and stepmother, Stuart and Mariel Robson; my sisters, Kate Robson and Molly Robson; and my beautiful children, Matthew and Daniela.

Most of all I want to thank my husband, Claudio, for once again making everything possible. I could never have taken this journey without you at my side.

About the author

About the book

Read on . . .

Insights,
Interviews
& More . . .

Meet Jennifer Robson

Natalie Brown / Tangerine Photo

JENNIFER ROBSON is the *USA Today* and #1 *Globe & Mail* bestselling author of *Somewhere in France, After the War is Over* and *Moonlight Over Paris.* She first learned about the Great War from her father, acclaimed historian Stuart Robson. In her late teens, she worked as an official guide at the Canadian National War Memorial at Vimy Ridge in France and had the honor of meeting a number of First World War veterans. After graduating from King's College at the University of Western Ontario, she attended Saint Antony's College, University of Oxford, where she earned a doctorate in British economic and social history. She was a Commonwealth Scholar and an SSHRC Doctoral Fellow while at Oxford. Jennifer lives in Toronto, Canada, with her husband and young children, and shares her home office with Sam the cat, Mika the kitten, and Ellie the sheepdog. ❧

Glossary of Terms and Places in *Goodnight from London*

The bombing that took place during the Second World War altered urban Britain dramatically; many of the streets and buildings I mention in this book have now vanished or have been so altered as to be unrecognizable. A project by the National Library of Scotland, freely available online, overlays historic maps on current maps of Great Britain, thereby allowing you to compare the before-and-after with ease. Go to maps.nls.uk/geo /explore or visit my website at www .jennifer-robson.com for the link.

If you're interested in seeing what the buildings I mention in *Goodnight from London* look like today (if they still exist), or are curious as to what replaced them, or if you would like to get a sense of where the places I mention are in relation to one another, I've created a *Goodnight from London* map via Google Maps. Feel free to visit (and use the Street View option to take a closer look). You can find it online at goo.gl/qZpW3i or via my website.

You may also be interested in visiting the bombsight.org website; its digitized bomb census maps provide a startling and powerful insight into the sheer volume of explosives that were dropped on London alone during the Blitz. ▸

Glossary of Terms and Places in
Goodnight from London (continued)

Ack-ack guns: Antiaircraft gun batteries were a familiar sight around Britain throughout the war; although the sound of their fire was considered a morale-booster, they were a largely ineffective deterrent against enemy bombers during the Blitz itself.

ATA: The Air Transport Auxiliary was a civilian organization that ferried military aircraft, for instance from factories to maintenance units, thereby freeing up combat pilots for military work. As many as one in eight of its pilots were women.

Anderson shelter: Named after government minister Sir John Anderson, these shelters were constructed of corrugated metal panels in a distinctive arched shape; more than 3.5 million were installed in private gardens across Britain, though they proved unpopular because of their tendency to flood in wet weather.

ARP: Air Raid Precautions was a civilian defense organization that enforced blackout regulations, managed air raid sirens, and assisted with first aid, rescue, and ambulance services. From 1941 onwards it was known officially as the Civil Defence Service, although the ARP acronym persisted.

Baby Austin: Nickname for the small, light, and economical Austin 7 motorcar that was produced between 1922–1939.

Barrage balloons: Large balloons, blimp-like in appearance, that were tethered above bombing targets as a deterrent against low-flying aircraft.

Boiler suit: A one-piece protective coverall; a variant on this was the siren suit (see below).

Cablese: A series of codes, almost a language unto themselves, used by telegraph operators and newspaper editors to shorten telegrams, or cables, to save on the costs of transmission; since cables were priced by the word, great efforts were made to combine words, create memorable acronyms, or mangle accepted rules of grammar to reduce costs.

Emergency Powers Act: First enacted in 1939, this act gave the government greatly extended powers during the war. Its provisions were not repealed until 1959.

Doodlebug: A nickname for the V-1 flying rocket, a form of guided missile used by Germany to attack targets in Britain in 1944–1945.

ENSA: The Entertainments National Service Association was founded in 1939 with the aim of providing entertainment to military personnel and people doing war work (munitions workers, for instance). Its performers included such well-known figures as John Gielgud, ▶

Glossary of Terms and Places in
Goodnight from London (continued)

Gertrude Lawrence, Vivien Leigh, Vera
Lynn, and Laurence Olivier.

Evacuation hospital: smaller and
ostensibly mobile field hospitals, broadly
similar to the casualty clearing stations
of WWI, that handled much of the
casualties in the wake of D-Day; soldiers
were stabilized and transferred to Britain
by sea or air as quickly as possible.

Falaise pocket: also known as the Falaise
gap, the battle for control of this area in
Normandy was a critical engagement
during Operation Overlord in August
1944.

Fifth columnist: Someone who works
to subvert the aims of a larger group
from within; suspicion of fifth column
activities ran high during the summer
of 1940, when a German invasion of
Britain was widely feared.

Free French: After the fall of France
to Germany in May 1940, the French
government in exile was led by Charles
de Gaulle and headquartered in Britain.

Incendiary bombs: As distinct from
high-explosive bombs, incendiaries
were smaller devices, often fueled with
magnesium, that burned fiercely upon
impact but didn't explode; the fires they
started not only caused damage to
property but also helped guide further
enemy bombardments.

Internment camps: In the early years of the war, tens of thousands of foreign-born nationals were interned in camps across Britain; a significant proportion were refugees from the Nazi regime in Germany and occupied Europe.

ISRB: The Inter-Services Research Bureau was one of the cover names used by the Special Operations Executive; other cover names included the Inter-Services Signals Unit, the Joint Technical Board, and the Ministry of Economic Warfare.

Jerry: Slang for a German soldier or the Germans in general.

LDV: The Local Defence Volunteers, established in 1940, were the first iteration of what later became the Home Guard.

Lend-lease: Enacted in March 1941, the United States' Lend-Lease program furnished Allied nations with war matériel, fuel, and food, altogether more than $50 billion worth, both before and after the U.S. entered the Second World War.

Milice: A paramilitary organization, created by the Vichy regime in occupied France, which fought the Resistance while furthering fascist aims (among them the deportation and murder of French Jews). ▶

Glossary of Terms and Places in
Goodnight from London (continued)

Military Cross: A British military decoration awarded for conspicuous gallantry.

Ministry of Food: This ministry oversaw the food supply chain during the war and was responsible for the program of food rationing that began in early 1940.

MOI: The Ministry of Information, headquartered at Senate House in central London, coordinated all government publicity and propaganda during the war.

Morrison sandwich: A communal surface shelter, built quickly in the early months of the war, with brick sides and a concrete or masonry roof; these were vulnerable to direct hits and the blast force of nearby explosions. Distinct from a Morrison shelter (see below).

Morrison shelter: Named after Herbert Morrison, the Minister of Home Security, these reinforced wooden structures with wire mesh sides resembled a large table and were used for shelter within the home.

Mulberry harbor: A temporary, movable harbor developed for use off the coast of Normandy in the wake of the D-Day invasion.

Musette bag: A canvas or leather bag, typically with a shoulder strap, favored by soldiers and war correspondents alike; often used instead of the heavier standard-issue haversack.

Off-ration: The term for foodstuffs and items not subject to rationing controls during the war; for example, fish and game meats remained off-ration during the war. Restaurant meals were off-ration, though subject to price controls.

Parachute mine: Highly destructive naval mines used by the Luftwaffe during the Blitz.

Phoney War: Also known as the Bore War, this was the eight-month period beginning in September 1939 after which war had been declared but little in the way of military offensives took place.

RAF: The Royal Air Force. The RAF pilots who prevailed against the German air force in the summer of 1940, at the height of the Battle of Britain, were the men of whom Churchill said, "never has so much been owed by so many to so few."

Rationing: Food, fuel, and clothing were rationed during the war; though on a day-to-day basis rationing was resented, it was generally accepted by the British people as the only practical way to ensure fair shares for all.

Scrag end: An inexpensive cut of lamb or mutton.

Siren suit: Similar to a boiler suit, this type of one-piece coverall provided warmth and protection against the ▶

9

elements during air raids; popularized by Winston Churchill, who delighted in wearing his suit when meeting dignitaries such as President Roosevelt.

SOE: The Special Operations Executive was founded in July 1940, in the dark days following the fall of France, with the aim of sending agents on covert missions to occupied Europe. It was a highly secretive operation, with an abundance of cover names, and everyone associated with it was constrained with vows of secrecy and threats of prosecution, imprisonment or worse if word leaked out. The operations of F Section (where Bennett works) focused on occupied France. Of 470 SOE agents sent into France, 118 failed to return; agents who were captured alive were invariably tortured before being executed. For many years after the war, little was known of the bravery and sacrifices of the men and women of the SOE, and only with the gradual declassification of the executive's records since the 1990s have historians been able to assess its significance to the war. For more information on the SOE, please see my suggestions for further reading.

Stenographer: A clerk or secretary trained in the use of shorthand.

Underground: The first stations in London's Underground subway system opened in the 1860s. By 1939 the Tube (it got the nickname in the 1890s) had hundreds of stations, though relatively few were used as shelters during the Blitz; most Londoners preferred to shelter at home or in communal aboveground shelters.

VE Day: Victory in Europe Day, which took place on 8 May 1945, marked the official end of the war in Europe. Across Britain an estimated one million people gathered in public places to celebrate.

WAAF: the Women's Auxiliary Air Force, which did not include women as aircrew (see the ATA above), was an auxiliary force that assisted RAF operations.

WAC: the Women's Army Corps (initially the WAAC) was founded in 1942, and was the women's branch of the U.S. Army, with more than 150,000 members over the course of the war.

Whitsun: also known as Whit Sunday, this is the seventh Sunday after Easter and a significant holiday in early twentieth-century Britain.

Wire services: another term for the news agencies, among them the Associated Press and Reuters, whose journalists' work is used by subscribing publications.

WPA: The Works Progress Administration was a New Deal Agency, formed in 1935, that employed millions of unemployed workers in public works projects. ▶

Glossary of Terms and Places in
Goodnight from London (continued)

A note on currency: Before British currency was decimalized in 1971—that is, before pounds and pence were measured in divisions of one hundred—it was measured in pounds, shillings, and pence. Twelve pence made up one shilling and twenty shillings made up one pound, with a total of 240 pence in a pound. Written in numeric form, a pound was symbolized by the term still in use, "£," while a shilling was "s" and a pence was "d". Other coins were circulated: the farthing (worth one quarter of one pence), the halfpenny, threepence and sixpence, the crown (worth five shillings) and the half-crown (worth two shillings and sixpence). Less commonly seen were the florin, worth two shillings, and the guinea, which actually referred to a gold coin no longer in circulation, and in practice was simply the amount of one pound and one shilling. In December 1940, the U.S. dollar/pound sterling exchange rate was fixed at $4.03=£1; this remained in place for the duration of the war. ∽

Reading Group Guide

1. How does Ruby's upbringing affect her work as a journalist?

2. Why do you think the Blitz, and stories associated with the sacrifices and heroism of that time, still resonate with us today?

3. The character of Nigel is a fairly antediluvian one, even in a 1940s setting. How typical do you think he is of men in male-dominated professions at that time?

4. At the end of Chapter 12, Ruby tells herself that the warm welcome from the Tremaine family is nothing more than a "fairy tale" that is destined to end. At what point do you think she finally is able to believe in the fairy tale? Or at least have confidence that she does belong with them?

5. What do you think Simon the cat represents to Ruby?

6. If you were Ruby, would you have tried harder to get to the bottom of Bennett's mysterious work? Was she right to decide not to investigate? Or do you think she ought to have persevered?

7. When Ruby tells Dan Mazur that wartime controls over the press, such as censorship, are a necessary evil, and that he should "just get ▶

on with it," is she right? Can such controls ever be justified, even at a time of total war?

8. If Mary had survived the war, do you think she would have eventually acknowledged her relationship with Kaz? Or would it have been reasonable for her to continue to believe that ambition was irreconcilable with marriage and motherhood?

9. When Ruby explains the reasons for her deceptions about her past, do you sympathize with her? Or do her actions anger you?

10. In the days and weeks following D-Day, do you think Ruby should have been more intrepid? Should she have tried harder to get to France, even if it meant breaking the rules?

11. Three characters from the author's previous books make cameo appearances in *Goodnight from London*. Do you like this reminder of previous stories or is it something you can do without?

12. How do you think Ruby and Bennett will make the adjustment to postwar life? Do you see Bennett making a return to life as a barrister? And how far do you think Ruby's ambition will take her? ❧

Voices from the Past

It's a question I get asked all the time: "How do you research your books?" It's a good question, and one that any writer of historical fiction should be prepared to answer.

I research my fiction the same way I once researched my doctoral thesis, and it's pretty typical of the approach that most historians use. I begin with general survey histories, which ensure I have a good overall understanding of the period, conflict, or region in question. From there, I move on to specialist histories, the sort of books that often begin life as a thesis for someone else's research degree. For this book, I was interested in such diverse topics as food rationing, the propaganda efforts of the Ministry of Information, and the covert work done by SOE agents in France, and I found a lot of the information I needed in specialist histories.

This stage of secondary-source research takes me months, and involves my plowing through scores of books and articles, all with a view to building a reasonably convincing portrait of life as it was lived at a certain time and place. But secondary sources alone aren't enough. At best, they're wallpaper in an empty room.

To fill that room, to attempt to understand the lives of people who inhabited the past, I need to hear from people with first-hand, direct, and personal experience of past events. ▶

Voices from the Past *(continued)*

Only through their recollections can I hope to even come close to the truth, and in so doing discover the stories at the heart of my books.

With *Goodnight from London*, there was no question of where I would begin: with my own grandmother, Myra Isabella Nicholson Moir, known as Nikki to her friends.

Nikki Moir with daughter Wendy, circa 1943.

Foncie Pulice/Courtesy John Moir

Born in Alloa, Scotland, Nikki emigrated to Vancouver, Canada, with her family when she was a girl. Although her early travels left her with an adventurous spirit, excitement was hard to come by in Depression-era Vancouver. After leaving school at sixteen, she did a secretarial course in typing and shorthand and soon landed a job at the Vancouver *News-Herald*. There she worked on the women's pages, "the usual spot for female reporters," as she later recalled. The *News-Herald* was run on a shoestring, and it showed.

"We were working for less than peanuts in the upstairs of an old building on Homer Street. You walked down an alley and up a long stairway into one big room. Along one side were some makeshift partitioned offices. There were hardly any typewriters, and it was always a fight between eager reporters to get their stories done without enough machines to go around. We had almost no library, or morgue as they used to be called. Instead we relied on an elderly newsman with a phenomenal memory."

Not long after, she met my grandfather, Reg Moir, who was working at the paper as a sports reporter. In 1940, their daughter Wendy, my mother, was born. In late 1942, Reg joined the Royal Canadian Air Force as an information officer, and was eventually posted to London. To save money, Nikki moved in with her parents, then went back to the *News-Herald* as a staff writer. "Most of our able-bodied men were gone," she recalled years later, "and I was given assignment beats that I would never have had otherwise. I had two major beats, the courthouse and the military." It was interesting but at times emotionally draining work, and she soon learned to ▶

Voices from the Past *(continued)*

stifle her own feelings when going after a story. "I was there to work, not to cry or show any other emotion. I was an observer who had to record what I saw and heard for my paper." And she also learned that there was no excuse for failing to get a story. "If you were sent out on an assignment, you came back with a story, no matter what."

She worked throughout the war, and after Reg returned from service abroad and decided he wanted to go to law school, Nikki supported the family (my aunt Terry and uncle John were born after the war) by working at the Vancouver *Province* as a feature writer. She was still working as a freelance feature writer in the 1970s when I was a little girl.

I loved looking through her clipping books, which bulged with the many stories she'd told over decades of work as a newspaperwoman, though sadly I never got around to asking her many questions about her work. To be honest, she was always a little cagey on the subject of being a woman in a male-dominated field, and I suspect it must have been pretty awful at times. In an era when women were expected to put up with unfair and sometimes outright harassing behavior, complaining was often seen as a tacit admission of not being able to handle the job. After being screamed at by one irascible editor of the most hard-bitten variety, for example, she kept her cool—it helped, she felt, that she'd grown up with five elder brothers—

and was rewarded, once he realized she "wasn't crumpling," with a smile and some rare words of praise.

Nikki never won any awards for her writing, for she worked in a business that prized speed over style and economy over poetry. But she was a pioneer in her field all the same, and she helped to pave the way for my friends who work as journalists today. Always curious, always learning, she even went back to school after Reg died in 1980, and graduated from Simon Fraser University with a bachelor's degree not long after her sixty-ninth birthday.

Goodnight from London was never meant to be Nikki's book, not least because she was a private person who didn't enjoy the spotlight; like most journalists, she preferred asking questions to answering them. She was my starting point, my inspiration, but she was never Ruby. I began with my grandmother, but I still had so much more to learn.

I particularly wanted to understand the experiences of women who lived in Britain during the war, so I returned to the oral history project I had conducted in 1993 as part of the research for my doctoral thesis. The project consisted of fifteen long-form interviews with a group of women living at a senior's residence in Oxford, and fortunately I had thought to save the transcriptions on every computer I've since owned. Reading through the hundreds of pages of interviews for the first time in almost twenty years, I was ▶

Voices from the Past *(continued)*

thrilled to find a treasure trove of details that added life and authenticity to my developing novel.

I have especially vivid memories of the hours I spent with one of the women, a Mrs. E.H. (I promised anonymity to the participants in 1993 and feel obliged to maintain it now.) Born in 1915 in Cardiff, she came to London with her sister in the late 1930s, both of them certain, as she recalled, that they'd soon be "digging up the gold out of the pavements." She worked as a secretary in a law office, and during the war was also a shelter warden and a Red Cross volunteer. Warm and chatty, with an amazing memory for details, she was an absolute fount of information about life in London during the war. Here she talks about the wearying routine of life during the Blitz:

"Warnings used to start as we left the office; as we came out of the Tube—they used to start at half past six. Well, you were lucky if you were home before that. And as soon as the warning went we were supposed to go to be on duty at the shelter, and then the all clear used to go about half past seven in the morning, so we'd come back, have a wash, and go to the office. We used to get *some* sleep— it was on a concrete floor, though!"

My own oral history project pales in scope, however, when set against the vast library of material held by the Imperial War Museum's Sound Archive, which was founded in 1972 and now holds more than sixty thousand hours of professionally recorded oral history evidence. Many thousands of hours of material have been digitized and are easily accessible via the museum's website, and while researching *Goodnight from London* I listened to dozens of interviews with people who lived through the Blitz, who served in the armed or auxiliary services, or who simply had memories to share of everyday life during the war.

I also returned to an archive that was familiar to me from my years as a graduate student: the Mass Observation holdings at the University of Sussex. Mass Observation was a social research organization, founded in 1937 and active until the 1950s (it has since been revived), which sought to collect information on the everyday lives of ordinary Britons. I made extensive use of its archive when working on my doctorate in the early 1990s, and then consulted its more limited online archive while researching this novel. It was from Mass Observation that I found the memories that informed my description of life in wartime Brighton, in Coventry after the November 1940 bombings, and in the Edge Hill neighborhood of Liverpool after the Durning Road disaster.

The personal recollections of people who lived through the war—direct, vivid, startlingly intimate at times— were critical to my understanding of the story I wanted to tell.

For example, it isn't enough to say, when describing a dinner during the war, that a family ate sausages. Who cares? ▶

Voices from the Past *(continued)*

If, however, the people eating the sausages complain about how they taste, and fret over what unsavory ingredients may be hiding in the sausages, and talk about their conversation with the butcher, and if all of that is based on the first-hand recollections of people who actually had such experiences, then the scene in question becomes more than a one-dimensional narrative. Then it becomes, ideally, something far closer to the truth.

Nearly all of the people whose reminiscences of the Second World War were captured by Mass Observation's interviewers, as well as by historians at the Imperial War Museum, are dead now, or too infirm to sit through extensive interviews with curious researchers. The youngest of the women I spoke with in 1993 would be well over a hundred years old today. Nikki, my grandmother, died at the age of ninety-five in December 2014. They are gone, but their memories endure. Their stories live on.

It was hard, at times, for me to write *Goodnight from London* and know that my grandmother would never have the chance to read it. I hope she'd have enjoyed it, and perhaps be secretly delighted by the parallels she found between her experiences and those of Ruby. Most of all, I hope she'd have known that I wrote it as a tribute not only to her, but also to my grandfather, to those who worked so hard for victory, and to everyone who endured those long, hard years of war. Their sacrifices will not be forgotten. ∽

Suggestions for Further Reading

The following represent only a fraction of the sources I consulted when researching *Goodnight from London*, but if you are interested in learning more about the Second World War, the people who lived through it, and the places that appear in my novel, these books are a good place to begin. Most should be easily available through your local library or bookseller, though some are now out of print.

I highly recommend Juliet Gardiner's *Wartime Britain*, which offers a lively and thorough history of Britain during the war. I also found *London at War* by Philip Ziegler, *The People's War* by Angus Calder, and the succinct *Britain in the Second World War* by Mark Donnelly very informative. For a sharper view of the Blitz, turn to *London Was Ours: Diaries and Memories of the London Blitz* by Amy Helen Bell, *Blackout* by Antonia Caroline Lant, and *The Blitz*, again by Juliet Gardiner.

For books that focus on women's experience of war, I recommend *Millions Like Us: Women's Lives in the Second World War* by Virginia Nicholson and *What Did You Do in the War, Mummy?* by Mavis Nicholson. ►

I found the following memoirs and diaries that center on the war years especially useful: *Among You Taking Notes* by Naomi Mitchison, *London War Notes* by Mollie Panter-Downes, *Nella Last's War* by Nella Last, and *Few Eggs and No Oranges* by Vere Hodgson.

To better understand the experiences of women journalists, I recommend *Battling for News* by Anne Sebba and *The Women Who Wrote the War* by Nancy Caldwell Sorel. The reminiscences of Clare Hollingworth in *Front Line* and Virginia Cowles in *Looking for Trouble,* both of them acclaimed war correspondents, are particularly informative. *Sketches from a Life by* Anne Scott-James offers an interesting perspective on work at daily newspapers and *Picture Post*, the magazine that was the model for *Picture Weekly*.

For works written by or about male journalists, I recommend *Of This Our Time* by Tom Hopkinson (an editor of *Picture Post*), *Ernie Pyle's War: America's Eyewitness to World War II* by James Tobin, *My War* by Andy Rooney, and *This is London* by Edward R. Murrow.

The history of the SOE has been imperfectly chronicled, for the organization remains steeped in secrecy and only a fraction of its official files escaped destruction after the war. Of those records that survive, many are still classified. I particularly recommend

The Secret Ministry of Ag. & Fish: My Life in Churchill's School for Spies by Noreen Riols; it is a highly entertaining memoir written by possibly the only surviving female employee of the SOE's F Section. Also worth consulting are *S.O.E.: An Outline History of the Special Operations Executive 1940–46* by M. R. D. Foot, as well as *Churchill's Wizards: The British Genius for Deception 1914–1945* by Nicholas Rankin.

If you'd like to learn more about life on the British home front, I recommend *Eating For Victory* by Jill Norman, *Make Do and Mend*, a reproduction of wartime pamphlets issued by the Ministry of Information, *Spuds, Spam and Eating for Victory* by Katherine Knight, and *The Wartime Kitchen Garden* by Jennifer Davies.

There is no shortage of novels on the subject of the Second World War, and it would be easy for me to fill the next ten pages with recommendations. I will instead confine myself to a handful of books that I find particularly inspiring: *Noonday* by Pat Barker, *The Heat of the Day* by Elizabeth Bowen, *The Race for Paris* by Meg Waite Clayton, *Everyone Brave is Forgiven* by Chris Cleave, *Coventry* by Helen Humphreys, and *The Last Summer at Chelsea Beach* by Pam Jenoff. ☙